KU-305-321

DO NO HARM

ROBERT POBI

HODDER &
STOUGHTON

First published in Great Britain in 2022 by Hodder & Stoughton
An Hachette UK company

First published in the United States in 2022 by Minotaur Books

1

Copyright © Robert Pobi 2022

The right of Robert Pobi to be identified as the Author of the Work has been asserted by
him in accordance with the Copyright, Designs and Patents Act 1988.

All rights reserved. No part of this publication may be reproduced, stored in a retrieval
system, or transmitted, in any form or by any means without the prior written permission
of the publisher, nor be otherwise circulated in any form of binding or cover other
than that in which it is published and without a similar condition being imposed on the
subsequent purchaser.

All characters in this publication are fictitious and any resemblance to real persons, living
or dead, is purely coincidental.

A CIP catalogue record for this title is available from the British Library

Hardback ISBN 978 1 529 34847 7
Trade Paperback ISBN 978 1 529 34848 4
eBook ISBN 978 1 529 34849 1

Typeset in Stempel Garamond by Michelle McMillian

Printed and bound in Great Britain by Clays Ltd, Elcograf S.p.A.

Hodder & Stoughton policy is to use papers that are natural, renewable and recyclable
products and made from wood grown in sustainable forests. The logging and
manufacturing processes are expected to conform to the environmental regulations of the
country of origin.

Hodder & Stoughton Ltd
Carmelite House
50 Victoria Embankment
London EC4Y 0DZ

www.hodder.co.uk

DO NO HARM

For my editor, Keith Kahla.
Who had the wisdom when I most needed it.

*In nothing do men more nearly approach the gods
than in giving health to men.*
—MARCUS TULLIUS CICERO

*Doctors are men who prescribe medicines of which they know little,
to cure diseases of which they know less, in human beings
of whom they know nothing.*
—VOLTAIRE

Either he's dead, or my watch has stopped.
—GROUCHO MARX

DO NO HARM

1

New York City
The Brooklyn Bridge Footpath

Dr. Jennifer Delmonico was approaching the second tower, which translated to somewhere around seventeen minutes at her usual pace. It took most people half an hour to cross the East River, but at six-foot-three, Delmonico's stride put her into NFL receiver territory. Which was one of the things about being a tall woman—the long bones were almost always of a greater proportionate length. Back in high school, when she had been the third tallest student out of twelve hundred kids, her height felt like a curse. But life out in the world had taught her that being the tallest woman in the room, and often the tallest person, came with all kinds of advantages—of both the social and biomechanical variety.

Old Man Winter was on the way. The cold air coming down from Canada this time of year hit the warm water surging up the East River with the tide, and the resulting condensation blossomed into a localized fogbank that blanketed the bridge. The effect was visually isolating, which was both comforting and unsettling.

She took the footpath almost every shift. Day or night. Rain or shine. Winter or summer. It helped her unwind the think box (and muscles) before (or after) hours spent putting patients back together in the OR. The tourists on the span were always a pain in the ass, but at three in the morning on a foggy night, the sober ones were off mining selfies in the warmer parts of the city.

Other than the errant jogger, the only other signs of life were the headlights and taillights of cars on the lower deck. If you ignored the cold, it was one of those New York movie moments that are part of the city's fabric.

It had been a long shift at the hospital, and the cool atmosphere out here was scrubbing the stale air from her lungs. Of course, in a metropolis with a population of eight and a half million souls, you were never—ever—alone in any true sense of the word. She could hear people behind her—or were they up ahead? The humid air messed with the acoustics and the fog conjured up all kinds of optical illusions, which had her doubting her own senses. The most jarring effect was the way the joggers materialized out of nowhere before passing back into the void, like ghosts racing to get to the afterlife.

And then it hit her—that weird sensation that every New Yorker experienced every now and then, at the most unpredictable times— that she actually *was* alone. It never lasted more than a few seconds. But it was very powerful.

All she could sense was her own presence. There were no other life-forms out in the mist. No cars thrumming by on the deck below. Even the wind seemed to be on pause just for her.

And then, as quickly as it had appeared, the sensation was driven away by the appearance of footsteps in the sonic vacuum—the rhythm of a jogger somewhere in the mist.

The steps came up on her left-hand flank. She stepped to the right.

And then. The rhythm changed.

There was a blip where her Spidey sense kicked in.

There was a loud electrical *CRACK!* beside her ear and her motor skills shorted out.

She fell.

Someone caught her, and she heard herself grunt.

She tried to focus on the undulating form haloed in the bridge lights.

She tried to move.

To breathe.

To scream.

But only squeezed out a weak squeak that she wasn't even sure had come from her own body.

But the jolt that scrambled her circuits had worked its way through her grid, and was beginning to fade. Thought became clearer.

And with thought, panic.

Her toes clunked over the wooden planks as he dragged her forward, toward the railing.

She tried to move. To scream again. And that tiny little squeak came out one more time.

Help! she screeched.

But only in her head.

"It's okay, Jennifer," a voice said.

She was hoisted up and her head fell forward.

And even paralyzed, she felt her weight shift as the fluids in her inner ear translated data to her brain.

And just like that, she was sitting on the edge.

Her head lolled back and all she could see were the suspension lines reaching up into the fog.

This time it actually came out when she said, "Please."

But he just let go.

Gravity embraced her. Pulled her back.

She began to fly.

And then the headlights were there. Right. There. And she began to close her eyes, but—

—the impact broke her neck.

Spine and skull.

Rib cage.

And drove everything she was into a tiny little hole in the universe that silently collapsed before disappearing forever.

And that.

Was that.

2

The Upper East Side

The Armory on Park Avenue was only a few blocks east and another handful south, and if the rain hadn't turned the city into a real-time film noir—and if Dr. Lucas Page weren't still recovering—they probably would have walked. Or at least his wife, Erin, would have walked; he would have limped. But the night was going to be boring enough as it was—he didn't need to add fatigue to the roster. So they were cabbing it.

Lucas hated these functions. They felt like excuses for the squares to drink too much, slap themselves on the back, and tell one another what a great job they were doing in the business of healing. But Erin, who was a pediatric orthopedic surgeon, insisted that she had to attend, although he could never really figure out precisely *why*.

The cabbie pulled a U-turn at 64th, then slammed to a halt in front of the Seventh Regiment Armory. They didn't have the klieg lights on, but the façade was adorned with a moving light show and the doormen were dressed as Yeomen Warders—which made absolutely no sense at all.

One of the Beefeaters opened the car door for Lucas, shielding him with an umbrella. Lucas got out, bolstered his footing with his cane, then extended his prosthetic for Erin. After she was out, he nodded a thanks to the man with the umbrella and slipped him a twenty—anyone who had to dress like that to make rent deserved a gratuity. And Lucas had experience with the people at these things; they were notoriously bad tippers.

As they ducked under the ivy tunnel that framed the door, Lucas asked, "What, specifically, are we here to celebrate?"

"Don't start."

Lucas held up his hands. "I forgot."

She stopped and gave him one of her bullshit-detector questions. "How many cycles does a cesium-one-thirty-three atom complete in a single second?"

He tried not to smile, but it got away from him. Or at least as much as was muscularly possible. "Nine billion, one hundred and ninety-two million, six hundred and thirty-one thousand, seven hundred and seventy."

"You don't forget things—you intentionally refuse to remember them. There's a difference." She stared him down for a second. "Do you have any other questions?"

"I'm still waiting for an answer to my first one."

"We're not celebrating anything. It's a charity gala—just like it was last year. And the year before. The money we raise goes to the poorer hospitals in the city. See?" she said, pointing up at the banner over the entrance. "It says so right there: *The Annual Sarah Rothstein Charity Dinner.*"

A heavyset couple decked out in non-rented evening wear shoehorned through the big double doors in front of them, and the woman's voice cracked into a high-pitched cackle that sounded like the dinner bell at a flying-monkey convention.

Lucas leaned over and said, "If I'm going to spend the evening with these people, I deserve a drinking problem." It wasn't that he didn't like doctors—he lumped them in with the general population, which meant that at least 30 percent of them were not just bad at their jobs, but dangerous. And in an occupation where people's actual lives were at stake, he thought more stringent competency requirements would do everyone some good.

Without turning to look at him, Erin said, "You have that turned around—if *I* am going to spend time with *you* while *you* spend time with *these people*, it is *I* who deserve a drinking problem."

Another man in an ugly red period costume held the door for them and Lucas stopped and handed him another twenty, doing his best to hide his pity.

"How do you explain the English flunky outfits if we're here to celebrate capitalism killing patients? Is there a theme? Is the medical profession advocating beheading those who can't pay their bills? Putting them in debtors' prison?"

"We're here because I have to come. Which means you will be nice." She snapped her fingers. "Look at me—*nice*, understood?"

He tried out his smile again. "I'm always nice."

Erin's goofy little snort was lost in the sound spilling through the doors. "Of course," she said. "Silly me."

The organizers had a string quartet going just inside the entrance and Lucas leaned over and said, "I guess Starcrawler was booked."

"And so it begins," Erin said humorlessly.

Neville Carpenter hollered their names, and came staggering over, drink in hand (and obviously a few had already passed through his blood/brain barrier).

Carpenter was a fixture at these events and Lucas could not remember a single one in the past ten years where he hadn't been present. He was a big drinker, a bigger talker, and Lucas didn't mind seeing the guy because it removed the burden of conversation. He was also smart and funny in a Henry Louis Mencken kind of way, which meant that Lucas could usually take him for an evening. Neville was Lorne Jacobi's boyfriend—Lorne was the ER administrator at Weill Cornell, where Erin worked. When Lucas had first met Neville, he had resembled a middle-aged David Bowie. But ten solid years of unhealthy living had vulcanized him into an elderly Mick

Jagger. Lorne was a Brooks Brothers and cap-toe Oxfords man who rarely said a word and Lucas had a hard time picturing the two of them in the same room, let alone smiling over Cheerios in the morning.

"Erin, you look *wonderful*. And non-medical Dr. Page, so do—" He looked up. And did not bother to hide his shock. *"You?"*

Erin smiled into her hand.

Lucas was used to people having trouble with the uncanny valley that his lost arm, leg, and eye presented—injuries from a decade-old accident that he referred to as the *Event*. But Neville was knocked back by the new layer of injuries added to the mix—his ear was freshly sewn back on, his hair was mostly burned off (what was left was dyed blond, the vestigial remnants of his daughter's Halloween costume gone awry), and he was using a cane—all of which had been recently collected during a temporary stint working with the FBI.

Lucas was not an investigator proper, not in the traditional sense. He was an astrophysicist by profession, but his facility with numbers made him a useful tool in many facets of the investigative process—both in the physical world and in the digital plane of raw data. So every now and then his unique competency pulled him back into the bureau's orbit. Unfortunately, his last sojourn had added a plethora of fresh injuries to the litany of old ones.

Neville gently took Lucas's prosthetic in his hand, as if it might come apart in his grip. "You do realize that there's a voodoo doll of you somewhere out there that is giving an unhappy person an awful lot of fun, don't you?"

Lucas tried out a smile, and by the way Neville cringed he could tell that his muscles hadn't cooperated. "You should see the *other* guy." What was left of him had been carted away in the modern equivalent of Canopic jars: Tupperware bins.

Erin punctuated the statement with a loud snort.

"I read about that." Neville leaned in and put a hand on Lucas's shoulder. "For once the *Post* held back the messy parts."

He then air-kissed Erin, apologizing for being distracted by Lucas's scrapes and scuffs. "And how is my favorite lady?"

"I'm good, Neville."

"And the kids?"

"They're good, too." Erin and Lucas had five adopted children, and there was no one in their lives who did not understand that they were a collective—one of those classic examples of the whole being greater than the sum of its parts. "Maude transferred to LaGuardia and she's doing well—she's got two paintings in the senior gallery, which is a big thing. Damien still looks like a young Noel Gallagher— girls are calling all the time, but he's got more important things to do. Hector's, well, just *Hector*—I think he's the most self-contained child I've ever met. And Laurie and Alisha keep reminding me to stop and smell the jelly beans."

Neville nodded in approval. "Sage advice."

One of the waitstaff was walking by—a short girl in penguin colors whose red eyes said she had taken a cannabis break before her shift—and Neville got her attention. "Can we please get—?" He arched an eyebrow at Erin, then redirected it to Lucas. "What are you two crazy kids having?"

"I'll have a Sauvignon Blanc," she said.

"Make mine a root beer. Lots of ice, please."

Neville shook his almost-empty glass. "And I'll have another bourbon, soda, rocks, please." He pulled out a fifty and tucked it under an empty wineglass on the cork-lined tray; evidently Neville was also over-tipping on behalf of the cheapskates in the place.

Neville had been a Wall Street banker with a penchant for vintage Ferraris, a habit he picked up once he started making what he liked to call *real money*. But two minor heart attacks had forced him to make one of those quality-of-life/fork-in-the-road choices, and hunting down Italian sports cars gave him more pleasure than simply shoveling all the zeros from clients' bank accounts straight into his own. He turned his hobby into a business and was now what Lucas considered a very fancy used-car salesman. It didn't pay as well as his former occupation, but he didn't wake up in the middle of the night having chewed through his mouth guard anymore, which was an amenable trade-off.

Neville picked up his glass and waved it in the air, indicating everything in general and nothing in specific. "So, once again, we find ourselves at an overpriced affair, populated by those without merit." He put the glass to his lips and finished what was left of his drink.

Erin asked, "Where is Lorne?"

Neville made the everything/nothing gesture again. "He's mingling," he said, dividing the word into two hard syllables.

As a child, Lucas had spent many evenings at these things with his adopted mother—the elderly Mrs. Page. She accepted every invitation sent her way, mostly because it gave her an excuse to dress up. As she got older, and her dwindling finances constricted her ability to contribute to whatever cause they were pushing, the invitations became scarcer. But even at the end, when she had been relegated to third-tier community hall events, she and Lucas always showed up dressed for the red carpet. Whenever he and Erin did one of these things, he wished Mrs. Page could be there with them. Which, in a way, he always felt she was.

Lucas was pulled back to the present when Lorne materialized out of the crowd, on his way from one conversation to another, and stopped to say hello. "How are the Pages tonight?" he asked, kissing Erin and giving Lucas one of their patented fist bumps—a habit they had developed to help Lorne with his carpal tunnel syndrome. But it was easy to see that he wasn't in the present at all—he looked tired and preoccupied.

After the fist bumping and kisses, he was gone, off to do more mingling.

Neville said, "He's pretty upset about Jennifer Delmonico," as he crunched an ice cube.

Erin nodded. "I know he and Jennifer were close."

Neville's tone changed. "He's friends with her mother, Dee Dee, from *way* back. The first time I met him he was with her. It was in the café at ABC Decorating. She set us up—two strangers who never would have met without her interference." He looked down into his empty glass. "And she just lost a daughter. Jesus. What a world, huh?" Then he looked up and nailed Lucas with his infectious smile. "Look who I'm telling that to, the luckiest unlucky person I've ever met."

Lucas said, "You need to get out more," just as the waitress came back with their drinks.

"One Sauvignon Blanc, one bourbon and soda, and a root beer—lots of ice." She smiled over the tray when she handed Lucas his soda—replete with tiny cocktail napkin—but when she saw his face, she blushed and turned away.

Neville slid another fifty under the empty glass he plopped down on the tray amid the wet rings. "For being so prompt," he said.

She scampered away before Lucas could throw another smile at her.

Neville raised the old-fashioned and said, "To Jennifer Delmonico, who I did not know very well, which I now regret."

Everyone raised their glasses, but the toast was interrupted when a hand clamped down on Lucas's shoulder. He winced as it torqued his frame, putting pressure on his still-cracked ribs, and he spilled some of his root beer. "What the fu—?"

Neville abandoned the toast and turned to the newcomer. "How is my favorite plastic surgeon?"

Dove Knox nodded a hello to the group but singled Lucas out for the first hug. "Hey, man! How's my grouchy buddy?" Knox had visited Lucas in the hospital a few weeks back, and he looked only mildly surprised by how banged up he still was.

"Swell." After the hug ended, Lucas put his root beer down on one of the tall bar tables and wiped his hand with a paper napkin as his ribs stopped tingling—a vestigial wound that he was starting to suspect might never heal.

Knox doled out two more hugs and greetings.

Lucas begrudgingly liked Knox. He and Erin had been friends since medical school—they had even dated for a while. But their romantic relationship never really worked and they had managed the not-always-simple transition from lovers to friends. He was now married to an internist named Carla and they were one of the few couples both Lucas and Erin liked to spend time with. Knox was smart and considerate, but he could be a little complicated. And he tended to drink too much.

"Have I missed anything?" Knox asked as he waved their red-eyed waitress back.

"We were just talking about Jennifer Delmonico."

Knox shook his head. "Don't know her."

Neville, who hated giving up the spotlight, said, "She was an orthopod at Weill Cornell."

Knox tilted his head at Erin. "Your haunt?"

"The sister ship in Lower Manhattan. So, yes, sort of."

Knox made the effort to raise one of his very nicely balanced eyebrows. "What happened to her?"

"She committed suicide last night."

Dove ordered a scotch-rocks from the server without acknowledging her, then directed his attention toward Erin. "Was she a friend of yours?" Knox was ridiculously handsome, a self-aware condition that he pushed over the top with a very good eye for clothes and a few small corrective surgeries—like the eyebrows. But he suffered from situational OCD that came out at the strangest times in the oddest little rituals. It did not control his life, but it controlled enough of his small habits that it could get annoying. Lucas had tried going to Rizzoli with him two Christmases back and it had been an exercise in line-up-the-books-just-so masochism. Knox tended to overcomplicate things—Erin said it was one of his core practices and had been one of the largest contributors to their demise, after his drinking. Even his tie knot was some obscure intricate affair.

"I didn't know her well, but she was a fixture at the hospital."

"What happened?"

Neville, in his role of resident expert since Lorne had been her administrator, answered. "Jumped in front of a truck after her shift last night."

Erin took a sip of wine that left a crescent of lipstick on the rim and Lucas could see she wasn't enjoying the conversation.

Neville shook his head and crunched more ice. "Lorne was really upset."

An electronic chime echoed through the space, and Neville nodded toward the main hall. "Shall we?" he asked, sticking his elbow out for Erin. "Lorne will join us."

Erin held up her phone. "First I want to take a picture of all of you—my favorite men all dressed up."

Neville pulled Lucas and Dove in, and Lucas was painfully aware that he looked like a reconstituted pallbearer against Neville's floral silk jacket and Dove's sartorial overreach.

Erin said, "Say 'cheese'!" and Lucas was the only one who didn't try to smile.

The phone made a simulated *click*, and she slipped it back into her pocketbook as they headed for the main hall, Knox dropping behind to talk with Lucas.

"Where's Carla?" Lucas asked.

"We got into a fight and she stayed out at the beach house." Knox put his hand back on Lucas's shoulder. "Which means I get to drink tonight."

Lucas rolled his single eye behind the dark lens. "Swell."

3

The Brooklyn Bridge

Detective Johnny "Jackets" Russo took another sip of vodka and Gatorade and realized that the seasonal hump was behind him, and it was time for his equinoctial switch to coffee and whiskey. Not that it made any difference—ethanol was ethanol. But the booze made the pointy little edges of the job a little duller, and the coffee would at least help keep him from freezing.

He was back on the bridge, doing a last run-through of the Delmonico suicide. After this, it was back to the precinct to see if the autopsy report had come back from the coroner. Once that last important piece of the puzzle was collected, he'd slip it into the file, close the cover, and forget all about this.

He stood at the spot Dr. Jennifer Delmonico would have used for her jumping-off point last night, where the footpath hooked around the support column at the stone tower closest to the Brooklyn side.

The body and accompanying mess had been cleaned up, and traffic once again hammered by, oblivious to what had happened here less than twenty-four hours ago.

Russo leaned over the railing and sighted down the lane to the east, facing the oncoming vehicle stream, and had the same thoughts as last night, beginning with all the things necessary to line up in order for this to have gone right. First the speed of oncoming cars had to be factored in. Then a good prelaunch position had to be lined up. And then the timing needed to be perfect. Any one of which could have gone south.

But all those things had unfolded seamlessly. Which was as good as you could expect in this particular situation. For everyone concerned.

He stood there for a moment, sipping from his travel mug and going through a longer list of what-ifs than these cases usually generated. He was no stranger to the bad things that happened to people. He had spent thirteen years incubating in the military before becoming a policeman, and that combined quarter century of trying to manage the completely unmanageable had allowed him to fill a mental scrapbook with enough disturbing memories to creep out George Romero. Russo had seen every permutation of death imaginable—and quite a few that weren't (the one with the fish tank, car battery, and real estate agent was a late-night staple that popped up when he drank too much—which was all the time these days). He had been witness to car accident decapitations and domestic crossbow shootings; he had pulled children who resembled boneless chickens out of washing machines and stepped over internal organs after building jumpers tested gravitational theory. Drone strikes and sniper hits. Never mind the stabbings and beatings and shootings that made up the bulk of his play dates. And each and every one of them reminded him of an epigraph he had read in college.

Such as thou art, sometime was I,
Such as I am, such shall thou be.

The bridge was not in his precinct, but he had been the first officer on the scene. When he arrived, it appeared as if the pickup blocking the right-hand westbound lane had hit a deer; there was a long black streak on the asphalt littered with splinters of bone and chunks of hair and parts that he knew belonged inside a large mammal. When he lit up the monkey magnets and got out of the car, he saw the shoe—there was *always* a shoe at these things. It didn't matter if it was a motorcycle accident or another Tesla that had caught fire and carbecued the occupants—he would unerringly find an errant piece of footwear nearby. Russo figured that it was just one of those bugs in the Matrix that no one would ever figure out—probably a little Easter egg that one of the original code writers had snuck past management. He was certain that if he went back two thousand years to a chariot crash on the Appian Way, he would find a sandal in the ditch. And in a hundred years from now, they would be finding space boots floating near the flying-car collisions—if humanity managed the miracle of not snuffing out its own pilot light before then.

The bridge police had arrived a few minutes before him, but he quickly established alpha status, which, he realized now, had been a smart move.

The bridge cops had been very helpful, immediately roping off the scene and diverting all eastbound traffic over to one of the westbound lanes. They had even put up privacy screens.

Russo phoned it in but was told that the Department of Transport's people had already been notified, which was still a relatively new procedure for him. But he didn't want anyone else handling this case, and he pushed back. Up until early 2021, all road accidents involving serious injury had been handled by the NYPD. But in one of those sweeping reforms designed to make New York a safer place, the city council had decided to hand investigative duties over to the Department of Transport. Everyone involved hoped that it would lead to safer streets and less work for the NYPD. But like all good intentions, it wasn't working out nearly as smoothly as everyone wanted.

It turned out that the fog and rain had performed a little black magic on the city and the DOT people were backlogged with more accidents than personnel; Russo was given the green light to coordinate things. Which was not the same as being in charge. But it was close enough for now.

Russo had interviewed the driver of the pickup, an electrician named Carl Moody. Moody was a thirty-seven-year-old father of two with a clean driving record and no criminal history. All through the interview process he shook as if he were reentering the atmosphere on a toboggan and Russo was pretty sure Moody's first call when he got home would be to find a therapist, so he gave the guy a card.

Moody had a dash cam and Russo had gone over the footage three or four times. The footage was relatively clear, and didn't leave much room for misinterpretation. So that was a plus.

After the ME's people showed up and Russo signed off, he headed back to the security office to review the CCTV footage. But he knew what he'd find before he got there.

And he was proved correct when they told him that the camera that should have caught her jump into traffic was down. But not broken — home to a raptors' nest. Russo asked what the fuck was going on and the security officer explained that the birds were endangered peregrine falcons and the city had passed a special bill preventing the removal of their nest.

So Russo watched the footage up until Delmonico moved off-camera, stage right, a final time. He watched her walk the footpath, focusing on her tall frame and long stride. He examined the people who got on before her. And after. He watched the people who passed her — all joggers. He saw the kids she had followed (and caught up to). But nothing appeared abnormal, or out of place — it was just a city footpath at night with people going about their lives. Which he had expected. And made his job a lot easier.

Then he thanked the Bridge Authority people and left the office for one more peek at the span to make sure he hadn't missed anything that might come back to haunt him later.

Russo looked up at the pair of arches that supported millions of tons of steel and history. And there it was — the falcons' nest.

But it wasn't the architectural marvel that David Attenborough had convinced him he would see—it was a simple wooden box—a *man-made* wooden box. With the designation *EKJ06* (which was the nest's designation in the national registry) neatly stenciled on the side in bright yellow paint. Apparently, there were four other nests on the structure.

The Bridge Authority people informed him that they didn't choose where the falcons nested—the birds made their own decisions. So the bird people (Russo knew they had a different name—probably the Manhattan Society for Avian Protection or something) had gathered a quarter of a million signatures in an effort to make the bridge more falcon-friendly. But the fix was a typical bureaucratic more-is-more approach, and all of the nests had been enclosed in protective plywood boxes.

But no one thought to move the security camera.

After running down the security footage problem, checking out falcons' nests that weren't nests and cameras that weren't there, he had taken a drive out to Delmonico's house in Brooklyn to speak with her husband. Greg Delmonico was everything that Russo thought he would be—tall, handsome, and boring, even in his grief. When Russo gave him the news, he sat down and stared at the floor. No crying. No yelling. Not even a curse. Just wide-eyed disbelief, which was more common than most people would have guessed.

Russo spent fifteen minutes talking with him, and the whole time Greg just kept staring like his eyelids had stopped functioning.

Russo had asked the easy questions and some of the difficult ones and tried to be as patient and understanding as a guy who didn't care could be. When they finished, Russo offered what he knew sounded like insincere condolences before walking back out to his car, pouring himself a fresh vodka and Gatorade from the box of supplies in the trunk, and heading back into the city where he had spent the night at the precinct doing paperwork.

Which meant that he had done his due diligence and he could now put Dr. Jennifer Delmonico away with the rest of the bad memories.

Russo took a sip of vodka and Gatorade from his mug and turned away from the traffic.

4

The Seventh Regiment Armory

Lucas's people-tolerance reserves had dwindled down to the dregs. As the backslapping started, he wondered aloud if they were here to honor Fred "the Dorf" Dorfman, and Erin kicked him under the table—but she got the wrong shin and connected with Dove Knox, who was having a hard time keeping a straight face. But he was so far in the bag that the kick just set off another paroxysm of laughter. Now, coming up on the end of the ceremonies, Lucas was ready to shout, *Fire!* just to get the fuck out of the place.

The main space of the building was in direct contrast to the well-appointed lobby, and resembled the inside of a Disney whale—the hot-riveted trusses and joists serving as backbone and ribs. All it needed was a little water on the floor and a wooden boy on a raft. And maybe an old puppet maker with a moustache to round out the theme.

The guest speakers were winding down—the final monologue of the night delivered by a neurosurgeon from Mount Sinai Beth Israel who said it was time to honor the members they had lost since last year's dinner.

Lucas hated this part.

Taking their cue from the in-memoriam presentation at the

Academy Awards, photographs and names began a slow fade-in-fade-out on the giant screen behind the podium while the string quartet played what Lucas had to admit was a very touching rendition of Handel's *Messiah*.

Three pictures in, the image of a young woman in her thirties cycled up. She was smiling, holding a cat, and looked like she spent her weekends on a kayak or a mountain bike.

Neville leaned in and said, "Daphne Bugliosi, urologist. She got locked out on her apartment balcony and tried to climb over to the next unit. She fell thirty-two stories with her cat, Rocky. The cat survived."

Lucas looked down at his now-flat root beer and wondered how long he had to sit here.

Four photographs later, Neville held up his scotch and said, "Eddie Lu, internist. Fell off his bike in Central Park and broke his neck."

Erin leaned over. "I didn't know Lu was dead. When did that happen?"

Neville's shrug was meant to illustrate that he was being approximate. "Two months ago? Three?"

The crowd was comprised of people who understood that death was one of the unbending mechanisms of life, and they cheered some photos, laughed at goofy poses in others, and raised glasses to most.

An image that could have been a stock photo came up. A man in his sixties sat behind a desk, a stethoscope around his neck.

Neville, in his de facto role as the table's MC, said, "Paul Ho, pediatrician. Carbon monoxide poisoning." He shook his head. "Got up in the middle of the night, walked into the garage, turned on the engine, and fell asleep in a lawn chair. What a way to go."

The dead faded in. The dead faded out. And Lucas unconsciously began noting the causes, the natural mathematician in him building a mental spreadsheet. For the younger people, the main causes of death were cancer; for the older, heart disease followed by cancer. In the cancer category, breast and prostate were pretty evenly divided, with lung having a large overlap between the sexes.

Every now and then Erin squeezed his arm as a signal that she knew the deceased and Lucas remembered many of the faces of the dead from various functions and parties and gatherings he had attended with her over the years. A few of them he knew personally — or at least well enough to remember their names.

The images cycled through another dozen faces before a photo of Jennifer Delmonico came up. She was on a corner somewhere in Brooklyn. With a Boston terrier and a baby stroller.

Neville raised his glass. "To Jennifer."

Delmonico looked about seven feet tall in the photo, as if the perspective had been fudged. She appeared unwilling to smile and Lucas figured that was the only photo they could find on such short notice. She stared at the camera as if she had somewhere else she would rather have been, which was incongruous with the balloon tied to the handle of the stroller, and Lucas wondered how she would have felt about them using that particular image. A digital time stamp on the bottom made it a week over five years old.

Lorne Jacobi's eyes filled with tears. "Sonofabitch."

"She was happy." Neville put his glass down. "This doesn't make any sense."

Lucas added her to the unintentional spreadsheet he was constructing in his head and one single digit on the counter clicked into place and he felt his onboard computer light up as the biological Nixie tubes started to glow.

Erin looked over at him and he wondered if she could see the orange heat filaments behind his sunglasses. She was the one person in the world who could unerringly figure out what he was thinking. But she just squeezed his arm and turned back to the screen.

A photograph of a man in his fifties came up. He was standing at the end of a dock with a fishing rod in his hand. A sweating beer sat on the planks beside him. He held up a nice-looking fish that Lucas assumed was a trout (but could have been a marlin for all he knew).

Neville said, "Artie Fossner, ob-gyn. Got his leg caught in the anchor line and got pulled over the side of his own boat."

The photos kept cycling by and Neville continued to demonstrate his command of the macabre, rattling off names, specialties, and causes of death. If he weren't a used-car salesman, he would have made a great mortician.

Cancer.

Heart disease.

More cancer.

And between the illnesses and natural causes came the accidents. And the suicides. Never two in a row. But never far enough apart that they could be completely ignored.

Leonard Ibicki. Pathologist. Drowned in his tub.

Dominic Rogers. Internist. Leukemia.

Isaiah Selmer. Neurologist. Hit by a car while crossing the street.

Mary Nguyen. ENT. Lupus.

Carol Villeneuve. Psychiatrist. Fell off a ladder while hanging a picture.

Chester Vance. Cardiothoracic surgeon. Tripped on his front stairs and impaled his skull on a cast-iron fence picket.

Janet Wilson. Ob-gyn. Breast cancer.

Dawn Ryan. Anesthesiologist. Motorcycle crash.

The faces of the dead faded in and out for what seemed way too long and when the final picture melted away—a young pediatric burn specialist named Zeke Ridley who died with his head in an oven—it took a few seconds for the string quartet to wind down and conversation to pick back up.

Neville and Lorne stood up, doled out their required portions of kisses and handshakes—and Lorne and Lucas went through their fist bump. Then they excused themselves and headed to the bar. Dove

Knox sat a little lopsided, listing to port as if his ballast was uneven. He had been working on his blood alcohol level all night and as usual he had done a stellar job.

Dove wasn't saying anything; he was just smiling and staring off into some indistinct point somewhere at the far end of the room.

"You okay, Dove?" Lucas asked.

Knox redirected his line of sight and hoisted his glass. "I'm gr-r-reat!" he Tony the Tigered.

Everyone else was either engaged in conversation, looking for the exits, or heading for the dance floor, where the string quartet had been replaced by a big band that was sliding into an old KC and the Sunshine Band number in a way that KC—and the Sunshine Band— would probably file a cease and desist order against.

After a few minutes of the trumpets telling the partygoers to *shake, shake, shake—shake, shake, shake—shake your booty*, Lucas poked Erin in the shoulder. "Either we leave or I put on my boogie shoes." He smiled at her. "And you do *not* want to see me dance."

Erin checked her watch, then surveyed the room. They had lost 10 percent of the guests immediately following dinner, another 10 had snuck out during the speech portion of the program, and another 10 had skipped during the in-memoriam segment (which even Lucas found to be in poor taste). Neville and Lorne hadn't come back. And it didn't look like Knox would care if they were being slowly licked to death by giant ground sloths.

"You want to leave?"

"I'm tired."

"Okay. You win." She leaned over the table to be heard above the big-band disco mash-up that was taking place. "Dove, we're leaving."

Knox smiled drunkenly.

"We're *leav-ing*," she said, a little louder.

Knox smiled again and held up his empty glass as a send-off. "I hear-eard you. Travel safe. Let's get together soon. Bring the kids out on the boat." He was obviously shit-faced, but his tie was still perfect, his hair still geometrically styled, and his shirt pressed and spotless.

"Okay. I'll put it together with Carla."

"She'll be back tomorrow; she'd love us all to get together." Even hammered, he was polite. He went to put the glass down but shifted the orientation of the cocktail napkin before he did in one of those little OCD tics that Lucas could never see coming.

They got up and Lucas went over and shook his hand and Erin gave him a kiss on the cheek with a promise to call Carla.

"Are you okay to get home?" Lucas asked.

Knox waved them away. "Go! The Royal Tenenbaum children need you." He held up his glass. "And I have more damage to inflict upon the scotch population."

Erin leaned in and said, "Forget it, Luke; Dove's got unparalleled smooth endoplasmic reticulum."

"Which means?"

She pulled his sleeve. "Which means he's a big boy and not our responsibility."

Lucas took off his sunglasses and put on his grumpy face, which enabled them to make it to the street without too many good-byes and promises of visits. Once they were out in the fresh air, he was grateful that the rain had died off; he needed to clear his head.

He put the Persols back on. "Care to walk home?" He pointed up Park Avenue with his cane. It had warmed up and more people were out than he thought there'd be.

"I thought you were tired."

He swung his cane around so it was pointing at the now-open door. "Only of the people in there."

Erin arched an eyebrow. "Maybe we need to rent you some friends."

"If you want to throw your money away, be my guest."

They headed up Park, leaving the evening wear crowd milling about the entry to the Armory—smoking cigarettes, texting, updating

Facebook, checking Tinder and Grindr and their favorite Instagram feeds.

She held the crook of his arm as they walked in silence and one of the side effects of her wearing heels was that every third or fourth step her fingers flexed on his bicep.

When the Armory was well in the rearview mirror, she said, "Thank you for coming. And for not complaining." She bumped his shoulder with the side of her head. "Too much."

"Am I that bad?"

She let out her goofy little snort again.

"I deserve that."

"Did you have *any* fun?"

"Sure. Loads. Especially the part where we left—that was the best." They crossed 68th Street, heading north. "The city lost a lot of doctors last year."

"It didn't really hit me until I saw all those faces up there; I knew a lot of those people. And they're only a fraction of the doctors who died last year—this city is huge." Her grip tightened again and she asked, "What are the chances of knowing so many people who died in such a short period of time?"

Lucas didn't say anything.

Because if he had, all that would have come out was, *Zero.*

5

The Meatpacking District

Dove Knox got out of the Town Car with a highball still in his hand. He put the glass down on the roof of the Lincoln and paid the driver in cash, leaving him the change because he didn't feel like bothering with things like counting right now. He staggered off, forgetting the glass on the vehicle's roof. The miracle was that he managed to walk into his building without accidentally crashing through the glass door (which had happened once, sort of).

The doorman, whose name was Poppy, watched Knox closely, no doubt to make sure he didn't stumble into one of the marble statues that lined the corridor to the elevator, converting it to smithereens. They were ugly sculptures, but apparently very valuable, and part of Poppy's rather loose job description was the protection of building property. Which he appeared to be taking seriously.

Outside, the Town Car left, and there was the high-pitched detonation of glass hitting sidewalk.

"I'llpayfordat!" Knox said as he deciphered the aural feedback. He turned and touched a finger to his brow in a military salute as the elevator doors slid closed. "G'nighPoppy," he said.

The wide industrial hallway on his floor of the converted factory was silent, which was always the case—as creative and eccentric as the patrons of the building liked to think they were, Knox knew all of his neighbors and they were some of the most boring people he had ever met. Not that the doctors he had spent the night with were any better—thank God Luke had been there, even if he was in one of his classic pissy moods.

Knox and his wife had been invited to a party upstairs at the Norwoods' tonight, but they had already committed to the charity event at the Armory. And even though Carla had bailed, he made good on his promise, which had to count for something. And he had spent time with Erin—who looked happier than he had ever seen her—along with Luke, whom Dove very much liked for no reason that he could figure out.

Dove wondered if he had missed anything at the Norwoods' party—even if his neighbors were boring, they were all very rich, and the food at the few soirees he had bothered to attend in the building were all four-star catered affairs. Everyone in the building used the same caterer; they had a retail space diagonally across the intersection. Every now and then, Dove watched the white-smocked staff from his living room, going through their rituals, dicing shallots, and throwing duck fat into skillets.

He arrived at his door and even inebriated was able to punch his entry code into the lockset in one go—one of the ingrained habits of a cosmetic surgeon was hands that refused to shake.

He got inside, sat down on the George Nakashima stool by the door, and carefully removed his close-laced Oxfords, amused at the *ba-boing* sound he imagined his feet made as they slipped free. He inserted the cedar trees, retied the laces so the knots would keep their form, then placed the shoes neatly on the small tray that was there for just such a purpose, but not before wiping them down— another habit.

But what he really wanted was another drink. So he pushed off the hardwood seat, and when the stool slid out of place in his wake he stopped, turned around, and returned it to its precise position in the corner; he was uncomfortable around disorder, which he understood defeated the purpose of drinking in the first place. But being able to identify a problem was not the same as being able to rectify it.

He walked into the living room and took a single step toward the bar when he realized that something was very wrong.

6

The 19th Precinct
East 67th Street

When Detective Russo got back from his field trip to the bridge it was late, and the detectives lounge was empty. But there was never any shortage of things to do, and Russo had plenty of paperwork to do while he waited for the Delmonico autopsy to come in.

Russo had never been much of a sleeper. Not when he was a kid, not through all his time in the service, and most definitely not these days. This Travis Bickle sleep schedule had a big upside—it enabled him to work more hours than anyone else in the shop. And anyone who knows investigative work understands that time is the single greatest commodity you can give a detective. So Russo took the optimist's route in considering his insomnia a gift.

He finished with his new notes from the bridge, put them in the Delmonico file, and pushed it to the corner of his desk, where it would sit until he got the autopsy report back from the Medical Examiner's office—which, as of fifteen minutes ago, was "on the way," whatever that meant. As long as the coroner didn't find any evidence to contradict Russo's judgment call, the records people would make digital copies of the handwritten portions to send to the appropriate departments before the original was sent off to the

Pearson Place Warehouse Facility out in Queens—the repository for all of the NYPD's physical capital files.

Russo was pouring himself another Gatorade and vodka when his phone buzzed with a new email. He finished mixing up the redneck cocktail and checked the message.

It was the autopsy report.

Russo knew what he was going to find before he opened it, but he went through the motions so no one could accuse him of being sloppy at some gotcha moment down the road.

Dr. Jennifer Delmonico had died from extensive blunt force trauma sustained by an impact with a vehicle. There were no drugs in her system and the Medical Examiner was siding with the Department of Transport in labeling this as a suicide.

The only thing that stuck out to the ME was that she had been pregnant—about six weeks.

Again, no surprise to Russo.

But her husband had not mentioned it. Which meant that either he hadn't known—a distinct possibility—or he hadn't felt like sharing. Both of which were understandable if approached from the correct perspective.

Russo printed up the ME's report, placed it in the file, and closed it. He then wrote three words on the cover—*Pregnant? Falcon? Joggers?*—all with question marks so it would look like he had been paying attention, and put it into the top drawer of his desk.

Then he threaded his arms through his overcoat, stuffed his scarf into his pocket, picked up his travel mug, and headed into another sleepless night.

7

Morningside Heights

It was one of those extraordinarily bright days that Dorothy Parker had insightfully declared made the world feel bigger, so Lucas had splurged on the comfort of a taxi instead of the subterranean migrating-salmon routine.

The cab stopped at 120th and Broadway and Lucas carded the fare, waited for the aluminum-finger-rejecting touch screen to yack out a receipt, and stepped out into the morning. The sidewalk in front of the vented glass and metal cube that housed his department was conspicuously devoid of students, and he made it to his office under the second miracle of not encountering anyone interested in speaking to him. Which meant that the day was indeed going well so far.

His assistant, Connie, was behind her desk, the landline to her ear. She nodded a good morning and cupped her hand over the mouthpiece. "Bobby Nadeel is in your office. And you have a departmental meeting at ten thirty."

"Don't let anyone bother me until Nadeel leaves."

"Yes, Dr. Page." And she went back to the call, which sounded like some kind of supplies problem with the school—he hoped she was tracking down the new printer he needed.

Nadeel was sitting behind Lucas's desk, sneakers up, arms behind his head. All that was missing was a cigar in his mouth.

Lucas said, "Get out of my chair," and hit the top of the desk with his cane.

The kid sprang up and almost capsized into the bookcase. "Sorry, Dr. Page, I was just trying it out."

Nadeel was one of Lucas's graduate students. He was laser smart, excellent at ignoring the superfluous to get to the important, and one of those digital natives who breathed algorithms. Lucas had used him in his work with the FBI a few times, and Nadeel's performance had earned him a job offer from the bureau—which he had turned down. His PhD would be finished in a few months and he had some of the most elite think tanks in the world courting him with job offers and promises of stardom. Unfortunately, the allure of fame appealed to him more than anything else.

Lucas dropped the cane onto the sofa, threw the ancient leather mailbag onto the desk, twisted out of his sports coat, hung it on the rack by the door, and sat down in his chair.

"Thanks for coming down, Bobby. I appreciate it."

Nadeel waved it away. "I've been here since you called last night." He took a hard drive out of the yellow nylon backpack on the floor and held it up. "I worked all night in the lab and have everything you asked for."

Lucas emptied the cash out of his wallet and put it down on the desk without counting it. "That's for your time and carfare." Nadeel lived on the Lower East Side with his parents and after an all-nighter Lucas didn't expect the kid to take the subway home.

Bobby stared down at the money as if he had no idea what it was. "I'd much rather use your beach house."

Lucas pushed the bills forward with his aluminum finger. "This isn't a feudal system; your time is valuable. And you can still use my beach house any time I'm not there with the family and if it's not rented out."

Nadeel picked up the cash. "Real money? I didn't know anyone carried this stuff anymore—I don't think I've seen any out in the wild." He counted it. "And this is too much."

"How many hours did you work?"

"Since you called me last night."

"That's barely more than minimum wage, Bobby. You deserve more."

Nadeel folded up the cash and forced it into the front pocket of his jeans. "If you say so." He handed the hard drive to Lucas. "I included a couple of basic cross-references like you asked for, but the majority of data is raw. It's chronological, but I don't see how that could pose any sort of a bias problem—you can shuffle it around if it makes things more objective for you."

Lucas turned the hard drive over in his hands.

"I included everything I could find on every doctor who died in the five boroughs over the past five years, regardless of cause of death. I started with the American Medical Association rosters, focusing on New York practitioners. I identified all the members who had been dropped; then I cross-referenced those against retirement announcements, filtering the fall-through against obituaries. When I had the list of deceased, I tailored an algo to collect all newspaper clippings and media references, including hospital newsletters and trade papers. I went through union rosters. I cross-referenced with real estate listings, apartment rentals, and social media posts. So this is mostly Big Data stuff—all findable if you're willing to go past the first page Google throws at you."

Not that Bobby couldn't figure out how to get into medical files or police reports, but Lucas had been clear that was verboten.

"Thanks, Bobby. I appreciate this."

"So, are you going to tell me what you're looking for? Is this another FBI thing?" By the way he said it, it was obvious he thought Lucas was still too banged up from the last time he had strapped on a badge and duked it out with the bad guys. Which, judging by his still-cracked ribs, cane, and fresh stitches, was not an unreasonable assumption.

Lucas leaned forward and nodded at the door. "Thank you for doing this. And don't forget to let me know when you want the beach house."

Nadeel looked at him for a few long seconds. Then he picked up his backpack, and saluted. "I know when I'm being told to fuck off."

"Then fuck off," Lucas said, and reached for his laptop.

8

Lucas wondered if the entire city—including the six-hundred-plus self-indulgent individuals at the Armory last night—were living a different reality than he. The doctors had missed this. The police had missed this. The Medical Examiner's office, the morgue, the journalists, morticians, and relatives had even missed it. Which made no kind of practical sense—it had been up on that screen during last night's overpriced dinner.

All you had to do was look.

Not calculate.

Not compare.

Not concentrate.

Hell, you didn't even have to *think*.

Just.

Fucking.

Look.

It was big. And bold. And daring someone to find it.

He went over to the printer that had been delivered half an hour ago. The sheaf of printouts was still warm, and smelled of ink. Taping them up was a pain in the ass; his hand was limited to a few basic grips and the microdexterity necessary to pull lengths of tape from a dispenser was beyond him.

It took a few minutes, and when he was done he had thirty pages up on the window in chronological order.

He took a step back to take in the Big Picture when someone knocked.

"Yes?"

Connie cracked the door and stuck her head in. "Your ten-thirty meeting is upstairs, in Judy's office." Dr. Judith Grabinski was the head of the astrophysics department.

Lucas shook his head. "I can't make it."

"It's a must-attend deal—she was specific."

"Then tell her—*specifically*—that I'm not coming. Tell them to send me the minutes."

"You won't bother reading them."

"Of course I won't bother reading them—I'm not interested. If I was, I'd attend the meeting."

Connie nodded like she understood, which she clearly didn't. "Can I tell them you'll be late?"

"No. Now go away."

She closed the door and he slipped back into the Now.

Lucas stood in the center of his office, facing the window. But he no longer saw the printouts. Or the data they contained. He could only see the results.

Thirty pages.

Thirty dates.

Thirty people.

Thirty doctors.

Thirty causes of death.

Thirty homicides.

9

26 Federal Plaza

Brett Kehoe was completely still, as if his central nervous system were on loan from an oil portrait. Lucas strongly suspected that Kehoe existed in one single dimension—that of the Special Agent in Charge of Manhattan. All of Kehoe's other attributes—classical pianist, wealthy West Coaster, family man, Yale graduate—could not compete with his core personality, that of a lawman. Lucas believed that Kehoe pictured himself in a similar capacity, which just augmented the menace.

Special Agent Otto Hoffner stood behind Lucas, his unusual height and general mass blocking out a good portion of the light coming in through the floor-to-ceiling glass wall that separated Kehoe's terrarium from the war room. Beyond the wall, agents busied themselves with all manner of crime solving, and the space looked like the accounting department of a multi-national. Hoffner was also preternaturally still.

Kehoe's eyes came back online and he looked down at the manila folder Lucas had dropped onto his desk.

"Thirty?" Kehoe said.

"Yes."

"Homicides?"

"Yes."

"Thirty homicides?"

"You're repeating yourself."

Kehoe took the sterling eyeglass frames from his pocket, unfolded them, and pushed them into place with his middle finger and thumb. He opened the manila file and began the rapid-eye dance of left-to-right-zig-back, repeat, without stopping for the full thirty pages.

He put six minutes and eleven seconds into the exercise, and when he finished he closed the folder and placed it back down on his desk.

Lucas didn't bother trying to calculate all the things going on in the man's head; he just waited. Kehoe was relatively efficient at parsing information. He was a broad-strokes kind of manager, and never needed a lot of nuance or detail to create a working model. But this entire story arc was built on details. Hundreds of small, circumstantial, highly improbable details that, when assembled, morphed into something much larger than the sum of its individual components.

So it wasn't really a question of if Kehoe *would* see it.

It was a question of if he *could* see it.

Kehoe folded his glasses and returned them to his pocket. "How can you be certain that they *aren't* accidents and suicides?"

"Anyone who lives in this city assumes that it's small, because you can see the edges from the top of any good skyscraper. But when you factor in a population of eight and a half million people, you have to measure demographics in terms of per-hundred-thousand. Which means that any subgroup that you can identify with the naked eye—and completely out of context—is a red flag."

Kehoe shrugged. "I don't see anything with my naked eye. Just thirty people whose time was up." He took a breath, then refocused on Lucas. "So convince me."

Lucas took a sip of coffee from the mug balanced on the wide leather armrest. "There is absolutely no pattern in their distribution."

"So?"

"A lack of pattern is a dead giveaway that you're looking at a pattern."

"How can a lack of a pattern be proof that there is a pattern?" He stared at Lucas, but his focus didn't switch from eye to eye, which was unusual. Even for him. "Explain it to me."

Lucas automatically shifted to lecture mode. "Randomness isn't the lack of a pattern in any given structure; it's the *apparent* lack of a pattern. At first glance, many sets of data appear to have no distribution pattern. But randomness—*true* randomness—is affected by something called probability, or, for this particular example, *probability distribution*. Which means that even in a series of true random events, there will be patterns. There will be repeats. There will be overlaps. And there will be coincidences." He nodded at the pages on Kehoe's desk. "Which this data set is missing—there are absolutely no patterns at all."

"All I see is thirty people who died in different ways: a bicycle accident, a drowning, a fall from a building, a trip down a flight of stairs, an overdose." Kehoe tapped the stack of paper. "Bad luck, worse luck, no luck, terrible luck, self-determination."

Lucas started a nod that converted into a shake of his head. "There's something called random selection that guarantees that there are patterns within true randomness. A mathematician named Motzkin said that even though randomness appears to be generally disordered, it is never *completely* disordered. I'll give you an example." Lucas turned to the war room beyond the glass terrarium of Kehoe's office.

"If you have a large group of people, say"—he did an instantaneous head count that was relatively accurate—"two hundred and thirty-one to two hundred and thirty-four individuals, what are the odds that two people in that group share the same birthday?"

Kehoe's eyes narrowed again. "One in three hundred and sixty-five?"

"Which I agree appears to be a roughly correct answer."

"But it's not?"

Lucas cantilevered out of the chair and went to the door that Hoffner was blocking. "Could you please pedal your oversized ass out of my way?"

Hoffner stepped aside and opened the door.

Lucas addressed the agents closest by. "Excuse me, could you people in this row stand up, all the way to you, right there." He indicated a female agent with brown hair two cubicles from the end, which made twenty individuals.

Everyone looked to Hoffner, who nodded. So they stood.

"Thank you." Lucas turned back to Kehoe. "A sample group of twenty that is more or less random, although they are all FBI agents, so the sampling isn't *truly* random, plus they all sit in the same row, which removes another layer, but it's close enough to serve our purposes. Special Agent Hoffner, since you know these people, would you please ask the first one in line what his birthday is?"

Hoffner's voice sounded like a seismic event when he said, "Agent Mayer?"

Mayer was a young man with a single eyebrow that peaked as if Shirley Jackson had just offered to sell him a lottery ticket. "February twenty-one, sir."

Lucas nodded a thank-you, then asked the group in general, "Who else in this row has a birthday on February twenty-first?"

An agent six places down the line raised his hand and nodded. "I do."

"Thank you."

Lucas stepped back into the office and Hoffner pulled the door closed, once again muting the activity beyond the glass.

"Six places"—he held up his aluminum fingers and added a thumb from his original hand—"*not* three hundred and sixty-five. Which is unusual, but that's the beauty of true randomness: it's never *completely random*. Why? Because in a truly random sampling, repetition is inevitable—that's the way the universe works. Which brings us back to Motzkin—" Lucas pointed a green anodized finger at the printouts on Kehoe's desk. "While disorder is more probable in general, complete disorder is *impossible*. To have that many deaths among individuals within a given group where none of them die on the same day of the month is so statistically unlikely as to be impossible. And none of them died on a Tuesday. Not one. The universe is a big place, and unusual and unlikely things happen all the time. But something is wrong here."

"That's it? You think that these are murders because none of the deceased died on the same day of the week? Or on the same date?" Kehoe was avoiding the word "victims."

"There's something else—every last one of those deaths happened during a routine in the victim's life, which is another overlap. Sure, if you examine them individually, there's nothing unusual about them—a fall off a bike, going overboard while fishing, getting locked out and falling from a balcony while trying to climb over to a neighbor's, tripping while walking down steps and getting a fence picket through the brainpan, overdosing on Oxy. Yes, people die in freaky-deaky ways all the time. But when you factor in that Dr. Lu took the same bike path he died on every day for the past five years, Dr. Fossner took his boat out three times a week, Dr. Bugliosi posted a selfie climbing from her balcony to the neighbor's on social media three months before she fell to her death, Dr. Vance climbed his steps at that particular time every day for the past twenty years, and Dr. Ibicki went to his cabin every weekend he had off, you start to see that these things happened when the victims were going through routines that were easy to identify and then follow."

"Like Jennifer"—Kehoe went to the last page in the pile—"Delmonico?" He looked up. "She didn't commit suicide?"

Lucas shook his head. "I can't figure that one out—it's not quite like the others. And it seems like it's too close to the last one, which was only two weeks back. There's some noise that I can't decipher. But she fits into the general dynamics of the whole."

Kehoe was no longer staring at Lucas like he was leaking oil. "If you are right—*if*—how come everyone else missed these deaths?"

"They're *homicides*, Brett."

"Homicides that were missed by the Medical Examiner's people, the NYPD, FDNY, the coroner's office, ATF, the New York City Department of Investigation, the Department of Transport, the Bridge Authority, the media, and the families of the deceased?" His face slipped into control mode and he looked at Lucas. "They've all been investigated." Kehoe understood that the world was imperfect, and that law enforcement made mistakes. But he was also a big believer in the bureau. And supremely overconfident in its efficacy. "So tell me, how can everyone else be wrong and only you be right?"

"I keep asking myself that very same question." Lucas reached into his bag and pulled out eight pages he had prepared for Kehoe, all handwritten on lavender legal paper. Lucas knew that he was being a little heavy-handed and sanctimonious, but sometimes the only way to drive the point home was with a hammer. He placed the pages on the corner of Kehoe's desk and stood up.

Kehoe took the pages, flipped through them, then looked up, his face conveying his confusion. "What's this?"

"Proof." Lucas stood up and slid his bag onto his shoulder. Then he took a final sip of coffee from the bureau mug on the armrest. "Now if you'll excuse me, I have somewhere else to be."

10

Kehoe picked up the papers that Page had given him before yet another melodramatic exit. The legal pages were tattooed with the most complicated mathematical formula Kehoe had ever seen—eight oversized sheets of heavily stylized ballpoint scrawl. The equation contained myriad symbols Kehoe didn't recognize that might as well have been the word "CROATOAN" carved into a tree.

He had no idea what he was looking at and no idea what the calculation was supposed to illustrate; as smart as he thought of himself, this was beyond his off-the-shelf math program.

So he dialed an internal extension that was answered before he heard it ring.

"Special Agent Li."

"Li, Brett Kehoe. I need you to come to my office."

"On the way, sir."

Kehoe hung up without saying anything else.

While he waited for Li, he made copies of Page's formula, then stamped and initialed both sets according to FBI protocol. He tucked the originals away in his top drawer as Li appeared at the far end of the war room, near the elevators.

Li was a tall, awkward man who had lousy people skills that

no one cared about because he was never required to work with people. His expertise was computational and applied mathematics, but he spent the bulk of his time in cryptanalysis, deciphering coded messages.

After checking in with Kehoe's assistant, Li was admitted to the glass office.

"What can I do for you, sir?" Even from across the desk he smelled of coffee and breath mints.

Kehoe held out the still-warm pages he had just printed.

Li took them and pushed his glasses up on his nose with his index before dropping unceremoniously into one of the chrome-and-leather cubes. "What is this?" he asked himself barely above a whisper.

Li spent a few silent minutes going over the pages, backtracking several times. When he finished, it was impossible to read his features beyond the general description of confusion. "Where did you get this?"

"I need you to tell me what it is."

"It's an equation, but—" Confusion was replaced by curiosity.

"*But* what?"

"But I don't understand it."

"What do you mean?"

"I, um, wow." His head ticktocked back and forth as he assembled an explanation. "Just because someone strings all these numbers together, it doesn't translate to them necessarily making sense. I can see that a lot of the terms work, but that doesn't mean they all fit together. It's possible that whatever this is, it's incorrect."

Kehoe was willing to believe that Page might be wrong about his doctor-killing conspiracy, but he could not accept Page being wrong about numbers. "I trust the source."

"I'll get to work on it."

"We don't have the time to *work on it*. Are we associated with anyone who can decipher this quickly?"

"It's not about deciphering this; it's about understanding it." Li looked up, and for a second Kehoe thought he had somehow figured the equation out. "Lucas Page would know how to work this out."

Kehoe shook his head. "Page can't be involved."

Li shrugged. "Then Corey Winslow at Stanford would be my bet."

Kehoe picked up the desk phone and held it out. "Call him."

11

The Hayden Planetarium
Museum of Natural History

Lucas paced the dark floor in slow, deliberate steps that allowed the bulk of his bandwidth to be directed at the cosmos overhead. The planetarium was temperature and humidity controlled, but it was no match for East Coast humidity, and the anchor pins for his prosthetics were transmitting the telltale low-voltage signal to his bones that it was once again raining and cold outside.

He was completely engrossed in the one passion that had commanded his life—the cosmos—taking in the high-definition three-dimensional projection that was part of the planetarium's latest push to educate a largely uninterested public about the universe in which they lived, no small feat when compared to the allure of memes on their phone screens. The model overhead was a pastiche of more than two hundred thousand images collected by radio telescopes around the world (including many photographs sent back to earth from distant robotic interstellar probes), then sewn together by tailor-made software, resulting in a breathtaking model of most of the known universe.

Two of his bestselling books had dealt with astrophysics—*reducing the complicated to the simple*, the dust jackets had declared—and he was here as a guest contributor. He was not a natural orator like past participants—he lacked the panache of Tom Hanks, Robert Redford, and Neil deGrasse Tyson—but he made up for it with a decade behind the professor's podium and a superb grasp of the material. Everyone involved in the project—including himself—was pleased with his performance thus far. He had already recorded four one-hour sessions and had another two to go, including this one— all of which would be edited for time, clarity, and application.

His unique ability to compartmentalize problems meant that even though he had scrubbed the thirty fresh murders from his RAM, they had simply been relegated to one of his secondary processors while his primary system narrated the discovery of the Witch Head Nebula.

Lucas automatically paced while he spoke, a habit he had developed early in his teaching career. He had traded his clunky Loakes for a pair of mesh Nikes to cut down on biomechanical clatter, but every now and then some part of him clicked or clunked or clanked and the sound engineer shook her head in the dim light of the console. But she never asked Lucas to repeat himself—stopping distorted his flow.

He was explaining why many astrophysicists believed that IC 2118 was an ancient supernova remnant when his phone buzzed in his pocket.

With five children and a wife who was an ER surgeon, he made it a rule to always answer calls.

It was Erin and he hit the green *answer* pictograph. "Hey, baby."

"Luke—" Her voice was calm, but he could tell she was forcing it.

He pushed a million imagined catastrophes out of his own way and said, "What?" a little louder than he intended to.

She was silent for a second.

"What is it?" he asked, louder still, and his arteries all stopped delivering blood to the various systems.

"I got a cryptic text from Carla and—" Her voice cracked and she paused. When she came back on, she was using her calm ER doctor voice. "Something happened to Dove."

Which meant nothing had happened to the kids.

His circulation started back up.

But the word "something" covered a lot of real estate in the bad-news department. "What kind of *something*?"

"He's dead."

12

The Meatpacking District

Lucas saw the emergency vehicles from a block out and the double adrenaline hit of dread and curiosity hit his system. There was an ambulance, a single police car, and a big black SUV that had to be a bureau ride.

The cab let him out on the opposite side of the street, and as he crossed the intersection the door to the SUV opened and the giant wedge of Special Agent Otto Hoffner stepped out. His facial expression and body language were just as lifeless as they had been earlier in the day and Lucas wondered if the guy had any other settings.

Hoffner didn't wave or smile or even nod—he just watched Lucas cane his way across the intersection one clickety-click at a time.

When Lucas made the intersection, Hoffner gave a perfunctory nod that had all the warmth of a jackbooted heel click. "Dr. Page."

Hoffner's size gave the automatic—and very incorrect—impression that he was a dumb man. It was true that he looked like he had had been designed to survive car accidents. But it was also true that he held degrees in both political science and labor law. And he was most definitely a man who could operate under pressure.

The combination of which explained why Kehoe depended on him as much as he would allow himself to depend on anyone.

Lucas skipped past the *I'm fine and how are yous?* with, "How long have you been here?"

"Six minutes." Hoffner looked up at the building—a renovated block of lofts where they had once manufactured clothing. "I spoke with the Medical Examiner's people and the police on-site; your friend hung himself with an extension cord—"

Lucas felt the oxygen in his lungs convert to a superfluid. And then it hit his blood. Every cell in his body, including the gel in his eyeball, stopped vibrating for a single zeptosecond.

And then it all started back up again.

"NYPD has been here a couple of hours now—the doorman called them after the housekeeper found the body. They did a quick walk-through, took photographs, then called the ME. Their people took a while to get here, and they weren't finished when I arrived. NYPD identified the body by his wallet, and they have notified his wife—who spoke to your wife."

"We're friends." Lucas hated having to explain himself, but there was a long line of telephones in this particular event.

"They're waiting to take your friend down until you've looked around." Hoffner closed the door to the Lincoln. "Another dead doctor."

"Are you starting to realize that I am right?"

Hoffner looked back up at the building. "Let's just say that I agree that there is not as much coincidence out there as people would like to believe."

• • •

The Medical Examiner's people were waiting in the hallway as Lucas did his walk-through.

The smell filled his lungs and coated his sinuses, the olfactory triggers embedded in ancestral memory conjuring all kinds of name-less fears. But Lucas had something to do, so he pushed all of his in-stincts into the back of the box and focused on the next few minutes.

He looked down at the shoes Dove had worn last night. Slim last, English-made cap-toe deals. Closed laces tied in one of Dove's classic boat-snob knots.

Lucas stared at the shoes as he acclimated to the smell he wouldn't be able to shake for hours, then entered the apartment proper.

But that was not to say that he was prepared for what he found.

Dove Knox hung from one of the structural joists that supported the floor above. His eyes were reduced to two sockets pressed into the clay of his skull and his tongue pushed out through his per-fect teeth. He was naked. One of the kitchen barstools was toppled over on the floor behind him, between two of the club chairs that framed the carpet.

There was a half-empty bottle of scotch on the coffee table—some obscure brand with one of those weird Islay spellings—and a single lowball on a coaster.

Lucas looked up, past his dead friend's cockeyed stare, to the extension cord that had been used as an improvised noose. The loop that held his neck was formed with a hangman's knot, but it was poorly done, and one of the loops had rolled over another.

The knot securing the cord to the truss was a complicated deal that Lucas didn't know the name of.

Hoffner sounded like he was making an effort to be sympathetic when he asked, "You okay?"

"No." Lucas shook his head and the movement helped him slip into character. "And would you please not talk to me."

Hoffner grumbled two inaudible syllables and walked away.

Lucas stood at the edge of the carpet, which was beige. Or taupe. Or mushroom. Or whatever the style pundits were calling that particular shade of unimposing not-quite-white-but-not-quite-tan these days.

After a few moments of staring up at the painted metal joist, Lucas began a walk around the apartment. On the single occasion that the whole family had come for dinner, the kids hadn't touched anything. But not because they were well-mannered—but because it felt like the order was built into the underlying code of the place, as if touching any of the objects on display would have ill consequences. Dove hadn't followed the kids around with coasters, but it wasn't hard to imagine him doing so. And it was the same now. Everything from the photographs on the wall leading to the master bedroom to the books on the shelves was very clearly aligned to some unseen grid.

Which Lucas could understand—there was safety in order.

The slick apartment could loosely be described as minimalism with the extras subtracted—the old ad agency slogan taken a step further: *Simplify* ~~Simplify~~. The loft was sculpted out of pure painter's white that lacked even a hint of hue to it, nothing to warm—or cool—the space. It was a background color. A gallery color. Chosen to showcase the objects, not compete with them. And it was one of the few indoor spaces where Lucas's sunglasses were actually necessary.

After touring the living and dining rooms, Lucas stopped at the photographs in the wide, well-lit hallway. They were framed, matted, and perfectly aligned. Photos of Dove and Carla, looking like what they were—successful Manhattanites, ridiculously handsome people with plenty of money and all the self-confidence that came with the gift baskets they had been allotted.

He had promised Erin he'd look around, and that was precisely what he was doing. There was no directive. No goal. Just the action of observation.

He walked through the guest room, then the bathroom, the master bedroom. He checked the medicine chest in the en suite. Toured the large walk-in that Dove and Carla shared—*His* and *Hers* sides.

Unlike the open sterility of the rest of the house, the closet was molecularly packed. But still laboratory clean and organized. Dove's shirts all hung precisely one inch apart—fifteen-barrel cuffs, ten single cuffs, and ten French cuffs—all white. Neckties filled a dozen cedar trays, rolled up and organized by hue—Dove had been disproportionately attracted to blues leaning into purple. No stripes in the bunch, not even a lone school tie. All of the shoes were bespoke, perfectly polished, and fitted with cedar trees branded with the logos of different makers. His cuff links and wristwatches were neatly arranged in three drawers. Nothing was out of place.

Lucas took a few photographs and went back to the living room.

There was an arrangement of fresh calla lilies in the middle of the big German Secessionist dining table. They were leaning toward the window, doing their best to offset the horror of Dove's body floating above his shadow on the carpet in a grotesque sundial.

Lucas looked beyond Dove, and focused on the negative space, looking for anything that might hold meaning.

And the only thing that stuck out was that one of the club chairs was off its mark.

Lucas looked at the room—at the six club chairs positioned around the carpet. There were two on each long side and one at each end, all at right angles, precisely six inches from the edge of the carpet.

He took a few photographs, then crouched down and examined the hardwood. A year's worth of UV light from the huge windows had bleached the exposed wood, leaving darkened position markers under the rug and chairs. One of the chairs was almost a full foot out of position, eight feet over from where Dove was hanging.

"Special Agent Hoffner, could you please ask the ME's people if that chair was like that when they arrived." Lucas turned to Hoffner, who was watching him with professional disinterest.

Without saying anything, Hoffner went to speak with the ME's people.

The cops had done a walk-through before the ME's people had arrived. Which meant anyone could have moved that chair.

Hoffner came back in and gave Lucas an odd look when he said, "That chair was exactly like that when they arrived. The NYPD is sending their walk-through photos over."

"Can we go to the basement?"

The big man shrugged. "We're the FBI; we can do whatever we want."

. . .

Hoffner was silent, which Lucas preferred over any forced conviviality—if they were going to be miserable around each other, they might as well be themselves.

Lucas unlocked the chain-link locker and stepped inside the eight-by-ten-foot space. Like the loft, everything was perfectly placed—all on plastic shelving, with nothing stacked on anything else, and nothing on the floor. There was a big Filson duffel that Lucas recognized as Dove's boat bag. He took it down, and rolled back the big brass zipper. Cotton boat rope was on top of the gear, tied in a neat figure-eight coil. Dove's boat shoes were beneath that, the laces threaded through the eyelets in a lattice pattern, the ends tied off in barrel knots. Lucas took a few photos of the coiled rope and the boat shoes with his cell phone, then closed the duffel and put it back in its place on the shelf. Beside it were two more coils of rope—both tied in figure eights—that he also photographed.

Lucas locked the gate with the padlock and gave it a few yanks because that's what everyone does.

Hoffner was staring at him. "And?"

"Dove Knox did not commit suicide."

13

26 Federal Plaza

Kehoe's earlier icy disinterest had been replaced with purpose and he was no longer treating Lucas like the mechanical boy who had cried doctor-killing wolf.

But that did not necessarily translate to Kehoe being in a good mood. "Was there any strategic value to your pissing off both the NYPD and the ME?"

Lucas opened his hands in a *That's the way it is* gesture. "Their emotions are misplaced; they shouldn't be angry, they should be embarrassed."

"The Medical Examiner's people said Dove Knox committed suicide. They found absolutely *zero* evidence of foul play."

"What do you want me to say, Brett? They're wrong. Has the CSI team got back to you?"

Kehoe looked up at Hoffner, who shook his head.

"So walk me through this," Kehoe said. There was no condescension in his tone, just a need to understand. It was his job to defend his people, and he could only perform that duty if he was informed. "What did you see at Knox's place that they didn't?"

"Knox was obsessive. He was a plastic surgeon, and I'd like to say that his professional ethos bled over into his personal life, but I think the actual truth is he became a plastic surgeon to accommodate his personal tics—something about correcting disorder. Dove ran his life like a German engineering app—everything he did was a combination of routine and precision. And I mean *everything*." Lucas pulled the ME's file over and flipped the pages a little too quickly with his metal fingers, ripping a few. When he found what he was looking for, he spun it around. "Look."

The image was a close-up of the extension cord around Dove's neck.

Kehoe picked up his tea, took a sip, and leaned forward, focusing on the picture. "What, precisely, am I looking for?"

"That cord and those knots."

"A hangman's knot on an extension cord. Not uncommon." Kehoe stared at him for a few long seconds that indicated he expected to have his opinion changed with something quantifiable.

Lucas took out his cell phone and scrolled through to the correct photo. "Here," he said, holding up the image Erin had taken of him, Neville Carpenter, and Dove Knox at the Armory last night. "That's Dove on the right. Look at that tie knot, Brett."

Kehoe took the phone and zoomed in with a thumb and index. "An Eldredge knot," he said matter-of-factly.

Lucas wasn't surprised that he knew what he was looking at—Kehoe was in one of his custom-tailored suits from Brioni and his shoes were bespoke, no doubt John Lobb according to preference. If anyone understood fashion minutiae, it was he.

"Look at the next couple of pictures."

Kehoe took another sip of tea as he swiped through the roll. He stopped on every frame—on the coils of rope and the intricate knots on Dove's boat sneakers, to the bespoke cap-toed deals in the front hallway. He finished the roll, put the phone down, and said, "He was good at knots." It was a statement, not a question.

Kehoe then turned back to the Medical Examiner's photographs. He leaned over the image and looked at the clumsy hangman's knot tied in the electrical cord.

Lucas nodded at his phone. "And the knot used to fasten the extension cord to the joist? I looked it up; it's called a—"

"Halyard bend," Kehoe finished for him. "And it's tied incorrectly."

Lucas nodded. "That's my point. He wouldn't screw up a knot. He tied them incorrectly on purpose. So that someone would know."

Kehoe looked at Lucas like he expected more.

"It's not just the knots," Lucas added. "Look at the position of the club chairs around the carpet in the first responder photograph, then look at the sun-bleached floor. Dove was maniacal about every little detail in his life—he would rotate his dinner plate until he found the right angle. He wouldn't order any food that was round, like peas—and if he ordered carrots, he had to have them julienned, not sliced. He had his Porsche cleaned twice a week—which meant he had to replace the carpets twice a year. And those chairs were always six inches from the carpet. Except when the first responders showed up."

Kehoe examined the picture. "He could have knocked this out of place when he kicked the chair away. Or stumbled into it before. He had been drinking all night from what the report said."

Lucas shook his head. "I've seen him put an entire bottle of scotch away in a night, Brett. The guy was like a funnel. Sure, he was half in the bag, but he wasn't fall-down drunk. Besides, I did the math, and there's no way he could have moved that club chair once he was up. Those suckers are heavy—hardwood frames with wire backs covered in horsehair and aged leather—they weigh a lot. Even if he had knocked the stool into that chair—which is impossible according to the laws of physics unless it bounced on the coffee table—it would not have moved. I'm not saying that he couldn't have left things like this, but he *wouldn't have*. Especially after a few drinks when he depended on routine. And his routine was to be obsessive about things like knots and furniture. Just look at the shoes he was wearing last night—they were placed neatly on the tray by the door; they had been retied, and even brushed off, all accomplished while he was drunk. So he didn't forget any of his habits. Plus, he had those three coils of rope in his locker—he never would have hung himself with an extension cord. He would have considered it poor form or something."

Kehoe picked up the photo the first responder had taken and examined the pushed-back chair. Then he thumbed back through the roll on Lucas's phone and examined the close-up of the sun-bleached pattern on the old factory floor.

Lucas considered Kehoe to be one of the smartest men in law enforcement and he knew Kehoe was lining everything up. "Whoever killed him sat down to watch him die, Brett—that's why the chair is moved back."

Kehoe stared at Lucas for a few moments and it was easy to see there were a lot of things going on behind the façade of calm. He took another sip of tea, but it was one of those little movements that he used to buy time as he thought things through. He put his hand down on the thirty pages Lucas had dropped off that morning. They had been repackaged with a clear plastic cover stamped with the bureau's seal. "Okay."

Kehoe then shifted focus to Hoffner. "I want you in charge for the next twenty-four hours. Put a team together and find a weakness in one of these cases that Page discovered."

Hoffner nodded. "Yessir."

"And I don't want this leaked, so pick the right people. If it gets out that we missed a string of murders before we know what we're looking at, it is going to take us a very long time to regain the public's trust—and rightfully so."

Another nod out of Hoffner just as his phone buzzed. "CSI from the Sixth," he said to Kehoe before answering with a professional, "FBI. Special Agent Hoffner here."

He listened.

"I appreciate this."

Pause.

"And you're certain?"

Pause.

"It's nothing personal." The turret of Hoffner's skull slowly swiveled until it was pointing at Lucas. "I'll tell him."

Pause.

"Send the report over ASAP."

Pause.

"Good-bye."

Hoffner pocketed the phone, and looked over at Kehoe. "That was Danny Holt, head of the CSI unit out of the Sixth. Holt believes that Page here is right. They're not classifying it as murder yet, but they've labeled it as *suspicious*."

Kehoe asked Hoffner, "What did they find?" but he was staring at Lucas.

Hoffner shrugged as if that explained everything. "They are going to call once they get toxicology back, and they're still waiting on the lab to analyze some powder, but the big lead is the extension cord. Knox's fingerprints were all over that cord—he definitely tied it himself. But he did something odd—he intentionally left his prints in a pattern: neat little rows all up and down the cord."

Lucas opened his hands. "Why would he do that if he didn't expect anyone to look into it? He was leaving clues, Brett. They're obscure. And a little hopeful. But whatever was happening forced him to improvise."

Hoffner nodded like that made sense. "Holt also said that they found some powder on the cord. They think it's cornstarch."

Lucas pointed a green aluminum hand at Kehoe. "I told you."

Kehoe's expression flattened out as he put things together. "Gloves powdered with cornstarch have been off the market for six or seven years—the starch was going airborne and causing allergic reactions. Were there any latex gloves in the place when you did your walk-through?"

"Under the sink. But I didn't check them for powder."

Kehoe directed a question at Hoffner. "Did they have anything else to add?"

Hoffner nodded matter-of-factly. "They asked if we could please keep Page away from their crime scenes in the future."

Kehoe allowed himself a small smile at that.

"Did they figure out the most obvious tell?" Lucas asked, wondering how it was possible that everyone else had missed this one final detail.

Hoffner's eyes dialed in on Lucas. "Most obvious tell?"

"Did anyone else notice that Dove was naked?"

"Of course."

"Then where the fuck are his clothes from the gala last night? Because they were nowhere in the apartment."

Hoffner let out a very low frequency "Sonofabitch."

Lucas stood up and pointed a green aluminum finger at Kehoe. "I told you—embarrassed."

14

East 70th Street

Dr. Arna Solomon shifted the big Benz into *park* and hit the shut-off button on the exotic wood dashboard with a finger she was using to air conduct Wagner's *Die Walküre*. She sat there for a moment, absorbing the sonic body blows of Iréne Theorin delivering a mountain-rending Brünnhilde. When the thunderstorm of heavy strings and deep brasses kicked in, Solomon brought both hands into the act, punctuating the crash of cymbals and subterranean roar of the bass drums with a few Victor Borge flourishes. Twain had been right—Wagner wasn't nearly as bad as he sounded. But there were still two hours left in the piece and Solomon did not have the luxury of time, so she turned off the sound system mid–lightning strike.

The sudden quiet triggered her work reflex, and she shut down her internal fantasy conductor, shifting into doctor mode. She collected her travel mug and the old Barneys leather messenger bag—the one that used to belong to her dead husband, Jacob—and stepped out into the garage.

It was close to dinnertime, which was both between shifts and before visiting hours, and the space was appropriately quiet. Solomon was not a woman given to melancholy. In point of fact, she was a card-carrying optimist—a necessary and indispensable personality trait in her field. But she had never liked the garage with its low ceilings, Soviet-airport lighting, and weird furtive echoes. But it was better than hunting for a spot on the street, especially when it was raining.

Solomon thumbed the lock function on the exterior door handle and the computerized nervous system of the vehicle blipped the park lights a single time. She adjusted the messenger bag on her shoulder, took a sip of coffee, and headed for the exit, which always felt farther than she remembered.

She had spent the past six weeks banking extra hours, which was a pleasant option rather than an unpleasant necessity at this point in her life. She was going away next month and didn't want any of her colleagues being forced to pick up the slack. Solomon had always functioned under the premise that health care was a vocation rather than a trade, and the idea of letting even a single patient down was anathema to her.

Today she was in a particularly good mood because she had spent the afternoon with her daughter, going over the final arrangements for her grandson Jacob's bar mitzvah. Of all her grandchildren, Jacob was her favorite—there was simply something about the boy that reached a little deeper into her heart. She didn't let it affect the way she treated the others, but it was something she was aware of. Maybe it had something to do with the way the boy wanted to be a doctor when he grew up, or maybe it had something to do with Jacob's uncanny resemblance—in looks, personality, and even name—to her late husband. Whatever the reason, it was one of those things that she filed away under the mysteries of the human heart.

Solomon was taking Jacob on a trip—two, actually. First they were going to Israel. They would spend a little time with family, but the aim was to teach Jacob a little more about his people. After that, they were off to Easter Island for ten days.

It was the same gift she and her late husband had given all their grandchildren when they turned thirteen—a trip to Israel followed by another anywhere they chose. All three of Solomon's eldest son Morton's kids had opted for Disney World. But what could you expect, they were *Morton's kids*. Benjamin, her other grandson, had opted for Paris, which was the perfect choice for someone who liked museums and shopping. But young Jacob? Once again, he had surprised and delighted her by choosing Easter Island; the bulk of their time would be spent among the Moai. It was in these small personal accomplishments that she was redefining herself in a way she had never imagined possible at this point in her life. After all, without family, life was little more than a spectator sport—she had learned that with her husband's death. Once again, he had been right—there were no happy endings for happy marriages.

Other than her own footsteps, there was some kind of mechanical clatter, almost out of range, that sounded like an electric motor trying not to die. Even the ambient noise of the city outside was dim, as if the volume had been dialed back. She sighted the yellow entrance to the stairwell in the corner, past the handicapped spaces, and zigged accordingly, stepping into the main lane.

Solomon was vaguely aware that something between the cars to her right moved. And she heard the beginnings of a noise—a soft scrape.

But she never had the chance to turn her head.

Or finish the thought.

Because the two bullets knocked her off her feet.

She slammed over into the floor.

Her head hit the cold deck.

And she was distantly aware that her teeth clattered off into the dimly lit nothing.

Arna Solomon lay on the concrete as her coffee mug rolled in a lazy circle a million miles away. She tried to focus on it. Managed to blink once. Then died.

15

The Upper East Side

Lucas walked beside the kids as they crossed Madison to the only place in the neighborhood (other than the 72nd Street playground) they considered to be hallowed ground—a tiny glass-fronted restaurant unceremoniously named Pizza! in typical New York get-to-the-point-ism. It was the textbook example of a hole-in-the-wall and, if examined from a real estate speculation perspective, wasn't large enough to park a car in. That it hadn't been absorbed by one of its neighbors was a zoning/legal miracle. To call it world famous would be slightly hyperbolic, but not completely inaccurate. It was also an excellent stopgap when a home-cooked meal went south.

And tonight's dinner had most definitely been a failure by any applicable metric.

Besides their five children, they had a tenant named (or, to be technically correct, nicknamed) Dingo. He and Lucas had become friends more than a decade ago, when they had both been doing mutual long-term stints at the rehabilitation center—Dingo had been a combat photographer and had lost both legs to a land mine in sub-Saharan Africa. When Lucas and Erin bought the house, there had never really been any sort of mystery as to who would live in the tiny apartment over the garage. Dingo reapplied his skill set to fashion photography and the occasional product shoot but spent the bulk of his time teaching a form of Brazilian Jiujutsu to other amputees. The kids loved him almost as much as he loved them, and he sometimes doubled as what Maude, in a rare Chuck Lorre flourish, liked to call their "manny."

The plan tonight had been for Dingo to teach Hector and Laurie how to make his famous spaghetti. After Dingo and the kids brought the two big serving dishes to the table, everyone was ceremoniously served and they settled in for what was loudly declared to be gourmet Nirvana.

Then Erin put a forkful of pasta into her mouth.

"Um, kids?" she said, her face playing around with an expression resembling a Renoir drunk. "What did you spice this with?" It wasn't hard to see that she was making a real effort not to spit the pasta out.

Hector gave the one teenage reply that had survived every generation gap since the evolution of opposable thumbs—a shrug. "Dunno. Just the stuff you put out."

Erin's mouth closed a little and she chewed, but she wasn't swallowing and Lucas took that as a cue and sniffed a forkful of what looked like perfectly fine spaghetti with meat sauce. It didn't smell *bad*—but it definitely smelled *odd*.

"Just the stuff I put out?" Erin asked.

Hector nodded. "Mostly."

Dingo nodded at Laurie. "I let her add some pepper flakes to give it more flavor." He sucked in a forkful of spaghetti and his face froze mid-chew like a baseball player working on a cheek full of tobacco.

"Which pepper flakes?" Erin asked.

Lucas put his fork down.

It was obvious that Dingo also couldn't swallow, so he spoke through his food. "The ones in the little container."

Erin tried not to treat Dingo like one of the kids, but sometimes it got away from her. "*Which* little container?" she asked after spitting the spaghetti into her napkin as politely as possible with seven people and two dogs watching her.

Laurie pushed off from the table, ran to the kitchen, and came back with a small plastic jar. "This one. The orange flakes."

Erin looked at the jar in Laurie's hand. Then down at her meal. Then over at Maude, who was smiling. Then at Damien, who was munching his pasta like it was the best thing in the world. Then over to Laurie, who was smelling her food but not eating it. Then back to Dingo. "That's goldfish food," she said.

Which was when Lucas pushed back from the table and enthusiastically said, "It's pizza night!"

So here they were.

As always, a small crowd stood outside, fucking around on their phones while they waited for their pizzas. Lucas pushed the door open for the two kids/Sherpas/assembly line supervisors and a warm cloud of steam carrying a mixture of herbs and garlic billowed out, setting off all the appropriate Pavlovian apps. Hector and Laurie ducked under his arm and marched formally to the counter in two synchronized goose steps, which got a smile from the little hairy dude in the white T-shirt behind the counter.

"Hey, guys, what'll it be this week?" he asked, reaching for his pad. Their routine was well-known, and Lucas tended to over-tip as a salve for their poor decision-making skills.

Lucas said, "Hello, Derrick. How's business?"

He shrugged. "Overworked. Underpaid."

Which Lucas knew went without saying—he couldn't understand how it was possible to sell an inexpensive commodity like pizza in a retail area that boasted one of the most expensive cost-per-foot ratios on the planet. The worst part was hearing customers complaining about their prices—when this place succumbed to the cheapskates, some fancy cupcake shop would move in where they would be happy to pay eleven bucks for a mouthful of sugar and flour while lamenting the loss of the pizza joint their stinginess had driven out of business.

Laurie looked up and nodded. "My dad says the same thing all the time. He works for the circus!" she said with great pride.

Derrick's eyebrow went up with that and he reframed his focus on Lucas. "I thought you were a teacher."

"He is!" Laurie said emphatically. "He teaches clowns—he's always talking about them."

"I see." Derrick smiled again. "Well, in that case, he and I deal with the same people all day. Present company excluded, of course."

Lucas nodded back. "Appreciated."

Laurie and Hector were comparing their handwritten notes—done in multiple Sharpie colors—to the menu. The place had a lousy website, so they couldn't order ahead of time, and he enjoyed watching the kids figure out the complicated process of trying to please seven people (eight, when Dingo joined them) without everyone getting a pizza of their own.

After a few moments of conspiring with Hector, Laurie turned and hollered, "We're ready!" to Lucas, as if he were across the street.

He tried to goose-step forward, but all he managed were three loud stomps that almost had him sliding into the garbage can. "Yes, ma'am?" he said, saluting with his alloy hand.

Laurie looked at their notes, shrugged, and pointed at Hector. "He's got it all figured out."

Hector shuffled the lists as if he were going over an important speech one last time, then looked up to the menu above the counter. "Okay—which is cheaper: three jumbos, one with pepperoni and bacon, one with only pepperoni, and one three-cheese with pineapple on half and anchovies on the other half, or . . . four larges, one with pepperoni and bacon, one with only pepperoni, one with three-cheese with pineapple on half, and one with cheese, mushrooms, and anchovies on half?"

Lucas scanned the menu and did the math. "The three jumbos work out to twenty-two-point-four cents a square inch and the four larges work out to twenty-two-point-six cents a square inch across-the-board." He also figured out that three larges and one jumbo—if tweaked appropriately—would have cost less and provided more, but that's not what Hector had asked and he didn't like confusing them.

Laurie threw her hands in the air as if she were explaining things to a child. "The pizzas are round, so we need *round inches*!"

Lucas smiled down at her. "That's not how it works."

"Well it should be!" she said, and crossed her arms defiantly.

Hector slapped the countertop. "Then jumbos it is, my good man!"

Derrick smiled at Lucas. "I have a couple of other clients who do that, but they count out loud and carry threes and all kinds of crap to figure it out. You're fast."

Laurie said, "He's good at numbers!"

Lucas leaned in. "With five kids, you try to save as much as you can."

Derrick paused with the pen over the order pad and gave Lucas a good once-over, starting with his green hand, then up at his face, locking in on his ceramic insert behind the ever-present sunglasses. "Something tells me you live an interesting life, Dr. Page."

Hector chimed in with, "You have *no* idea."

Lucas stepped back to let Hector go over the order with Derrick, and the first thing the kid said was, "First of all, I want you to slap so much cheese on these things that you get fired."

The menu board above the counter lit up in bursts of red and white, and Lucas turned to a spotless obsidian SUV rolling up onto the sidewalk, the wide chrome snout aimed at the restaurant. The door opened, and a tall black woman in a tracksuit and bright white Air Force 1s got out—Special Agent Alice Whitaker.

Lucas accidentally let a soft "Fuck" slip out.

"Your girlfriend's here," Laurie said, doing a pretty good job of sounding like Erin.

Derrick looked over at Whitaker, who was using a cane as she came toward the door, then back at Lucas. "Interesting *and* complicated."

Lucas went outside and Special Agent Whitaker took a few solid steps toward him. Her mouth unzipped, exposing that ridiculously large smile of hers. "Dr. Page, I am sorry to bother you during dinner."

He stuck out his hand and smiled without meaning to. "You're looking good." He hadn't seen her since she had been released from the hospital a couple of weeks ago and she was mending pretty well. Even down twenty pounds she looked like she was once again ready to chew through a chain-link fence. "Can I assume that you're here for something specific?"

Her smile disappeared. "Someone murdered a doctor a few blocks from here."

Lucas turned back to the restaurant, to the kids going over their color-coded pizza instructions with Derrick. "I am getting tired of always being right."

16

East 76th Street

The street was an example of protecting and serving—all that was missing was the Ken Burns voice-over accompanied by a Trent Reznor score. There were half a dozen police cruisers idling on the pavement, their lights generating an off-kilter seizure-inducing rhythm. But the big attraction was the black NYPD command vehicle in front of the garage doors, the side cabins rolled out and various power lines running to electrical feeds, like a mobile answer-seeking machine.

Whitaker blipped her siren for two short chortles, scattering the amateur necrophiles at the tape. She shook her head in disgust, then jammed the Lincoln up onto the sidewalk between two police cruisers.

"Ready?"

Lucas looked at the cop cars and the rubberneckers. "Nope."

"Now, we will both be nice, right?"

"Do you have a mouse in your pocket?"

"Technically I'm still on leave, so I would appreciate you not harshing my mellow."

. . .

Lacking the backdrop of an exterior sky, the concrete interior was the kind of place where time adapted to an alternate clock. Unlike most of the parking facilities in the city—eighteenth- and nineteenth-century buildings that had been retrofitted in fits and starts as America's fetish with the automobile evolved—the space avoided the New York architectural truism of function complicating form. The structure was clean and relatively well lit, even if the ceilings were low. It was directly across the street from the Weill Cornell Medical Center, which gave it a captive audience—people visiting dying relatives and sick loved ones didn't go price shopping—and the hourly rates mimicked the vampiric thinking fueling the health-for-profit model.

Whitaker announced their arrival by throwing the metal fire door open into a group of cops staring wide-eyed like a family of lemurs.

A short plainclothesman with thick gray hair and a pair of clunky slip-ons with rubber soles decided that he was the spokesman. "I help you?"

Lucas said, "Is that a question or a statement?"

Whitaker stepped in front of him, badge out. "Special Agent Whitaker, FBI."

The cop in the bad shoes said, "Mark Burger. Detective First Class—Nineteenth."

Whitaker took a few steps forward. "Who's your lead?" Contrasted against all the bad suits, her tracksuit and bright white Air Force 1s looked out of place.

Burger gave her a once-over, then leaned in and checked out Lucas, his focus locking on Lucas's bad eye. "He's over there. Johnny Russo." He pointed at a group of men in suits near the Medical Examiner's van. "You can't miss him; he's the one with—" He stopped and shifted focus to Lucas's other eye before switching back. "You can't miss him," he said again, smiling for some reason.

They were ten feet from the group of suits when one broke formation and stepped forward to greet them. "Can I help you?" he asked, sounding like he was in charge. He was of medium height and wore a pair of shoes not dissimilar to those of the first cop, which must have been a new thing in police circles. He carried a travel mug decorated with a happy face and the slogan *World's #1 Ex-Husband!* on the side.

Whitaker did the thing with the badge again. "Special Agent Whitaker, FBI. You Russo?"

"That's me," the world's number one ex-husband said, taking off his tinted glasses.

Which caused everyone—Whitaker, Lucas, and even Russo—to freeze.

Because Detective Russo sported a very obvious, and very poorly directed, prosthetic eyeball.

It was Russo who broke the brief silence with, "It's weird to see another one out in the wild, isn't it?" in a heavy Long Island accent.

Whitaker didn't bother dialing back her smile when she said, "This is Dr. Lucas Page."

They shook hands all around, and when Russo latched onto Lucas's prosthetic he leaned in and pointedly examined Lucas's eye behind the ever-present sunglasses. "How'd you lose yours?"

"I didn't *lose* it; I know exactly where it went." Lucas shifted focus down to Russo's mug, which was off-gassing alcohol mixed with some kind of fruit punch.

Russo nodded like he understood. "Mine was—"

Lucas said, "I don't care," and Whitaker gave him one of her *please shut the fuck up* looks.

But Russo obviously wasn't the kind of man to be deterred, and he kept his focus on Lucas for a few disappointed seconds. "Did it run off with your manners?"

Whitaker stepped in with, "We're not trying to stake a claim here. We're just trying to figure out if this murder has any bearing on an investigation we're involved with." She indicated the big red

Rorschach focal point that was taped off and lit up. "What can you tell us?"

Russo, who was still giving Lucas a four-letter stare, pivoted toward the crime scene, where all the little plastic grid markers were still out like Lego tombstones. "Female. Sixty-eight years of age. Solomon, Arna. Surgeon at Weill Cornell, across the street. Arrived for her shift at five fourteen P.M.—that's her Mercedes over there." Russo did another pivot, and pointed to a dark green G-class SUV four parking spaces over. "Shot twice between the shoulder blades after she got out. We don't have the caliber back from the lab yet, but it was larger than a twenty-two. Security footage gave us a big fucking zero—excuse my French—and we're assuming that the perp hid in the back of a pickup truck that was filmed leaving the front gates shortly after Solomon was shot: silver Chevy Avalanche. We're interviewing the owner right now and my CSI people are going through the bed of his truck."

Lucas asked, "How many cameras on-site?"

Russo tapped his foot on the concrete. "The garage itself has seven in total—two outside the main entrance/exit and two inside. Then there's one inside each staircase that leads to the street—" He indicated points behind Lucas, index and forefingers out on both hands, air host–style. "And one on the roof, but it only faces the rooftop to the east of the emergency door, so it's got a blind spot. The surveillance system doesn't have audio and nobody heard a thing until the lady who found Solomon—Mrs. Bhavna Reddy—ran down screaming at five fifteen thirty-nine P.M. Me and my partner got here within four mikes."

"Was Solomon a regular?"

Russo's good eye cycled up as he picked at his memory. His bad one stayed pointed roughly straight ahead, which resulted in the funhouse eyeball thing that Lucas used to make people uncomfortable. He had never been on the receiving end before and he had to consciously stop himself from laughing. "Monthly pass. For the past six weeks she's been doing four days on, one off. We checked the garage footage going back a week and she always arrives between five ten and five sixteen P.M.

"Five people left the garage on foot in the time between the victim's arrival and Mrs. Reddy's screaming. We tracked them all down: four were going to the hospital across the street; the other walked down Seventieth to one of the satellite facilities that houses imaging—she works there and didn't know the vic."

Whitaker turned back to Russo. "Any idea about motive?"

Lucas knew it was a ridiculous question if this murder factored into the others—but there was no reason to suspect either way—and it was the kind of question that Russo would expect. It was also the kind of question where an experienced detective's perspective might lead to better, smarter questions.

"Mugging." Russo took another slug from his mug and shrugged. "She had fifteen grand on her. Now she doesn't."

"Fifteen thousand dollars?" Whitaker asked.

"Her grandson has a bar mitzvah coming up and she was supposed to pay the DJ and a few other suppliers. We talked with the family and bank."

Lucas wondered how much was signal and how much was noise. Russo struck him as smart, but that particular bone was often hampered by the myopic groupthink that resulted from a homogenous approach to crime solving (the FBI suffered from similar creative hobbling).

"Is there anything unusual we're not aware of?" Lucas asked.

Russo thought about that one for a little pulse of silence. "I mean, it's fucked up and senseless and, other than a lack of suspects, textbook."

"Can I see the photos?" Lucas asked, avoiding eye contact.

Russo turned to the group of cops who were clearly getting ready to send the ME's van off to autopsy land. "Monty? Bring over the tablet."

A small bald man in another lousy suit and more terrible shoes headed over.

While Monty came toward them, Russo said, "I gotta say, this is weird—Solomon's my second doctor of the week."

This time Lucas did make eye contact.

"The other one's a suicide, but still, it's unusual." Russo took a sip of his travel mug cocktail. "Jennifer Delmonico. Walking home on the Brooklyn Bridge footpath after her shift and jumped into traffic. Ended up eating the grill of a pickup." Russo looked over at Lucas as if he were supposed to say something.

He didn't.

"Anyhow," Russo said as if that were some kind of an explanation, and turned to the man with the tablet. "Detective Cristo, Special Agent Alice Whitaker and Dr. Page from the FBI."

The detective with the unfortunate name stuck out his hand and they shook all around. "What is the FBI doing here?"

Without taking his focus from Lucas, Russo said, "They haven't really said."

When Cristo got to Whitaker, she pulled out her smile again. "Unusual name."

Detective Monty Cristo shrugged with the excitement of his ten thousandth explanation. "My mother taught gym; my father taught English; the name was a compromise. Yeah, school was rough."

Russo passworded into the tablet, brought up the film roll, and held the tablet out for Lucas.

Lucas pushed his sunglasses up onto his forehead and flipped through the crime scene photographs as he walked toward the chalk outline connected to the patch of blood on the cement. He downloaded myriad details about the body's location in the garage, its orientation, and the placement of the wounds. He plugged in all the pertinent waypoints, and when he was finished he put the tablet down on the roof of a nearby car.

He squatted down, putting all of his weight on his original leg and steadying himself with his hand. He focused on several blemishes in the concrete, using them to orient the real world against the photographs.

He then reached out and touched the concrete where Arna Solomon's left foot was outlined. The surface was dry. Cool.

Lucas was still as the current from his transformers migrated to the vacuum tubes, and they began to glow. He pushed himself up, and by the time he was standing, his processor was at performance level.

Lucas closed his eyes.

Filled his lungs with oxygen that tasted like car exhaust, humidity, and bad cologne.

When he opened his eyes, all Lucas could do was let it happen. So he did.

He spun slowly in place and—

—to describe what occurred as happening without his participation was both true and untrue. It was autonomous and involuntary—like his heart rate—but more intimate. He could actually hear his neurons sizzling as they converted visual pixels into usable data before projecting the results onto the back of his skull.

The space was absorbed by the numbers as everything recognizable was swallowed by the equation taking place. Lucas no longer saw the cars or the concrete, the walls or Whitaker or the detectives in the cheap shoes. Everything was simply a complicated skein of digits.

He looked down, and Dr. Arna Solomon was on the floor at his feet, her torso twisted, one flat beside her foot, the insole sticking out like a distended tongue. Numbers carpeted her body, swirling over her like digital insects.

Lucas looked up.

Closed his eyes.

Took a breath.

And then—like a star imploding—the chaos ceased and there was instant nothing. Not even light.

When he opened his eyes, Whitaker and Russo were staring at him.

Russo opened his mouth to say something, but Lucas cut him off with a soft, "Shut up."

Whitaker added a soft, "Please."

Solomon had parked close to one of the two stairwell exits.

Even if the killer *had* left in the back of a pickup truck, it didn't explain how he had made it into the building. Which did not make sense. There was too much sleight of hand involved in the premise. And this wasn't something sneaky.

Or complicated.

Which was why Russo couldn't see it.

Lucas pointed at the stairs. "That's where the killer headed."

"Why?" Russo asked, and stepped forward.

"He walked across the street to the hospital."

Russo's voice took on a bemused tone. "Who said the killer entered the hospital?"

"I just did."

17

The NYPD command vehicle was on par with the units the FBI used, illustrating that the line of demarcation between the two agencies was purely jurisdictional and not tied to financial constraints.

Lucas sat in front of a wall of monitors as the digital footage from both the parking garage and the Weill Cornell security cameras played out simultaneously. There were twelve feeds from the hospital—one both inside and outside at each of the six entrances closest to the parking garage—but "closest" was a relative term with a building the size of two city blocks.

Detective Russo had already gone through the footage and insisted that Dr. Arna Solomon appeared to have been killed by no one at all.

Lucas had his criticisms of the way cops did things, but when it came to investigative know-how, the NYPD was a very close second to the bureau. Russo didn't strike him as dead weight, but he was unusual in that he talked a lot—a rare subspecies in the detective taxon.

Russo said they had gone over the tapes—which was just an anachronistic term for digital source files—a dozen times. They concluded that the murderer was not on film, which was a classic example of bad thinking compounded by overconfidence. After all, if you don't know what you're looking for, anything will do.

They were running the video from ten minutes before the arrival of the police, which gave them roughly a five-minute window on either side of the homicide. The positive takeaway was that the NYPD had identified each individual caught on camera through a combination of facial recognition software, hospital logs, cell phone data, license plates, credit card data, and old-fashioned legwork. The killing had happened before peak rush hour, but even with the low volume of traffic, the exercise netted a hundred and three individuals who had walked through the doors of the hospital. All of whom had to be matched against the parking garage tapes.

Lucas was sitting back from the monitors so he could take in all the visual real estate. His sunglasses were off as his eye cycled from screen to screen, feed to feed, image to image, detail to detail, positioning each byte of information in its place.

As the figures moved on- and offscreen, the software automatically enhanced their faces and brought up a bubble denoting their name and a description such as "patient," "doctor," "nurse," "visitor," "hospital employee," "retail worker," "unknown."

Lucas consciously tracked and catalogued myriad details, automatically factoring them into the mental map he was assembling. He watched people leave the garage; he watched people enter the hospital; he watched people leave the hospital.

He focused on the macro.

And the micro.

The obvious.

The inobvious.

The counter ticked off the last few seconds and Lucas kept focused on the screens until they all paused with the arrival of the police.

He sat there, staring at the frozen images.

"See anything?" Whitaker asked.

Lucas was silent for a moment as everything came together in his head—the crime scene, the mental map of the garage, and the footage he had just viewed.

"At all?"

Lucas put his sunglasses back on and looked up at Russo, who was examining him with what appeared to be amused interest. The detective leaned in and asked, "So, was the trip worth it?" There was something going on behind the carefree grizzled veteran-of-a-thousand-wars act and Lucas wondered if it was just a lack of familiarity with the man or if it was a signal he was unable to receive.

Lucas let the footage swirl around in his developing tank and picked up the cup of shitty coffee that the NYPD had been kind enough to supply. He took a sip, wished he hadn't, and pointed at one of the monitors. "A man entered the hospital on camera thirty-one-B at two minutes, nine seconds after the modeled time of Solomon's murder. The heads-up display identified him as Albert Hess. From the time Hess drove into the parking garage, to the time he crossed the street and walked into the hospital, is seven minutes and eleven seconds. Which was a long time."

Russo said, "It's a hospital. Maybe he's sick."

"Of course he's sick—the heads-up said he was a patient."

Russo came back with, "We already cleared him."

Lucas mouse-clicked back in the footage to where Albert Hess walked through the hospital doors.

Hess froze mid-stride. From this distance out, he looked to be in his mid-sixties, one of those gaunt men strung together from the stuff butchers cut off the beef tenderloin. He wore a down-filled parka that was too large and carried a paper bag in his hand.

"That," Lucas said, pointing at the bag in his hand. "There's a logo on it."

Russo said, "So?"

Lucas leaned forward, grabbed the mouse, and zoomed in on the bag, enhancing the graphic. The design was folded into the bag, almost entirely hidden. But like most children of the TV era, Lucas had had thousands of commercial brands and trademarks burned into his memory by Madison Avenue advertising, and even with most of the logo hidden, it was impossible not to recognize it. "Burger King."

"So?" Russo repeated.

Lucas looked at the image for a few seconds, then closed the screen and cantilevered out of the chair bolted to the floor. "Nothing."

Russo, who was now focusing on Lucas's good eye, asked, "So, does this murder have anything to do with that lateral case you are working on?"

"I don't know."

"Yeah, well, 'I don't know' sounds an awful lot like 'Go fuck yourself.'"

Lucas headed for the door. "Thank you for your time, Detective Russo."

18

Once outside, Lucas threw the now empty cup of coffee into a wire garbage can.

Whitaker was side-eyeing him. "What is it?"

"What is *what*?"

"You have that trying-to-figure-out-the-Gordian-knot look on your face."

"It's a Conway knot."

"The difference being?"

"You wouldn't understand."

"Oh. Good. For a second there I was worried that you might be condescending."

"What? No." Lucas stopped and pointed at her. "Albert Hess."

"The sick guy? What about him?"

"The heads-up said he is a patient at the hospital."

Whitaker stopped and flipped through the roster that Russo had printed up for them. "Yes. Right here. In Oncology."

Lucas climbed into the Lincoln. "And what was he doing there?"

Whitaker opened the driver's door and passed the sheaf of papers over the console. "It says here he was visiting a Dr. Rathke."

Lucas took out his cell and dialed Lorne Jacobi.

Jacobi answered in two rings.

"Lorne, Lucas Page."

"Hey, Luke. What's going on?"

Lucas closed his eyes to let some of the tension bleed off. "Have you heard about Arna Solomon?"

His voice went flat. "Yeah."

"I need some information that can't wait and you're the only person who can help."

"Name it."

"Do you know a Dr. Rathke?"

"Desmond Rathke? Sure. So does Erin. I think you met him at the Nguyens' party two years back. He's a couple of departments downstream, and I don't work with him very often, but he's a good guy. Oncologist. Why?"

"He was visited by a patient named Albert Hess this afternoon. Can you find out why? I'm not asking for him to break patient/client privilege; I just need to know that Hess had a good reason to be at the hospital."

"Is this about Dr. Solomon?"

Truth usually got more mileage than a lie. "Very much so."

"Give me a few minutes."

Lucas hung up and Whitaker started the SUV. "Are you going to tell me what you're thinking, or is it a secret?"

"Did you see anything unusual in the way Hess moved?"

She shrugged, slid the transmission into *reverse*, and backed off the sidewalk with two honks to scatter the rubberneckers behind them. "He looked sick."

"It was more than that. I know that look. He was fucked up but trying to look like everything was aces. Like it was just another day in paradise. Trying to fit in. Which makes sense out in the world, but not in a hospital—that's home turf if you're ill."

Whitaker pulled around the command vehicle and accompanying police cruisers, heading east. "If you say so."

They made the corner when Lucas's phone buzzed. He answered with, "And?"

Jacobi said, "Hess was Rathke's patient for more than a year."

"So he was there for a treatment?"

"He stopped treatment a month ago."

"Did he have an appointment?"

"He just dropped in. I explained to Rathke why I was asking and he didn't see a problem revealing that Mr. Hess was heading to hospice care tonight. Out in Westchester. Rathke trusts me. Which means he trusts you. So don't let this get out."

"Did Rathke tell you what kind of cancer?"

"Started out as esophageal but metastasized to his stomach, liver, kidneys, and bones."

Lucas filed the information away and said, "Thanks, Lorne. I owe you."

"Just find this guy, Luke."

"I'm working on it."

Lucas pocketed his phone and turned to Whitaker, who was once again side-eyeing him over the console. "Well?" she said.

"Stage-five cancer. Esophageal and stomach, among others."

"It's a hospital. Sick people come and go."

"Why would a man with esophageal and stomach cancer be carrying a Burger King bag?"

"Because he was hungry?"

"You don't chow down on cheeseburgers and fries when you have stomach cancer. Which means he was probably carrying something else."

"Like?"

Lucas circled his aluminum finger in the air, signaling her to turn around. "Let's go."

"It's ten o'clock at night. Where are you going?"

"*We*, Special Agent Whitaker—where are *we* going? You, me, the mouse in your pocket, and those terrible shoes of yours."

"So where are *we* going?"

"Westchester."

Whitaker was no doubt trying her best to sound buoyant when she said, "This time, how about we try to not blow up a bunch of stuff."

Lucas waved her concerns away with green aluminum fingers. "I try not to make promises I can't keep."

19

Westchester

Lucas closed the digital file on Albert Hess, turned off the tablet, and shut his eyes to recalibrate his night vision. Hess had been married for forty-two years and was now a widower. No children. Taught chemistry at a Bronx high school for thirty-six years. Coached Little League. Volunteered with the Boy Scouts of America for three decades. Made charitable donations each quarter, all to children's causes, including significant sums (compared to his salary) for the Shriners and the Make-A-Wish Foundation. No speeding tickets. No parking tickets. No late fees at the library.

Lucas opened his eyes, and they were long off the highway, delving deep into sub-suburbia.

"So you still think a man with stage-five cancer killed Arna Solomon?" Whitaker glanced over at him.

"I do."

"Even if I discount how shitty he looked in that surveillance video—and he looked worse than you do right now—do you know how sick he had to be in order to check himself into hospice *tonight*?"

"Very."

"Which could arguably be construed as his lacking the *means*.

And I assume that our people cross-referenced Mr. Hess's personal history with that of Arna Solomon."

"They have."

"And they didn't find a connection?"

"They did not."

"Which could arguably be construed as his lacking the *motive*."

"It's not a complicated equation." Outside, it looked like Sleepy Hollow country, replete with naked trees, skittering leaves, and the windows of houses flickering like predatory eyes in the distance. "We have five people on camera coming out of that garage. If we ignore Russo's ridiculous Hollywood escape in the back of a pickup theory, one of the people we have on camera killed Solomon. And Hess is the only one who checks *any* of the boxes."

"All this because he was carrying a Burger King bag?" Whitaker didn't sound like she had an opinion.

"No. All this because the timing is right—and it isn't with the other four possible suspects."

"Which only gives us *opportunity* out of the crime trifecta."

The chemical fuel of focus was succumbing to fatigue. "We have no obvious motive, but one exists. We have opportunity and, if you think about it, means; even a man with cancer can pull a trigger."

They were heading down a country road that appeared to be going absolutely nowhere when the disinterested narrator in the GPS directed them to a drive bookended by a pair of stone pillars supporting an open iron gate that was fully in keeping with the Ichabod Crane vibe.

Whitaker swung the SUV into the drive, and her lights swept over the pillars, then an empty field. "And Hess also killed your friend Knox?"

Whitaker's question was interrupted by a call from Hoffner. "Dr. Page here."

"Page, Hoffner. We came up with something on your friend Knox's murder. But I don't think it's going to make you happy."

"Try me."

"We collected cell data from his neighborhood last night and a phone that was most likely in his apartment placed a call about ten minutes after he arrived home. The call went to a cell phone in the Hamptons, and the location pinpoints Knox's place out there—specifically the master bedroom. Both phones were prepaid and their numbers were offset by a single digit. It looks like they came from an AT and T retail store. We should have the location, purchase date, and—if we're really lucky—receipts by the morning. The line was open for eight minutes and four seconds and it appears as if it was a data link and not a call."

Lucas closed his eyes and pushed the new information into the master narrative he was assembling. "And how are you interpreting this?" He could already predict the crime-solving-by-numbers approach Hoffner had probably employed.

Hoffner didn't disappoint when he said, "Stats say that Knox's killer is most likely his wife."

"Statistics also say that one hundred percent of people who breathe oxygen are guaranteed to die. It's how you interpret the numbers that counts."

"You don't think Knox's wife spoke to his killer, or maybe spoke directly to her husband to tell him that she was responsible for having his button punched in front of the killer?"

Lucas allowed himself an audible sigh but tried to remain polite when he said, "What I think is that Dove was tag-teamed. One of the killers got into his apartment somehow—either they were waiting for him when he got home, or they forced themselves in once he arrived. They confronted him, maybe with a weapon, and then showed him that there was an accomplice out in Montauk—through a video link. They told him that if he didn't commit suicide, they were going to kill Carla and then him anyway. So Dove incorrectly tied the knots, intentionally left his fingerprints all over that extension cord, and sacrificed himself."

Lucas could tell he had dented Hoffner's certainty by the big man's silence.

"So how about you start hunting down CCTV and traffic footage in Knox's neighborhood to see if you can find us a suspect. See if you can place Hess anywhere near the scene—even a sick old man can kill someone with a cell phone. Or, if you want, I'll take care of it when I get back. You know, just so you don't have to do any heavy lifting." He hung up and resisted the temptation to throw the phone through the windshield.

"So Hess had the means to kill both Knox and Solomon?" Whitaker asked.

Lucas ignored the question for a few seconds as he recalibrated his frustration. "It would appear so, yes."

The Westchester palliative care center was another half mile down a well-tended gravel road and Lucas wondered what the hourly rate was because the grounds would be the envy of any top-tier golf course on the planet. Even in the dark, the tight landscaping, pruned bushes, sculpted shrubbery, and nursed trees looked like they were lifted from a brochure for the Overlook Hotel.

The building itself was an Edwardian stone manor with a copper roof and a dozen decorative chimneys—none of them belting out smoke. Lucas was certain it had been used as an English estate in a film he had seen a long time ago.

There was a lone car in the visitor section, parking lights on, engine idling. A man sat behind the wheel, the screen on the phone he was staring into having the same effect as a flashlight under his chin. The license plates denoted it as a police vehicle, and when they pulled in beside the car Detective John Russo looked up and smiled.

While Lucas and Russo were staring at each other, Whitaker said, "Hey, look, it's your stunt double."

"Swell."

It was colder up here than in the city—or maybe that was the fatigue talking—and Lucas realized it was time to dig out the winter clothing.

"Dr. Page, Special Agent Whitaker," Russo said through a big smile as he climbed out, putting his travel mug down on the roof of the car. He tied off his scarf and buttoned his boiled-wool coat.

Lucas zeroed in on the important. "What do you want?"

Russo looked up at him. "I thought we should pool our resources."

Whitaker looped around the front of the car and they all stood staring at one another in a replay of their first meeting back in the parking garage.

Lucas shook his head. "We're the FBI: we have all the resources we need."

Russo picked his mug off the roof of the sedan and took a sip. "I'm not here to be a pain in the ass."

"Then you need to change tactics."

Russo turned to Whitaker and jabbed a thumb at Lucas. "Does he *ever* chill out?"

Whitaker shrugged. "Define 'chill out.'"

The fingers in Lucas's original hand were starting to get cold. "What do you want?" he repeated.

Russo gave him a pretty good rendition of a cherubic smile. "I want to help you solve the thirty homicides you're not telling any-one about."

20

Lucas didn't break character when he calmly said, "Thirty homicides?"

Russo shrugged, and the gas lantern at the edge of the parking lot behind him finger-puppeted weird shadows onto the asphalt. "Well, if you want to be a stickler, it's thirty-two. But I'm not big on being a stickler."

Whitaker said, "Then you're not going to get along with Dr. Page."

Russo's cherubic smile was still hanging on his face, but that errant eyeball made him look like a badly restored statue. He pointed at Lucas. "I did some research, and they don't pull someone like you out of mothballs, especially after you just won the smash-up derby awards"—he did a game show prize wave with his hand, indicating Lucas's relatively fresh injuries—"unless it's important. So I tried to figure out what other investigation the Solomon murder could be related to that would warrant the participation of someone of your particular reputation. And for no reason other than it seemed the smart money, I checked with the records department. I found out that today you guys—and by 'you guys' I mean the FBI—requested the physical files on seven deaths in my precinct. By the time I got to the third file, I saw it. By the seventh, I had you cold. Five accidents, two suicides. All doctors." He paused, indicating that the applause sign was now on.

Lucas just stared at him, and when Russo turned to Whitaker she had her stink eye going, which was like trying to get a sketch to smile.

Russo's optimism peeled away and fluttered off into the wind. "Okay. Be like that."

Lucas shook his head. "Seven deaths do not thirty-two murders make." But he waited to see what Russo could contribute other than speculation.

Russo shook a finger at him and that smile came back. "No, they don't. But then I checked with all of the other precincts in the five boroughs before moving on to the Medical Examiner. And beginning this morning, the FBI has requested the files on thirty deaths in the city where the deadsters are all . . . drumroll please . . . *doctors*."

Neither Lucas nor Whitaker said anything.

"You guys are a tough crowd."

"What do you want?" Lucas asked again.

"When I put your recent file-gathering marathon together with your presence at the Solomon murder, it's not much of a leap to figure out that Solomon's murder is part of a broader problem. And since you're the FBI, I don't think the broader problem is bad luck."

"That still doesn't explain why you are here."

Whitaker opened the passenger door and leaned in against the seat to take the weight off her bad foot.

Russo took another drink from his mug. "If I have seven murders that I missed in my own precinct, I'm going to be looking for a new job in the food service industry. Especially since my people were first on-site in all seven deaths. And if this makes it to the news— and anything you guys work on always makes it to the news—I'm the guy they tie to the post and start throwing lawn darts at. So I need this to go away. More than you do."

Lucas slowly said, "What. Do. You. Want?"

"I have something that you don't—invisibility. You start showing up all over town with the guys in the sunglasses and windbreakers and it won't take long until we're all reading about this in the *Times*. There's still a lot of shell-shocked people out there from the bombings last month, so that will buy you a little camouflage, but not blanket immunity. Me? No one notices a guy in a bad suit and cheap shoes stumbling through a crime scene with a Gatorade and vodka in his hand. So I get to clear those seven murders—if they *are* murders—in my precinct, and you guys go on to fame and fortune with the others. And of course, I am completely at your disposal."

Their gazes intersected and Lucas saw the mindfuck that came from trying to suss emotion out of a glass eyeball.

Whitaker shifted on her feet and Lucas looked over and she shrugged in an *It's your call* way.

Lucas knew Kehoe wouldn't be happy about their partnering with Russo, but there was nothing he'd be able to do about it. And part of him liked the idea of pissing Kehoe off—there was nothing the man hated more than giving up even a morsel of control, no matter the context. Especially to somebody like this. But Russo had already demonstrated that he was curious and smart, which was never a bad combination when it was on your side of the equation. And if he proved to be problematic, they could always open the car door and push his ass out into traffic. "I need to think about this."

Russo nodded like that at least represented movement, if not actual motion. "Okay. So let me give you something that you don't have. Jennifer Delmonico was pregnant."

"I know."

"What you don't know is that her husband isn't the father."

Which only surprised Lucas because it was new information; it contained no shock value. But it was the kind of detail that might prove useful somewhere downstream. "Do you know who is?"

Russo delivered his shrug with a side order of smile. "Nope." Russo kept his eye locked on Lucas for a second, then turned the smile off. "And what if I could give you the Solomon murder weapon?"

"Do you *have* the murder weapon?"

Russo went to his phone, pulled up a photograph, and turned the screen toward Lucas.

It was a plastic device that looked like a homemade hair dryer. Lucas recognized it as a 3-D printed pistol. "Where did you find that?" he asked.

"My people found it in one of the hospital dumpsters an hour ago. In a Burger King bag. Three-D printed pistol in a nine mil. It's made from a polymer and doesn't have any metal parts. My people just started looking at it, but they already think that it was produced on a Crealty Ender-Six, which is a plug-and-play printer that runs about five hundred bucks. The plastic appears to be another Ender product and they sold somewhere around three hundred thousand pounds last year. So it's basically untraceable. But we called the school where Hess taught and they have two of these—one in their computer lab, one in their biology department. Hess was a biology teacher."

Lucas thought that one out for a second. "Prints? DNA?"

"Nope. The grip is crosshatched and they didn't find anything on the rest of the gun or the two spent shells that were in it—but the lands and grooves matched the slugs the ME took out of Solomon."

Either this worked or it didn't—discussing it in a cold parking lot all night wasn't going to swing the needle one way or the other. "Okay."

"Okay?"

Whitaker gave Lucas a fast look of surprise, then turned to Russo. "And if we hadn't shown up here?"

Russo waved it away. "I wasn't motivated by hope. I kept hearing your voice in the back of my head saying that the killer walked out of the parking garage, across the street, and into Weill Cornell. And Hess was the only one who checked any of the boxes. I can't figure out motive, but I think that's where you might come in."

Lucas shook his head. "It's not. Which begets your first contribution—do you have anything to offer as to why someone might be killing doctors?"

Russo and Lucas locked dead stares again and Lucas realized that the two of them could stand out here all night doing this.

"That seems like kind of a stupid question. I mean, a better question would be why aren't more doctors murdered? From the fifty thousand deaths a year in the US from wrongly prescribed medication, to the other fifty thousand deaths caused by opioid overdoses, to having the wrong limbs amputated, to female patients having a twenty-three percent higher mortality rate when they are operated on by male surgeons, to all the malpractice suits due to sheer incompetence, to the cost of medical care, to the laundry list of experiments the medical community has performed on unsuspecting Americans over the years, I'm surprised we don't have a national doctor-hunting lottery. And the first line of the Hippocratic oath? *Do no harm*? Who came up with that—Vinnie Boombatz? No, I don't have much of a problem imagining a hundred motives."

Lucas dead-eyed him again. "I don't want a hundred imagined motives—I want the correct *one*."

21

Albert Hess could have been his own grandfather. He barely approached the basic parameters of a grown man and looked exactly like what he was, someone being eaten alive by his own cells.

The caregiver—a tall man named Mario who wore a puka shell necklace and looked like he would rather be playing Dungeons and Dragons—introduced Lucas and Whitaker to Hess. But the sick man didn't say hello. Or nod. Or even acknowledge them. He just watched them with a pair of eyes that looked like they were getting ready to close forever.

After Mario excused himself, Lucas took off his sunglasses and sat down beside the bed. "Mr. Hess, we appreciate you making the time to see us. Especially now. We'll make this as short as possible."

Hess looked up at Lucas, but it appeared to be a reflex and Lucas wondered if he had made a mistake and wasted their time coming out here. He put his hand on the rail. "We understand that you've already spoken to the police about Dr. Solomon's murder today, but there have been some developments and you might be the only witness we have. I apologize for coming at such a late hour during such a difficult time."

Something moved around behind Hess's eyes, but Lucas could

not decipher its meaning. "Are you certain that you didn't see any-one else in the garage?"

Hess slowly lifted his hand—a translucent claw underscored with blue veins—as if gravity were giving him permission. He pointed at the pitcher of water and glass on the nightstand.

Lucas filled the glass by a third, then helped Hess take a few tentative sips that barely dented the volume.

When Hess was finished, he coughed once before weakly shaking his head. "I didn't see . . . anyone else." His voice was distant, as if the sound waves were affected by the same general gravity pulling him into an ever-diminishing space in the universe. "I parked . . . and left. That's all. The police already asked me about all of this. A detective named Russo." Hess pointed up at Lucas's prosthetic eye. "He had a glass eye as well. But the other side."

Lucas took out his phone, and brought up a photograph. He leaned forward and held the screen in front of Hess's face. "Did you see this man?" he asked, as if he expected a yes.

Hess shook his head without looking at the photograph. "I didn't see *anyone*."

"Please, Mr. Hess, this is important. Just take a look."

Hess rolled his eyes over and focused on the screen. After a couple of seconds of nothing, he shook his head. "That's not a man; that's a child. And no, I didn't see him."

"He would have been dressed just like this. In jeans and a pilot jacket and a white T-shirt with an RAF roundel on it."

Hess took a deep breath that sounded like his teeth were rattling loose. "I did not see that boy."

Lucas pretended to look at the photo—but he knew the image intimately because he had shot it four days ago, when he had taken his son Damien out for hot dogs after his guitar lesson. He was uneasy about using a picture of his son to lie to a dying man, but there were bigger things at play here, and he didn't have time to fashion the appropriate wedge to get into Hess's head. "Semantics."

Hess narrowed his eyes at that.

Lucas swiped through to the photograph of the DIY pistol Russo had just sent him. "He might have had this in his hand." He held the screen in front of Hess's face again. "I know it looks like a toy or a tool, but it's a homemade handgun."

Hess's eyes locked on the screen and a tide of microexpressions surged through his tight facial muscles. He stared at the image for a few moments, then closed his eyes and shook his head.

Whitaker saved the scene. "Page, it's okay. We have everything we need to put that man, I mean *kid*, away. The arrest will stick." She turned to Mr. Hess. "We're sorry for bothering you, sir."

With that, Hess's eyes came back to life. "You . . . arrested him?"

Lucas once again held up the photo of Damien. "He's a nobody who doesn't have a future. He's got a record, arrested four times for theft. He shoplifted some food from a bodega last spring. He was arrested again in the summer for stealing food stamps. He's not going to be missed. People like this need to be stopped." Lucas tapped the screen. "The lab has ascertained the make and model of printer used to manufacture the pistol, and this boy's school has one."

Hess waved the point away with that translucent hand. "Every school has a three-D printer these days."

Lucas shrugged. "It still looks like this man is going to jail for a very long time."

"That's not a man; that's a . . . child," Hess repeated, this time more forcefully. There was lightning behind his eyes, but something was preventing it from making its way to his features, as if the cancer were sticking its fingers into the power lines and bleeding off current.

Lucas forced a small smile. "Technically, yes. But they'll be charging him as an adult. Don't worry—we have this guy. We don't make the laws; we simply enforce them." Lucas hoped that sounded as cynical and broken to Hess as it did to him.

Evidently it did, because Hess leveled an ugly stare at him. "That was their defense at Nuremberg."

"We caught this kid with the murder weapon on him. I think we all know where this is going."

Hess's eyes brightened as his system allotted them a little more current. "The police told me they didn't have a suspect! They said the killer hid in the bed of a pickup truck they had on film!" Hess was alive, angry. "What about the money?" he asked.

"What money?"

Hess's face went into a question mark setting again. "The police said that woman had been robbed of fifteen thousand dollars."

Lucas gave another disinterested shrug. "He probably spent it. We'll figure all of that out. Or not. It doesn't really matter."

Hess's focus shifted up to Whitaker, who had her combat face on, then back to Lucas, who looked like he had passed *I don't give a fuck* a long time ago. They had foregone *good cop/bad cop* in exchange for *terrible cop/terrible cop*, to deny Hess any sort of an ally. They needed him boxed into an emotional corner.

Hess slowly turned his head back to face Lucas and nodded at the water. Lucas once again helped him take a drink. This time Hess was able to put a few swallows away, finishing the relatively empty glass.

Then the old man looked up at Lucas and all of his defenses seemed to fall away. "Why are you really here?"

"I want to know if you killed Arna Solomon, Dove Knox, and the others."

22

Lucas and Whitaker moved quietly through the dimly lit hallway, past the open doors with the sleeping patients, toward the entrance. Mario, the attendant, had stayed behind with Hess.

"You really think that sick old man killed Arna Solomon and your friend Dove Knox and thirty other doctors?"

"I don't know anything. I don't even suspect anything. It's all just data."

"Well, using a picture of your son was ballsy; I'll give you that."

"You don't have to give me anything."

"You need to lighten up."

They hung a left, and as they passed the receptionist she looked up from her Harlan Coben novel. She nodded a good night to Whitaker, then tried the same with Lucas but froze up when he smiled back and the scar tissue pulled his mouth into a grimace.

"Thank you," Whitaker said. "We appreciate you making this easy for us."

The receptionist managed to salvage the smile. "Well, you were certainly nicer than the other two who tried to visit Mr. Hess tonight."

Lucas and Whitaker stopped and pivoted as if they had practiced the move in front of a mirror.

"Other two?" Whitaker asked.

The woman put her book down. "Two men. Forties or fifties, I guess—I can't really tell; all old people kinda look the same age to me. Average height—shorter than both of you. One had a big moustache—you know, one of those Freddie Mercury thingies. Looked like hockey players."

"When?"

"About an hour ago."

"Did they sign in?" Whitaker asked.

She shook her head. "I asked for identification—we don't let just anyone visit our patients in the middle of the night—and they said they were friends of Mr. Hess. I told them they had to come back during visiting hours."

Lucas dispensed with any efforts to smile and simply nodded at the security camera in the corner. "Do you have them on that camera?"

"Yes, I think so."

Whitaker opened her hands in an *It's all good* gesture, but it was evident that she wasn't asking when she said, "Can we take a look?"

The receptionist summoned security—which was a misnomer for a sleepy-looking young man with a name tag that read *Alan*. After being brought up to speed, Alan led them to the security office—which was another misnomer, this time for a small closet outfitted with a rack of computer servers that was in line with the price tag of the place.

Alan took a step toward the rack of tech, stopped, and turned around with his mouth hanging open. "They're gone."

"What do you mean *gone*?"

Alan flicked one of the hard drive slots with his finger. It swung in, then out. "Empty. No hard drives." He flicked a few more to demonstrate his point. "See—the little green lights are off. Empty."

"Are you sure they were on earlier?"

Alan looked over at Whitaker and pinched his face into smarty-pants mode. "They're never off. We gotta keep them for legal reasons."

"So where are they?"

Alan looked back at the empty server rack. "Um, gone."

Whitaker turned to Lucas, but he had already stormed out.

23

It was so gray outside that Lucas momentarily thought his graphics card had shit the bed. Even the natural gas torchères lining the cobble pathway looked like a black-and-white pop-up book.

"Page?" Whitaker put a hand on his shoulder. "You're mumbling to yourself."

Lucas blinked and the world came back online in color. "It's rude to interrupt a conversation."

Russo had been waiting outside by the door. He was walking backwards, arms open, and his coat was open, exposing a very nice Cousin Eddie mock-turtleneck beneath a white — *Was that angora?* — sweater. "Are we going to tell the detective what's going on?"

The gas lanterns carved Russo's face with heavy shadow emphasizing his sockets, and his ceramic eye kicked off less light than his original equipment. Lucas wondered if he looked as odd to Erin and the children as Russo did to him.

Whitaker opened with, "Hess set off all my alarm bells. I think he killed Solomon."

"And Knox?" Lucas asked.

She shrugged.

"Because after Solomon and Knox, there are thirty other deaths that need explaining. Do you think our friend in there is a prolific serial killer?"

"You're not concerned about Hess?" Whitaker asked Lucas.

"I'm more concerned about the two yahoos who tried to muscle their way in to see Hess tonight before stealing the entire surveillance system."

Which got Russo's attention. "What?"

Whitaker filled him in on the security room and the tracksuited hockey-playing Freddie Mercury and his partner.

Russo was still moving backwards and was on a direct azimuth to collide with one of the lantern posts and Lucas raised his green aluminum hand. "Post."

Russo took a single step to his left. "Thanks."

Lucas knew that monocular vision was counter to the way the human brain had evolved. During rehabilitation, he had learned that his acute sense of spatial awareness was a software strength that could compensate for missing hardware. But Russo—like everyone else—had not been allotted the same gift and was destined to be a little clumsy with half his field of vision erased.

Whitaker was moving relatively well with the cane and the big white Nike anti-gravitational space sneakers. "So what's next?" she asked.

Lucas had been working that out. "We have thirty successful murders, enough of a sample group to suggest that there was an unsuccessful one along the way."

Russo waved his mug at Lucas. "I don't understand."

"We need to find out if there were any attempted murders against doctors in the past three years. If we find one, this gets upgraded from murder—or even serial murder—to conspiracy."

Whitaker tucked her cane under her arm, and her gait evened out. "Why is nothing ever simple with you?"

24

The Upper East Side

It was the middle of the night and the city was nowhere near waking when Whitaker pulled up in front of the Page home. A light snow was falling, but it was melting as soon as it touched down, which gave the impression of slow-motion rain.

Whitaker killed the engine. "Dr. Page, I would like to say it has been a pleasure, but"—she looked over and shook her head—"I'd be lying."

"You and me both." Turning his head required too much battery power, so he kept his focus straight ahead. "How are you holding up?"

"What do you mean?"

"You were supposed to be recuperating, enjoying a Jamba Juice and reading crime novels—not driving me around the city looking for murderers."

"I don't need to read crime novels—I'm a character in one."

That got a smile. "Noted."

"Look at you, pretending to be all caring and shit."

"Seriously, are you up to this?" It was impossible to miss the irony of the question coming from him.

"The foot is not nearly as bad as I thought it would be. My neck is fine. And I can't sit around anymore. Yesterday I caught myself looking at cat videos." She turned, and by the way she moved, Lucas understood that her neck was giving her more problems than she was admitting. "And I'm not much of a cat person."

"I got that."

"What's next on our agenda? I mean *after* sleep."

"Hoffner and his people have to deconstruct the lives of thirty-two murder victims to try to find a commonality that everyone has missed for two years. And we're going to stick with the ancillary task of sniffing out any attempted murders of doctors that fall into our parameters." There were a million things that needed to get done, and then a million more that needed to line up before he could put Dove's death to bed. "Look, Dove is the perfect starting point. And so is Solomon. Those two will be more than enough to keep us busy."

"And Russo?"

"Let's wait and see if he can shake something loose in the Delmonico case."

"You trust him?"

"I don't trust anyone who walks around with a mug of vodka and a gun—it's not what I would describe as a recipe for success."

"People with glass eyes shouldn't throw stones."

Lucas laughed despite his fatigue and opened the door. He checked his Submariner. "Pick me up in forty-eight hours."

Whitaker saluted as she started the engine. "I'll wait until nine."

Lucas stopped the door from swinging wide and denting one of his neighbors' cars. "Once again, I wish I could say it has been fun, but it hasn't." He closed the door and headed up the steps, unable to shake off the effects of his anti-fatigue software hitting a paywall.

It was so late that it was early, which he realized he could turn into an exercise to explain the nature of imaginary time to his students.

Once inside, he smelled coffee, and headed back through the house, to the kitchen, to find Erin at the island, sitting in the dark.

He walked over and gave her a hug without hitting the lights. "Hey, baby."

She put her mug down and leaned into his chest without getting up. "Hey, Mr. Man. I've been sitting here, beating myself up. After all the grief I've given you about working for the bureau, I can't believe that *I* get to be the hypocrite and ask you to go back."

Lucas took off his coat, draped it over one of the barstools, then walked over to the cupboard and took out his *World's Greatest Dad—from world's greatest kids (and Hector)! WE LUV YOU!* mug—which he realized was some kind of weird counterpart to Russo's *World's #1 Ex-Husband!* mug. He put it under the spout and hit the appropriate buttons on the stainless coffee robot.

He watched as the various multi-colored lights came to life and the machine began to hum.

"How was your day?"

There was no way he could answer the question, so he ignored it. "I need you to do me a favor—don't talk to anyone about what's happening."

"What do you mean by 'anyone'? And what *is* happening?"

"I mean don't talk to colleagues or friends about these deaths. Not about Knox or Solomon or Delmonico."

"You think Delmonico was murdered, too?"

He nodded. "Possibly."

"That's not the confidence I'm used to." Erin was eyeing him quizzically, the blinking lights highlighting her freckles.

He gave her another shrug. "Something is off with her death. The details are wrong by just enough to make me doubt that she's part of this."

"So what's going on?"

"I don't know." The best possible outcome for everyone would be if Hess actually did turn out to be a prolific serial killer, which still wasn't a hard no. "Not yet."

The machine finished converting hope into caffeine and Lucas picked up his mug and a few drops plinked in the dark.

"What do you mean?"

Lucas shrugged again, which bothered him—he much preferred yes or no answers. "What's the one reason you can imagine someone killing a doctor?" The coffee was perfect, and he felt his battery bars go up.

"There isn't one."

Lucas was once again surprised by her optimism; Erin never thought that there were good reasons for bad behavior. But this wasn't an exercise in optimism; it was an exercise in realism. "Okay, if you were a bad person, what's a reason you can think of to go after a doctor?"

"Anger?"

"At what?"

It was her turn to shrug. "Carelessness, negligence, incompetence, criminal misconduct, wrongful death—any of the usual causes cited in malpractice litigation—either perceived or real."

Lucas tipped his mug at her. "Which all amount to revenge."

"I guess."

"Which is a viable motive when examining any of these on their own. But it loses any scope of probability when you factor in thirty-two deaths. I think it's highly unlikely that one person committed all of these murders." He thought back to Albert Hess and the way gravity was pulling him into the void. "And I find it highly unlikely that it's a group because there is no communal motive that I can think of."

"So it's not a group?"

"Nope."

"And it's not an individual?"

"Nope."

"This sounds like one of your quantum physics problems."

Lucas pulled in a mouthful of coffee and it went straight to the pistons driving the machinery. "If it was, I'd have figured it out by now."

25

Lucas woke to the sound of deep snoring and the smell of bacon and . . . and . . . was that fish? He opened his eyes and Lemmy's snout was an inch from his nose. "Christ," he grumbled, and pushed the dog's face away with the palm of his hand.

Lemmy generated some inarticulate warble that could have meant anything, opened his big soulful eyes, stretched, and yawned.

"Yeah, good morning to you, too, dummy."

The clatter of the family getting ready for the day was going on beyond the closed bedroom door and Erin must have told the kids to let him sleep; otherwise Alisha and Laurie would have been in to jump on the bed with enough enthusiasm to shake his prosthetic eye loose—which they had actually accomplished on one occasion. Lucas rolled over and came face-to-face with another reward—Bean's butt. The little dog was expressing about ten thousand volts of happy with his spinning cigar nub tail and Lucas wondered how he got up on the bed. His legs were only about six inches long, which meant that one of the kids had probably given him a little ballistic help. "Great. Sure. Thanks." He rolled Bean aside and sat up.

He felt remarkably solvent and hoped it was a sign he was getting stronger. He snapped in his leg, took a fast shower, brushed his teeth, mounted his arm, and managed to get into a fresh suit without tearing off a button. Which was as good as it got.

Lemmy and Bean were already downstairs, where there was bacon, and Lucas hoped there would be a few pieces left. The way he felt, uncooked would do.

The kids were lined up at the island, watching Dingo at the stove. He wore a chef's hat, an apron decorated with very large—and very ugly—cabbage roses, and had the stub of a frozen breakfast sausage wedged into the corner of his mouth like a cigar. He was scrambling eggs in one skillet while bacon sizzled in another as he simultaneously buttered toast and dealt out plates like Lars Ulrich channeling Durga. He was wearing his performance blades instead of his street feet, which Lucas knew he much preferred.

"Good morning, Dr. Page!" Dingo said without looking up, and the kids all repeated, "Good morning, Dr. Page!" like they were used to doing for their teachers.

"Good morning, family!" he yodeled back with as much enthusiasm as he could muster sans caffeine.

Erin, who was at the table, held her mug up in a toast. "Ah, the mummy moves."

Lucas gave her a kiss that the younger kids mimicked with smooching noises.

"So, how is everyone?" Lucas asked, feeling like they were all in on something that he wasn't, which was not unusual.

Dingo put a mug in his hand.

"Thanks."

Dingo danced back to the stove, pulled the skillet off the heat, and began spooning eggs onto plates with the precision of Lucy on the chocolate assembly line. But the eggs got delivered, and he dealt out bacon and toast that he punctuated with, "Good night, Cleveland!"

The kids clapped and Lucas sat down at the table while they went at their breakfasts.

Dingo came over and laid a plate of eggs and one single strip of bacon down in front of Lucas. "Here ya go, mate. Fuel for the day."

Lucas poured coffee into the pipe and felt the battery bars on his voice top up. "Any more bacon?" He was really craving bacon, which was unusual.

"Sixteen strips of bacon in a package, divided among five kids, three strips a kid, leaves you with one strip of bacon, my man."

"Alisha won't eat three strips of bacon."

Dingo nodded at that. "She gave one of her strips to Lemmy and the other to Bean."

Lucas looked down at his plate and shook his head. "Swell." He picked up the lone piece he had been allotted and began to raise it to his mouth. It snapped off in his fingers, bounced off the table, then spun off toward the floor where Lemmy snapped it up before it hit the tiles.

Lucas stared at the dog for a few heartbroken seconds. "Really?" Lemmy sat down, thinking there might be more where that came from. "Forget it."

Maude held out a crispy strip of her bacon. "Here."

Once again, Lucas was amazed at how much she looked like Erin—the thick red hair, the freckles, the expression on her face, and the exasperation in her eyes—which was a testament to Jungian thought, because all of their children were adopted.

Lucas smiled and she smiled back and he reached out and took it. "Thanks, kiddo."

Damien shielded his plate, prison-style. "Touch my bacon and you'll need another fake hand."

Lucas feigned a grab and asked, "Aren't you guys all going to be late?" It seemed too relaxed for a school morning.

Alisha turned around in her chair and pointed her one crispy strip of bacon at him to emphasize her point. "It's Satu-day."

"Saturday?" How had he missed that?

Dingo came over and sat down at the table. Evidently the title of stand-in chef didn't guarantee him any more bacon than Lucas—he had eggs and the single sausage that he had been coddling, the end looking as if Lemmy had taken a chomp. "It's after Friday but before Sunday."

"So what's on the clock today?" On Saturdays they usually got whatever supplies the kids needed for the week, and sometimes he was allowed to talk them into a movie. But with five children, the hours tended to get used up more frequently than banked. And there was always grocery shopping to do. They were all just grateful that Erin rarely worked weekend shifts.

Erin pointed at Laurie, Hector, and Alisha. "Well, we four are going grocery shopping."

Maude kicked in with, "Which leaves me and Damien at home. I have plenty to do." She turned to Damien, who wasn't paying attention, and gave him a light punch in the arm. "And you, Wes Borland?"

Damien handled it like he handled most questions—with a cryptic smile and a shrug. "If you guys are all going out, Ima play my guitar."

Erin turned to Lucas. "And you, Brother Theodore? What are *your* plans?"

Which was precisely when his cell phone rang. It was Russo.

Lucas tried to sound pleasant when he answered, "Dr. Page here."

"Page, Russo. And how is the grumpy man today?"

"What do you want?" He pushed himself up from the table and walked down the hall.

"Don't you ever stop to smell the flowers?"

"That's exactly what you were interrupting."

"Okay. It's Saturday. I understand. I just thought that we should get together and compare notes. You know, on account of us investigating a bunch of murders and all."

Lucas checked his watch, did the math, and figured that Russo probably hadn't slept, which earned him a gold sticker. "Whitaker will be here to pick me up in a few minutes and we can swing by."

"I'm going home to get a little sleep. Make it this afternoon. But there's something you should know—I followed through on your theory of there being an attempted murder of a doctor out there in the system and found one. A woman named Denise Moth tried to kill one Leonard Ibicki nine months before he died of an opioid overdose in his tub. She tried to poison him at a bar."

"Ibicki drowned in his tub at his cabin. Oxy overdose."

"That's the one—nine months after Moth tried to kill him."

Lucas was impressed with Russo's *Sitzfleisch*. "You've been busy."

"I'm good at my job. Before this I was in the service, and I was good at that, too. I promise I'm not dead weight."

Lucas heard a honk from out front, and figured that it was Whitaker. "I gotta go."

26

Mother Nature still hadn't made up her mind on art direction and it was back to bright skies and sunshine. But the wind was still coming in from the north and the air was crisp. Which meant there could be snow. Or rain. Or hail. Or even frozen grasshoppers given the way the year had gone so far.

Lucas came down the steps without his cane—he realized that both he and Whitaker using the same prop was a bad look. Besides, his leg wasn't giving him that much trouble, and experience taught him that the only way to move forward after an accident was to *actually* move forward. Which meant that the training wheels needed to come off at some point, even if it increased the statistical likelihood of kissing the pavement.

Whitaker looked up from behind the wheel, smiled, and pushed the door open, filling the street with 1980s pop.

Lucas climbed in and punched the sound system with his aluminum hand, killing the music.

Whitaker sounded ridiculously cheery when she said, "Someone's clearly not ready to rock down to Electric Avenue."

Lucas pulled the door closed. "If that someone is me, you are correct."

She pulled away from the curb. "And how did the inimitable Dr. Page sleep last night?"

"With his eyes closed."

"I don't know why I keep trying."

"Neither do I."

Whitaker nodded at a box on the dashboard, then at a cardboard cup in the console. "Bagels and coffee." She checked the mirror, pulled away from the curb, and caught the green light at the corner.

Lucas peeled the lid of the coffee back. "Very much appreciated."

They punched east into the morning, but the autumn orbit was to the south and the light was not yet making it down between the buildings.

After a few sips of molten caffeine, Lucas turned to ask if they had lined up all the available surveillance footage from Dove Knox's apartment like he had asked, but Whitaker cut him off with one of her pre-answer answers. "We're not going to the office. We're going to Brooklyn. After your call last night, Hoffner put a room full of junior agents on the data sets and they hit every citywide arrest docket for the past three years. And guess what?"

He kept forgetting about that little magic trick of hers—the way she could predict questions. Her frequency detector only had one-way reception, so she could only preemptively sense questions, not answers, which gave it a limited use. Lucas knew that nothing paranormal was going on—because there was no such thing—and Whitaker never gave it any supernatural properties; she simply called it "That thing I do." Lucas thought it was a neat trick, and figured he'd eventually work out how she did it.

He took another sip of the still-too-hot coffee and said, "A woman named Denise Moth tried to kill one of the doctors on our list—Leonard Ibicki—nine months before he accidentally over-dosed in his tub."

She double-glanced over at him. "Just how the *h*-*e*-double-fuck did you know that?"

"In both quantum and astrophysics, there's an accepted precept that even though a force isn't visible or measurable through familiar means, it's still possible to observe—and therefore often predict—its effect. I'd like to say this is all an unorganized mess, but there's a form, an underlying order, to what's happening." He took a sip of coffee. "Oh, and Russo told me."

He pulled the doctor's stats from memory. "Leonard Ibicki was an accidental suicide. Light opioid user—his sister said that it had been a habit for years. He had been before the medical board three times, the last resulting in a stint in rehab. Not a very good doctor, which I think he probably knew and is more than likely the reason he stayed away from direct patient care."

Whitaker said, "That's the one," and pulled a paper file from between the seat and console.

Lucas cracked the jacket and began to read.

Denise Moth had been caught stirring a lethal dose of 06-monoacetylmorphine into Ibicki's drink at a bar he frequented. A waiter saw her and notified an off-duty police officer who was also a regular. Moth wasn't arrested, but she was questioned. Ibicki decided to cover lab costs—the NYPD didn't foot the bill on every suspected roofie that came their way—and once they got toxicology reports back, Ibicki pressed charges. Moth was arrested for attempted murder. She pleaded no contest, and received a seven-year sentence. She did two years in an upstate facility before being transferred back to the city, where she was slated to spend the rest of her sentence at the Metropolitan Detention Center in Brooklyn.

"Well?" Whitaker asked as she took the ramp onto the FDR.

"It fits the general dynamics of this thing—the bar where this happened was part of his regular routine and the guy was already playing with Oxy, which is how he eventually died, even if it was nine months later. And both his attempted murder and eventual murder didn't happen on a Tuesday. So it fits."

"So while Moth was in prison, someone else killed Leonard Ibicki?"

"Smurf-xactly."

"Could it be Hess?"

Lucas looked out the window at the people firing up their Saturday mornings. "It could be anyone."

27

Metropolitan Detention Center
Brooklyn

The interview room was a ten-by-twelve-foot gray cell with one single window that looked out onto the courtyard, parking lot, large redbrick wall, and Gowanus Expressway. The smell was a physical manifestation of the color palette, and Lucas wondered why he kept ending up in places like this, speaking to the broken, defective, and angry.

Hoffner had made the appropriate calls and Denise Moth was accompanied by her lawyer, a young black attorney named Dennis Jones who seemed to be as interested in being here as Lucas was. But he pretended to pay attention and didn't complain about having his Saturday morning blown by the FBI.

Denise Moth was small according to almost every conceivable metric—size, demeanor, and personality. Whatever intelligence she possessed was well masked with cold disinterest.

Ms. Moth once again said, "I don't care."

Her attorney leaned over and whispered something in her ear, but she shook her head. "No."

Whitaker leaned forward. "You've already been through enough, Ms. Moth. And there is a valid argument to be made that you are not a threat to the public at large—but that only comes to light if we know *why* you tried to murder Dr. Ibicki."

Moth had been an accountant at a Queens pigment distributor. She had been married to a man named Mark. They had a son named Matthew. But an accident on the Robert Kennedy Bridge ten years ago put Matthew on life support that they had withdrawn four years in. Her marriage fell apart. Three years after that she tried to murder Dr. Ibicki, a man with whom she had no apparent connection. And there was no real-world way to connect any of these things together—they were just random backscatter noise thrown up by the universe.

But people rarely killed random strangers for no reason. Not unless there was some sort of psychopathy involved. And Moth certainly did not fit any of the necessary criteria for that particular mental pathology. At least not according to her file.

Whitaker filled the dead air with, "Look, Ms. Moth, Dr. Ibicki is dead. And you certainly didn't kill him because you were in here when he *accidentally* overdosed. So whatever was going on with Dr. Ibicki is over. He's dead. And there is no reason for you to keep this to yourself." Whitaker opened her hands. "We're trying to look forward here, not back. What we do care about is who else was involved. And why."

Moth stared at her. "I'm not particularly concerned about what you or *Dr.* Page care about." The way she said the word "doctor" made it sound like a curse.

"Ms. Moth, believe me when I say that I have a pretty good idea of what you've gone through."

She opened her mouth to protest, but Lucas just kept her locked in his stare and she looked down at his hand, then back up at his eye, and he knew his point had been taken.

Lucas went for their only prop, pulling out a photograph of Albert Hess. He placed it on the table, spun it around, and pushed it across the scratched metal. "Do you know this man?"

She didn't look down.

Lucas prodded her again. "Just take a look."

Moth glanced at the picture, looked up, and shook her head. "No."

"Are you—"

"I said *no*."

Whitaker stepped in with, "If you help us out in a quantifiable way, we will take this to the judge and see that you get time served. There is no reason for you to spend another four years in here. And there is no one out there worth protecting. I think we're being more than fair. And you could be out enjoying your life by Christmas."

Lucas watched her for a moment, then added, "Because we're going to figure this out. With or without you."

The lawyer leaned in again and whispered in her ear, but she shook her head and leveled a stare at Lucas that was as inanimate as his own. "You can't figure out something that isn't there. And if no one will talk to you about it, that's all you have." And that was when she disengaged from the conversation, got up from the table, and signaled the corrections officer through the small glass window in the door.

28

FDR Drive

Traffic was unusually heavy for a Saturday morning, and the fog rolling in off the East River transformed the sea of taillights ahead into an armada of bioluminescent organisms. But Brett Kehoe was not paying attention to the meteorological sleight of hand or the traffic—his focus was on the files that Hoffner had given him to read on the way in.

Kehoe had risen at his genetically preprogramed time of 5:00 A.M. After a jog with his two-man security detail—the route of which he changed randomly (or at least he had thought it random before Page had redefined the term)—he showered, dressed, and had a breakfast of four poached egg whites, three ounces of lamb's liver, half a cantaloupe, and two cups of coffee. But instead of the usual routine where he met Hoffner at the front door at precisely 6:45 A.M., he had used a few weekend hours to field email and declutter his schedule.

Kehoe always used his morning drives to catch up on the night's activity and, without exception, this daily exercise reminded him that Sinatra had been right, and the city never slept.

With Hoffner taking lead on the Page case, another agent should have picked him up. But in the early stages of an investigation he didn't want any lag time between the questions asked and the answers received—part of his shortest distance between two points approach.

Hoffner had gone over the dust that Page had kicked up and Kehoe was trying to place the details in context, starting with the twin cell phones at the Knox murder, moving on to the Hess interview, then the two mystery men who had tried to visit him, and ending with the discovery of Denise Moth and her failed attempt at murdering Dr. Leonard Ibicki. All garnished with the participation of a cyclopic NYPD detective named Johnny Russo.

Kehoe tapped the folder in his lap. "If nothing else, Page is insightful."

The big man at the wheel grunted in the affirmative and it sounded like a mechanical noise off the exhaust system. "Of the thirteen suicides mixed into this thing, not a single one left a note, which our people say is too skewed to be a coincidence." Hoffner sounded annoyed that Page had been right, which was not an unusual reaction to his acumen.

"Three of the deaths that presented as heart attacks have turned out to be homicides—one insulin overdose and two hydrocyanic poisonings.

"We've also questioned four of the likeliest suspects in the cases where there were acrimonious court battles over accusations of malpractice—you know, the obvious choices in the suspect category— just to see if shaking the trees produced anything of value. All of them have alibis. I mean airtight, recorded, ridiculously reliable alibis."

"Which is a point *against* Page's acumen." Kehoe's phone rang and routine overrode consideration and he picked it up without checking the display. "FBI. Special Agent in Charge Kehoe."

"Special Agent Kehoe, Dr. Corey Winslow. Stanford University."

"Yes, Dr. Winslow." Kehoe had been wondering when Winslow would call back.

"I've finished working on that equation you sent over." Winslow's voice was delivered on a deep open southern frequency that sounded like it did not know how to express stress. "I was just about to email my results to Special Agent Li but wanted to ask you a question before I did—who wrote this?"

"I'm afraid I can't share that information."

Winslow was silent for a few seconds before giving a very slow, "I see."

"Dr. Winslow—"

"Yes, of course. Sorry. I don't know the specifics about what this is related to because I wasn't given the context, but those eight pages were an equation proving that thirty individual events within a sample group of sixteen hundred and eleven individual events are not random and did not occur naturally like the others."

"Forgive me, Dr. Winslow, because I'm not a mathematician, but that seemed like a lot of numbers for a one-sentence summary."

Winslow delivered the dry chuckle academics substitute for a laugh when they want to emphasize that they know more than you do. "That wasn't a summary; that was the answer to the equation. A summary would take me days to explain."

"Why was it so complicated?"

Winslow's southern delivery slowed down as he went into TED Talk mode. "There is a famous quote by Carl Sagan that goes, 'If you wish to make an apple pie from scratch, you must first invent the universe.' This equation is the equivalent of a recipe for Sagan's apple pie—Sagan's *complete* apple pie, beginning with the Big Bang, going on to explain how the universe, and eventually our planet, formed, highlighting how life began, moving up through evolutionary biology to explain the development of the apple along with its chemical composition, working out the molecular formula of the plate the pie should be baked in, and going through a dissertation on the thermal properties harnessed by the oven in which it will be baked, after providing blueprints on how to build said oven—including the composition of raw materials. Of course it's truncated, and there are gaps, but he—or she—did their job."

Kehoe rolled his eyes; the only time he tolerated folksiness was when it came from John Prine. "Why would the author do that?"

"I think they're trying to make a point."

"And that point would be?"

"I'm not a psychiatrist, but this comes across as, oh, I don't know—frustrated, I guess." There was a bemused tone in his voice again. "Because it appears as if this was written by a very smart individual who feels like they are being forced to explain something elemental to people who can't grasp basic concepts—that would explain the condescending overkill, I suppose."

"I wasn't aware that numbers could be condescending."

"Numbers are like words, Mr. Kehoe, and how you use them says a lot about you."

"Dr. Winslow, I appreciate your help. Please, let me know if I can ever return the favor."

"Well, if this individual isn't a criminal, tell them I have a job for them."

"Doing what?"

Winslow let out a long, slow laugh that had more Texas written into it. "Whatever they want."

Kehoe disconnected and looked up to see Hoffner eyeing him in the mirror. The big man's facial muscles barely moved when he asked, "So Page is playing some hopped-up three-dimensional game of Super Mario Mouse Trap in his head?"

Kehoe turned back to the world outside, and the sea of taillights in the fog. "There are *glass-half-full* people; there are *glass-half-empty* people; there are even *glass-is-too-big* people. But Dr. Page is the only *glass-is-incorrectly-designed-for-the-application* person I have ever met. Which means he approaches the world—and more importantly its problems—from a *Let's redesign the glass* perspective. Which makes him the avatar for Shaw's Unreasonable Man, upon whom all progress is dependent."

"He's still a supreme pain in the ass, sir."

Kehoe smiled at that. He had once asked Page how he saw the world almost uniquely through the prism of mathematics, and his response was typical Page: *Understanding how to operate a complicated piece of machinery is not the same as understanding how a complicated piece of machinery operates.* "It helps that he's right most of the time."

29

Queens

Quaralco Pigments was located in an industrial park in Queens, close to the East River and not nearly far enough from a residential area should a fire break out. It was operating on a weekend skeleton shift, and as Lucas and Whitaker walked the length of the warehouse on the way to the shipping office, he inventoried the chemical labels and had a hard time believing anyone would keep so many potential disasters under one roof. The facility was equipped with a foam sprinkler system and fire doors, but the building didn't look like it was anywhere near code. There were barrels and boxes, cans and jars, bottles and pallets—and with one good spark, the entire thing would become a poisonous crater.

Mark Moth was in his office near the loading dock. He was on the phone when they walked in and he hung up with a quick "I'll call you back" after Whitaker held up her badge.

"You guys find those two trucks?" he asked.

Whitaker shook her head. "We're not here about any trucks, Mr. Moth. We would like to ask you a few questions about your ex-wife."

And just like that, his demeanor changed. "Aw, shit. Tell me she's okay."

Whitaker held up her hand. "She's fine. But we're looking into why she would try to kill Dr. Ibicki."

"Yeah. Well," he said, as if those two words held the answers to any question they might have.

"Can you help us at all?"

"What happened? I mean, this is all old new news."

"It's possible that your wife knows something about another case involving Ibicki."

"He died, you know," Moth said without emotion. "Overdosed nine months after Denise's trial. How's that for irony?" He shook his head. "I still don't know what all that was about."

The man leaned back in his chair and studied them for a moment. Like his ex-wife, Mark Moth looked like he had been reduced in some material way. It was in his movements and eye contact, as if simply existing was an encumbrance. "Denise and I don't talk anymore. And even before she"—he paused—"*allegedly* tried to drug that man, we hadn't talked in a couple of years. I don't see how I can help." He shook his head. "At all."

"You were married. Which means you probably know her better than anyone. Besides, we spoke to her, and she does not come across as a murderer. We're trying to figure out her motivation."

"You and me both," he said, popping forward in his chair and putting his elbows on the desk. "Honestly, after our accident—you know about our accident?"

Whitaker said, "Only that you were in a collision on the Robert Kennedy Bridge with a drunk driver. The driver was killed and your son was badly injured."

"If you want to call a crushed skull and severed spinal column *injured*, you be my guest. Matty was killed. And then Denise disappeared. I'm not blaming her and I'm not saying I don't understand. I'm just saying she didn't bounce back."

Whitaker levered into one of the mismatched folding chairs. "Do you know why she'd try to drug Dr. Ibicki?"

He shrugged. "I don't know why she did anything at the end there. And Ibicki? That made no sense at all. I mean she didn't know him. At all. We never met him. She never had an affair with him. He lived in a different neighborhood, worked at a hospital we never went to, worked with people we didn't know. I mean, it was a big fucking mystery and one of the key points the defense wanted to offer. Think about it—why would anyone try to murder someone they didn't know and had never met? I have a lot of issues with Denise, but she's not a psychopath; she's just broken."

"And she didn't have anything to offer during sentencing?"

Moth shook his head slowly. "She took a deal. Didn't even fight it. She just stared at the table in front of her waiting for the inevitable. She can be stubborn."

"We noticed." Lucas stayed in the doorway, with his back to the forklift noise in the warehouse. "Was she injured in the accident? Is it possible she had some undiagnosed brain trauma?"

Moth shook his head. "She was checked out. A bunch of times. We were both fine." He looked up when he realized what he had just said. "Physically fine, I mean."

"What happened that day?"

Moth shrugged. "It was one of those things where you think that maybe God has it in for you, know what I mean? We were at the tollbooths, back before everything went E-ZPass and electronic and shit, and I was digging some change out of the ashtray. And this guy—name of Wayne Minister, sounded like a country singer to me—had a few too many and didn't see the booth. Or us. Or anything, I guess. Because he plowed his minivan into the back of our Golf at about seventy miles an hour and flipped over top of us, landing his van on the roof of the booth. There's this big fucking smash and for a few seconds all I could hear was nothing. Then I look over at Denise and Denise looks over at me, and the roof of the Volks is gone and it's obvious that we're both all right and we both have this surprised look on our faces and I'm about to smile with how lucky we were when we both turned to the back seat at the same time—" And he stopped. Just stopped. And his eyes filled with tears. "I'm sorry, I haven't talked about this in a long time. It's funny, isn't it, how something that defines your life, that you try not to think about, but is running in the back of your head on replay while you walk and sleep and eat and work, stays under control until you try to talk about it? Fuck me." He shook his head as if that would somehow reset the needle. "And fuck you for coming here."

Lucas gave the man a few moments to recalibrate his system before asking, "Did she have any friends who might be able to help? Relatives? People she worked with? Anyone other than you who she was close with and might have confided in?" He leaned forward and tried to convey the import of what he was saying. "We really would like to help, Mr. Moth. And if we can find out why she did what she did, and if it factors into our other case, it might help her out legally."

Moth shook his head. "Me and Matty were her whole life. I mean, it's been ten years since those times, and I know I'm not remembering them the way they actually happened, but we were happy. And after we got nailed by that drunk asshole it all just went straight to shit. Like, not even a pause or anything. She tried one of those group things—you know those pamphlets they have at the community center? That lasted all of one week. She tried exercise. She tried prescription pills. She tried booze. She even tried meditation. Nothing helped and she eventually just disappeared. From me. From herself. From everyone."

"And you got divorced?"

"We stayed together until they took Matty off of life support. After that, she wasn't there anymore. We were both so chewed up from what had happened that we were too tired to bother with a divorce. But it was over. We both knew it. She moved out as soon as they pulled the plug. I didn't see her for a couple more years until she asked for a divorce through a lawyer. Nothing ugly—just a

Please sign this and we're divorced thing. I tried to stay in touch, but she wasn't interested. And, I guess, neither was I, really. The next time I hear anything about Denise it's from her defense lawyer asking if I'd be a character witness for the judge. Like I said, she took a deal and it never went to trial."

"You ever visit her in prison?"

Moth nodded. "I tried. I went to see her when she was upstate, once a week for the first six months or so. Every Sunday on visitors' day. She wouldn't see me. Wouldn't even come out to the booth. I tried again when she was shipped to Metro DC over here in Brooklyn last year. Same thing. I gave up. It's not like we both aren't carting this thing around. And it gets to a point where you have to take care of yourself, you know?"

Lucas knew. He took out the photograph of Albert Hess he had shown Denise Moth an hour ago and put it down on the desk. "Do you know this man?"

Moth leaned forward and gave it a cursory glance. He looked up with an expression that had no discernible meaning, then back at the photograph to give it what looked like honest attention. He shook his head and pushed the photo back. "Who is he?"

"We thought he might be a friend of your wife's."

"I told you, she doesn't have any friends. She doesn't have anything anymore."

"Would you try talking to her for us?"

"If Denise has made up her mind, I'm not changing it for her."

"Does that mean you *can't* help, or that you *won't*?"

The hurt was still playing around with his eyes, but it had dimmed a little. "Take your pick."

30

The Upper East Side

The worst part about grocery shopping in the city on a Saturday was that it was *grocery shopping*. And it was *in the city*. That it was on a Saturday factored in, but only marginally. Erin understood that with a family of seven, hunting down food was an endless task. But she was a transplant from Chadds Ford, Pennsylvania, via Boston, and even after all this time she still wasn't used to the sheer volume of demands Manhattan made on people just trying to stock the fridge for the week. With such a large TV brood, coupon shopping was a must. Which turned their Saturdays into a scavenger hunt with restrictive parking.

They did the bulk of their shopping at Fairway Market, but detours to Citarella for specialty things like Maude's favorite frozen yogurt had to be factored in. Every now and then they did Gristedes, but Lucas had been banned and she could only go when she was alone or with the kids—like today. Bulk items like toilet paper and paper towels were delivered by FreshDirect and every now and then she gave in and picked up a pallet of stuff from Costco—it was a nice change to not be the only person in the parking lot who looked like they ran an orphanage—but it was way uptown.

Lucas had tried to take the task off her roster; when he wasn't slumming with the FBI, his schedule was a lot more open, particularly in the summer when he only touched base with his PhD students every couple of weeks. He was a whiz with coupons but lousy at things like checking tomatoes. But if she handed the rounds over to him, it was only a matter of time before they were banned from *every* grocery store in the five boroughs—he wasn't what Erin (or anyone else, really) considered a *people person*.

It was coming up on noon and she and the kids had somehow finished up the last part of the run, a final stop at their favorite bakery, a small French place on Madison. The window was always full of pastry alligators and pastry chickens and pastry *thises* and pastry *thats*—and they tasted as good as they looked. So four or five times a year they splurged.

Erin pulled around the corner and into the tight entrance to the alley behind their house. The little lane was a holdover from the nineteenth century, back when horse and carriage had been the standard vehicle of convenience. Theirs was one of the few alleys in the entire neighborhood, and it allowed the very great privilege of a garage in the city, which most people considered to be an urban legend.

Even though the Volvo was relatively narrow compared to the vehicles of thirty years ago, she often felt like taking the corner into the alley was like trying to park an Akula-class submarine in a bathtub.

"So?" Erin asked, nodding at the pastry box that Hector was protectively cradling in his lap. "What did you get?"

He smiled over. "Stuff."

"What stuff?!" Alisha hollered from the back.

Erin glanced up into the mirror. "Today is no-yelling day."

"What stuff?" Alisha delicately whispered before smiling up.

Hector put on his best Little Lord Fauntleroy face. "*Awesome* stuff."

Erin finished the corner, then straightened out. She always took it slow through here to avoid collisions with garbage cans or neighbors out back walking their tiny angry dogs.

A man was in the alley, just past their place, speaking on his phone. When they entered the lane, he turned away and cupped his hand over his ear.

Hector automatically reached for the garage door opener clipped to the visor and the movement caught Erin's attention. She glanced over and smiled, then turned back to the alley.

And to the man on the phone, who was now aiming a pistol at them.

There was a moment.

An instant.

A tiny grain of time.

When Erin and the man with the gun saw each other. Their eyes locked and something sparked between them.

It held.

And then.

He fired.

And the world broke into little pieces.

31

Whitaker pulled up to the house, rolled to a stop, and turned off the engine. "You have any coffee?" she asked.

Lucas pushed the door open with his shoulder. "Coffee, apple juice, milk—all the staples." He looked up at the house. "Except bacon."

They stepped out at the same time and Whitaker hit him with, "If Hess is responsible for all of this—"

"He's not. If he was, we wouldn't have Denise Moth in the storyline. It's not just Hess. There's a—"

And that was when the unmistakable crack of gunshots close by punched a hole in the day.

Followed by a child's scream.

32

Erin screamed, "Get down!" and the round grunted through the windshield and she was walloped into the seat, punched by an asteroid.

Everything—
  —unfolded—
    —at—
      —half—
        —speed.
Blood misted—
  —the windshield—
    —the mirror—
      —and Hector.
Laurie—
  —and Alisha—
    —shrieked.
The seat absorbed Erin—
  —reached the point where it had nothing left to give—
    —and threw her forward.

Where she was hit by—
  —a second bullet—
    —that scrambled her circuits.
The man—
  —took a step—
    —toward her—
      —and the children and—
        —raised the pistol.
Erin screamed, "Stay down!"
Stomped her foot into the floor—
  —gasoline converted to torque—
The wagon—
  —launched.
The muzzle—
  —flashed.
The side mirror disappeared.
Erin put the car into the shooter.
He folded—
  —and rolled up—
    —over the hood—
      —and *CRACK!* over—
        —the windshield—
          —and then—
            —the roof.

She kept her foot down—
  —he hit the pavement behind them—
    —rolled and—
      —Erin planted the car into a utility pole.
The hood buckled.
Groceries exploded forward.
The children screamed again.
Erin turned and—
  —Hector was covered with—

—blood.

—His?

—Hers?

Oh no. Oh no.
OH NO.
"AreyouokayHecctorsaysomethingisthatyourbloodLaurieare
youokaysaysomethingAlsihaAlsihaALISHAIT'SOKAYSWEETIE
IT'S—"

—And—

—the shooter rose off the pavement—

—and lifted the pistol.

33

Lucas ran up the steps.

Almost snapped his key off in the lock. Threw the door wide and it crashed into the wall, obliterating a framed painting.

"Erin!" he screamed when he got inside.

From upstairs Maude said, "Did you hear that?"

Damien galloped down with his guitar as Lucas ran by, Lemmy following.

"What is it?" the kid asked, mid-chord.

"Where's Mom?" Lucas yelled.

"Shopping. Why?" But that last word came out frightened.

Lucas blew through the main floor and into the kitchen, where he collided with a barstool. The chrome and Perspex seat skidded across the floor, upended when it reached the carpet, and shattered the glass on the oven door.

"Erin!" he screamed. And tore the back door open.

When he saw the smoke, panic shifted into terror.

When he heard the next gunshot, terror shifted into rage.

He bolted.

And fell down the steps.

34

Erin watched death unfold from the pavement, reconstituting like damaged origami demonically pushing out its folds. It was a herky-jerky seesaw process that blew every circuit in the vestigial fight-or-flight mechanism overheating her skull.

The engine was still running, but it was a dyssynchronous grinding of noises. Smoke slithered around the car.

They had to move.

She had to get the kids out of the car.

Blood was everywhere. Even on the mirror that she couldn't stop staring at.

What do I do?

What Do I Do?

WHATDOIDO?

The shooter was on his feet now, but one of his ankles was folded, and without meaning to, the medical encyclopedia in her head analyzed his condition: *foot crush injury*.

But his arm looked like it worked. And his arm controlled the hand that held the pistol.

Erin was filled with a primitive memory from a thousand

generations ago, from an ancestor who knew that if she didn't do something, they would all die.

She said, "Stay down," one more time, and shifted the transmission from *drive*—where it was still planted—into *reverse*.

The kids ducked and Erin double-footed the gas. The Volvo whined and refused to disengage from the pole.

Then there was a frightening *CRACK!* and the car peeled away, leaving the front grill nailed to the post.

The wagon launched in reverse, one bent wheel with a flat tire squealing out a long fan of sparks. Smoke billowed from the engine.

Erin fought the car and the bones were grinding around in her shoulder.

She kept the gas straight into the floor, the pedal bending against the force.

The car sped backwards.

"Stay down!" she said again, calmly this time, and the dissociated surgeon who lived in her head told her that the chemical spike of shock was filling her pistons.

There was a single sharp report as the man fired again and the back window shattered.

The kids screamed.

Erin ducked as they collided.

There was a crunch and the back bumper took out his knees.

He folded under.

There were two more gunshots on top of each other.

One zipped up through the trunk, detonating cans of soda and plinking out the roof.

There was a flash.

And a horrid crunch and the car buckled as the wheels ate bones. Organs. Intentions. And options.

A *whump* as the fire erupted.

And the car planted into the brick wall.

The momentum threw her into the seat, and there was a loud snap inside her as something else broke and she screamed.

And the kids screamed.

And the still-running engine screamed.

But the real screams came from outside.

From the man on fire in the middle of the alley.

One of his legs kicked back and forth; the other was pointed straight up, bent the wrong way at the knee. Shrieking like a sentient insect set ablaze by a child.

An arm pointed up at the sky, the wick effect melting his hand as it involuntarily emptied the pistol into the sky.

—*BANG!BANG!BANG!BANG!BANG!BANG!BANG!*—

Erin watched, was absorbed by the terminal moment before realizing that the fire was crawling lazily toward the car.

She tried to reach for her seat belt, but her arm wouldn't move. She tried with the other but stopped when a liquid sac of pain burst somewhere in her chest and she coughed up blood.

Alisha was screaming—an irrational, single note of terror.

Hector was clutching the crushed pastry box to his chest, little glazed alligators oozing out at the corners.

"Hector?"

He looked over at her in slow motion, perfectly disinterested. "Yes?" he said, as if politely answering the phone.

"Hector, listen to me. *Listen!*" she said, louder, to be heard over Alisha's shriek.

But his expression didn't change; he was in shock.

"You have to help your sisters." She couldn't move her arms and the fear dynamo in her chest cranked up.

She heard Laurie unbuckle herself in the back. "I can do it!" the little girl said.

The flames were crawling across the alley floor, looking for something to feed on.

All Erin could smell was her own blood. And gas.

The only sound was her own heartbeat. And Alisha's screaming.

"Please, Hector." She watched the fire coming for them. "I know you're scared, but listen to me—*listen to me!*"

That shook him loose and he nodded a definitive time. "Okay."

"Take off your seat belt. Get in the back. Help the girls out. Fast." She tried not to let the terror come out.

Hector absentmindedly placed the crushed pastry box on the blood-and-glass-spattered, dashboard, unbuckled himself, and crawled over the seat into the back. When his sneaker hit her shoulder, she screamed.

There was the sound of the baby seat buckles being disengaged.

The flames were at the hood now, smoke starting to chug through the vents.

"Get out."

"What about you?"

"I'm fine." It stung her—physically *hurt* her—that her first lie to the children would also be her last.

Hector wrapped his fingers around the handle and pulled and— nothing happened.

"It's stuck!" he said.

Erin's program switched to mother mode. "Get out! GET OUT! Kick it open! Go through the window. Please pleasepleaseplease. Please. Kids. Go. Go."

The hood was on fire and smoked pumped through the vents and the shattered windshield. Flames were snaking into the car, the heat intimate.

Hector grunted as he planted his foot into the door one . . . two . . . three—*aha! Open!*

But with the rush of air came the rush of oxygen.

Which fed the fire.

"*Ruuuuuuuuuuuun!*" she screamed.

The kids spilled out.

Fire burst in.

And Erin closed her eyes to welcome the inevitable.

35

Lucas scrambled to his feet.

Stumbled forward, bounced off the swing set, and lurched for the gate.

To the alley.

To the smoke.

To the fire.

To Alisha's high-pitched screech on loop.

He had to punch the code in twice before the lock gave and he yanked the wrought-iron door open.

When he hit the alley, the heat from the conflagration wrapped him in its arms and time sped up, slowed down, and folded all at once.

Hector was half carrying/half dragging Alisha toward the house. The little girl was screeching as if she were being taken apart. Laurie stood by the burning car, frozen and immobile as Lot's wife.

Alisha was pointing at the fireball and a single high-pitched shock wave poured from her mouth.

A body was on fire in the alley, amid a patch of charred asphalt that danced with flame. The corpse's arm was pointed at the sun, a pistol fried into its fingers.

Lucas ran past Hector. Past Laurie. Past the burning body holding the gun.

The flames were in the car, licking up against the windows. The dashboard was on fire.

Erin's shadow was behind the wheel. Unmoving.

Black smoke blocked out the world and all Lucas could see was the nothing in front of him. He ran to the door and the smoke filled his lungs.

He couldn't see the driver's window. The heat was pushing him back.

Lucas pulled at the handle and it came off in his hands.

The flames were on his pants now. On his legs.

Alisha was still shrieking somewhere out beyond the smoke.

He put his metal hand through the window. But it had no feeling, and he couldn't find her in there.

She's two fucking feet away!

He fumbled around in the molten air and somehow found her seat belt and punched the buckle and pulled on her and as he got her through the window there was a supercharge of air and he tried to step away and the whole thing let go and the force blew him back across the alley and he hit the fence and all of a sudden he was lying in the daylight with Erin, who was on fire.

He slapped at her. Trying to put her out with his own flaming arm.

And then something pummeled him and Whitaker screamed, "Roll! Roll!" as she hit him with her coat and then there was another explosion as what was left of the car was reduced to molecules and he was on the asphalt beneath the sky inked over with smoke from the burning gasoline and he could barely see through the tears.

"You're good. You're good."

He coughed violently. Rolled over. Tried to breathe and rise at the same time. But his code was skipping, and he shuddered as another wracking cough twisted his ribs and he collapsed.

He forced his eyes open and everything rippled through the tears from the smoke.

Whitaker was beside him and even though her mouth wasn't moving he recognized her voice telling him that it was okay and he heard the children somewhere far away and Dingo was telling them to stay back and Lucas rolled over and put his hand on Erin and screamed.

36

"Are you okay?" Dingo yelled, and Lucas realized that he was expected to answer.

But he could only nod. So he did. And with an academic clarity it dawned on him that he was in shock. And sitting on the pavement. Erin lay on the ground with her head in his lap. Tears cut light fissures through her soot maquillage.

Smoke was everywhere. And the stench of burning gasoline in the morning air smelled nothing like victory. And something else that he recognized but did not want to name.

His lungs were filled with ants.

He held Dingo's balled-up shirt to the holes in Erin's shoulder. Her wounds were pissing blood all over her chest—when he had turned her over on the pavement, the shattered bone ends ground around in her muscles like white teeth trying to chew their way out of her body.

But she was alive.

Dingo had corralled the kids into his apartment over the garage. Lucas couldn't see them, but he could feel their eyes on him and Erin. Alisha had stopped screaming. And the sound of sirens blipped in the distance.

The security team from the French consulate was outside, small machine pistols at the ready as they held a perimeter. One of them was on his phone with a cigarette fastened to his bottom lip and he was summoning an ambulance in perfect English.

Lucas cradled Erin's head and tried not to look at the blood-soaked charred clothing.

"Where's Whitaker?" he asked with a voice that he didn't recognize.

Dingo raised an arm, gesturing to some point behind Lucas's shoulder, and he turned.

Whitaker's shiny SUV four-wheel-drifted around the far corner of the alley and the back end slammed into a convertible Audi, knocking it into a fence. She rocketed up the lane toward them, pulling wet leaves in her jet stream, lights on, siren off.

She slammed to a stop, dusting them with dirt, and Dingo did most of the work in lifting Erin off the pavement and into the back seat as smoke swirled around them.

Erin's head lolled forward as they drunk-walked her to the Navigator and Dingo said, "I got the kids."

Whitaker jumped out and yanked the back door open and Lucas climbed in, pulling Erin like a wet carpet. Dingo fed her in while Lucas tried to keep the sopping shirt to her wounds.

Lucas looked at Dingo, then back up at the kids just before Whitaker slammed the door and they were gone.

She lit up the siren and they rocketed out of the alley in a screech of rubber, straight into Saturday traffic.

Whitaker counter-steered out of the skid, sideswiped a parked Prius, and blew east, toward the hospital.

Erin said, "I'm okay," but she was staring up at something beyond him. She didn't sound convincing. Or convinced. But there was no missing the hope.

He gave her his smallest smile that he wasn't sure she could see. "I know."

"I'm okay," she repeated.

She was covered in soot and blood and her singed hair framed her now-eyebrowless-eyelashless face and all Lucas could smell was burnt everything.

She swallowed, then calmly said, "I'm in shock right now. But I was hit in the axillary artery, so you have to slow the bleeding." Even in shock, all she knew how to do was deal with things. "You need to plug the holes, Luke."

He looked around. "With what?"

"Your fingers."

Lucas's original hand was filthy. He wiped it on his shirt and it only got worse. "I need disinfectant!" he yelled in frustration.

Whitaker threw a bottle of hand sanitizer into the back. "That's all I got."

Time was not an available luxury, so without checking the alcohol content, Lucas tore the cap off with his teeth and shot a load of sanitizer into his hand. He pulled the bloody shirt away and hesitated just long enough to see her heart pump out a burst of black and he said, "Okay," and took a breath. Then he shoved his fingers into the two fresh tunnels drilled into her body.

Erin arched her back and screamed, "*Mother...fucker that hurts!*"

He put the shirt back over his hand and reapplied pressure as best he could with his prosthetic. He looked up just as Whitaker jumped a light and nearly clipped a cab.

When he turned back, Erin looked into his left eye—the sunglasses were somewhere back in the alley. "I think we need to move...somewhere with...trees."

Lucas smiled down at her. Tears broke loose. "I'm in. Wherever you want to go."

"How about the hospital?" She found that hilarious and snorted, and her goofy little laugh was cut short by a cough that brought up blood.

She looked up at him and all he saw was her fear. "It's okay. You're okay."

She tried to smile and a red drop left the corner of her mouth and trailed down into her hair. "I know more about this stuff than you do."

"Only in theory."

"Take care of the kids. Lie to them—tell them that I am going to be fine."

"You are."

"I'm cold, Luke. I've lost a lot of blood and it's in my lungs. I'm not okay," she said. "Something is *wrong*."

Whitaker cut around a Town Car that was unloading suitcases on 74th Street, and she plowed through them, sending them spinning into orbit. They were gone before the sound wave of the driver's curse could pace them.

Whitaker glanced up into the mirror. "How is she?"

"I . . . I . . ." He could hear the panic in his own voice. "I . . . don't know."

Lucas looked up and the city moved by outside faster than he had ever seen it before. They were flying.

He looked back down at Erin, but she had passed out.

37

Weill Cornell Medical Center

Whitaker was doing close to eighty heading east when the geometry of the city shifted and the hospital materialized out of the concrete camouflage like a piece of Magic Eye op art. It was a little farther than Lenox Hill, but it was familiar ground, and Lucas knew the people there—which he grimly understood was not the same as trusting them.

Whitaker swung the SUV around the corner to the ER entrance in a precise Bill Hickman drift that missed all the stationary objects in their arc.

She kicked down and they rocketed toward the doors, where a formation of hospital personnel was waiting.

She hit the brakes and they fishtailed and the Emergency team rushed forward from the scrimmage line before the SUV came to a complete, but crooked, stop.

All the doors were pulled open and an octopus of human hands reached for Erin with experienced gloved tentacles. She was pulled out and fed into a waiting gurney with Lucas still attached.

He told them about the two gunshot wounds to her shoulder—that he didn't know if there were more. After three rapid-fire questions, one of the doctors got Lucas to remove his fingers, then pushed him out of the way and took over.

Lorne Jacobi stood back while his people did their thing, and when Lucas took a few steps back to give them room, his prosthetic foot hit the asphalt with an uncharacteristic mechanical clank. He looked down and his boot was . . . just gone.

Lucas watched Erin as they rolled her for the door, and for a single byte of time the line was right, and he thought their eyes intersected.

It felt like they were together.

And then her orientation changed, and they were once again apart.

He wiped his bloody fingers on his charred lapel.

Jacobi reached out and his hand went high, to Lucas's shoulder. "Luke, all of Emerge is ready for her. Chance and Walker are scrubbed in and waiting. They're the best. And this is one of the finest care facilities in the world."

Lucas didn't want to hear brochure blurbs right now, but he nodded a thank-you and tried to stay in the moment. He knew Ellie Chance through Erin, and her peers considered her a superb surgeon; he didn't know this Walker character, but he understood that he had to trust Jacobi; this was out of his area of expertise.

Lucas ran after the gurney and got inside as they wheeled Erin past the desk and off to the operating room. Lucas yelled, "I'll be right here!" as they rolled her through the doors.

He thought he saw her flutter her fingers at him, but that might just have been hope fucking with him.

He was staring at the *Staff Only* sign on the automatic glass door when Jacobi grabbed his forearm and steered him away. "She's going to be in there awhile, Luke." He held up his phone. "They'll keep me updated: as soon as I know something, you'll know something. Go have a coffee. Make calls. If you need anything—food, a shower, something to help you sleep, something to help you stay awake—let me know. Give me ten minutes to get you some clothes."

"I appreciate everything." And he did. "But my clothes are fine, Lorne."

But Lorne was already somewhere else. "I love Erin—I didn't know they made people like her."

Lucas knew what Jacobi meant, but his RAM was dedicated to dealing with the short-term goal of Erin making it through surgery. After that, they could discuss how swell she was.

Jacobi shook his head and his eyes filled with tears. "What the hell happened?"

Lucas had more questions than Jacobi ever would. "Someone tried to kill her."

"And?"

"And you know as much as I do."

"And her attacker?"

Lucas looked at him for a long second as he rewound his memories. "She ran over him and he's dead."

Lorne turned in the direction they had just wheeled Erin. "Then that's one less thing we all have to worry about."

Lucas shuffled back to the waiting room and Kehoe was unexpectedly there, talking with Whitaker. The whole reception area was staring at her, and when Lucas entered the frame they shifted focus to him. Half of his suit was burned away and what was left looked like a dragon's lung with pockets. In perfect theatrical fashion, his prosthetic arm and legs stuck out of the charred sleeve and leg, exposing his mechanical prosthetics, and it was impossible to miss the uncanny valley effect he was having. If it had been another time, or another place, he might have asked if Sarah Connor was in the house.

"How are you doing?" Kehoe asked through a very sincere facsimile of concern.

"I need a phone."

Whitaker handed hers over.

Lucas stepped away, dialed, and Dingo immediately answered, "Page residence."

"She's in surgery. How are the kids?"

Before answering, Dingo spoke to the gaggle of background voices asking questions. "She's in surgery. She's going to be okay. I need to talk to your dad." He came back with, "They're fine. What can I do?"

"Just take care of them. Can I speak to Maude?"

Maude came on with, "Yes?" It was tentative and filled with a million questions, none of which Lucas had the answers to.

"Hey, kiddo. You okay?"

Maude answered him with, "What's happening?" and the children's voices ramped back up with a hundred new questions that she cut off with a harsh, *"Shut up! I'm talking!"*

"Mom's in surgery. She's going to be okay."

"Is that real talk or don't-scare-the-kids talk?"

Lucas tried not to think about the answer too long. "Both," he said. "We got here pretty fast and she's got the best people in the world working on her."

Again, Maude said, *"Shut up! I'm talking!"* to the others.

"Is everybody okay?"

"No."

"I need you to take care of everyone while I'm here. Can you do that?"

"I'll try."

"Thank you." He felt himself start to cry, but it was a distant, unconnected thing that was happening to someone else. He tried to keep the tremble out of his voice when he said, "She's going to be okay," again.

Maude said, "Uh-huh."

"I'll call every half hour whether I have news or not."

"Damien wants to talk to you."

There were some muffled voices before Damien said, "Is she going to be okay?"

Maude's voice overrode his question with an irritated, "*I told you she's going to be fine!*"

Lucas repeated, "She's going to be okay. But she's going to be in surgery for a while—hours. I'll call every half hour or so just to check in. Can you help Maude take care of the others?"

"I guess, yeah."

"Okay. Good. I have to go, but I'll keep you guys updated."

"Okay. Bye."

Dingo was back with, "Don't worry about us. And call if you need anything."

"Thanks, Darren," he said, using Dingo's given name for only the second time he could remember in the dozen years they'd known each other.

Lucas hung up and walked the phone back to Whitaker. She was eyeing him with concern and opened her mouth to say something when Russo came barreling in. He scanned the entry, admission desk, then ran into the waiting room.

Russo skidded to a stop and put a hand on Lucas's shoulder, which seemed to be the standard response to tragedy today. "Page, are you okay? What the fuck happened?"

Whitaker said, "How did you know we were here?"

"This is my precinct—Cristo and I got the call and were first on the scene. I saw your name on the address info and the French guys in the alley with the machine pistols said you had taken off, so I put one and three together and figured you'd come here, even though it's farther than Lenox Hill." He was examining Lucas and there was no missing the concern in his tone or expression. "What the fuck happened?" he repeated.

Lucas pointed a green aluminum finger at him. "I'm making somebody nervous."

38

Lucas paced the corridors, trying to find the logic in the colored lines that intercepted nonsensically at the various transepts, like an old Microsoft screen saver. What did color-blind people do? Why hadn't they opted for a system based on numbers? *Follow line 3 then go left at line 9* seemed like a friendlier UX—and it had the added benefit of being easy to explain to non-English speakers with nothing more than a fast diagram. Or they could use both, which he was certain would be more efficient—*Follow yellow/3 then turn left at blue/9* had a built-in redundancy, because the chances of someone being both illiterate *and* color-blind were relatively slim, even in America.

But all of that was simply a distraction from reality. And reality was most definitely where he needed to be.

Erin had been on the table for almost six hours now. Jacobi kept his word on the updates, and he had given Lucas progress reports at least twice an hour since she had gone in. Jacobi had remained after his shift and Lucas appreciated that he was handling this personally; it wasn't like Lorne didn't have enough to do already, but he was a classic example of asking a busy person. Lucas had taken a shower in one of the patient bathrooms and Lorne had brought him a fresh change of clothes, borrowed from an intern who was close to Lucas's six-foot-three height and, remarkably, just as slim. Lorne had even scrounged up a pair of sneakers from Lost and Found to replace the single fire-eaten brogue that Lucas had hobbled in on.

Whitaker had gone home for a shower and a change of clothes. And she said something about trading in the Navigator for another—in less than ten blocks she had managed to take out three of the four quarter panels, both bumpers, two mags, the grill, and one mirror.

Lucas knew she'd also check in with the office to see if they had anything on Erin's shooter. Lucas could see Whitaker was tired and still not 100 percent ready for prime-time duties—that she insisted on being part of this said a lot about their friendship.

Russo had stayed for about an hour, spent too much money on hospital coffee for Lucas, Whitaker, and Kehoe, asked a bunch of questions, said he was going to find out just what the fuck was going on, and disappeared. Which was appreciated.

Lucas hit the end of the corridor, then turned left on the pumpkin orange line, which brought him back to the waiting room.

Lucas knew that from an absolute perspective (if you could apply that specific term to the human experience in any meaningful way) they would ID the shooter. The guy was now missing from his life, and someone knew he was gone. But it might take a little time. Which was the one commodity that you couldn't amass.

And it wasn't Albert Hess. Not unless he had crawled down here from Westchester to carry out one last act of murder in service to whatever emotional demons had talked him into killing Arna Solomon—an event that still made no kind of sense.

Hoffner had a pair of agents monitoring Hess just in case the two hockey players came back. Maybe they were something. Maybe they were nothing. In that respect investigations were very similar to advertising—90 percent of your efforts were wasted; the problem was figuring out *which* 90 percent.

He began another tour of the color-coded linoleum when Whitaker materialized at his side. She had changed. The tracksuit and Air

Force 1s had been upgraded to a business casual suit and a pair of polished black boots that were almost military. And the cane was gone. But it wasn't just her appearance that had changed, it was her body language, and Lucas could see the anger moving around beneath her skin.

"How is she?" Whitaker pushed a coffee into his hand and held up a paper bag leaching grease to convey the message that he needed fuel.

Lucas was so tired at this point that he was running on some primitive genetic response inherited from sharks—if he didn't keep swimming, he'd simply settle on the bottom of the ocean and die. He took the coffee without breaking his stride, and nodded a thank-you. "I don't know. Every update I get is the same as the last one. 'It's going well, but we don't know yet.'"

They turned a corner and Lorne Jacobi was coming through the doors at the end of the hallway, looking like someone had deoxygenated his blood. He moved with a slow, tired walk and his suit appeared too large for him.

Jacobi walked over, reached out, and once again put his hand on Lucas's shoulder. "They're done." He looked up and smiled. "She's going to be okay."

Lucas looked down at Jacobi. Then over at Whitaker. Then back at Jacobi. And began to cry.

39

Kehoe stepped into the elevator, followed by his assistant—Special Agent Carlo Dillman, a new addition to his administrative factotum class—who pressed the button for the appropriate floor. The mirrored doors slid closed, assembling him like two half molds out of Westworld, and Kehoe automatically checked his appearance in the polished panel.

He didn't watch the floor numbers cycle by, or use the time to reply to texts and email—he used it to prepare for his meeting. Because every time Page interacted with the world, catastrophe was inevitable, and something—or someone—ended up in pieces.

Not that Kehoe expected a struggle-free landscape; he understood that life delivered worst-case scenarios all the time. But that was his strength—seeing the solutions through the chaos. But with Page, his predictive powers never aligned with the real-world outcome, and the fallout was always of a completely different variety than he had planned for.

And of all the things in Page's life, nothing meant as much to him as his family. So even though Kehoe had no idea what was coming, he had to prepare. And get in front of it. Or at least shape enough of the narrative going forward so Page's ends aligned with the bureau's.

But Page wasn't a thirty-year-old field agent. He was a beat-up middle-aged man quickly approaching the point where any runway left in front of him existed in name only. It was getting to the point where they were running out of parts to replace.

A lot of it traced back to Page's childhood; when you read his file, it was impossible to miss the Shakespeare intertwined with Dickens—along with a little Groucho Marx to keep it bearable. As much of a mystery as Page was—and there was a lot about him that no one would ever figure out—he was a classic study in Freudian psychology (Kehoe strongly suspected that Freud had stolen his entire gig from Shakespeare anyway, so his theories supported each other).

Page had spent his first five years bouncing around the foster system until he had managed the miracle of being adopted by an aging socialite who saw promise in him. And it had paid off. But along with the promise came the rest of the baggage of a kid who was abandoned. When you looked at Page's life now—and the kids he was collecting—it was impossible to miss that he was trying to both pay back the kindness and faith that old Mrs. Page had put into him as well as give these kids a reason to become part of the solution instead of the usual cliché.

Kehoe felt himself lift a little as the car slowed, then dinged, and the doors opened, once again disassembling his reflection into two parts that slid sideways and disappeared.

He stepped out into the hall and was immediately hit by how quiet things were, even for a hospital.

As he and Dillman passed the desk, one of the attendants stood up and asked for ID. Dillman flashed his badge, and pointed to their agent down the hallway who had swiveled her head around to watch them—more of that field precision at work that Kehoe liked to foster in his people.

When they arrived at the room, the agent nodded a silent greeting to Kehoe, then stepped aside and opened the door for him. Kehoe walked in, leaving Dillman and the auxiliary agent out in the hallway.

Page was at the foot of the bed, his hands on the rail, watching Erin.

40

The door opened quietly and Lucas turned to see Kehoe standing half in the room, half in the hall, his body language conveying his usual indecipherable emotional liquidity. Lucas did not have one single fuck left to give toward Kehoe's motivation—this was now about Erin—and Kehoe would become part of the solution, or he could get pegged. Lucas didn't care which.

Kehoe nodded at the hallway beyond the room, signaling that they needed to talk.

As Lucas cleared the transom, he was suddenly aware that a noticeable portion of his corporeal microadjustments were not trimming correctly. Which meant that he was past tired and entering exhaustion.

They left Kehoe's assistant and the sentry by Erin's room and began a slow walk to the far end of the hall.

The floor was silent except for an undercurrent of low-frequency hum emanating from the air itself. This portion of the facility was dedicated to neurology, specifically patients who were suspended in medically induced comas while waiting for damaged tissue to regroup or jump-start, and there was no human noise. Jacobi had arranged for Erin to be moved here under the name of Jane Doe, where she would be invisible; Lucas knew that anyone hunting doctors might have access to either hospital or patient records, and Jacobi had come up with this as a solution.

"How is she?" Kehoe asked.

"Barring any other unforeseen fuckery, the surgeons are relatively optimistic. But what else can they be? It's like she was hit in the shoulder with an axe. Twice."

"Is there anything more you need from my end?"

Lucas didn't look over—he didn't want Kehoe to see the emotions surging through his circuits; the man wouldn't be able to stop himself from leveraging a weakness.

"Yes. I just don't know what. Or when."

"Whatever it is, just ask." Kehoe put his hands in his pockets. "I haven't been able to figure out exactly *why* yet, but you and I owe one another."

Lucas knew what he meant because in some awkward way, he felt it, too. But Kehoe wasn't being honest with himself if he couldn't frame the why of things because it all straight-lined back to that afternoon when the universe had momentarily slipped its moorings and altered the destinies of everyone involved. "Yeah, well." And that was that—their version of a hug.

"So what do you want to do?" Which was an unusual question coming from a man who tended to be a taker, not a giver.

"What have your people learned about the shooter?" For the past twelve hours, he had been dedicated to Erin. But now that the conversations had shifted from survival to recovery, it was time to go after answers.

Which, in this particular case, meant people.

"Your friend Russo spent the night on missing persons reports and found a man he thinks is a match. His name was Ira Alan White. Forty-eight. Residential installer for Verizon. No priors. No arrests. No known association with the wrong kinds of people. Lived in Astoria with his wife. One daughter. A mortgage and a minivan and about five thousand dollars of credit card debt. Just a regular guy with a regular job." He looked over at Lucas. "Does that fit in with your expectations?"

Lucas thought about Albert Hess, the schoolteacher, and Denise Moth, who had worked at a pigment company. Just regular people. With regular jobs. Who had killed—or tried to kill—total strangers. "My expectations have nothing to do with the way this thing operates." Between Kehoe's leather-soled shoes and Lucas's tired, off-kilter gait, they sounded like a long-nailed critter skittering down the hallway. "How long until you know if it was White?"

"Twelve, maybe fifteen, hours until the lab can give us a definitive answer—they're comparing DNA from the shooter to a toothbrush we got from his wife."

"What about the pistol the shooter used? Did it lead anywhere?"

Kehoe shook his head. "It looks like it came up the Iron Pipeline," which was an in-house term for the six states along I-95 that had lax gun laws. "It was purchased in Ohio by a Brooklyn man who used it in a murder-suicide with his wife and three young children two years back. It was impounded by the NYPD and slated for their recovery program. The paperwork is good, and it was supposed to have been melted down."

"But it wasn't."

"No," Kehoe said. "It wasn't."

"Dead end number one."

Kehoe allowed himself one of his patented cryptic smiles that meant whatever he wanted it to at any particular moment. "Your friend Russo is quite a character."

"We're not friends."

Kehoe nodded as if he had expected that response. "I looked into him. He's a good cop. Before that he was in the forces, and he had an exemplary record. Can you control him?"

Lucas didn't bother with a shrug because it required too much juice. "I'm not interested in controlling him."

"You might need to."

"No, Brett, I won't. He's either an asset or a liability, and that's as far as this goes. He doesn't work out and he's gone. I'm not doing this to make friends, I'm doing this for Dove. And Erin. That's as complicated as this gets." Which they both knew was not completely truthful.

"You can sit this one out, Luke. My people have this. Take care of Erin and the kids and go back to teaching; I've taken my pound of flesh and I don't expect any more vig."

"I need to know she's safe. And as much as I trust your people—which I don't—I need to end this."

Kehoe nodded as if he had expected that. "Okay." He reached into his inside jacket pocket and pulled out a folded piece of paper. He held it out. "Then you should see this."

Lucas stopped under one of the dimmed overheads and unfolded a handwritten letter—a single page with six lines of tight, painful scrawl in ballpoint.

Dr. Page:
I killed Arna Solomon.
The money I took from her briefcase should be all the proof you need to know that boy didn't kill her.
The motive is none of your business.
Albert Hess

After reading it through again, Lucas handed it back. "How did you get that?"

"Albert Hess died last night."

"I see."

"You must have made an impression; he left that specifically for you."

"And Solomon's bar mitzvah money?"

"Hess's brother was here, staying at his house. He was alone with Hess most of the morning. We interviewed the brother, and he told us Hess told him that he had some money stashed under the floor of his shed that needed to go to the appropriate people; his brother handed it to our people, who were watching Hess to see if the two men who visited him came back. Apparently after killing Solomon, Hess went home, stashed the cash, then took a cab straight to hospice." Kehoe stopped and looked over at Lucas. "Which took dedication and determination."

"Did your people learn anything from the note?"

"Tranter in Forensic Linguistics said that by calling it '*the* motive' instead of '*my* motive' he was trying to distance himself from *full* responsibility." Kehoe examined Lucas and he knew that meant a question was coming. "How did you know that Hess killed Arna Solomon?"

"It was obvious."

Kehoe shook his head. "Not to anyone but you."

"Whitaker and I weren't the first law-enforcement people on-site—the NYPD were. And they were convinced that the killer wasn't on surveillance footage. So I knew that whoever was responsible was invisible to law enforcement."

"How did you know to look for Hess?"

"I didn't." Lucas shrugged and realized it was like explaining how to breathe—it was an unconscious and involuntary process. "The least obvious place for the killer to go was the hospital—no one expected him to go there. So it was the perfect choice. And what's more invisible than a sick old man walking into a hospital to say good-bye to his oncologist? You'd have to be a cynic to think he had just killed a doctor and then walked straight into a camera feed. Besides, there was nothing in his history to suggest he might be responsible—he was a law-abiding civil servant his entire life. Cops can't make that kind of connection because there isn't one to make. Hess was completely invisible on all the scales. No one could have seen it."

"You did."

"I'm not no one." Lucas tried the best smile he could manage after two days on his feet, but he could feel his *check engine* light flickering. He turned back to Kehoe. To his taxidermied eyeballs. "Look, Brett, for two years these murders have been disguised as accidents or suicides. And they were spread out. Which means that the person or people who committed them didn't want credit. And generating fear in consecutive victims wasn't a component—this wasn't advertising. These people wanted the victims dead—that's as evolved as this was. They were simple executions meant to get lost in the static." He stopped and turned to Kehoe. "But that changed in the past little while. Jennifer Delmonico was murdered late Wednesday night/early Thursday morning, Dove Knox was murdered late Thursday night/early Friday morning, Arna Solomon was murdered on Friday afternoon, and then Ira Alan White tried to kill Erin on Saturday morning. Which has nothing to do with the formula I came to you with."

"Any thoughts as to what changed?"

Lucas shook his head.

"So what's next?"

"We throw the one thing at this that they didn't plan for."

"Which is?"

"Me."

41

It was a little after 6:00 A.M. when Erin's eyes slowly cracked like tiny garage doors going up. She was cross-eyed for a second. Then she blinked, and her optical mode reset.

Lucas reached out and took her hand and she saw him for the first time. She didn't move her head, but her eyes rotated up and she gave him a smile. It was weak and conveyed that she didn't feel so good.

"Hey," Lucas said, and opened one of the plastic water bottles he had brought up from the food court. He had a long career of hospital stays under his belt—sometimes he thought he held some kind of a record—and the institutional sippy cups leaked all over your chest if you drank lying down.

He held the bottle to Erin's mouth and she took a sip, licked her lips, and said, "Hey," back.

She lay there for a moment and the only expression he could read was confusion.

"You're okay," he said. "Do you remember what happened?"

And then her circuitry connected enough of the appropriate dots. "Hector and Laurie and Alisha were with me and—"

He leaned in. "They're good. Everybody is okay. They're at home with Dingo."

She sunk back into herself and went quiet as her eyes narrowed and he knew she was trying to access memories of what had happened.

He stood there, holding her hand and being both still and silent as she went through the process. After the *Event*, full petabytes of his memory were scrambled or completely scrubbed by the wallop his brain had taken. It was a creepy madness that fucked with him at the most inobvious times over the most inconsequential things. It had taken more than a year until he felt like he wasn't hobbling around with gaping holes in his overlap with consensus reality. But that had been a traumatic brain injury—a piece of metal had crushed his orbit, pulverized his eyeball, and speared his brain, somehow missing anything of true import. The doctors said that Erin hadn't suffered a concussion, which took a TBI off the table, but that did not mean that her brain wasn't pissed off over what it had endured. Or the medications that had been run through it.

She was silent for a few minutes, and Lucas just let the clock do its job without interrupting her.

She looked up at him. "Someone tried to kill us. A man. He had a gun and he shot the car. We were coming home. I remember him shooting. The car. And the windshield. And then I . . . I . . . did I hit him with the car?" She looked up and the tears blossomed.

He squeezed her hand and nodded. "Yes."

"And there was a fire. I remember the fire." She looked over and saw her arm for the first time. She tried to move it and the cast didn't budge and she winced and closed her eyes. "Ouch."

Lucas wondered if he should call a nurse to let her know that Erin was awake. He had done this enough times to understand that the heart of the business lay with the nursing staff—without them, the entire medical profession would collapse under the weight of its own hubris. They had come around several times last night to check on her, and he made it a point to thank them each visit—he was horrified when he heard stories of how they were often treated by patients. And often the doctors.

He was about to step away to summon a nurse when Erin said, "Did I kill that man?"

The way her voice trembled broke his heart and he almost lied to her. "He killed himself with his decisions."

"There was a fire. The car was on fire. How did I get out?" The way she was parsing out her words was off, and he recognized the residual confusion—of both the trauma and the anesthetic variety— poking at her brain.

"I pulled you out."

And she looked up and noticed that his hair—which had yet to recover from Maude's Halloween dye experiment, then had the added trauma of last month's car accident followed by his grand fi- nale with the Machine Bomber—had been badly sculpted by the fire. She ran her eyes down his frame, looking for more damage. "Are you okay?"

He smiled at that and held up his hand. "You should know by now that they can't kill me."

That smile came back and she looked down at her body. "What's my condition?" The doctor was now in the house and she nodded at the water in Lucas's hand.

He held it to her mouth and she took a few decent pulls without spilling any of it. "You got shot twice. You were in surgery for six hours and they installed three braces, thirteen screws, and five pins. Ellie Chance and someone named Walker worked on you."

She nodded in approval. "Naomi Walker. She's good. Not as good as *me*, but good."

He faked his impressed face. "Wow. You were worked on by *two* girl surgeons? What is the world coming to?" It still pissed him off that people couldn't believe Erin was a surgeon based simply on her sex.

Erin bit her lip—which he knew was a sign she was about to cry. But she looked down and wiggled her fingers, and that seemed to stop her fear.

"You'll be operating on patients in no time." Which was the first partial lie of the day. The doctors said that she had a lot of work ahead of her and that there were no guarantees about anything, as if that were some sort of special insight.

"Can I see my chart?"

He took it from the wall, opened it, and held it up in front of her.

"Jane Doe?" She looked up. "What the fuck's going on, Luke?"

"We didn't know why you were attacked. If it has something to do with my past, I wanted you removed from the equation. And if you were targeted by the same people who killed Dove Knox, I wanted you removed from the equation."

"But if I killed the man who was after me, I'm safe, right?"

"That's a tricky question." He closed her chart. "Do you remember the shooter?"

She nodded emphatically and Lucas could tell it made her dizzy because she closed her eyes and paused. When she opened them, she kept her head still when she said, "I can picture his face like he's right here."

"Describe him."

Her eyes went up as she retrieved the clip of mental footage. "Late forties. Medium height. A little paunchy. Dark hair. Leather jacket."

He took out his phone and showed her a photo of Ira Alan White. "This the guy?"

"Yes."

"Do you know him?"

"Nope."

"His name was Ira Alan White. We're waiting for confirmation from the lab. When we get it, the warrants open up his life." Lucas zoomed in on the photo. "Are you certain you don't know him?"

"I said no."

He could see that she was getting tired and he needed to give her some downtime.

And evidently she was reverse-engineering the problem, because she said, "You need to sleep. Go home. Be with the kids. I'll be fine. All I need is rest for a few days. Then I start physio." She looked down at her hand and wiggled her fingers. "Ouch."

How was it that she was the one in the hospital bed with two repaired holes in her corpus and she was taking care of him?

"Seriously," she said, "you look beat. Get some rest. I'm not going anywhere. The kids need you."

He leaned in and gave her a kiss. "I'm sure that Dingo's got everything under control."

"I'm sure he does; in three days our kids will be swilling beer and breaking furniture with karate chops." She gave his fingers a weak squeeze and her expression changed gears. "But you're not going to catch these people by sitting around in a hospital."

Lucas opened his mouth to disagree. But couldn't.

42

The Upper East Side

The house was dark and silent, but Lucas didn't bother with the lights. The taxi ride home from the hospital had only been a few minutes, but he had fallen asleep. If he didn't lie down, he'd start seeing swarms of bats.

There were no kids' sounds and even the dogs were staying upstairs, which made sense; it was much better to hang out with people who scratched your belly, let you sleep in the bed, and didn't call you dummy all the time.

Lucas stood in front of the coffeemaker, feeling like Oliver Twist with his *World's Greatest Dad—from world's greatest kids (and Hector)! WE LUV YOU!* mug in his hands. It was impossible to pull his attention from the substitute adrenaline dripping into the carafe while the fan blades in his head tried to keep the entire system from overheating. He needed sleep, but there were things to accomplish before the family got up.

The glass from the broken oven door had been cleaned up and Maude (judging by the handwriting) had put a piece of masking tape over the control panel with *DO NOT USE OVEN!!!* written on it.

When the machine finally crossed the horizon of converting his hope into coffee, he filled his mug and sat down at the island. The backyard swings were wet with rain and the garden was reduced to a few sticks and some dead flowers that had done their duty for the season. A piece of police tape hung on the back gate and it brought back thoughts of the man Erin had killed in the alley. A man probably named Ira Alan White who probably worked for the phone company and probably had a family of his own. A man she had never met.

Lucas was staring into his mug, trying to find the will to stand up and go to bed, when Lemmy and Bean ran into the kitchen. They danced around his legs and he sent them out back for their morning poop.

Dingo came into the kitchen, wearing a hoodie under one of Lucas's robes. His street prosthetics, which looked less mechanical than his blades, poked out the bottom. "Hey." He didn't sound like he had been asleep.

"Hey back." Lucas was watching the dogs sniff all over the tiny backyard and thinking about how Erin had screamed when he jammed his fingers into the bloody holes chopped into her shoulder and about how he was certain that she was going to die in his arms.

"Are you okay?"

"Tippy-top."

"Of course you are." Dingo eyed him for a moment in the almost dark, and it was impossible to figure out what he was thinking. "What happens if the supergenius just picks up his toys and goes home?"

Lucas shrugged as Lemmy squatted outside, killing what was left of the garden. "More people die."

Dingo poured himself a coffee and sat down at the island. "The FBI has their own folks, Luke. You could—and I know this is just crazy talk on my part—but you really could let *them* take care of this. It is what they do, after all."

"This job isn't like that. There's something about finding the right combination of people to do this that can't be replicated by forcing square pegs into round holes."

"So let them find new round pegs. Apple continued without Steve Jobs; James Bond went on without Sean Connery; hell, even Dave Grohl went on without Kurt Cobain."

And once again, Lucas wondered how everyone in his life thought the same way. Well, everyone but *him*. "I need to know that these people won't come back after Erin."

"You think they might?"

"I don't know who they are or why they're doing this, so I can't even factor in probability. All I know is if they're not stopped, I am going to worry every time Erin leaves the house or is late coming home or doesn't answer her phone. And so will the kids. I need this put to bed and the only person I trust with her life is me."

Lemmy and Bean came up the back steps and Lucas waved them through the door.

"Do you realize how that sounds? I mean, I heard the same thing not too long ago when you came out to my place and told me you were working on the Machine Bomber."

It was too early, but Lucas was running on autopilot and he pulled out the dog bowls. He doled out their portions—Bean's puppy kibble a fraction of the health pellets that Lemmy the mastodon needed to keep his ass in gear—and realized that if something happened to Erin he wouldn't even know where to buy dog food. And that drove home the uncomfortable realization that Dingo was, in no small part, right.

Dingo wasn't finished. "Yet here we are, a month later, with your boo-boos barely beginning to heal, and you're already downloading new ones. It's like you have one of those strings on your chest with the little plastic loop on the end and you just keep pulling it and pulling it and spewing prerecorded horseshit."

"You're dating yourself with your analogies."

Dingo shook his head. "Look, man, I'm your fucking friend and I sat up half the night with your kids talking to them about why a man shot their mother and why their father was out there looking for the people responsible and you should have seen them. They're terrified. And they deserve better."

That got to Lucas and he took a step toward Dingo. "You see this?" He held up his duralumin and titanium hand. "You think *I* think this was worth it? You think *I* think this was a fair trade for not disintegrating with five of my friends?" He tightened his mental grip on the anger, and squeezed. "I want a boring life, Dingo. I want to teach and spend Saturdays with my kids and grow old with Erin with all my parts and walk the dogs and have a beer with you out back every now and then. But it doesn't feel like I'm allowed to have that. It's like I'm some tiny Lucas Page living in a snow globe on a shelf and every now and then someone walks by, picks it up, and shakes the shit out of it just to see if I can hold on. I feel like I only exist for some angry god's entertainment. It's fucking exhausting.

"After that thing last month, *I was quit*. And then someone— maybe a man named Albert Hess, maybe a man named Ira Alan White—killed Dove Knox and Erin asked me to look into it and that's when the invisible hand picked up the little glass ball and here we fucking are. So it doesn't seem to matter one tiny bit what I want because—"

He stopped. Maude was standing in the doorway, looking eerily like Erin, her gaze penetrating skin and bone and metal to get to the truth underneath.

Their eyes met and Lucas said, "I'm sorry. You weren't supposed to hear that."

She shrugged. "At least now I know all of this is out of my hands."

She came over, and gave him a hug, and he stopped the anger and fear in his chest and put his metal hand on her back.

"You can't stop," she said. "If you do, CPS will come and take us all away." There was an attempt at humor in her voice, but she was not completely wrong.

She pushed off him and pointed at the ceiling. "Come on," she said, grabbing his hand—the real one.

"Where?"

"You can't walk around looking like that," she said, once again sounding an awful lot like Erin. "Someone needs to cut your hair." She let out a sigh that had the weight of a fifteen-year-old's universe in it—which is the densest kind according to astrophysics. "And then you are going to get some sleep."

43

He was aware of two things, and the twin sensations happened so close to each other that he assumed they were part of the same event—there was chirping, and he could not move.

Chirping.

Paralysis.

Chirping.

Paralysis.

And then he was awake. And aware that his cell phone was bleating nearby. And when he opened his eyes he understood why he could not move—the kids had piled on after he got home and the bed was packed with little bodies strewn about like a clan of cave people in footsie pajamas. Lemmy was there, the spirit animal of the clan, snoring like a bear with lung cancer. Even Bean had made the cut, and was curled up like a warm furry water bottle between Lucas and Damien.

Lucas's cell phone continued dancing around on the nightstand.

Lucas took a breath, then tried to jimmy out from under the covers. But the movement pulled the covers tight over his ribs and it took him a few jabs before he could get his arm out from under the pile of kids that were starting to respond to the noise and movement.

It was Russo's number.

"Yeah?" he said, foregoing formalities.

"Is it Mom?" Laurie asked through a big yawn.

Lucas cupped his hand over the phone. "It's a friend of mine."

With his eyes still closed, Hector mumbled, "You don't *have* any friends."

Lucas refocused on Russo. "Yeah?"

"How's your wife?"

The question killed Lucas's natural grumpy response mechanism. "She's going to be okay."

"And the kids?" Which earned him another point.

"We're all okay. Thanks."

"Anything I can do?"

"You could get to the point."

"Jeez. Sorry. Yeah, so I wanted you to know that I asked around at Delmonico's hospital, and doctors like talking to cops less than gangbangers do. I spoke to everyone she worked with and I got nowhere with nobody."

Lucas didn't feel like giving him grammar pointers, so he said, "There's someone I can ask." Lorne Jacobi was now firmly involved in this thing, and Lucas knew he could be useful. Which brought about the second—and very uncomfortable—realization that he was starting to think like Kehoe.

Last night, after Maude cut his hair, he took a shower and crawled into bed with both his prosthetic limbs on, just in case there was a middle-of-naptime emergency and one of the kids came ripping in. Which meant that this morning, after pushing three small legs, one small arm, and a dog off him, he was able to sit up without listing to port, starboard, headboard, or footboard.

When he was sitting solidly on the edge of the mattress, he said, "Have you pulled her cell phone records?" He would have brought up credit cards, but married people tended to not put afternoon hotel stays on the Amex.

"Got 'em and ran 'em. The only people she seems to talk to are other doctors. Nothing sticks out. Nothing looks odd."

Lucas knew that most doctors worked ridiculously long hours and they tended to gravitate toward one another—it was one of those captive audience situations. "I'll take a look at them; maybe there's a pattern there."

Russo, either unaware or intentionally obtuse, said, "I'm pretty good with numbers and shit. Besides, we ran them through a computer."

"I want to look at them anyway. Did you get text transcripts?"

"Yep. And they gave us a big fat nothing."

Which meant that Delmonico had been very careful with whatever she had been doing, with whomever she had been doing it, wherever they had been doing it, for however long they had been doing it.

Or that Russo had missed something.

Lucas was fully awake now, and aware that the cave clan behind him were stretching and yawning and starting to babble in hushed tones, which translated to questions. But his phone buzzed with another call. "I have another call. I'll hunt you down later."

Russo started to say something, but Lucas disconnected, saw that the new call was from Whitaker, and answered. "Good morning."

"How was your night?"

Lucas hated it when people asked how he was, no doubt a vestigial response from waking up in the hospital after the *Event*, missing a lot of his factory-installed components. Back then, all everyone had wanted to know was how he was doing. Everyone. All the fucking time. "I'm fine. What's up?"

"We found some security footage from a building on your friend Knox's block that might be something. Hoffner wanted to know if you were interested in checking it out, or if he should just send a pair of agents down?"

"Pick me up in an hour." He once again hung up without saying good-bye and the kids swirled around him like australopithecines approaching the monolith in *2001*, yammering a million machine-gun questions that could all be reduced to "When is Mom coming home?"

He held up his phone, found the thirty-second video that Erin had recorded in the hospital where she was smiling and blowing kisses and making mom faces, and pressed *play*.

44

After doing his best to make breakfast for the kids—microwaved pizza bagels and milk—Lucas spent fifteen minutes at the table with the children, hoping they didn't notice that he was watching the clock.

He told them wonderful stories about how great the hospital was—Mom got to eat all the ice cream and Jell-O that she wanted! Laurie shook her head and said too bad she couldn't get all the wine she wanted and Lucas had laughed a little too hard. Dingo then took over, so Lucas went upstairs, showered, and tried to talk himself into facing a new day.

After getting into a new suit, he put in a call to Lorne Jacobi. Lucas felt a little guilty calling him on a Sunday morning after the man had sacrificed yesterday and most of last night to keep him company at the hospital. But that was all he allowed himself—a *little* guilt—as he dialed the number.

Lorne answered in two rings, and didn't bother trying to hide that he had been sleeping—he answered in the midst of knocking things over (it sounded like a collection of bottles). "Lucas? Is everything okay? The hospital hasn't called me about anythi—"

"Everything's fine, Lorne. But I need another favor."

Lorne yawned. "Sure. Of course."

Somewhere in the background Neville said, "Tell Luke I can help out with the kids if he needs," and Lucas smiled and promised himself to be nicer to the guy from now on.

"Lorne . . ." Lucas hesitated because there was no polite way to do this. Or at least no gentle way. "I'm sorry for asking you, but the police have hit a wall with your staff and I said I'd try."

Lorne let out a laugh at the other end of the line. "I can't believe that Lucas Page is trying to be delicate. Jesus, Luke, just ask."

"The lead detective who's looking into Jennifer Delmonico's death said he asked around at the hospital, but no one would talk to him. I can't give you all the details, but I need to know if she was seeing somebody."

Lorne was silent for a moment. "I see." But it was clear from his tone that he didn't. "I mean, I knew Jennifer pretty well. Maybe as well as anyone at work. And she never said anything to *me*. Are you certain?"

"Lorne, I need you to be discreet with this information—we haven't released it to the public. She was murdered."

"Does this have to do with the man who shot Erin?" He sucked in a deep breath. "Or Arna Solomon? Jesus. What's going on, Luke?"

"I can't tell you anything because I don't know. But I need you to find out if Delmonico was seeing anyone. Like I said, the detective said he couldn't get anyone at the hospital to speak to him."

"I'll talk to her mother. Dee Dee and I have been friends forever and she and Jenny were close."

"Close enough that she'd tell her that she was having an affair?"

"I guess we'll find out."

"Thank you, Lorne, I appreciate this. And please, like I said—discreet."

"Of course."

"Thank you. Again. Call me as soon as you know anything."

45

The Meatpacking District

When Lucas got out of the cab, Whitaker's face scrunched into a knot and she ticktocked her head from side to side to take in his new haircut. "Where did you find a barber between this morning and this morning?"

"Maude did it."

She nodded, but the action conveyed neither approval nor disapproval—it was simply an acknowledgment that yes, indeed, that was most certainly a haircut.

Which Lucas understood. Because even if he examined his reflection with subjective optimism, the best he could come up with was a mix of Julius Caesar imagined by Rob Bottin. But in a better suit.

She smiled, said, "I think it's time you considered getting into hats," and pointed at the door to the building.

• • •

Aida Gourmanderie was situated in a corner unit diagonally across the intersection from Dove Knox's loft, on the same floor. The establishment had five-star Yelp reviews across the board, which was quite the achievement in the age of you-can't-please-any-of-the-people-most-of-the-time. The space was redbrick with high ceilings and a dozen stainless-steel worktables where they hosted weeknight cooking classes and a monthly wine tasting. The general impression was not dissimilar to a coroner's workroom but smelled of duck fat and sautéed garlic.

The owner, Ms. Nita Vanier, was a small, thin woman of Vietnamese and French ancestry who still had a strong Parisian accent after twenty years stateside and seemed like she would be no fun to work for. She wore the standard outfit of her trade—checkered pants, a white smock, a brimless cap, and once-pink Crocs that could have belonged to a painter or welder. The one feature that Lucas kept gravitating toward was the burn marks on her hands and forearms, earned over a lifetime in front of a hot pan. While they spoke, she kept glancing at the kitchen as if she were afraid the employees might light the place on fire—or steal recipes—in her absence.

Whitaker showed Vanier a photograph that had been recorded on the night Knox died, eighteen minutes after he was dropped off by the car service. It had been captured by a security camera in the lobby of a building across the street—it had a long focal point, and faced the garage and service entrance to Knox's building.

The image was grainy in the way that they almost always are, and showed a black woman who was anywhere between twenty and forty years of age. She was thin and stood approximately five-foot-four to five-foot-six and had her hair pulled back into a bun. The giveaway had been the black pants, white shirt, and black bow tie that denoted her as help from the Norwoods' party.

Vanier glanced at the photograph and said matter-of-factly, "That's Trina Moncrieff." Curiosity started to massage her features. "Is Trina in trouble?"

Whitaker didn't want to give anything away, so she said, "We need her help with something."

Vanier's eyes narrowed as if she didn't quite believe that.

"How long has she worked for you?"

Vanier shrugged in the way the French have mastered to mean whatever it is supposed to at the time. "Seven months."

"And she worked the Norwoods' party across the street two nights ago?"

"Yes."

"What can you tell us about the party?"

She gave that French shrug again. "It was a small to medium event for us—they were supposed to have sixty guests, but I counted about eighty. Mrs. Norwood planned it back in June. A decent menu—eight types of canapés followed by a buffet: lobster ravioli in vodka sauce; shaved beef; duck confit—"

Lucas wasn't interested in the menu, but he had done this enough times to know that it was impossible to gauge where the important details would come from—he never forgot that David Berkowitz had been caught because of a parking ticket that was almost overlooked.

"—white wine; and our ratatouille, which Mrs. Norwood ordered for her vegan friends. I had eight servers and four kitchen staff there to handle the cocktails and appetizers, another four kitchen staff for the main; then we went down to eight people for the remainder of the night—to take care of the bar and cleanup. By eleven we were down to four people, mostly serving drinks and cigars."

"Cigars?"

"Cigars and scotch are experiencing *another* revival," she said, rolling her eyes. "I prefer a cheese plate and a good sauterne, but I'm not American."

"And Trina was there the whole night?"

She gave another shrug, this one meaning *of course*. "She's very conscientious—she understands presentation, which a lot of people don't."

"Do you cater a lot of events in that building?"

"I tend to be the go-to; I'm close and this company has a reputation that goes back to 1953. They're mostly new-money people in that building, and they don't really understand food." Her eyes narrowed. "Of course many of them read Chowhound and *consider* themselves to be foodies—whatever *that* means—but anyone who takes pictures of their food and posts it to social media doesn't understand the true nature of food."

Lucas thought that statement was pretty rich coming from a woman who had a Facebook page, TikTok, and both a Snapchat and Instagram account—loaded with nothing *but* photographs of food.

"Anything unusual about that night? Either with Trina or the party?"

Another shrug, this one with no discernible meaning. "No."

"What time did you clear out?"

"I left at ten, but the party was over by eleven, which is early, even for a weeknight. Cigars and scotch stopped by midnight. The staff stayed behind to clean up. They brought our things back here and locked up. Next morning I came to work and Trina was already here and everything was cleaned and put away, from the stemware to the chafing dishes. Mrs. Norwood came by with a two-thousand-dollar tip, and I split it among the staff, with a little extra for Trina."

"So Trina came back with the rest of the staff?"

This time she shook her head. "She stayed behind to clean up the Norwoods' kitchen and ended up leaving later than the others. She's good that way—I can trust her with clients and I can trust her with the business."

"Do your staff have their phones on at work?"

"I don't allow it."

"Does Trina always work late?"

An emphatic nod this time. "She's a very hard worker. I think she picked it up in school."

"Which culinary school did she attend?"

Nita shook her head. "She didn't go to culinary school; she went to medical school."

46

Washington Heights

The elevator was not the kind of place a claustrophobe would enter by choice. It had no ventilation and was lit by a single low-watt bulb that cut the space into shadows reminiscent of H. R. Giger. As the tiny cell was pulled up through the core of the building, it vibrated with a mechanical clatter that suggested the stairs might have been a smarter choice.

Half of the red LEDs on the control panel were burned out, adding to the science fiction vibe, and when they passed what was either the sixth or the eighth floor, Whitaker took out her side arm, checked the chamber, and returned it to the pressure holster on her belt.

"What's that for?" Lucas was still surprised that guns had not yet been relegated to the same technological dustbin as sticks and stones. It was only a matter of time before they gave way to robotic solutions that a man with a gun would be completely defenseless against.

"I have come to learn that if I hang out with you, I need to adopt a shoot-first-ask-questions-later approach." Now that her hands were free, she pointed at the ceiling, indicating their destination somewhere up in the building. "You think this Trina Moncrieff woman killed your friend Dove?"

"She was caught on camera leaving the building an hour after the

Norwoods' party. Which coincides with Dove's TOD. So she had opportunity. I don't see motive, but that fits in with the rest of the killings; I still can't figure out why Hess killed Arna Solomon."

Whitaker looked at the console, looked away, then did a second take and shook her head—evidently her Klingon was rusty as well. "You think that she and an accomplice killed your friend Dove with cell phones?" She didn't look skeptical, but she didn't look convinced.

"Why not? It's the most logical answer to the two cell phone signals Hoffner found." But Lucas had slightly more insight into the situation than the average observer—he had been friends with Knox, and knew how he thought. And Lucas most certainly knew how much Dove and Carla were in love—the one argument that kept her at the beach house that lousy night notwithstanding. And Erin had dated him. So Lucas had a few fingers inside of the dead man's head, a perspective that wasn't afforded to many others.

She pointed at the floor. "And you really think we need those two policemen downstairs?"

"I don't know what we need. But I'm never walking into a problem again without some sort of backup, even if it's just an emotional security blanket like two guys with clubs."

"See? Look at that—we've both learned something." She smiled at him. "But only because you, my friend, are a jinx."

The red display came up on what looked to be the seventy-fifth floor in alien code but was in reality the twenty-eighth in Arabic, and the car slammed to a stop with a noise that could loosely be described as dinosaur-ish.

The hallway was filled with a broad palette of cooking smells—none of them isolatable.

They found the unit and Whitaker knocked and stepped back and to the side.

The peephole went dark before the locks did their thing and the woman from the surveillance video pulled the door open by six inches. Trina Moncrieff looked up at Lucas, then over to Whitaker. "Yes?"

Whitaker held up her FBI identification. "Mrs. Moncrieff, I am Special Agent Whitaker, FBI. This is Dr. Page. May we speak with you?"

Moncrieff's face registered neither surprise nor concern. "What is this about?"

Whitaker backed up by a footstep. "We would like to talk to you about the night you worked the Norwoods' party."

Moncrieff examined them for a moment, and her eyes went to Lucas's aluminum hand, then up to the scar tissue surrounding his sunglasses, and she tilted her head to look at the side of his head where his ear had been sewn back on. Then she looked back at Whitaker. "Did something go missing?"

"No, not at all."

"Do I need a lawyer?"

Lucas said, "Why would you need a lawyer?"

"Being black?"

Which caused Whitaker to side-eye Lucas with her *I understand* face.

But Trina Moncrieff pulled the door open and stepped aside. "You might as well come in."

The one-bedroom apartment was small, tidy, clean, and sad. A line of sagging bookcases that Lucas recognized as Ikea from his college days took up an entire wall in the small living room. They were filled with medical textbooks, cookbooks, and repair manuals for every year and model of Toyota that Lucas had ever heard of. He did that thing he did with instantaneous counting and came up with 107 textbooks, 141 cookbooks, and 151 automotive repair manuals. The two bottom shelves on the first bookcase contained 41 children's books, most of which Lucas's kids could recite from memory.

The rest of the furniture in the room fell in with the overall gestalt, but the view from up here was spectacular. The tiny balcony contained a child's bicycle, a plant that was either dead or hibernating, and a small laundry rack that took up most of the space. There was no television and the only personal touches other than the books were the photographs covering the end tables—images of Moncrieff and her husband and their son.

Moncrieff gestured to the sofa with the phone in her hand. "Please," she said.

Lucas and Whitaker took up position at either end and Moncrieff flexed her catering muscles with, "Would you like a . . . water? It's all I have."

"I'm fine. Special Agent Whitaker?"

Whitaker shook her head.

With no other seating options, Moncrieff dropped into the chair facing them. But she didn't say anything—she just stared and waited and Lucas could tell that all kinds of things were going on in her head. She looked down at her phone, shook her head like now was not the time to answer a text. She said, "Excuse me," then plunked out something with her thumbs before tucking the phone into her back pocket.

Lucas decided to start with the easily deniable. "Did you know a Dr. Arna Solomon?"

Moncrieff stared Lucas in the eyes, doing that thing where she couldn't decide which was the one to focus on. "I heard about that one on Channel Seven. She was killed Friday, I think. Mugged."

Lucas nodded with the same expression he used on the rare occasion one of his students impressed him. "What about a Mr. Hess?"

Moncrieff looked like she thought about the name for a moment. "No. I don't think so."

"Dr. Jennifer Delmonico?"

That one seemed to stop her, but only for a second, because she slowly shook her head again. "Were they guests at the Norwoods'?"

"Why would you think that?"

"My boss texted that you visited. I assume something went missing from the Norwoods'.″ She held up her hands. "I've worked for Nita for seven months." She eyed them both sternly. "I'm not a thief."

Whitaker leaned forward, putting her forearms on her knees. "No one is accusing you of theft, Mrs. Moncrieff. We just have some questions that we need answered. They might have nothing to do with you." She smiled. "Or they might."

Lucas's patience was already worn down from three days of running around, chasing motiveless crimes, and plugging his wife's gunshot wounds with his fingers. He was in no mood for niceties or slow dancing. "What about a Dr. Dove Knox?"

"Dr. Dove Knox?" she repeated. "I don't think so, no."

"What kind of a phone do you have, Mrs. Moncrieff?" He already knew the answer—Whitaker had given him a report from Hoffner's people; when it came to digital bread crumbs, the bureau was an apex bloodhound in sniffing out misdirection and plain old horseshit. As he always said to his students—data didn't lie.

She took out her phone and shook it at Lucas. Her wallpaper was an image of the boy whose photographs filled the side tables. "Old iPhone."

"And you had it with you the night of the Norwood party?"

She shook her head. "No. It was back in the kitchen. In my locker. Nita doesn't like us having phones at work."

Both of which were true. The bureau had geolocated her phone on the night that Knox had been killed and it had indeed been in her locker—or at least within a few feet of it—all night.

But that presented Trina Moncrieff with a new problem.

Lucas leaned forward and took off his glasses for impact and the move had the desired effect; Moncrieff shifted uncomfortably in her chair. "Do you own another phone?" he asked.

She locked focus on Lucas's bad eye and shook her phone. "I can barely afford this one." She shifted back to his good eye. "Why?"

"What about your husband? What kind of phone does he have?"

Now the circuits behind her face were doing their thing and Lucas could see her thinking. "Same thing—an iPhone. His is even older."

"Mrs. Moncrieff," Lucas said, and pulled out his own cell. He cycled through a film roll and brought up a photograph from the Norwoods' party. It was one of three that had been gleaned from social media profiles that belonged to guests. "Can you please take a look at this?" He held the phone out so she could see the first image.

It was a photo of her at the Norwoods' party. She was carrying a tray through the room, but she was a background element, not the focal point. Her hips were twisted as she negotiated her way between two groups of people who had their backs to her.

Lucas had zoomed in, and there was no missing the telltale shape of a phone in her back pocket.

Moncrieff leaned forward, took his cell, and looked at the image. Her eyes locked on it, and she stared blankly for a few moments.

"Now are you certain you don't know any of the people I mentioned? Lying to a federal agent is in itself a felony with a mandatory two-year conviction." He stared her down. "Take a moment to think about that."

"I told you. I never heard of them." She looked up, and there were all kinds of little fireworks going on under her skin. "Not Arna Solomon or Albert Hess or Dove Knox."

Lucas stared intently at her, which he knew could be unnerving. "I never said Albert Hess—I only said *Mr.* Hess."

The pyrotechnics going on beneath her skin migrated to the surface, and her face played around with myriad microexpressions for a few seconds.

And then, as if someone snapped their fingers, her features reset and she looked out the big balcony window, to the world beyond, where it had started to rain. "It's raining. I have to bring my laundry in. I have a shift tonight."

Moncrieff got up from her chair and handed Lucas's phone back.

She opened the sliding door and stepped out, turned to Lucas and Whitaker. Smiled.

There was an instant when everything was okay. She looked at her cell phone—at the photo of her little boy—and kissed it.

She looked at them again and gave Lucas a smile he would remember forever because it looked defeated.

And then she jumped off the balcony.

47

The world outside the police tape was chaos come to life. People played music and took selfies and dictated Instagram and TikTok posts at warp speed. The crowd screamed insults at the first responders. A hundred phones were held above the fray, lenses turned toward the action in an attempt to record Trina Moncrieff's body.

Moncrieff had plummeted twenty-eight stories, which would have given her a final speed of somewhere around eighty miles per hour, depending on the precise amount of resistance she had generated. In practical terms, she had impacted with the full force available to her by the laws of gravity. But her trajectory hadn't been without its imperfections, and she had clipped a lamppost just before reaching the pavement. At the speed she was traveling, that little pre-impact generated a significant amount of centrifugal force, which spun her around with enough pull to fling off both her shoes. But the most meaningful effect the lamppost had had on the equation governing her trajectory was that it slowed her just enough so that she hadn't gone completely through the roof of Whitaker's SUV, which had been parked up on the sidewalk. But that did not mean that she—or the Lincoln—was not mangled beyond any reasonable sense of recognition.

Lucas watched the first responders as they tried to disentangle Trina Moncrieff's parts from the vehicle. When one of her legs peeled away and flopped onto the ground, the crowd cheered, causing Lucas to turn away and head outside the wire, where the howling of the ghouls would be a little less grotesque.

He headed to the corner of 178th Street, where he could watch traffic, try to clear his head, and resist the urge to move to the North Pole.

Lucas's irritation at the pandemonium back at the tape was exacerbated by the half-hour grilling he and Whitaker had endured by the two detectives from the local precinct—the 33rd. It had been a slow, surreal, time-wasting process of convincing the police that they hadn't, in fact, thrown Trina Moncrieff off her balcony. But when enough question marks had been expended, the process morphed into promises to call if there were any developments. When the bureau personnel finally arrived, the cops had simply faded away.

Whitaker came up on his flank, still in shock over Moncrieff's jump into the Great Wide Open, as Tom Petty had so poetically called it. "That escalated real fast."

"Yeah. Well." And that was all he had to offer.

"So she killed Knox?"

Lucas nodded. "I think that's a fair assumption."

"So why are you the only one seeing this for what it is?"

"I'm not seeing it for what it is—I'm seeing individual events within the larger narrative for what they are. When Hoffner told me about the dual cell phone signals—one from Knox's and one at his beach house—there was only one reasonable answer. And it wasn't that Carla had Dove killed, regardless of statistical likelihood.

"Trina Moncrieff and someone—most likely her husband—were on those phones. And they used Carla as a hostage to get Knox to do what they wanted, which was hang himself. She made him take off his clothes, get up on a stool, tie his own noose, and hang himself. And when he was swinging, Trina Moncrieff pushed back a chair, sat down, and watched him slowly asphyxiate." He stopped and turned to Whitaker, making a conscious effort not to look back at the partying crowd. "Is anyone on the way to pick up her husband?"

"Hoffner has two men headed there now. You and I can interview him at the office."

"He won't be able to tell us anything."

"You can be pretty persuasive."

No shit, he thought. *I just persuaded a woman to jump to her death.* He started for the corner, which he hoped was far enough to lose the noise of the crowd.

Whitaker put a hand on his mechanical elbow and pulled him to a stop. "She jumped off the fucking balcony."

"Yes. I know. I was there."

"Why would she do that?"

"It was planned."

"What do you mean, *planned*?"

"A contingency plan—in case someone came around asking. She had to know it was a possibility." Lucas thought of that last moment when she kissed the picture of her son before diving off into the sky. He looked back, up at the building, and zeroed in on the balcony.

"But you hadn't even got into the heavy-lifting part of the interview yet. It could have gone in a million directions."

"I shouldn't have tipped her off about Hess. I shouldn't have shown her the pictures of her with the phone at the Norwoods' party. I should have walked her into a corner and we'd know more than we do. She wasn't a hardened criminal. She wasn't a psychopath. She wasn't a contract killer. She was just a person who took on more than she knew she could handle if things went south. Which means that her motivation for killing Knox was strong—because no one kills another human being and *plans* on getting caught. But she knew it was a possibility, mathed out the consequences, and did it anyway." Lucas put his hands into his pockets and picked up his direction. "This entire case lies in the motivation. So far, no one is connected to anyone else, which makes no kind of practical sense. The forced randomness that tipped me off to these murders is also somehow applied to the relationships between the victims and their killers, only I haven't figured out what it is. When I do, this entire thing comes apart at the seams and I go back to being a grumpy professor with five kids and too many dogs."

"You don't think her husband is going to help us? He has a kid to think of."

"Does he?"

"What's with all these riddles?"

Lucas glanced back at the EMT crew extricating the body from Whitaker's Lincoln, which would be out of commission until it got a new windshield, bodywork, interior, paint, and an exorcism. "Have the analysts dig up everything they can on Trina Moncrieff. On her. Her kid. The husband. Their medical history. Everything from high school, college, and medical school transcripts to the reason she didn't finish. Any papers she wrote. Anything her professors can remember. Internet history. Phone records. Credit card and bank statements. But most important, find out what happened to her son."

"I'm sure he'll turn up."

"Just find out where the fucking kid is."

"Don't get pissy; I didn't enjoy watching that any more than you did."

Lucas worked things over in his head. "It's not just that—it's that I missed this. I should have known."

"Do you feel like sharing what's going on in that melon of yours?"

"Do you remember what Denise Moth said to us in the interview room at Metro DC?"

"She said that we couldn't figure out something that isn't there. And if no one talked to us about it, that's all we had."

Lucas lifted his metal arm and pointed at the crowd who were cheering as parts of Trina Moncrieff were being loaded into a bag. "And Trina Moncrieff can't tell us anything."

Whitaker's phone buzzed and she checked the screen, then said, "It's the office," before answering with, "Whitaker."

She said, "Yes."

Pause.

"Really?"

Pause.

"No."

Pause.

"How?"

Pause.

"Before they got there?"

Long pause.

"Page said that would happen."

Pause.

"Yeah. Always. He can't help it."

Pause.

"Really."

Pause.

"Oh fuck."

Pause.

"When was this?"

Pause.

"Okay."

Pause.

"What kind of footage?"

Pause.

"Excellent. Okay."

Pause.

"Yeah. Of course." She cupped a hand over her other ear to block out the shrieks of the crowd behind them. "We're waiting for the forensics team to finish going through the Delmonico residence, and then we're doing a walk-through." She checked her watch. "If my new ride shows up, I'd say an hour."

Pause.

"And what did Russo have to say?"

Pause.

"Sure. I'll tell him." And she hung up.

Whitaker stared blankly at her phone for a few moments, then dropped it into her pocket. "That was Hoffner. When our people showed up at Trina Moncrieff's husband's place of employment—"

"He was dead."

She looked skeptical. "How did you know *that* was coming?"

"What's a common trope in espionage movies or novels when a spy is about to be interrogated? What do they do?"

"Swallow cyanide." There were all kinds of uncomfortable things going on in her eyes. "But he wasn't a spy. And this isn't an espionage novel."

He shrugged. "Okay."

"You knew this was going to happen?"

"I suspected."

"How?"

There were a million little things that had made no sense before Trina Moncrieff jumped off the balcony. But now, with clear footage of the rearview mirror, those small particles were coalescing into a cogent line of code. "That text she sent when we showed up—I figured she reached out to her partner in the Knox killing—which, I think I correctly predicted, is her husband. When the phone records come through you'll see I'm right. Also, their child is dead—has Hoffner found that out yet?"

"You got a crystal ball in your head?"

"I'm just starting to see the effects of whatever is driving this thing. There's an order, a rhythm, to the entropy. Which is not the way the universe is supposed to work."

48

178th Street and St. Nicholas Avenue

Lucas sat in the booth, staring into his fifth coffee and ignoring the corned-beef sandwich he had ordered but wasn't even mildly interested in eating; he hated being the guy using up valuable square footage for very little return—and places like this were being slowly euthanized by focus-group corporations like Starbucks and Pret. He had ordered a tuna melt for Whitaker, who was outside speaking with the next person on her list to boss around. Or ask something of.

Then again, maybe she was just picking out the options on her next SUV.

Lucas stared at the coffee, watching the cream swirl in a diaphanous weather system that was quickly coming together. When it had achieved the perfect color he took a sip. It tasted exactly like the previous four, which was a testament to both the waitress and his mixology skills.

He was still staring into the tiny caffeine vortex when Whitaker slid onto the bench across from him. "Our people are done tossing the Moncrieff apartment."

He looked up. "And?"

Whitaker cleaned her hands with a disposable alcohol wipe—one of those residual COVID habits that many people had permanently added to their routines—then pushed her tuna melt aside and pulled his sandwich over. "They didn't find Knox's clothes."

"What *did* they find?"

"A box of latex gloves—the old kind with the cornstarch on them." She picked up one of the wedges of rye and corned cow, shot a load of mustard on it from the packet, and took a big unhealthy bite.

"Maybe I was going to eat that."

She nodded and chewed and after swallowing said, "Sure you were. Us humans need food; you just need your batteries topped off every couple of hours." Whitaker held up the sandwich, and a glop of mustard plopped out, onto the plate. "This is great."

"I'm so pleased."

She took another big bite. When she finished washing it down with her coffee, she pointed the half-gone sandwich at him. "We'll take a run-through; then we'll head back to the office."

Lucas's phone rang and this time he recognized the number. He held it up and said, "It's our gimp-eyed detective."

"You're not allowed to say shit like that."

Lucas tapped his ceramic eye with a metal fingertip, and it clinked three distinct times. "Try to stop me," he said before answering the call with, "Dr. Page here."

"Page—Russo. I heard you and your partner threw a suspect off of a balcony."

"That's not funny."

"I didn't say it was, only that it happened."

"Well, it didn't."

"So what *did* happen?"

"She jumped."

"You really have an impact on people." Even in chuckle mode, Russo's laugh had a cackle quality to it. "And then those people have an impact with the sidewalk."

"Can you get to the point, or are you too drunk to talk?"

"I bet you were a sunny child, amIright or *amIright*?"

"*What do you want?*"

"Sheesh. Okay. Fuck. I went back and spoke to Delmonico's husband—he didn't know she was pregnant."

Which presented all kinds of new questions. But no answers. "Anything else?"

"Yeah, I just saw the rec your people put in for the surveillance footage from the Brooklyn Bridge on the night that Jennifer Delmonico was killed and there's some sister footage that I got from a dash cam that you'll want to see as well."

"I wasn't aware of any security from the bridge."

"Well, there was and the bureau asked for it. But I just got my hands on some corroborating footage and you'll want to see it as well."

"Can you send it over?"

"It's not entered into evidence yet—I wanted you to see it first. Can you swing by? Or should I meet you somewhere?"

Lucas looked over at Whitaker, who was chewing her way through the second half of the sandwich. "We're finishing up lunch and then we're going to do a walk-through of the Moncrieffs' apartment." He checked his Rolex. "Give us an hour. We'll meet you at the precinct." And he once again hung up without saying good-bye.

49

The bureau people had been through the Moncrieffs' apartment and come up with very little. They were still there, but in the process of packing up.

They had gone through every book in the bookcase—people often hid things in books—but found nothing at all. The office drawer in the little desk in the bedroom had yielded nothing of value, not even an address book. No diaries or journals. There were a few albums of family photos in the bedroom, which seemed anachronistic for people in their thirties, and Lucas had them shipped back to the office.

The only two items of note were a semi-automatic pistol and a box of latex gloves, both under the sink in the kitchen. The latex gloves were the now-discontinued kind that were dusted with cornstarch, and the lab would see if they could match the powder to the compound found on the extension cord that Dove Knox had hanged himself with. The gun, a Polish P64 in a Makarov 9mm, only had three rounds in the magazine. The pistol was one of those invasive species from the former Eastern Bloc that had been showing up in the US for the past thirty years, and topped out at about a hundred and fifty dollars retail, seventy-five on the street. The weapon was not registered to either Trina Moncrieff or her husband, and once again, they would ship it off to the ballistics lab to see if the gun had a history that might broaden the parameters of the case.

The apartment could have belonged to anyone, and other than those two items, there was nothing at all to suggest that these people had anything to hide.

Which was jarring for its disassociation from reality.

Lucas was leaning against the little counter that separated the tiny galley kitchen from the living room/dining room and staring at a photograph that was up on the fridge. It had been taken in a bar or a pub with a bunch of friends—one of those ubiquitous strip-mall sports bars that purchased their décor from eBay and garage sales. Trina Moncrieff held up a glass of wine, and her husband had his arm around her, a beer in his hand. They were smiling, but it wasn't making it to Trina's eyes. Or her husband's. There were three other people in the frame, all hoisting glasses and doing a better job of looking like they wanted to be there. A television was on in the background and a soccer game was going on—a World Cup game, judging by the graphics.

Whitaker came over and held up a new key fob. "Hoffner had our new ride delivered."

Lucas handed the photograph to one of the evidence people, who labeled it and put it into a plastic evidence sleeve. "Then let's go visit the inimitable Detective Johnny Russo."

50

The 19th Precinct
East 67th Street

Russo was waiting for them on the sidewalk in front of the precinct. Police cars and SUVs were parked up and down the street and uniformed cops in bulletproof vests stood around, staring into their phones and nursing cups of coffee. All that was missing was a donut wagon and some opening credits.

Russo was in yet another suit that looked like it had been stolen from a Goodwill mannequin that had been outfitted as an extra from a 1970s sitcom. It was blue. And it fit. But that was as complimentary as one could be. He had his signature *World's #1 Ex-Husband!* mug in his hand and looked like he hadn't slept. Ever.

Russo directed Whitaker to a designated parking spot on the street just east of the internal garage entrance and he was on top of Lucas before he had cleared the transom. "Dr. Page!" Russo's Long Island accent seemed to be getting stronger the longer Lucas knew the man.

Russo slapped him on the shoulder and said, "Thanks for coming up here. Saves me a lotta time, brother," the last word ending in a phonetic "uh."

Lucas stuck out his prosthetic and Russo slowly rotated their grip so he could get a better view. "That's something."

Lucas yanked it away. "Yes. It's called a hand."

Russo turned to Whitaker, who was coming around the back bumper. "He always this rude?"

"No." She and Russo shook hands. "He's usually worse."

Russo nodded at the shiny new Lincoln, which only had seventy-four miles on the odometer. "Nice ride. What happened to the other one?"

Lucas flatly said, "Trina Moncrieff went through the roof," which effectively wiped the grin off Russo's face.

Russo had one of those classic the-world-doesn't-make-sense looks on his face as he held the door. "That sucks."

The precinct had been designed around the same aesthetic principles as Swedish cars—it would never be called pretty, but it was most definitely utilitarian.

Lucas passed through the big double doors. "So you've decided that Delmonico was murdered?"

Russo looked to Whitaker for a little moral support. "No sense of humor. No small talk. How do you take this guy?"

She shrugged as they hit the steps. "In small well-paid doses."

While they signed in, Russo and the big duty officer exchanged shop talk, and the officer kept calling Russo "Jackets," which made no sense.

As they headed upstairs, Whitaker asked Russo, "What's with the name Jackets?"

"Nickname." He flicked his monumentally ugly blazer. "I always wear jackets. So I can carry stuff. You know, glasses and handcuffs and smokes and shit. I did this fishing thing with some of the other guys a few years back—we went to Key West. The other guys all got snazzed up in midlife crisis chic—you know, Tommy Bahama shirts and cargo shorts and Crocs and stupid ball caps with smiling turtles on them. Me? I'm in shorts and black socks and a sports coat because I need a place to carry all my shit. Like I said. So the guys start calling me 'Jackets' and, well, it kinda stuck."

Lucas said, "That's fascinating. Really. I mean that. Very engrossing story. But can we get back to business? What are we about to look at? Or is it some kind of a secret?"

Russo deflated, shook his head, then took a pull off his mug before dropping his volume conspiratorially. "Okay, so I got a list of license plates for all the vehicles that were on the span when Delmonico was hit by that pickup truck. My people spent the last three days hunting them all down and of one hundred and sixty-one vehicles that were on the span, one hundred and nineteen had dash cams. We got the footage from all but one, which is on a two-hour loop. One hundred and seventeen of the one hundred and eighteen were dead ends, but one made money for us. I just entered it in evidence, but we're not releasing it to the public and I haven't talked with Delmonico's husband about it yet—the guy's still not cleared as a suspect."

"It's not the husband," said Lucas.

"Yeah, well, statistics ain't on your side with this one."

Lucas nodded at him. "Congratulations."

"On what?"

"On correctly coming to the incorrect conclusion."

They made the third floor and Whitaker was doing well without the cane, which Lucas knew had probably developed beyond a purely physical crutch into being a mental one.

Russo led them down a hall, through a room that had been reproduced in thousands of Hollywood films over the past century with very little variance. The space was filled with gray metal tanker desks parked in a grid, each one paired to a different kind of office chair— some metal, some upholstered, some oak. There were old-school in-out paper trays. A water cooler. File cabinets. A few tabletop electric fans. And state-of-the art flat-panel monitors everywhere.

A few detectives in suits sat at desks, filling out forms in bulk—an activity that Hollywood ignored in favor of car chases that took out vegetable stands, shootings on busy streets, and the occasional cultural landmark being obliterated in an explosive fireball. No one looked up or gave them a nod, which Lucas found oddly refreshing.

They were taken to a back office where the plainclothesman with the odd name from the Solomon murder—Detective Monty Cristo—was examining a screen and taking notes on a legal pad with a pencil.

"Special Agent Whitaker, Dr. Page, you remember Detective Cristo."

Cristo half rose out of his chair and shook hands all around before dropping back into the seat. "Nice to see you guys again," he said, not even making an effort to sound sincere.

Russo directed Lucas and Whitaker around the desk, then put a hand on Monty Cristo's shoulder. "Would you please show these wonderful folks from the FBI what good old-fashioned police work has produced."

Cristo brought up an off-the-shelf video player, then selected the last file in the playlist. He double-clicked, and they were suddenly behind the wheel of a low-riding compact. Latin talk radio was on in the background, and the sound of crunching cellophane crackled out of the speakers. The car was on the Brooklyn Bridge, heading east in the peculiar golden light that is only produced by incandescent lighting shrouded in fog. The cars ahead were blurred by the miasma of condensation, taillights blinking like bloodshot eyes in the mist. The digital time stamp on the bottom right of the screen read *2:23:34 . . . 35 . . . 36.*

"This is the dash cam from a car that belongs to a man named Antonio Marquez. He's a custodian at the Empire State Building and was heading in for his three A.M. shift. He's eating pork chips and, I strongly suspect, cracking a beer in another three . . . two . . . one—"

Which was when the unmistakable sound of a can being popped echoed through the speakers. Followed by the sound of drinking. More crinkling of cellophane. Munching. And Spanish talk radio.

Lucas focused his attention on the footpath in the upper left-hand corner of the screen. Every now and then he was able to pick out a shadow in the mist that represented a human being, but there was no missing the otherworldly vibe the bridge had had that night.

Marquez was approaching the first tower from the Brooklyn side and Lucas willed the mist to clear so he could make out details on the footpath above.

But all he saw was more fog.

And the errant phantasm.

Then the stone tower materialized and there was an instant—a blip in time—when something in the mist on the footpath moved.

A figure.

Near the railing, above traffic.

Then a ghostly mitosis occurred. And it split. Became two. And the second figure peeled off from the first.

Began to tumble over the railing.

Toward traffic.

Then the car moved by the vantage point.

And everything became the past.

Detective Cristo stopped the video and leaned back in his chair.

"What did I just see?" Whitaker asked.

Lucas reached out and tapped the screen with his alloy finger. "Someone throwing Dr. Jennifer Delmonico off of the Brooklyn Bridge footpath."

Whitaker turned back to the monitor before refocusing on Lucas. "This is all unfolding like you said it would."

"No. Not with Delmonico."

Russo stepped in with, "What do you mean, *not with Delmonico*? She was murdered just like the other doctors."

Lucas gave a nod that converted into a shake. "She was murdered, but not like the others. Her homicide doesn't fit the patterns other than she was killed during a routine. Unlike every other doctor on the list, she had never had a malpractice case filed against her; she never had a single disciplinary action taken against her in any professional capacity; she's younger than all the other victims, if only by a few months of the next-youngest; she was pregnant; she had been practicing for a shorter period than every other doctor on my list. And on and on. She doesn't fit the criteria." He pointed a metal finger at Russo. "And neither did Erin."

Russo's mouth was doing that amused-at-the-world smile he had. "What are you saying?"

"Only that Erin and Delmonico seem to be outliers in the chaos. They don't fit."

Russo pointed at the computer screen, where Delmonico's shadow was frozen in the process of splitting off from the other one. "Well, somebody sure fucking killed her."

Lucas couldn't argue with that. And he didn't try. "They certainly did."

Whitaker's phone rang and she stepped away to take the call.

Russo led Lucas away from Cristo and quietly asked, "You don't think that Delmonico is part of this we're looking at?"

Lucas had been wondering about how Delmonico fit in for some time. And now that Erin occupied the same unknown part of the equation, Delmonico's murder looked even more dyssynchronous. "No, I don't."

"And you haven't seen the security footage from the Brooklyn Bridge that goes along with this?"

Lucas shook his head. "I wasn't even aware that there was any." Besides, he was letting Russo run point on Delmonico while he and Whitaker picked up the slack on Knox, Solomon, and now Erin.

"Well, look at it. And let me know what you think."

"What does it show?"

"I don't know. Until I saw this video, I thought it didn't show a thing. Now I'm not so sure. You want Monty here to cue it up?"

Monty looked up and smiled benignly, like a dog hearing its name but not knowing the context.

Whitaker came back and said, "No time." She poked Lucas in the shoulder.

"Our people have IDed the guy who tried to kill Erin. DNA confirms that it was Ira Alan White." She headed for the door. "Kehoe and Hoffner want you to interview his wife."

After thanking Russo and asking him to send copies of the dashcam video to the bureau, the detective walked them down to the new SUV.

As Lucas climbed in, Russo smiled at him and said, "Now remember, don't throw this one off a balcony."

51

26 Federal Plaza

Lucas and Whitaker stepped off the elevator and he was hit by the sheer volume of activity. The bureau office was one of those contained systems where the macro barely represented the activity occurring below the surface; for every agent walking the halls, there were ten sequestered away in cubicles, laboratories, conference rooms, and lecture spaces; and for every one of those, there were another ten out in the field, gathering the data necessary to feed the machine. The bureau employed more than thirty-five thousand people, and that was separate from the automatic systems that were continually operating at a molecular level, always on, always hungry, always analyzing — pulling data in from social media, news outlets, and every other facet of society.

Hoffner saw them from across the room and came over, covering the eighty feet in what looked to be three long strides. "Page, Whitaker."

Lucas was too tired for small talk, so he gave Hoffner an alloy salute.

Hoffner looked him over. "You okay?" The usual hardness was gone from his voice, but he still sounded like a piece of heavy machinery firing up.

"I'm good. Thanks."

"How's your wife?"

Lucas was suddenly aware that Hoffner was being both polite and the bigger man, and he was embarrassed at his past snarkiness. "She's going to be okay. Thank you."

Hoffner took a step in and looked down at Lucas. "You need anything from me, you ask."

Lucas was confused, and he didn't try to hide it. "Sure. Okay. I, um, I will."

Hoffner stared at him for a moment. "Anything, okay?"

Lucas nodded. "Okay."

Niceties over, the big man headed for the operations room. Lucas followed silently in his wake, letting Hoffner's superior mass pull him along as the two agents traded information.

Whitaker was still doing pretty well with the foot and Lucas wondered if it would start to bother her by the end of the day or if she really was ready to lose the cane.

Whitaker and Hoffner went through the usual information exchange that substituted as small talk on the job. "Is Ira Alan White's wife here yet?"

Three yards of fabric shifted as Hoffner took a corner at an intersection of upholstered cubicles. "She's on the way. Should be about fifteen minutes. We've got people at their house and the digital folks are going at their lives. So far there are no red flags."

Except that fucker tried to kill my wife, Lucas thought.

"Russo told us that the bureau requested some CCTV footage from the Brooklyn Bridge, taken on the night Delmonico was murdered."

"We did."

"And?"

"And I think Page should see it before I go making any declarations about what it contains."

After slaloming through the war room proper, Hoffner carded

them into the operations room, which now looked like mission control hopped up on livestock steroids and determination. But for a space so alive, it was remarkably quiet.

Hoffner pointed up to the wall of whiteboards. "We've reclassified nine deaths—six accidents, three suicides—as homicides. We're close on four more. Bodies are being exhumed all over the five boroughs and the lab is getting ready to chalk up a lot of overtime on their necromancy."

Hoffner pointed at the digital whiteboards. "We have two hydrocyanic poisonings. There's a suicide that looks wrong from almost every angle—Marvin Shapiro cut his wrists in the bathtub but had two broken fingers on each hand due to unknown causes. A guy doesn't break his fingers before slashing his wrists with a Ginsu. I don't know how that one got by the ME."

Hoffner indicated another victim—Dr. Luther Tanner, pediatrician. "Collapsed on the doorstep to his house and his wife found him. She called nine-one-one. Ambo delivered him to Gracie Square, where they tried to resuscitate him. Died an hour later. But the hospital still had his blood sample on file. The guy died from heart failure brought on by an insulin overdose—but by the time he died his body had metabolized it, and the autopsy missed it. That their lab still had a blood sample from when he was admitted is nothing more than dumb luck." Hoffner looked down at Lucas. "You were right about this. All of it."

There was nothing to be gained by the *I told you so* dance. "And the Delmonico footage?"

Hoffner nodded over at the far side of the room, to a row of monitors across the long wall. Agents of various ages, sizes, and sexes worked on keyboards, digitally combing the virtual salt mines of data that existed in unidentifiable quadrants of cyberspace.

Hoffner stopped at the seat occupied by a junior agent who looked like he spent his weekends doing bong hits and cutting his own hair. "Mace, could you please show Dr. Page and Special Agent

Whitaker the tapes on the Delmonico murder we got from the Bridge Authority?"

Mace brought up a dozen different recordings and they automatically self-organized into a row. He hit *play* and the tall form of Dr. Jennifer Delmonico—identified by a floating red crosshair—walked onto the first screen in the herky-jerky movements that sped-up video produces. "These are from the security cameras on the bridge footpath, from west to east, played at five-times speed. Delmonico takes about eighteen minutes from the time she steps onto the bridge proper to make it to the second suspension tower, where camera four-one-three-five-T is."

Delmonico crossed from the first into the second frame, then onto the third, unaware that in a few truncated minutes she would be dead.

Mace said, "The interesting part is our jogger, Freddie Mercury."

He brought the same dozen camera feeds up—the one difference being the time stamps. The red crosshair identified a figure who walked into the first frame with the single word *suspect* hovering over him as he moved—he wore black pants, black sneakers, and a black hoodie that hid the top half of his face. But Mace was right about the stylized moustache—he looked like he was most definitely channeling the late singer.

Mace continued, "Freddie follows Delmonico onto the bridge, which could be coincidental. He pauses here—" Mace reached out and tapped the screen. The figure paused, stretching out his quads near a gaggle of late-night tourists ogling the fog where Lower Manhattan should have been. "While Delmonico continues on her way. He stretches for seven minutes, nine seconds, and never looks up so we can get a peek at his face. Then, right here—"

Mace slowed the footage down, and the figure's head cocked to one side like a dog tuning into an invisible whistle, and he took off running.

"He starts."

Mace hit the command and the figure picked up pace, running at five-times speed across the different camera feeds. "The guy's a runner—we clocked him and he's at about six-point-one miles per hour, which is athlete level."

The recording resembled the Patterson-Gimlin film, only this was reality.

Delmonico moved with a long, easy stride.

The suspect was now six cameras behind.

Then five.

Then four.

Lucas watched as time unwound.

Three cameras.

Then two.

"Right here," Mace said, slowing down the footage, "is where Delmonico and Mercury both cross onto the dark side of the moon."

Both crosshairs denoting Delmonico and the jogger moved out of the frame at almost the same instant and into the blind spot where the camera was blocked by the falcons' nest.

Mace held up his hand and counted, ". . . Twenty-two . . . twenty-three . . . twenty-four . . . and this"—he snapped his fingers, converting his forefinger and thumb into a gun that pointed at the next screen where Mr. Mercury entered the frame stage left—"is where our suspect comes out, by which time Jennifer Delmonico has been thrown into traffic."

Mace fast-forwarded the rest of the tapes showing the jogger moving from left to right in a steady gait. He hit the end of the bridge, cut through the throngs of people heading for the center— and the commotion—and off into the night.

"We checked traffic cameras and CCTV footage from the area around the ramp and this guy just disappeared."

Lucas stared at the monitor, replaying what he had just seen in his cranial screening room. He edited the footage together with the dash-cam video that Russo had shown them, then ran through it in his head one more time. Something wasn't right.

Lucas leaned forward, pointing at the first camera in the frame. "Bring this back to seven minutes and fifteen seconds."

Mace clicked through the commands and Freddie appeared back near the entrance to the bridge, stretching out his quads.

Mace started the footage and three seconds later, when Freddie's head cocked to one side, Lucas said, "Stop."

Mace froze the frame, and Freddie stood suspended in what looked to be a dance move, head cocked to one side while simultaneously dropping his foot and beginning a pivot. All that was missing was a little bit of dirty guitar and a bass line.

"See that?" Lucas asked.

Whitaker was the only one who said, "Nope."

"If Freddie Mercury here is our killer, and since the dash-cam footage that Russo showed us proved that someone *was* definitely up there with her when she went over the edge, he knew he had to overtake and overpower her *off-camera*. And that particular location is the only point on the bridge where surveillance is down."

"So?" Hoffner asked.

Lucas turned on the tone he used with the kids when they were being intentionally difficult. "It's a math problem. You know what math is?"

Hoffner gave him a look that could only be described as a scowl.

Lucas pointed at the screen, as if the problem were obvious. "Speed is simply distance divided by time. Think back to grade school, before they decided that you were more suited to chewing on tires. Two people leave Lower Manhattan, both bound for Brooklyn—one a pedestrian, the other a jogger. The pedestrian walks at roughly three-point-four miles per hour; the jogger runs at six-point-one miles per hour. In order for the jogger to catch the pedestrian precisely at camera four-one-three-five-T—how many minutes after the pedestrian departs does the jogger have to leave, assuming that both of their speeds will remain constant?"

Hoffner's face was chopped into large planes of irritation that he wasn't bothering to hide.

Whitaker shrugged. "I was an anthropology major."

But Mace looked up, his lopsided haircut adding a maniacal edge to his grin. "You're right!"

Lucas nodded down at Mace. "Freddie here needed to know *precisely* where Delmonico was on the span before he took off after her, and he had to know her usual walking speed, or he would have been caught on-camera throwing her into traffic. So we know this is premeditated."

The lights behind Hoffner's eyes got a little brighter with that. "So how does he know where she is? Did he time her from when she started her walk?"

"He could have, but the longer he relied on her rate remaining constant, the greater the chances were that it changed—interruptions, people in front of her, people taking selfies; maybe she got a phone call. The surest way for him to be as accurate as possible is"—Lucas tapped the screen with a green anodized finger—"to know where she hits the point where he has to go after her so that their speeds and times intersect in that blind spot in the most natural-appearing manner possible. So here"—he once again tapped the screen—"is where someone signals him. Someone was on the bridge waiting for Delmonico. And when she passed a certain point, they signaled Freddie so he and Delmonico would arrive at the tower—and that blind spot—at the *same time*." Lucas flicked the screen again. "He's on a call. Someone's doing reconnaissance for him. Where is Delmonico at five seconds before he cocks his head to the side? Eight minutes, eighteen seconds after he starts stretching."

Mace went to the footage and enlarged the video from the fourth camera in the series. Delmonico was mid-frame, passing a man. He was leaning against the railing, looking out at the East River, his head moving with the motion of an animated conversation.

When Delmonico walked by, his head bobbed with some unknown snippet of dialogue. Then he pocketed the phone and walked away, toward Lower Manhattan.

Mace zoomed in, enhancing the man's face. It was grainy. But there. He was anywhere from thirty to fifty-five and wore a pair of oversized aviators.

Lucas said, "Freddie Mercury and his pal here tag-teamed Delmonico."

He looked up and Hoffner was examining him with renewed interest. "Does this fit in with everything else?"

Lucas looked back to the screen, to the two men who had killed Delmonico. "Albert Hess and Trina Moncrieff and Ira Alan White are just average people with lives and jobs. But these two guys," he said, flicking the screen with an aluminum finger—an act that irritated Mace, who slapped his hand away—"are professionals." He looked up, at the faces of the dead doctors wallpapering the room.

Hoffner held up his phone. "Okay. Ira Alan White's wife was just brought in. Time to put you into a room with her."

Lucas was staring at the two men frozen on different monitors. "Let's see if she knows Freddie Mercury and his friend from the Brooklyn Illuminati."

52

Lucas and Whitaker were in the interview room with Ira Alan White's wife, Sharona. It was one of the nicer rooms, the kind with upholstered chairs instead of the usual metal suckers. They weren't treating her as hostile, but that small initial courtesy could change with one wrong answer. Which everyone present seemed acutely aware of.

But Sharona White appeared to be as genuinely surprised as everyone else that her husband was a would-be murderer who had burned to death in a pool of gasoline.

"You don't understand," she said, wiping her nose for the hundredth time with the hundredth fistful of tissue. "Ira wouldn't hurt anyone. It was one of the things that attracted me to him. We argued about it before we had Kyle—I didn't see anything wrong with smacking a kid if they got out of line. Ira said it was barbaric, and that if I wanted children with him, I had to promise that I'd *never* hit them. He was right—Kyle's the most polite thirteen-year-old in the world." She blew her nose into the wad of Kleenex, threw it into the can beside the interview table, and reached for a preemptive refill.

Lucas tapped the photo of Erin on the table. "And you're certain that you don't know this woman?"

She leaned over and repeated the process they had already gone through four times. She took her time, appeared to search her memory card, and once again shook her head. "I told you—I've never seen her before and he never mentioned her." She looked up and her eyes went wide. "Oh my God, was he having an affair with her?"

Lucas shook his head. "Not as far as we know." And he realized that in absolute terms it was possible that he knew Erin as well as Sharona knew Ira. They shared a life and a family and a car, but who knew what kinds of secrets were floating around out there in the ether? That he allowed himself some sort of internal superior smugness over this woman's relationship might be pure delusion. After all, Mark Twain had said that it wasn't what you didn't know that would get you, but what you knew for certain that just wasn't so.

"And these people?" Lucas asked, dealing out eight-by-tens of Albert Hess, Denise Moth, and Trina and Darrel Moncrieff.

She looked up, her eyes suddenly panicky. "Did he try to kill them, too?"

"No. But there seems to be a connection between your husband and these people that we can't work out."

"So they're still alive?"

Her comment made him realize that he hadn't seen that very obvious commonality between the victims and most of the killers they had found—they were all dead. How had he missed that? "Mrs. White, your husband was not a mass murderer. From what we know so far, the attempted murder yesterday was his only crime. But he might have known one—or all—of these people. Maybe he mentioned them. Please take a look."

She leaned over and as she moved through the photo lineup, Lucas tapped each one, giving them names.

Mrs. White once again appeared to make a thorough memory

search and shook her head. "I don't think I've ever seen any of these people and I don't remember Ira mentioning any of them."

"What about these men?" Lucas asked, producing photographs of their Brooklyn-bound Freddie Mercury and his accomplice. They were grainy surveillance camera stills that weren't very good, but if she knew either of the men, they would probably get her there.

He slid them across the table, tapping each one in turn with his metal finger. "I know they are terrible photos, but look at the general characteristics."

She stared at his finger for a moment, as if seeing it for the first time. She then blinked once, and shifted focus to the pictures. She stared intently, like she was trying to see past the likenesses of the two men to the reasons her life had ended up here, speaking with the FBI about her dead husband. She finally tapped one of them and said, "That guy looks like Freddie Mercury."

"So you haven't seen them before?"

She shook her head. "Sorry. No."

Mrs. White had reached the end of her confusion reservoir and she leaned back and her emotional gears ground to a halt. "None of these people ring any bells." She looked up at Lucas, and went through the left-eye-or-right-eye game that put most people on edge. After a little back-and-forth she said, "Which eye am I supposed to look into?" She wasn't being rude—it just sounded like she was too tired to guess.

Lucas took off his glasses and pointed up at his left with his original biomechanical hand. "This one."

She focused on it. "I will sit here all year if you people need because I want to know what happened to my husband. And I want to know why he tried to kill someone. We had a mostly good marriage. And he was a good father to Kyle. Things got tough when his brother died, but he got over that. It took three years and a lot of work, but it happened. Or it felt like it happened. He seemed so . . . okay with things. I still can't see him killing anyone. Especially a stranger. Not after all that time he spent in therapy." She gave Lucas one of those looks that he knew came from the invisible sun people don't even know they have access to.

Lucas put his glasses back on and said, "Therapy?"

53

Robert F. Kennedy Bridge

Lucas and Whitaker rode in one of the metal blood cells clogging up the arteries of the Robert F. Kennedy Bridge. It was raining and the roadway appeared to be suspended in the clouds. Everything beyond the guardrails—or more than three car lengths ahead or behind—didn't exist. And traffic was at a complete stop, which made for a very weird sense of isolation.

They were on the way to visit Ira Alan White's psychiatrist, Dr. Matthias Vaughan. Vaughan had a private practice in the city but spent the bulk of his working life at the Manhattan Psychiatric Center on Randalls and Wards Islands, where he was head of psychiatry. Maybe he could help them figure out White's motivation for trying to kill Erin. Which might lead them to an answer to one of the big questions that they had.

Lucas was lost in the particles zipping through his gray matter, trying to see how they related to one another. To thirty-two dead doctors. To Albert Hess. Trina and Darrel Moncrieff. Denise Moth. Ira Alan White.

And Erin.

But no matter how he approached this thing, or how he assembled the pieces, the mechanistic levers that were powering it were invisible. He could observe the effects, but not the root cause. And like Newton had demonstrated, a body at rest doesn't begin to move without a force being exerted on it—something has to push, or pull, it.

"So those two guys on the bridge killed Delmonico?"

"Yes."

"But Hess killed Arna Solomon?"

"Yes."

"And Moncrieff killed your friend Knox?"

"Yes."

"How are they connected to Ira Alan White?"

"I don't know."

"Is it possible that our unknown killers, Mr. Wint and Mr. Kidd, took out Leonard Ibicki?"

"I don't know."

The automotive cholesterol started moving again, and Whitaker switched lanes toward the 278 West for Wards Island. "Which gives us three *yeses* and two *I don't knows*. That's not the Dr. Page we all fear."

"I don't guess. The only certainties—and I mean the only *I bet my life on it* certainties—are that Denise Moth *did not* kill Dr. Ibicki, and that Freddie Mercury and his friend did kill Jennifer Delmonico. What doesn't fit is that Denise Moth didn't seem to care that Leonard Ibicki died later, which is not how someone who has a motive to want him dead would react."

"Maybe she's not part of this."

Lucas thought about that for a few moments. "Everyone I mentioned is connected. I just haven't figured out how yet."

Whitaker pulled the SUV through the turn on the off-ramp and Lucas steadied himself against the centrifugal pull by grabbing the holy shit handle. At the stop sign at the end of the final arc, Whitaker swung them south, toward Hell Gate.

Considering that Randalls and Wards Islands were adjacent to

Manhattan and home to two hospitals and several public service departments, including an FDNY training academy, a police station, a water treatment plant, and an arena, it felt like a deserted former East Bloc closed city, empty flagpoles and all. The bulk of the island's space was allocated to soccer fields, baseball diamonds, and various sports areas that were used by the schools of the five boroughs, but they were all empty in the late November weather. And there were no joggers or cyclists, which was unusual, especially on a Sunday.

Whitaker looped through the crescent on Hell Gate Circle at the southern tip of the island, then pulled back up and into the fenced lot of the hospital. "This place is cheery."

Lucas looked up at the structure. "It's just a building. And it's raining. And there are no people visible."

"What about the barbed-wire fence, the bars on the windows, and the words 'Psychiatric Hospital' on their website?"

"Would you rather it be shaped like a giant Mickey Mouse?"

Whitaker snapped her fingers. "Actually, yes."

Lucas pulled up the collar on his overcoat, and they both stepped out into the rain coming down in the friscalating dusk light.

Even on the island visibility was almost nil, but the traffic on the bridge to the north was audible through the rain and wind that made up the bulk of the ambient background noise. They ran for the building as well as a man with a prosthetic leg and a woman recovering from a bullet wound to the foot can.

When they presented their badges at the front desk, they were unceremoniously handed clipboards preloaded with generic visitor's forms for civil servants.

They filled in all the appropriate fields and Whitaker was asked to relinquish her side arm. She removed the clip, popped the cartridge out of the chamber and thumbed it into the magazine, put the two components into the little plastic tray, and pushed it across the counter—all while giving the desk guard a very poignant grimace. They were issued laminated visitor passes and directed to the elevators.

The fourth floor was clean, tidy, and updated, including motivational posters and a rack of pamphlets by the elevator doors—along with the standard hand sanitizer dispenser that had been granted permanent status in all public spaces with the arrival of COVID.

The desk facing the elevator was behind screen-impregnated glass, emphasizing the true character of the institution. It was much more civilized than what its nineteenth-century counterpart had no doubt been. They might not be using truncheons and beatings for treatment, but the space still conveyed all the mental baggage that accompanied that particular image. And of all the illnesses, Lucas realized that diseases of the mind were both still the least understood and, correspondingly, the most feared. Mrs. Page used to call places like this Gourd Wards.

The building branched off to the left and right, but the wings were secured by magnetic security doors that could only be operated from the desk.

The receptionist was a heavyset black man with big muttonchops in keeping with the nineteenth-century vibe. His name tag read *Wallace*—which could have been a first, last, or nickname, and he was reading a paperback copy of Hemingway's *Islands in the Stream.* He put the novel down and asked, "May I help you?" through a small speaker built into the glass, exposing a gold-rimmed incisor.

Whitaker held up her pass and bureau identification. "Special Agent Whitaker and Dr. Page, FBI. We're here to see Dr. Vaughan."

Wallace looked over at Lucas and he held up his pass.

When Wallace had finished checking whatever he was supposed to, he nodded at the door on his left, which was south. "Dr. Vaughan's office is down the hall, the fifth door on the left. His receptionist, Dr. Anderson, will take care of you and Dr. Page."

There was a low-frequency hum as the magnetic lock was disengaged, and Lucas pulled the door open and held it for Whitaker.

Whitaker said, "Is that what it's like at your Christmas parties, with two Dr. Pages and all of your doctor friends? 'Merry Christmas, Doctor.' 'No, Merry Christmas to you, Doctor!' 'Sorry, Doctor, I was speaking to the other doctor. Apologies, Doctor.' 'No, Doctor, the fault is mine.' 'Apology accepted, Doctor!'"

Lucas thought about the charity gig at the Armory the other night. "Actually, we just call all of our friends bud."

There was no music on the wing, which Lucas had expected for some reason. The place was quiet, and only a few patients were in the hall, each accompanied by hospital staff.

Dr. Anderson was waiting for them in the hallway, in front of a poster emphasizing that there was always a tomorrow if you wanted there to be, which Lucas knew was a complete lie for at least eight thousand American citizens each and every day, historically unusual pandemics notwithstanding.

"Special Agent Whitaker, is it?" Anderson asked with a friendly smile that looked like it got a lot of use.

Whitaker nodded a greeting, and gestured to Lucas. "This is my associate, Dr. Page."

No one shook hands—another COVID holdover—and Anderson directed them to the office with a genuine smile. "I was told you were coming, but not the reason." Anderson was one of those people who could be anywhere between forty and sixty-five, and probably hadn't changed her haircut since junior high. She was short, and thin, and nothing about her presentation suggested either a medical, or academic, degree. She looked like she spent her weekends reading romance novels and baking cookies. Or playing boogie-woogie piano for her cats. Or doing whatever little old ladies in sweaters were into these days.

Very matter-of-factly, Whitaker said, "It's a private matter for Dr. Vaughan."

She nodded and smiled—typical Non-Player Character behavior—and said, "I see," when it was clear that she didn't.

Anderson led them back into a small institutional reception office that didn't have a single personal touch factored in. "Dr. Vaughan will be free in a little while," she said.

Lucas wondered what "a little while" meant—because in astrophysics, like geology, a million years wasn't even a blip on the clock.

After a few silent minutes in the interconnected airport lounge chairs facing the desk, the door to the inner office opened, and a middle-aged man who looked like his mind was occupied with a complicated protein-folding equation came out. He looked down at them and shook his head as if they weren't supposed to be there, and said, "You do understand that it's happening, don't you? I mean, it's all around us, you just have to—"

Dr. Anderson cut him off with, "We'll see you later in group, Mr. Evans. After supper. Don't forget."

Mr. Evans stopped his monologue and stepped out into the hallway where a tall black attendant steered him away by the elbow.

Without looking at them, Anderson got up and went to the inner office door. "Dr. Vaughan, the people from the FBI are here. A Special Agent Whitaker and a Dr. Page."

A voice that could have sold Courvoisier on the radio said, "Dr. *Lucas* Page?"

"I believe so, yes."

"Far out! Please send them in. And hold my calls."

54

Lucas had no idea what to expect of Dr. Matthias Vaughan, but it wasn't a big fuzzy Chewbacca-looking dude in a Joy Division T-shirt, Birkenstocks, and a gold Rolex—an assembly of contradictions by any measure. He had a gentle smile the size of a mail slot that made you understand why he went into the business of helping people. But the big surprise was that his voice sounded better in here, at the source, than it had from the outer office.

Vaughan came around the desk to meet them, taking Lucas's prosthetic in both of his very large hirsute oven mitts. He held on to the alloy appliance as if deriving information from it, and looked into Lucas's good eye behind the dark lens. "I'm Dr. Matthias Vaughan. I've read all of your books, Dr. Page, and it is very much a pleasure to meet you, man." His teeth sparkled amid the massive Viking beard.

Lucas wasn't sure how to respond, so he just nodded. "Okay."

Vaughan then turned to Whitaker, who introduced herself with the usual, "Special Agent Whitaker, FBI."

Vaughan and Whitaker shook hands and he gave her the same gentle smile and two-mittened handshake. "It is nice to meet you."

He was somewhere in his sixties but had younger teeth, older eyes, and age-appropriate skin.

Vaughan gestured to the sofa facing the institutional armchair he no doubt used as his perch during mental-coaching sessions. He sat down and crossed his ankle over his knee, exposing brightly striped Paul Smith socks. "So, how may I help the FBI?" Whatever personality had been missing in Anderson's tiny institutional closet out front was made up for in here. Vaughan's décor had an ethnographic bent and it was easy to see that he had an interest in primitive healers, represented in everything from the fleam collection in the display case to the reproduction Venus of Willendorf he kept under a glass dome on the edge of his desk. There were tribal masks and examples of pre-Columbian pottery, all dealing with classic Mesoamerican human-to-god and animal-to-god metamorphoses.

Lucas handed the doctor a warrant granting them access to Ira Alan White's medical files, then folded into the sofa. "You were Ira Alan White's psychiatrist?"

Whitaker took up position at the opposite end of the sofa, which had recently been sprayed with disinfectant.

Vaughan's big fuzzy face looked confused and he peeled back the flap on the envelope and read the warrant. He spent a moment going over the text, and when he was satisfied by its contents he folded it up and placed it on the coffee table. "Not *were*—am. What is this about? Is Mr. White in some sort of trouble?"

Technically, the question had both a *yes* and *no* answer. "Mr. White is dead."

Which did a pretty good job of surprising Vaughan. "What happened?"

Whitaker gestured to Lucas, who went into answer mode. "Just before noon yesterday, Mr. White tried to shoot my wife as she was coming home from grocery shopping with three of our children. He shot her twice through the windshield of our car and she returned the favor by running over him. Twice."

Even behind all the facial hair, Vaughan's face was doing a pretty good job of conveying a mixture of shock and horror. But he was silent as he waited for Lucas to finish filling him in and Lucas realized that he was probably a decent therapist.

"At some point the gas tank ruptured and Mr. White burned to death."

Vaughan waited a few seconds as he metabolized the information. Then he blinked, took a deep breath, and leaned forward, looking into Lucas's good eye. "How is your wife doing?"

"She's fine. Thank you for asking. But we're not here about my wife; we're here about Ira Alan White."

Vaughan nodded like he understood, but his expression indicated that he didn't. "And how may I help?"

"We think that the attack on my wife may be connected to a current bureau investigation and we were hoping you might help us figure out Mr. White's motivation. Maybe he said something to you."

Vaughan sat back in the chair as if he had been pushed, but he did a competent job of not looking insulted, even if it came out in his tone. "I'm sorry, Dr. Page, I can only pretend to understand what you must be going through, but I can assure you that if Ira had hinted that he was even fantasizing—never mind actually considering carrying out—what you have told me, I would have contacted the appropriate agencies immediately. Doctor/patient confidentiality ends when a patient expresses any desire to harm themselves or others. If Ira had said anything at all to me, you would have known before yesterday." Vaughan remained seated as he stared into Lucas's original eye.

"Did he mention a group of friends? People he spent time with? We're looking for possible accomplices or even his motives to commit a murder."

Another shake of the big bison head. "Ira lost a brother a few years back, and that tended to be the focus of our sessions. He had typical twenty-first-century midlife problems like everyone else—the occasional issue with work, trouble paying the occasional bill, arguments with his wife, stress about his son. But nothing that ever raised a flag. And certainly never any talk or hints of murder. I can send you my notes and his file if you want."

"Could we get it now?"

Vaughan looked like he was still recovering from the initial shock. "I'm sorry. The work I do here at the hospital is completely independent from the work I do in my private practice. And the two filing systems are independent of one another. Everything here falls under the parameters of the new H Two O program, which is Health and Hospitals Online, and the system uses traditional electronic medical records. I don't use EMRs in my private practice unless a patient requests it, and that is unusual." Vaughan picked up his cell and typed something into it. "I've just left myself a note. I can have those to you tonight if you would like, after my shift here. Both my apartment and office are on the Upper East Side. Say, ten o'clock. If it's urgent, I can have Dr. Anderson run up to my place to get it."

Lucas checked his watch. "Ten is fine." He held out a card and said, "Is it possible that someone exploited Mr. White in some way—blackmail, maybe? Is it possible he was manipulated?"

"I don't understand; why would you say that?"

Lucas shrugged. "I don't know. I'm just trying to figure out why he would try to kill my wife."

"I'd like to say that psychiatry is a window into the human mind, but that's not entirely true—it's more like a peephole. And if people don't talk to you, it's hard to figure out what's going on with them."

Everyone was starting to sound the same. Or they were at least buying their thoughts from the same supplier.

"So you don't think it possible that he was manipulated into trying to kill my wife?"

Vaughan took in another lungful of air and let it roll around in his system for a moment. "I never saw any indicators." He looked at Lucas, and the concern was dialed back up. "I'm sorry, but this is a little disconcerting. I spent more than seventy sessions with Ira over the past year and a half and I can't reconcile the gentle—if somewhat sad—man that I knew with the would-be murderer you're describing. He was making progress—*real* progress. It was obvious." He stared at Lucas and he looked perplexed. "And I lost a friend to mental illness last week, so please excuse my melancholy—even psychiatrists have their troubles."

There was a gentle knock on the door and Dr. Anderson poked her head in. "Dr. Vaughan, you have group downstairs in ten minutes."

Vaughan looked up and smiled warmly. "Thank you, Dr. Anderson."

She closed the door and Vaughan held up Lucas's card. "Do I need to drop Ira White's file by the office?"

Both Lucas and Whitaker stood, he favoring his right leg, she the left.

"We can have it picked up." Lucas stuck out his hand. "Thank you for your time."

Vaughan waved the card at him. "If I think of anything else, I promise to let you know. But may I ask a favor?" He eyed Lucas with a sheepish grin that actually made him look like a smiling sheep.

"Of course."

Vaughan gestured to the wall of books that made up his office library. "Would you be so kind as to sign one of your books?"

• • •

They were on the ramp back up to the Robert Kennedy Bridge and rain had arrived with the darkness.

Lucas was trying to find something useful in their conversation with Dr. Chewbacca, but it wasn't happening.

"So?" Whitaker asked. "Was that worth driving all the way up here?"

Lucas looked out at the dark and all he saw was rain dancing on the pavement and red taillights blinking through the downpour. "At least that guy will buy a copy of my next book."

55

Midtown

It was blustery and cold and drizzly in what the kids would call a perfect Winnie the Pooh day. But maybe the shit would burn off— with everything that had happened in the past couple of days, Lucas needed a little sunshine.

There were miles and miles of concrete and asphalt and glass and dented cars and bodies hunched under the weight of their lives. Maybe Erin was right—maybe they needed to leave New York. She had said some place with trees, but that covered a lot of bases. The town of Redbud in Vermont had trees. But so did Iceland. And Entmoot.

Canada was the easy option—they had health care and affordable education and updated infrastructure and no guns on the street and it was close enough to drive to. But it was a polite country filled with mostly polite people and Lucas knew *that* would get *real* old, *real* fast. Besides, he didn't like maple syrup. Or hockey. And with Neil Peart and Gord Downie gone, they only played Celine Dion on the radio—so that was out.

Lorne Jacobi had called him back at home earlier. He had spoken to Jennifer Delmonico's mother last night, who, after half an hour of small talk, admitted that her daughter had indeed been having some trouble at home. And she had been seeing someone. She didn't mention Jennifer's pregnancy and she didn't know who the man was, only that he was older, a widower, he treated her well and had a good sense of humor. He lived somewhere on the Upper East Side. Which was a whole lot and nothing, all at the same time.

Lucas had also asked Lorne if he knew Dr. Matthias Vaughan, and he had been rewarded with a warm chuckle. Apparently Vaughan was considered to be a psychiatrist's psychiatrist (which Lucas found to be more of an indictment of the discipline than a celebration), and Lorne told Lucas to say hello for him if their paths crossed again.

Before leaving home, he had loaded another video of Erin onto the kitchen iPad, which he hoped would help mitigate the effects of what had been another long night for the kids. He wanted to be home, but until this was put to bed, it would be his residence in name only. The plan from here on out was to make everyone's life miserable, starting with Kehoe.

Pedestrians thinned out the closer he got to the office, which was partially owing to the neighborhood; you needed places people could buy things if you wanted to attract them.

As usual, traffic was being rerouted around FBI headquarters for security measures, and when Lucas got out of the cab on the corner of Thomas Street, Whitaker was waiting for him across the intersection, on the east side of Broadway. A group of protesters had been corralled behind portable metal barriers to the south, and they were yelling insults and waving signs, and one look at the camouflage established an instant stereotype.

Lucas ignored the shouting simpletons and headed across the street to where Whitaker was sitting on one of the dragon's teeth, the only civilian in the loose line of sentries clad in tactical gear. She was in a long camel-hair coat and the shoes from yesterday that looked more like combat boots than street wear. But she had added a red scarf for a little flair. Or to make it easier for snipers.

They met in the middle of the intersection and shook hands.

"How are the kids?"

He shrugged. "Better than I am."

Whitaker glanced over at the protesters and shook her head. "It's the Proud Boys today. Why don't these mooks protest something important, like America being behind the rest of the first world in education?"

Lucas didn't bother following her line of sight; he saw enough impotent rage on television. "I think their presence demonstrates your point pretty well, although the subtlety might be lost on them."

They slalomed through the dragon's teeth and Whitaker started to fill him in. "Vaughan sent Ira Alan White's file over last night and the behavioral people have gone through it. There were no warning signs that White had the potential to turn violent. He was suffering from depression and anxiety, but he presented as neither angry nor paranoid."

"His attempt to murder Erin didn't just spin up out of the blue."

Whitaker shrugged. "Like the Great Man once said, 'The heart is sorely charged.'"

"Have the analysts gone at his life?"

"Everything from his tax returns to his Amazon purchase history."

"And your people found nothing?"

"You mean *our* people."

"Semantics."

"They couldn't find a single link between Ira Alan White and Erin. Like Hess, Moncrieff, and Moth, the one necessary component is missing—motive."

"Any connection to Hess and Moncrieff?"

"Nyet."

When they badged through the security desk, the sentry gave Lucas a *What the fuck happened to you?* up and down. "You in bomb disposal?" he asked, as if that was the best joke anyone had ever made.

Lucas reached down with his biomechanical hand, folded up his alloy thumb and three of his fingers, then gave the guy a metal middle-finger salute before walking away.

The ground floor was empty owing to the early hour, and there were two elevator cars waiting with the doors open. They stepped in and Lucas swiped his ID, then hit the floor button with his still-extended middle finger.

Whitaker settled against the back wall and the doors slid closed. "Russo's upstairs, waiting for us."

"Swell."

"You know, I think the guy actually *likes* you."

"So what."

"*So what?* So besides Erin, he might be the only person on the planet. Maybe the *entire universe* if we ever discover intelligent life elsewhere. I would think that would make him statistically important to a numbers geek like you."

"Stop it."

She smiled up at him. "Can you at least be nice to the guy?"

He stared at the numbers accelerating on the panel. "I'm always nice."

Whitaker looked down at his alloy hand for a moment. "Oh yeah, I forgot." She reached out and gently folded back his middle finger.

56

26 Federal Plaza

They came out of the elevators to find Hoffner and Russo immersed in discussion at the line of demarcation between the carpeted cubicle work farm and the polished terrazzo foot traffic beltway. The size differential between the two men contrasted so deeply that they could have been unrelated species—Russo descending from a long-lost Mediterranean dwarfine haplogroup, Hoffner an evolutionary relic from an extinct branch of antediluvian warmongering protohumans. All that was missing were little Latin signs denoting genus for the museum diorama.

When Russo saw them, he smiled and waved.

Hoffner did neither.

Russo carried his *World's #1 Ex-Husband!* mug. Once again, he was wedged into badly made slip-ons and a Men's Wearhouse special. He wasn't wearing a tie, which Lucas found oddly anti-establishment for an Italian Catholic detective. As always, Hoffner looked like he had been retrieved from a seventeenth-century German battlefield and forced into modern clothes against his will.

"Luke, my man!" Russo said as if they were long-lost friends from the neighborhood. Followed by, "And Special Agent Whitaker!" delivered at almost the same level of enthusiasm.

Hoffner nodded warmly at Whitaker and then glanced down at Lucas and dipped his head once. "Page."

The first thing Russo said was, "How's your wife?"

"She's good. Thank you for asking. What are you doing here?"

Russo shook his head as if he should have known better. "I know you don't think that Delmonico's murder fits in with the others, but a homicide is a homicide, and they all get treated equally."

Lucas repeated the question.

Russo held up the inch-and-a-half-thick stack of paper he was carrying. "My people ran through Delmonico's cell records a bunch of times and nothing sticks out. The one number she called more than her husband was a Dr. Joyce Carmichael, but even if they were doing furry triangle rides it's pretty safe to assume that Carmichael didn't father Delmonico's baby."

Lucas said, "Furry triangle rides?" and rolled his eyes.

"We've only known each other a coupla days, but I think I can safely assume that you're one of those *Let the light from my burning bridges guide my way* kind of guys, *amIright*?"

Whitaker interrupted the exchange with, "Can we get back to the furry triangle rides?"

Russo smiled at her. "She was supercareful with her texts, nothing that could be used against her in a court of law. I mean CIA-level careful. Nothing in there about her being knocked up . . . I'm sorry, I meant to say 'with child.' Anyway, I've drawn blanks all around. I sent a copy of her transcripts over this morning and was just discussing it with Special Agent Hoffner here."

Lucas had some news of his own on Delmonico. "Jennifer Delmonico's supervisor—Lorne Jacobi—called me back. He spoke to Delmonico's mother and she *was* seeing someone. The mother didn't know who, only that he was older, a widower, lived on the Upper East Side, and made her laugh a lot."

Russo's glass eye seemed to dilate when he said, "That's it? Older? Widower? Upper East Side? Funny? Shit, I'm an older widower on the Upper East Side and I'm hilarious." Russo smiled, and it made him appear as if he were letting the crazy out of the bag. "Like *really* funny." He shook his head. "Us short guys never get the chicks."

Lucas stared him down. "Are you coming back to the conversation we were having any time soon?"

"Sorry. I forgot—no downers, no frowners." Russo's smile faded away.

Whitaker said, "What about those two guys who tag-teamed her on the bridge?"

Hoffner shook his washing-machine-sized head. "We ran their faces through every database we have on file, from the military to the Department of Corrections to Costco, and they don't exist."

Lucas put his attention back on Russo and held out his hand. "Let me take a look at Delmonico's phone records, and I'll tell you if I see anything."

Russo laughed and said, "There's almost twenty-two thousand calls in here; you're going to be reading for a month. And you still won't be able to remember shit."

Whitaker smiled and said, "Detective Russo, are you a betting man?"

Lucas took the printouts from Russo and went to an empty desk at the edge of the cubicle neighborhood and sat down. He could do this digitally, but the time it would take to cue it all up would probably be longer than simply flipping through it.

As careful as people thought themselves, they always left something behind in the way of binary bread crumbs. And probability dictated that Jennifer Delmonico would be no different.

The files went back two years, which was a good way to build a profile of her call habits, with a total log size of 21,131 separate transactions, slightly tilted toward outgoing over incoming at 11,301 and 9,830, respectively. Besides the calls, there was a list of 5,800 text messages that were cross-indexed to transcripts that weren't included.

Lucas took a breath, removed his sunglasses, closed his eyes, and let himself slip into that place that always made sense.

And he was drawn in. To the pages. To the lines of numbers. Where everything worked as it was supposed to and there were no errors, or expectations. Questions or doubts. Just absolutes.

The idea of unique time stopped and he disappeared.

. . .

Hoffner was gone when Lucas came back.

Russo checked his watch and said, "Twelve minutes, eleven seconds." But there was no missing his curiosity.

"Learn anything?" she asked, and Lucas could hear that she was in show-off mode.

But he didn't give her the chance to win whatever wager she had going with Russo; he just said, "Come on," and headed for the elevators.

"Where are we going?"

"Back to the Manhattan Psychiatric Center." Lucas hit the button with a green finger. "Over the past two years, Dr. Matthias Vaughan called Jennifer Delmonico forty-one times. All on Wednesday afternoons."

57

Wards Island

The pavement outside once again danced in the rain as they passed the toll cameras on the Robert Kennedy Bridge. Whitaker piloted and Lucas rode shotgun, which relegated Russo to the back, which had the unintended consequence of reminding Lucas of his son Damien every time the detective asked a question.

Lucas was looking beyond the rain, ignoring the macro while his processor chewed on the micro. He took a sip of coffee and had mixed emotions about travel mug manufacturers effectively harnessing the laws of thermodynamics when he inadvertently seared the lining of his mouth.

Russo said, "Bullshit. There's no way you memorized twenty thousand calls."

Lucas shrugged. "It was twenty-one thousand one hundred and thirty-one calls." But he wasn't thinking about numbers; he was thinking about Vaughan. And how he was now mixed into this thing.

Russo snickered. "I stared at those things all night and put them through five different spreadsheets. You can't learn shit in twelve minutes."

"It was the extra eleven seconds that did it."

Whitaker readjusted her mirror and looked up at Russo. "You have the call log on your phone?"

"In my email."

"Pick a call. Give him the time and date."

Russo took out his phone and clicked up the information as if this were all a huge waste of time. After thumb scrolling for a few seconds, he nodded unenthusiastically. "November twenty-four, a year ago. Six twenty-two P.M."

Lucas had no idea where the number had been stored, but it floated to the front of his consciousness. "Bellamy Dry Cleaners. The call lasted for two minutes, thirteen seconds. It's listed nineteen times in the data set. The first time it was encountered was May eleventh, the previous year, at eight oh seven A.M. That call lasted ninety-one seconds."

Russo was silent for a few moments as he vigorously scrolled back and forth to get to the relevant places. When he looked up, his glass eye almost fell out. "Holy motherfuckin' shitcakes."

Lucas was still staring out the window at the rain when he said, "The call immediately before that one was to her babysitter, and lasted three minutes, eleven seconds, and that number appears seventy-two times in the log. The following call was to her sister in Connecticut, and lasted ten minutes nine seconds. She called her sister twice a week and her sister called her three times a month on average—a pattern that was broken only four times in two years on the sister's end." Lucas gave Russo the numbers for both the babysitter and the sister.

Russo said, "That is . . ." He paused, then smiled. "Have you ever thought about going to Atlantic City?"

Still keeping her attention on the road, Whitaker held her hand back over her shoulder, as if balancing an invisible tray. Russo took his wallet out, thumbed through his bills, plucked out a hundred, slapped it into her palm, and said to Lucas, "How do you do that?"

Lucas took another sip of molten caffeine magma, swallowed, and shrugged. "I have no idea."

"Well, do you have any ideas about why we're going to see this Dr. Vaughan guy?"

"I'm hoping that he can lead us to some sort of a hub where these people are connected."

Russo jabbed his *World's #1 Ex-Husband!* mug through the seats. "The victims or the killers?"

"Vaughan was seeing Ira Alan White as a patient. It's possible that Jennifer Delmonico was also a patient. If that's the case, he was treating both a victim and a perp, which makes him the only connection we've found so far. But it's possible he only knew Delmonico professionally, as a fellow doctor, which might make him useful from another perspective."

"Wanna know what I think?" Russo asked.

Russo was waving the mug around between the seats and Lucas was tempted to yank it away and throw it out the window. "Enlighten me."

"I think that we're gonna find out that Vaughan was boinking Delmonico. That's why they talked so much."

Lucas turned back to the world outside. "Anything is possible."

Whitaker signaled onto the 278 West for the second time in as many days.

"Maybe it's some kind of secret cult or something!" Russo smacked his mug. "The Doctor Death Club. And the first rule of Doctor Death Club is that you don't talk about Doctor Death Club! The second rule of Doctor Death Club is that you don't talk about Doctor Death Club! Which would explain why Trina Moncrieff jumped off the balcony; you can't ask a corpse any questions."

Denise Moth had said that they wouldn't be able to figure things out if no one would talk to them, which made Russo righter than he knew. "Stop being ridiculous. All I'm saying is that there is a unifying geometry to all the killers we've found so far. They all have the same habits, which they did not develop independently of one another."

"So they know one another?"

"So far I can't find anything to suggest that they might."

Russo said, "You mean *we*?"

"No. I don't."

Russo leaned forward, between the seats, and Lucas could smell the fruit punch (or whatever that was) and vodka on his breath. "For a guy who's taking all the credit for not having any answers, you are asking a lot of questions."

"The only way to get the right answers is to ask the *correct* questions, and at this point I can't even begin to do that. The data we do have support no conclusions; we're still missing too much information. Or I'm just not seeing it."

Russo once again said, "You mean *we*?"

"No, I don't."

Russo opened his mouth to say something, but Whitaker cut him off with, "Don't waste your breath."

Whitaker pulled the SUV through the final turn on the ramp and they were swallowed by the shadow of the bridge as they headed south on Central Road, toward the psychiatric center.

The island had the same East Bloc closed-city feel to it today, and Whitaker didn't bother with the loop around Hell Gate Circle this time; she just cut into the parking lot and everyone got out of their respective doors.

Russo stopped and looked up. "You know, I understand that these places help people, but why do they have to make them look like prisons?"

Whitaker pointed at Lucas. "Yesterday, Dr. Page suggested that they make them look like giant Mickey Mouses. Or is that Mickey Mice? Mices?"

Russo slapped him on the back a little too hard. "I like that idea."

"Too bad, because I never said that. I'm completely fine with them looking like what they are—institutions."

Russo threw his arms in the air. "Your problem is that you're not embarrassed of the jerk that lives inside." His exasperation converted to a smile. "Which is both refreshing and disheartening."

Lucas walked off toward the entrance. "Too bad, I'm aiming for *practical*."

They went through the same sign-in procedure as yesterday, and both Whitaker and Russo relinquished their side arms—Whitaker her Glock, Russo his SIG Sauer. The detective followed the semiautomatic with a small revolver. When he pushed it across the counter, he gave Lucas his squirrelly smile and said, "That's my just-in-case piece."

"Just in case what?"

"If I knew, I'd call it that."

Lucas took his pass and headed for the elevators.

They took the same elevator car as yesterday, but this time it smelled heavily of the same disinfectant that had wafted off Vaughan's sofa. But it was riding on an undercurrent of a sour organic sub-odor that Lucas tried to ignore.

"So how are we doing this?" Russo asked.

Whitaker said, "Vaughan likes Dr. Page."

Russo sounded surprised when he said, "Really?"

"He even had him sign a book the last time we were here."

Russo turned to Lucas, obviously impressed. "You wrote a book?"

"Five, actually."

"What were they about?"

"About four hundred pages."

"With pictures?" Russo waved his mug at Lucas. "Come on, what were they about?"

"The pointlessness of trying to assign meaning to the universe; how science can be used to make better decisions in a world filled with misinformation; how science is misinterpreted by the scientifi-cally illiterate to serve illogical arguments. That kind of stuff."

"Oh, airport reads."

Lucas dead-eyed him and Whitaker smiled into her hand.

They were once again greeted by Wallace behind the bulletproof glass and they all held up their passes. He had moved on from Hem-ingway to Brontë's *Wuthering Heights*, which was a perfect choice for today's weather.

Whitaker said, "FBI and NYPD. We're here to see Dr. Vaughan. He's not expecting us."

Wallace nodded at the south wing and said, "You know where it is," once again exposing a single gold incisor.

As opposed to their weekend visit, the floor was now a humming hive of patients on the move.

As last time, Dr. Anderson was waiting for them in the hallway in front of the office, looking like she smelled of cookies and had cat treats in her pocket. "Dr. Page, Special Agent Whitaker, nice to see you again," she said, sounding like an emissary from Munchkin Land.

"We apologize for the short notice and promise not to keep Dr. Vaughan very long."

She looked at her watch. "Your timing is perfect. But he only has about ten minutes until his next appointment. If you need more time, I can shuffle it by a few minutes, but we're very busy on Mon-days with all the group sessions and assessments."

Lucas held up his hand. "We promise to be quick."

They were once again chaperoned through the small outer office to Dr. Vaughan's sanctum.

Vaughan came out from behind the slab of mid-century teak, this time with his arms wide as if meeting old friends. "Dr. Page, Special Agent Whitaker." He shifted focus to Russo and his eyebrows went up. "And the NYPD?"

He was once again assembled out of conflicting data points—today it was an aubergine suit that had to be either Etro or Paul

Smith judging by the unconventional fabric, a Pearl Jam T-shirt, and checkered Vans. His hair was pulled into a ponytail held by a hammered sterling clasp, and a big Navajo squash blossom necklace hung over the T-shirt.

Lucas extended his prosthetic. Once again, Vaughan shook with both hands, and this time his wrist was fitted with a bunch of bead and string bracelets like the kind Lucas's kids made at summer camp—the Generation Alpha version of the macaroni necklace. "Dr. Vaughan, we appreciate you taking the time to see us again."

Lucas had just finished thanking Vaughan when Russo inserted himself into the space between them. "Hey, Dr. Vaughan, nice to meet you. I'm Detective Russo with the Nineteenth."

Vaughan and Russo went through greetings, and the psychiatrist said, "It is rare I get a visit by representatives of the FBI, the NYPD, and Columbia University all at the same time," he said, his eyes locking on Russo for a few ticks of the clock.

Lucas corrected Vaughan with, "Once again, I am here under the auspices of the FBI."

Vaughan turned away from Russo and nodded as if greeting a visiting dignitary. "Of course. My apologies." He once again gestured to the sofa as he took up position in the industrial armchair. But not before pointedly checking the multi-colored Swatch chronograph he was wearing—a marked change from the gold Rolex of yesterday. "So, what brings you back here?" Once again, he had a gentle smile that made it easy to understand how people could tell him their secrets. "I assume you have questions about Ira White's file. You can always call—I know you are no doubt very busy." He stopped, and swiveled his big bushy head toward Lucas. "But first, how is your wife?"

"She's doing well, thank you."

"Good. Good. That's what counts."

Lucas focused on the little fertility goddess on the edge of Vaughan's desk. "Did you know Jennifer Delmonico?"

If Vaughan had a surprise mechanism, it was disengaged. "Of course. We've been friends—or we *were* friends—for years. I think I mentioned her yesterday." He stopped and looked up at Lucas. "Yes, I am certain that I mentioned I lost a friend to mental illness last week."

"Well, we're investigating her murder."

"I . . . I thought she . . . committed suicide."

Lucas aimed an alloy finger at Russo. "Detective Russo has upgraded it to a murder investigation. And it's tied into the attack on my wife."

Which did trigger his surprise response, and he looked at Lucas with an expression that covered a range of emotions that all went on behind his professional calm. "I don't know what to say. I'm sorry. I assume that you feel I can help somehow, but like I said, and I'm sure your people at the FBI saw in the file, Ira White never gave me *any* reason to suspect that he was a danger to anyone. Do you think he killed Jennifer Delmonico?"

"No."

Whitaker took out the photographs and lined them up on the coffee table, their orientation directed at Dr. Vaughan. "Do you know any of these people?" she asked, and lined up shots of Albert Hess, Denise Moth, Freddie Mercury, and his friend in the sunglasses.

When Vaughan leaned forward, he looked like a bison going to take a drink. He scanned the images and nodded. "Yes," he said, and pointed at the photograph of Denise Moth. "This woman. I believe her name is Moth—I can't recall her first name. I was slated to be an expert witness at her trial, but I was never called. I interviewed her for three hours. She was arrested for attempted murder. She tried to kill a—oh my God—" Vaughan froze, and looked up at Lucas. "Doctor."

58

"That's why you are here." Vaughan's big bison head was immobile as he lined everything up. "I'm a link between Ira White and Denise Moth—and they are both accused of trying to murder doctors." There was no denial, only cold realization.

Russo, not one to ignore terrible timing, said, "Were you fucking Jennifer Delmonico?"

Vaughan didn't sound defensive when he said, "What does Jennifer's death have to do with two attempted murders?" And then the third lock clicked into place and shock filled his features. He looked up and all the color was gone from his skin. Even his hair looked like it had lost pigment. "If Jennifer Delmonico was murdered, that makes *three* doctors you are inquiring about. Am I to assume that there's a fourth?"

Lucas hadn't wanted to open this up, but Vaughan was no more likely to spill this to the news than they were. He was bound by doctor/patient confidentiality and, if he had any common sense, a duty to remain employed. Because if any of this got out, the newspapers would cobble everything together into a very ugly narrative—true or not.

"So?" Russo asked. "Were you? Fucking her, that is."

Vaughan had used up most of his emotional reserves, but he still had a little in the tank, and he looked at Russo like he had just defecated in the planter by the door. "That's a terrible thing to ask."

"I apologize." Russo gave one of his many smiles, and it was hard to tell if he was truly sorry, or just fucking with the psychiatrist. "Were you and Jennifer Delmonico having an affair?"

"We were friends." He looked upset, which did not appear to be an emotion that came easily to him.

Russo cranked up that weirdo smile of his again. "So if I check credit card records and follow up with hotel bills and put those against phone records, I'm not going to find that you two were *neuken in de keuken*?"

"I appreciate your directness, Detective Russo, but no."

"Are you married?"

"I'm a widower." He smiled wistfully and it wasn't hard to see that he slipped into a happier time.

"When did you last see Jennifer Delmonico?"

"Maybe a week ago. Three days before her death. We had lunch."

"How did she seem?"

"She seemed fine."

"What did you two talk about?"

Vaughan was staring straight into Russo. "What do friends talk about over lunch? Work. Life. The usual topics. Did she mention that she was considering jumping in front of a car? No. Did she say she was nervous because someone had been following her or calling and hanging up? No."

"Was she in a good mood? A bad mood? Happy? Stressed? Preoccupied?"

"I told you, she seemed fine. Nothing appeared to be off—and I'm trained to see if things are off, Detective."

"Did you know she was having an affair?"

Vaughan was silent for a bit. Then he nodded. "Yes, I did."

"Can you tell us anything about the man she was seeing?"

He shook his head. "I asked once, but she didn't want to talk about him. I respected her privacy. I don't know his name, or where they met, or how long they were involved."

"And you were under the impression that she committed suicide?"

"It wasn't an impression—*that's what I was told.*"

"By whom?"

"Her mother. She and my wife were friends."

"One more thing." Russo gave Vaughan one of those goofy lopsided stares that Lucas knew threw most people off their game. "During your lunch, did Dr. Delmonico mention that she was pregnant?"

All the relaxed nonchalance dropped out of Vaughan's body language and his features went brittle. He opened his mouth, then closed it. And shook his head. "I'm sorry I couldn't be of more help." Then he rose, and pointed at the door.

59

The Bronx

It was coming down as snow but quickly converted to rain, forcing Whitaker to forego her usual Ricky Bobby vehicular performance art in deference to safety. But Lucas had to make a conscious effort not to instinctively reach for the holy shit handle—some habits are easier to develop than unlearn.

After their reconnaissance mission with Russo, they had dropped him off at his precinct, then pulled a U-turn, and headed up here. Albert Hess's house was a little three-bedroom/one-and-a-half-bathroom that looked scripted by Hollywood as the archetypical New York sitcom suburban dwelling, complete with red brick, white siding, and shutters. A single FBI van was in the driveway and a local police cruiser was parked on the street, two cops in the front seat staring at their phones, the engine running and wipers on.

The bureau had taken the place apart, and any and all relevant material had been carted to the various departments. But there hadn't been much, and what there was had provided no answers at all.

When they entered the house, two FBI agents were in the living room, a heavyset man who introduced himself as Corbett, and a short, thin woman named Radcliffe. Both sat on the sofa looking at their phones and neither got up to shake hands.

A small man who clocked out in his late sixties or early seventies came through the kitchen door at the back of the house, holding a mug. He wore red corduroy pants and a plaid flannel shirt that were both at least two sizes too large for him—the cuffs on each were rolled and the sleeves still went to his knuckles. He had gray hair combed straight back, so thick it could have been upholstered, and Lucas caught himself trying to see the tacks holding the fabric down. There was no missing his resemblance to Albert Hess.

The little guy came forward, the cuffs on his pants *zheek-zheek-zheek*ing on the carpet. He looked down at Lucas's hand, then up at his face, then took a sip from his mug. "I'm Tommy Hess, Albert's brother."

"I'm Dr. Page; this is Special Agent Whitaker. We're with the FBI. I'm sorry for your loss."

Albert eyed him for a moment before, "Ah, yes, the man he wrote the letter to." Tommy stared at Lucas as if he, too, was searching for answers about his brother. "We weren't close." Tommy shrugged. "Not for the last five years." He tilted his mug toward them. "Coffee?"

"That would be great."

Whitaker shook her head. "I'm good. Thank you."

While Tommy went to the kitchen, Lucas began his walk-through.

He was immediately struck by an inherent weirdness in the home. It took a few rooms to identify the root cause—at first glance, it was implied that human beings lived there, but only until you started to look for the personal details behind the set dressing. The place felt like one of those rooms at Ikea where everything from the fruit to the television were vacuum-formed fakery. There were no personal touches, and what was there painted a portrait of a man intent on dying with his secrets.

Lucas scanned the inventory sheets detailing the items that had been taken back to the office and there wasn't anything of evident value in the lot. Even the bedroom nightstand had been missing the medication and personal doodads usually present for a person who was elderly, sick, or both.

But very few people were true minimalists, and if he looked around Lucas saw that a lot of things had been removed in the not-too-distant past.

There was no computer. No cell phone. Not even an address book, which made no kind of practical sense for someone who owned neither a cell phone nor a computer.

Lucas knew that there *had been* an address book, or a cell phone, or a computer—or all three—and they were now gone.

Lucas called Whitaker over. "There is a lot missing."

Whitaker nodded. "The team says he scrubbed the place. Which isn't uncommon."

"For criminals or people who are terminally ill?"

"Both, I suppose."

The library was the one place that Albert Hess seemed to exist. Maybe because by the time he got around to it he had been too weak to schlep boxes of books to the curb or donation center or wherever the rest of his life had ended up. He had been big on non-fiction with a focus on biographies. There were a few books on science, but they were pop market books, not academic treatises. All of the titles had been read, but some were sticking out a little, a sign that the bureau people had tossed the shelves, shaking out the pages—standard procedure that, most of the time, ended up netting nothing of value except the occasional memento photo that had been forgotten.

The basement was unfinished and contained an ancient oil furnace, a wall of plywood shelving, and a small workshop that held little more than a single toolbox, one handsaw, and a coffee can full of mismatched screws and nails. The shelves held a few empty boxes marked *X-mas Decorations* in a floral cursive and *Camping Gear* in crooked uppercase block letters, but that was it. Judging by the dust rings, the rest of the crap had been jettisoned relatively recently.

Back upstairs, Tommy was in the kitchen finishing up Lucas's mug of coffee. There was a book on entomology on the table. When Lucas walked in, he looked up but didn't say anything and Lucas saw the family resemblance again.

"Cream? Sugar?"

"Black is perfect," Lucas said, and gratefully accepted the Coney Island tourist mug. "Thank you."

Tommy rolled up his sleeves another turn and looked up at Lucas. "Please excuse my clothes; they belonged to Albert—I'm from California and I'm not used to this weather anymore. I flew in on short notice and thought I'd have time to pick up a few things, but that all went sideways when the FBI showed up."

There was a photo on the fridge of Albert Hess at a restaurant with a group of friends—four people of similar age. There were a few hoisted beers and a neon sign in the background under a moose head. Lucas tapped it with his knuckle. "That's how you need to think of your brother." Hess looked healthier in the photo. More alive. Or at least less sick.

Tommy looked up from the coffeemaker and shook his head. "I'm glad he had *some* friends."

The coffee was excellent. "This is great."

"I own a string of coffee shops; it's the one thing I take seriously. Well, that and good weed." He smiled. "California, what can I say?"

Lucas kept staring at the photograph on the fridge, and even when he was healthy and alive Albert Hess looked like he wasn't having any fun—not even at an event that had meant enough not only to record but also to put up on the fridge. His smile looked forced, like one of those journalist-who-took-a-wrong-turn-in-the-Middle-East hostage photos that made the rounds on the news every couple of years. "So you came out to help Albert?"

"Help?" Tommy sat back down at the table, marked his spot in the insect book, and rubbed the bridge of his nose. "It's funny, I hadn't heard from Al in five years. At all. Not a Christmas card. Not a text. He didn't even call me when Sherry died. Then, four days ago, he calls to tell me he's dying." Tommy paused and looked into his mug as if the coffee held answers to the unanswerable. "He said he had a week, maybe two, and would I come out to say good-bye. I got a flight three hours after his call. He was already in care when I arrived. He left a key for me in the mailbox along with a note."

"What did it say?"

Tommy shrugged again. "Absolutely nothing of import." He took a piece of paper out of his pocket and handed it to Lucas. "That's it. Well, a photocopy anyway—your people have the original."

It was a single Post-it with three short lines of handwriting in a cursive script that matched the letter Hess had written Lucas the morning he had died, but it was stronger, and didn't fade out in the middle of words.

Tom, thanks for coming. My will is in the safe—the combination is the last two digits of Mom's birth year, the date of the month you were born, and the last two digits of the address we lived at when you graduated college. Al.

Like his confession, it was bare bones, and missing even the hint of a personality. Lucas flipped it over to see if there was anything on the back. There wasn't.

Tommy said, "How do you like that? We don't talk in five years and that's what I get as a good-bye—'thanks for coming.'" He stood up and put his mug in the sink. "I'm surprised it didn't say: 'So long and thanks for all the fish.' Jesus. I have no idea why he asked me to make the trip. All of this is a little overwhelming, not to mention pretty goddamned awful. That poor family, losing a mother, a grandmother. Not only do I not get to connect with my brother on his deathbed, but I find out that he's a murderer.

"It's funny, when Al asked me to come out I thought that maybe we'd talk a little. Figure out what went wrong. We were raised to believe that blood means something, you know? But he wasn't interested in talking about *anything*. He didn't ask about my kids, and when I tried to tell him, he just waved it away, like it was a nuisance.

Which I guess I understand, considering what happened to him. So I stopped trying—I mean, he was dying, so it's up to him what he wants to talk about, right? I didn't want to bring up any things that brought him more pain."

"Cancer isn't easy. Not even when it is."

"It wasn't just that. His wife's death was the last in a long line of bad exclamation marks in his life, you know? That's pretty much when he fell off the face of the earth. I tried to keep in touch but—"

Lucas recognized the rhetorical *What was I supposed to do?* built into the question. "And the money he asked you to bring to him?"

"I wanted to stay out there, near the place he was at, but he told me he wanted someone at his house, just in case." He looked around the kitchen. "Just in case *what*? There's nothing here worth stealing. And no one has come by with casseroles or booze. Then the next morning he calls and tells me that there's a stack of money under the plywood floor of the shed and I need to bring it to him immediately. I asked him what for, and he told me it was none of my business— exact words 'none of your business.' How's that?"

"And you took it out to him?"

Tommy looked at Lucas across the table. "I cabbed it down. I knew something was off, but I didn't suspect that he had *murdered* someone. He wouldn't even go fishing with our dad when we were kids because he was afraid that the hooks hurt the fish. He wouldn't play the game Operation because the guy's eyes were open and he was worried about hurting him. Remember that game?" He shook his head. "Just look at the backyard—there has to be fifty bird feeders out there. I can't see him killing anything, let alone *anyone*."

"Does the name Arna Solomon mean anything to you?" As soon as it was out Lucas realized that he had asked that same question to too many people over the past four days and he wondered if maybe, just maybe, he was looking at this entire thing through the wrong end of the telescope.

"The woman he killed?" Tommy shook his head. "I've been

wracking my brain about that one for three days. But like I said, we hadn't talked for years. There's no one I would recognize from his life, not even his best friend—if he even had one."

Lucas took the photograph of Hess and his friends at a bar off the fridge and turned it toward Tommy. "He had some friends. And he thought enough of them to put this up."

There was a date on the back—November 24 the previous year. Lucas was about to put it back on the fridge when it hit him.

November 24. The previous year. Almost exactly twelve months ago.

"Fuck," he said.

Tommy leaned forward. "Did you say 'fuck'?"

Lucas yelled, "Whitaker!" a little too loud.

She came in with her hand on her holster. "You okay?" But she wasn't watching Lucas; her hand was on her holster and she was eyeing Tommy Hess as if he were a paper silhouette tacked up to a wall.

Lucas held up the photograph.

Albert Hess stared back, an untouched pint of beer in his hand, everyone else at the table smiling. Lucas recognized the look of disinterest—it was similar to his the night Erin had taken a photo of him and Neville and Dove at the fundraiser. He didn't *want* to be there—he *had* to be there. "There was a photograph on Trina Moncrieff's fridge that I put into an evidence sleeve. It went to the office. Find it. Her and her husband having drinks with another couple in a bar. There was a television on in the background. Have Hoffner send us a scan—front and back."

60

They sat in the SUV in front of Albert Hess's house as the snow gained a little traction with the colder temperatures and was now coming down in lazy clumps that were melting on the windshield and street, but sticking to the lawn and trees. They were waiting for the email from Hoffner to come in.

Three minutes, sixteen seconds later, it did.

Lucas snatched the tablet away from Whitaker before the notification chime died out and snapped the message open. He retrieved the photo, and blew it up to full screen, then placed it on the dash.

Trina Moncrieff and her husband, Darrel, smiled back from the grave, drinks in their hands, smiles on their faces, breath in their lungs, and friends by their side.

Lucas reached out and expanded the image with his original thumb and forefinger, zooming in on the television.

"What's that?" he said.

"Looks like a soccer game. Except a stickler like you will call it football. Why?"

"When was this photograph taken?"

She shrugged. "I don't know."

He flicked the screen and the tablet shifted on the wide leather dash. "That's Brazil and Egypt. When did they play?"

Whitaker fired up Google. "February eleven, three years back. In Qatar."

"February eleventh, three years ago." He shook his head and smiled. "How did I miss this?"

Whitaker was examining him like he was speaking gibberish. "Miss *what*?"

Lucas picked up the photograph that had been on Albert Hess's fridge and flipped it over. He pointed out the digital time stamp on the back. "This."

She took the picture, checked the date, and shrugged. "November twenty-fourth? So what?"

Lucas snatched the picture out of her hand and placed it on the dash beside the photograph from Moncrieff. "February eleventh, three years back; November twenty-fourth, last year."

"Okay. They're the dates that Albert Hess and Trina and Darrel Moncrieff went out for drinks with their friends. What am I missing?"

"On February eleventh, three years back, Dr. Leonard Ibicki died of an accidental overdose at his cabin upstate." Lucas remembered something that Neville Carpenter said less than a week ago, at the Armory fundraiser. "November twenty-fourth, last year, Dr. Daphne Bugliosi, urologist, got locked out on her apartment balcony and tried to climb over to the next unit. She fell thirty-two stories with her cat, Rocky. The cat survived." Lucas bucked in his seat when he flicked the screen again, and the tablet fell over. "Don't you get it?"

"No."

"Jesus Christ. Look—none of them are happy in these pictures. Not Hess and not the Moncrieffs. They didn't want to take these photos—they *had* to take these photos."

"I'm missing something."

"Hess needed to prove he was busy on the night Ibicki died—Hess is connected to him. I don't know how, but he fucking is, and *he* wanted Ibicki dead. And the Moncrieffs needed to have a record of where they were on the night that Bugliosi died, because *they* wanted her dead. These aren't their friends—they're alibis."

"Which means what?"

"Which means we now know how this thing is put together." He looked up and realized that he was no longer tired. "And knowing how something is put together makes it much easier to take apart."

61

"It's revenge. Every fucking last one of them." Lucas was so keyed up that he wasn't bothered by Whitaker's velocity. In point of fact, he wished she would speed up so they could get to Federal Plaza. "Petty juvenile one-dimensional *I should have seen it* Agatha Christie revenge."

"How did we miss it?"

"Because we've been trying to find the link between the killers we have and their known victims—links that don't exist, and can't be found."

"What about the other murders? Hoffner's been sending agents out on a rotating basis since they opened this investigation last Friday."

Lucas was still marveling at the simplistic brilliance of the way this was put together. "That's just it—it's a fool's errand. Take Dr. Paul Ho. He's the pediatrician who committed suicide in his garage. Hoffner's people found an anomaly—he had booze in his system, but he was a known teetotaler. So Hoffner rightfully assumed that someone put a funnel in Ho's mouth, filled him up with vodka, then put him in his car and fired up the engine. Hoffner then looks at the victim's history, looking for anyone who might wish the good

doctor harm, and sees that a family named Crenshaw spent years su-
ing him for wrongful death—they had a grandfather who died, and
something about the case meant that they didn't collect life insurance.
They fought Ho in court for six years and eventually lost. Hoffner's
people interviewed everyone in the Crenshaw family. And each and
every one of them had a bulletproof alibi—they were all in Phoenix at
a resort when Ho died. So Hoffner's people scratch them off the list,
and move on. But that's just it—the Crenshaws probably *are* responsible for Ho's murder, but someone else committed it for them."

"This seems overly complicated, not simple."

Lucas shook his head and nodded. "That's the true beauty of
simplicity—sometimes it takes a while to see it."

"So who did kill Ho?"

"I don't know. But it's someone that doesn't have any sort of a
motive."

"But Hess really did kill Solomon?" Whitaker sounded confused.

"We *assumed* that Moncrieff and her husband had a motive to kill
Dove Knox; we *assumed* that Hess had a motive to kill Arna Solomon; we *assumed* that Denise Moth had a motive to kill Dr. Ibicki;
we *assumed* that Ira Alan White had a motive to go after Erin. So we
looked for their motives."

"But there weren't any." It was expressed as a statement but
meant as a question.

"Whoever organized this—and believe me, someone has most
definitely organized this—removed the one sacrosanct element that
has been present in absolutely every non-random murder in the history of our species—motive. Motive is the fuel that keeps the whole
equation up in the air."

"But Hess said he had a motive and it was none of our business."

He reached into his pocket and pulled out the copy of the confession that he had been carting around out of morbid curiosity.
"Listen—

"Dr. Page:

"I killed Arna Solomon.

"The money I took from her briefcase should be all the proof
you need to know that boy didn't kill her.

"The motive is none of your business.

"Albert Hess"

Whitaker shook her head, hit the index, and pulled around a taxi. "And he mentions the motive—the one you say he *doesn't* have."

"He doesn't say: '*My* motive is none of your business'—he says: '*The* motive is none of your business.' Because *he* didn't have a goddamned motive! Tranter in Forensic Linguistics thought that he wrote '*The* motive' instead of '*My* motive' because he could not accept responsibility. Which never made sense to me because the first line in the confession is that he killed Solomon. He wasn't trying to escape responsibility; he was being factual. There *was* a motive; it just wasn't *his*. The guy was a teacher, and meaning was important to him."

Whitaker was no longer looking at him like he had forgotten to take his anti-psychotic medication. "If this is true, then Russo was correct with his Doctor Death Club idea."

"I know." He hated the idea of Russo out-thinking him.

"So to find out who killed Ibicki for Hess, all we have to do is figure out who wanted Solomon dead? They traded murders?"

"No. Probably not."

"Jesus!" she snapped. "Now what am I missing?"

"That's too simple. Too, I don't know—uncreative. Or too much of a straight line for whoever put this together. And probably simple enough for the FBI to pick up on. Because as we already know, they figured someone would be coming around sooner or later."

"So what are you thinking?"

"I'm thinking that we have to figure out why Albert Hess would have wanted Leonard Ibicki dead. We need a motive. And if we can come up with one, then my hypothesis is solid. And if I'm right— and I'm willing to say that it's a big *if*—then we need to figure out how these people are trading murders. Because it certainly wasn't on craigslist."

62

26 Federal Plaza

Kehoe stood in front of the wall of monitors with his hands clasped behind his back, haloed in light particles. The glow almost overpowered his presence and the effect was not dissimilar to how the Kepler telescope detected distant exoplanets by measuring small changes in a star's total light output as objects passed in front of it.

Hoffner stood to the side, looking like he had been kidnapped from a mastodon hunt and was wondering where they had put his spear.

After several long minutes of inactivity, Kehoe turned his head and said, "I assume that you have double-checked this."

"Fuck you."

Hoffner rotated his skull toward Lucas and raised an eyebrow. But didn't say anything.

Kehoe calmly said, "I'm just being thorough."

"Yeah, well, don't do that with me."

Kehoe turned back to the screen, back to the highlighted fields in the spreadsheet Lucas had cooked up, and once again disappeared into the glow. "So they're not related?"

"No."

"But they all follow the same general approach."

"Yes."

Three nights ago, Erin had asked, "So it's not a group?"

And Lucas had said, "Nope."

Then she had asked, "And it's not an individual?"

And the underlying code had dictated that it couldn't be, so he had said, "Nope," again.

But he had missed that she had given him the only possible solution that unified the conflicting information: If it wasn't a group, and it wasn't an individual, the answer was: A group. Of individuals.

Lucas stretched, taking his weight off his good leg and shifting it to his prosthetic. His spinal column unfurled in a series of centipede clicks, telling him it would soon be Tylenol Time. "Which means that we have a group of independent people with the same basic goal who have absolutely zero reason to carry out that goal other than it is the defining reason they belong to the group."

"What kind of group?"

"I don't know."

"How many in the group?"

"I don't know."

"How do they get together?"

"I don't know."

Kehoe turned his back on the screen, which put both Lucas and Hoffner in his line of sight. "Then don't you two have some work to do?"

63

Weill Cornell Medical Center

Lucas realized that he had spent an inordinate amount of time in hospitals over the span of his life—both as a spectator and participant.

"What?" Erin asked.

Even tired she looked ready to sit for a Dante Gabriel Rossetti painting.

"I was just watching you sleep."

"You never *just watch* anything. That noggin of yours is always working."

He shrugged. "It's supposed to be a feature, not a bug."

She yawned and rubbed her eye with her free hand. "How are the kids?"

"They want to come see you. They're worried that you're getting a prosthetic arm."

She laughed. "Great. What did you tell them?"

"I said that you'll be home soon and they can see you then."

She looked disappointed; she missed them. "You need rest; you look like one of those Japanese soldiers that just found out World War Two is over." But it was delivered through a smile so it wouldn't sting too much. "Or the guy who tried to put the *Kaboom!* back into the dynamite."

He wanted to smile, but he was worried that his muscles would malfunction and his eye would pop out. "I'm tired."

"Go home. Get some rest. I'm fine."

He reached out and touched her cheek with his hand. "I need to talk to you first. I think I've figured out what's going on with the case. Or cases. Or whatever you want to call the organized murder of thirty-two people. And I need your help."

She raised the mattress so she was sitting and Lucas helped her adjust the pillow behind her head.

"So you know why that man tried to kill me?"

"Revenge."

"For what? I never saw him before in my life."

"He wasn't mad at you; someone else was. Or is. I think that this is a group of people who trade their grievances—it's vertically inte-grated murder, a soup-to-nuts thing. Someone out there from your past blames you for something and Ira Alan White tried to kill you on their behalf. In exchange, I think someone else killed a doctor that he had a grievance with."

"Jesus."

"The problem was that I spent the past four days trying to con-nect Hess to Solomon, Moncrieff to Knox, White to you. But it wasn't Hess who wanted Solomon dead; it wasn't Moncrieff who wanted Knox dead; it wasn't White who wanted you dead. They traded murders. And that removed the motive, which made them invisible."

Erin's eyes had unfocused and she was no longer looking at him. "Crisscross," she said very softly.

He brushed a thick red curl of singed hair out of her face. "Like you said, it's not a group and it's not an individual; it's a group of individuals."

"What kind of people—?" And she never finished the sentence because there was no answer that would be comprehensive enough. "Wow."

"The bureau is reengineering their approach; they'll find the people responsible."

She was pulled back from wherever she had been, and looked up at him. The lightbulb over her head changed hue. "Which means I'm still in danger."

He took her hand and it was cold, but she gave his fingers a gentle squeeze.

"The agent in the hall won't let anyone in here. You're safe."

She looked up at him. "If you say so."

"Can you think of any patients you've had who might think they have a reason to come after you? Angry letters? Anything like that?" He knew that she had never faced litigation, but that didn't mean he knew every problem she had ever had with work—sometimes the little inconsequential things were the ones that came back to bite you in the ass.

"Angry letters? How the hell do you go from sending an angry letter to trying to kill someone?" She tried to shrug, but the action was cut off when her shoulder moved, and Lucas knew exactly what she was feeling and wished that he could somehow transfer the pain to his own system. "No."

"Any reprimands? Complaints? Maybe even colleagues?"

She was silent for a moment. "No."

"No angry parents? You've never been threatened?" As she was a pediatric orthopedic surgeon, her patients were all children.

"No."

"Well, someone out there thinks they have a reason and I need you to figure out what it might be."

"Luke, nothing comes to mind. Nothing sticks out. I'm not saying that I haven't had days that I wish I could do over, but none of them were because of something I misjudged or miscalculated or did wrong. You know this more than anyone—sometimes you do everything right and the whole thing goes sideways for reasons you can't even figure out in hindsight."

"Do you know a Dr. Matthias Vaughan?"

Her eyes narrowed and she mouthed the name silently before shaking her head. "Nope."

Which was the end of his questions. "Then I have nothing else to ask."

She gently squeezed his fingers again. "What's wrong?"

"I can feel my mind shifting, I'm becoming like Kehoe, trying to work out how people can benefit me. I don't like it."

"You're nothing like Brett Kehoe, Luke. He's a prick, you're not."

Lucas smiled, then laughed at that. "There are a lot of people who would disagree with you on that."

She waved his statement away. "You want to know the difference between you and Kehoe? It's simple—Kehoe is polite, but he's rarely kind; you're kind, but rarely polite." She smiled. "And that's an important difference."

"If you say so." He checked his watch, and saw that if he wanted to catch the kids before they were in bed he had to leave.

She said, "Go. Leave. Smooch the kids for me." But there was something else going on behind her smile.

"What?" he asked.

"They're going to come after me again, aren't they?"

He thought about Denise Moth, and her attempted murder of Dr. Ibicki. He survived, but only until someone else finished the job. "I'll close them down before they get a chance."

She watched him for a moment but didn't look like she was buying any of it. "Then why do you look worried?"

64

The Upper East Side

Lucas was immersed in the files he had carted home from the office. He preferred computers for dealing with data, paper when reading—and he understood that a reasonable explanation for this split had something to do with him not technically meeting the definition of "digital native."

He was digging through three inches of paper summarizing the life of one Dr. Matthias Vaughan when his phone rang and he tried not to yawn as he answered. "Dr. Page."

"Page, it's Hoffner." The praetorian sounded tired. "You were right."

The dogs lay by the hearth, but the fire had gone out. "You'll need to be more specific." Lemmy's slumber looked graceful compared to that of Bean, who was on his back at the edge of the rug, balls to the wind.

"Hess wasn't angry with Solomon. Or even *his* doctor. So we went through the usual six degrees, beginning with his wife, who died of cancer. And came up with nothing. So the analysts family-treed him and went to work. He had a great-niece who died seven years ago—his sister's granddaughter. She went in for a biopsy and the lab pathologist misread her sample. By the time it became apparent the path had made a mistake, the kid was terminal. Died at thirteen. The health-care provider settled for an undisclosed amount, but Hess's sister went into a tailspin after that. Major depression, attempted suicide. Lost her marriage. Died of cirrhosis. Understandably, Hess was very angry about it. We called his brother and it checks out."

Hoffner didn't bother sounding surprised. "You were right, it was Leonard Ibicki."

"Who Denise Moth tried to poison in a bar and who subsequently died in what the coroner declared to be an accidental drowning brought on by an opioid overdose." Lucas checked his Submariner. It was already after three in the morning. "And Moth said she didn't know Hess."

Hoffner took a line from Kehoe when he asked, "What aren't you telling me?"

"Your people are in trouble."

"How so?"

"If Hess went after a doctor that he believes wronged his great-niece, that adds a lot of potential space between the suspects and the victims."

"How?"

"Let's assume that all the cases are like Hess's—family oriented. And let's use your regular American nuclear family as our case study, which means a mother, father, and two children. Then add in all the people that spring off from that core. Grandparents—on *both* sides. Uncles and aunts. Then factor in cousins and their spouses. Friends of the family. Exes. Boyfriends and girlfriends. And pretty soon you're looking at an easy forty potential suspects *per family*. And that's only assuming the nuclear family you use as a starting point is comprised of parents and two children. Add in multiple divorces and people with six or eight children, and some will be a hundred and twenty suspects strong. Of course, some will be sixty, and others ten. But I'd say forty is a realistic number if you include two or three generations.

"The thirty-two doctors on our victims' list had an average of four-point-three malpractice suits filed against them, not including wrongful death or civil cases. Thirty-two doctors, multiplied by four-point-three malpractice suits, multiplied by forty possible suspects per dissatisfied family involved in the suit, brings you to five thousand, five hundred, and four possible suspects. And that's just using malpractice suits as the jumping-off point. If we add in another factor—say, people who feel they were screwed over by one of our doctors but *didn't* voice their anger, let alone pursue legal action—I assume that we can double that; everyone I know has a horror story about an incompetent quack. Which gives you a potential suspect gene pool of eleven thousand individuals. And you can immediately assume that one percent of those potential suspects are actual psychotic individuals, which nets you a hundred and ten crazies."

Hoffner was silent for a moment before coming back with, "Great."

"But that's assuming that I'm right."

Hoffner stayed in work gear. "What did I interrupt?"

"I'm reading the file on the psychiatrist. See if you can connect Hess or his sister to Vaughan. Or anyone else on your list of his family members."

"That won't be easy."

Which Lucas already understood. In any other profession other than law, a court order could generate a look at a client list. And from there, it would only be a matter of matching the suspects to the victims through association. But doctor/patient confidentiality protected against blanket requests—not even the federal government had the legal right to see a patient list. They could request a single name—and even then, only after providing a judge with very strong proof that it had direct bearing on a crime. "Look at tax returns— there might be some medical receipts that will corroborate his involvement."

"You think he's part of this?"

"He's definitely part of it. I just don't know if he's active, passive, or peripheral. He treated Ira Alan White, was slated to be a witness at Denise Moth's attempted murder trial, and was friends with Jennifer Delmonico—Russo is convinced they were canoodling, but that could just be wishful thinking."

Hoffner let out a sigh to demonstrate that they were expending a lot of fuel on this. "You find anything useful in the file?"

"Yes. No. I don't know. Not yet."

"Get some rest. I have people on this. Spend time with the family. You can leave this alone."

Lucas said, "No, I can't," then hung up without saying goodbye, a habit that was starting to save him a lot of time in very small increments.

After a few minutes of sitting with his own silence, he cranked out of the sofa and fed three logs onto the mat of red embers. The noise woke Bean, who looked up like he had been roused out of a dream where he was alone in a Scooby Snack factory. He eyed Lucas suspiciously for a few seconds before dropping his head back onto the floor with a heavy thud and a sigh.

Lucas knew he needed to get to bed but automatically—and stubbornly—dropped back into the sofa to continue with the file.

Like many people of his generation and class, Matthias Vaughan's life had unfolded as if the world owed him special treatment. He had been born in Los Angeles and raised in Malibu. His father had been a radio broadcaster, his mother a soap opera actress.

After graduating from Malibu High School with good, but not perfect, grades, Vaughan spent two years at a prominent East Coast prep school before shoehorning into Harvard Medical School as a legacy student—his father was a journalism alumnus and, by this point, a regular fixture on national syndicated radio.

Vaughan earned a BSC, then a doctorate from Harvard, interned at Massachusetts General, then transferred to Johns Hopkins before being recruited by the American Medical Association. His job

with the AMA was gathering data from prison psychiatry departments around the country. From there he accepted a position with
the Mountain Meadows Research Institute, a thinly disguised think
tank for the NSA. At Mountain Meadows he became the go-to man
for various special warfare departments of the US military, mostly
under the catchall of "adviser"—a term that Lucas understood to be
code for something the government didn't want advertised.

After reading the very detailed but ultimately unenlightening file
the bureau had put together, Lucas went to the Internet, where he
was able to find several academic papers.

None of which squared with the big burly man in the Joy Division T-shirt, Paul Smith socks, and perpetually caring voice who had
welcomed Lucas like an old friend.

His phone chimed with Erin's ringtone.

"Hey, baby."

"Hey yourself, Mr. Man."

"What are you doing up?"

"I was thinking about hot dogs."

"Hot dogs?"

"Yeah. The hot dogs you are going to bring me tomorrow."

"I can do that. Any specific kind?"

"*Good* hot dogs."

And he suddenly understood that their talk earlier had scared up
the monsters and she was probably calling to hear a friendly voice.
"Are you okay?"

"Lorne dropped by after you left. He's not looking good—I
think that he's more concerned about these murders than you are."

"That's why you called? To tell me Lorne is upset and you need
hot dogs?"

"I just miss you guys. And I want to come home."

"You're getting out in a couple of days."

"Three, probably."

"You want me to come back? I can sleep in the corner."

"The kids need you. How were they tonight?"

He sifted through his personal footage of the evening for something good and came up with, "Laurie opened up a Sharpie tattoo shop this afternoon, and all the kids have some very nice barbed wire. Except for Damien—he has a flaming eight ball on his forearm."

"That's exactly what I needed to hear." Her voice was distant, alone. "Now go back to bed."

"I love you."

"I know."

"All right, baby. I'll see you tomorrow. With hot dogs."

She said, "Utah, get me two," and hung up.

65

Lucas opened his eyes and Alisha was standing in the middle of the big Persian, smiling at him. She was in a little nightgown exposing the Sharpie barbed-wire tattoo and holding up his phone, which was singing, "Clowns to the left of me—"

"Mr. Lucas—phone's ringing."

He stretched and yawned. Then looked around. "How did you get out of bed?"

"Laurie helped me."

Lucas reached out and took the phone from her. "I'll take you back up."

"Can I have Lemmy and Bean?" She pointed at the dogs, who were still asleep in front of the once-again dead fire.

"Let me answer this," he said, then swiped the screen with his thumb. "Yeah?"

"I wake you?" Hoffner sounded as tired and annoyed as he had earlier and Lucas realized the guy hadn't slept.

"No." Lucas checked his Submariner. It was almost 6:00 A.M. "What's up?"

"Albert Hess visited Dr. Matthias Vaughan. They had at least one session together."

Lucas was now fully awake. "How did you find this out?"

"My people spoke to Hess's oncologist, Dr. Rathke. When Hess first started treatment, he was having a hard time. Rathke recommended he see someone. That someone was Vaughan. Rathke brought it up a few weeks later and Hess said the visit had been very productive. But Hess's medical records don't show him visiting Vaughan. Not once."

Laurie lay down and curled up on the rug with an arm over Lemmy.

"Vaughan said he didn't know Hess."

"Well, someone's lying." And he saved himself the two and a half seconds once again.

Lucas thought things through for a moment and realized that they needed to answer some of the questions that were piling up. And something that Russo said came back to him, so he picked up the phone and dialed the detective's number.

It rang three times before Russo came on, "Dave's not here, man."

"It's Page. I need a favor."

"Chicks? Amyl Nitrate?"

"Stop it."

"Just trying to be friendly."

"Yeah, well, don't."

"Fine. What do you need, Dr. Page?" Russo said, sounding very officious.

"Just be here in fifteen minutes. Don't be late." He hung up before Russo could give him any more bullshit.

66

The Upper East Side

Dr. Matthias Vaughan's expression said that he wasn't surprised to be woken up by a grumpy one-legged, one-armed, one-eyed astrophysicist with bad hair.

"Dr. Page, is everything all right?" he asked warmly. Or maybe that was rhetorically. Lucas couldn't really tell.

The psychiatrist was in a large robe that had Sgt. Pepper epaulettes on the shoulders. Beneath the robe he wore striped silk pajamas and black velvet slippers with a skull-and-crossbones motif, all of which seemed oddly fitting. But the real theater was the doctor's hair and beard. For a moment Lucas wondered if he'd slept with a plasma globe in his bed, or if the static generated by his silk pajamas while he walked over a wool carpet had created an electric charge, because he looked like he was storing sparks in his head.

Lucas said, "You and I need to talk."

Vaughan gave him a couple of barn owl blinks, then swung the door wide. "Of course. Come in."

Lucas paused beside him and made a point of shaking the man's hand with his prosthetic. "Thank you for seeing me."

"Welcome to my home." Vaughan pointed down the hall.

But Lucas was in no way prepared for what he would find inside.

The apartment wasn't a living space; it was a film set. The ten-foot walls were painted a warm velvet black that offset the objects and photographs that defined the décor. Vaughan's interest in social anthropology, and specifically its subsets of visual anthropology and ethnography that had been on display at the office, was eclipsed by his home collection. Lucas wondered how he afforded or even found some of the things on display—they belonged in museums. Or burial grounds.

As Lucas followed Vaughan down the hall to the kitchen, he was once again reminded about all the unique and unusual things hidden in the city. The hallway was decorated from floor to ceiling with photographs, mostly late-nineteenth-century gold tones of Native Americans by Edward Sheriff Curtis, an odd choice since Curtis had been notorious for tweaking costumes and adding flair to his subjects, a habit that purists and academics still faulted him over.

Vaughan led Lucas into the kitchen and it took a few moments for him to metabolize the scene. The room was a classic example of a large New York prewar remodel, with five miles of subway tile, big nickel-plated faucets, and enough Holophane fixtures to light up an airport. But what stopped him was the antique English brass and glass display case that separated the cooking area from the eating area. It was ten feet tall by ten wide, and eighteen inches thick. Whatever the piece had started its life as—probably storage for medical implements—it was now a controlled environment for a collection of shrunken human heads, each under a glass dome and neatly labeled with a tag.

Lucas stared at the wall of diminutive faces, expecting them to stare back. But they couldn't; all of the eyes had been sewn shut with cotton string tied off in very precise knots. The mouths were also sealed in the same manner. All but one of the inhabitants of the glass case looked to be South American indigenous peoples, and every one seemed to be male—although it was difficult to be certain.

Some had long hair, others short—most jet black. The few that had facial hair only exhibited sparse patches. There was a single outsider who had the red hair and bushy moustache of a European, and when Lucas leaned in to read the tag—which was stamped with the seal of a Peruvian museum—he learned that it had come from a German missionary named Hans Klopek.

It took Lucas a minute to put the faces in the case into some sort of relatable context that didn't automatically generate the word "monster." It wasn't easy.

Vaughan interrupted his moment of internal horror with, "I'm sorry. I usually warn people about . . . them. But you caught me off guard." He yawned, and Lucas half expected the signature Chewbacca mewl-roar. "Would you like some coffee?"

"Please," Lucas said, and turned away from the bodiless crowd.

"They are all very old. And none of them were killed just for their heads."

"How comforting for them."

"When Europeans discovered the Jivaro people in northern Peru and southern Ecuador, they became fascinated by their custom of taking and shrinking the heads of their enemies—they are known as tsantsas—which was a process to harness their spirits. Europeans began to trade for them as curiosities, and the Jivaro did what any enterprising capitalist would—they went from occasionally acquiring a head to becoming very proficient headhunters, turning their religious practice into a commercial endeavor."

Lucas had his back to the case, but he couldn't help feel that the eyeless dead were somehow observing him, which was an unusual feeling in that he was not the least bit superstitious. "It's called perverse incentive—when people are inadvertently rewarded for exacerbating a problem they were supposedly trying to fix. In India, during British rule, the English offered a bounty for cobra heads in order to cull the population. Industrious citizens began farming them for profit, and once the British found out, they ended the program. The now-worthless cobras were released into the wild, which had the opposite effect of the initial bounty."

Vaughan pulled a can of coffee out of the cupboard. "I only purchase true ceremonial examples."

"How ethical of you." Lucas glanced back at the case. "My wife is like that with coffee—she only buys fair-trade beans."

Vaughan turned and looked at him like he couldn't figure out if he was being insulted, joked with, or both. "Why did you come here, Dr. Page?"

"I want to know if you're the guy I'm going to be arresting."

Vaughan popped the foil seal and grabbed a filter. "Why would you be arresting me?" Even in front of the forest of human heads, being accused of wrongdoing before his first coffee of the day, he sounded at ease, relaxed, and ready to help.

Lucas took off his sunglasses and nailed Vaughan with his glass eye. "You are at the center of thirty-two homicides."

"Thirty-two murders?" His surprise had the added feature of sounding genuine. "I'm a clinical professor of psychiatry at Harvard Medical School, and an attending psychiatrist at the Manhattan Psychiatric Center, where I am also chief of their social psychiatry division. I'm a contributing editor to both the *Journal of the American Psychiatric Association* and *Social Psychiatry and Psychiatric Epidemiology*—and have published eighty professional articles and written twenty-three chapters between the two. I write and lecture widely on psychiatric research and the relationships between psychiatry and public policy. I'm a fellow of the American Psychiatric Association, and am chair of the Object Relations Institute of New York."

Lucas didn't miss a beat when he said, "And Einstein was a patent clerk; I don't get your point."

"I don't like being accused."

"And I don't like airport metal detectors; tough shit, life isn't fair."

The good doctor was silent as he took in a few deep breaths. His expression quickly neutralized, and he sounded a lot calmer when he asked, "What thirty-two murders are you talking about?"

"In the past two years, thirty-two doctors have been killed. Of the four people we have identified as murderers and would-be murderers, three of them saw you at some point in their lives. You already confirmed that you treated Ira Alan White and had a few sessions with Denise Moth in preparation as a professional witness in her trial. This morning I found out that Albert Hess—who you said you didn't know when I showed you his picture—was recommended to you by Desmond Rathke, Hess's oncologist."

Vaughan had moved back against the counter and crossed his arms. There was no missing the concentration on his face, even behind the facial shrubbery.

"And I'm betting that you know Trina Moncrieff somehow."

Vaughan stared at him for a few moments while the coffeemaker added background noise. "I have no idea who Albert Hess is. I told you, I didn't know the man. And Trina Moncrieff? No recollection whatsoever."

Lucas slipped the thick-framed Persols back on. "Albert Hess shot and killed Arna Solomon in a parking garage on Seventy-first four days back; Trina Moncrieff killed my friend Dove Knox in the Meatpacking District five nights ago."

"Of which I know nothing."

"But you *did* know Jennifer Delmonico, who was killed last Wednesday. I haven't quite figured out *why* yet—because she most definitely does not fit in with the others—but I will." Lucas decided that he was no longer interested in a coffee.

Vaughan regarded him thoughtfully for a few seconds, as if he could see through the questions to the answers. "You say this Trina Moncrieff murdered your friend and Ira Alan White tried to kill your wife." He smiled. It was a small, gentle smile that seemed loaded with meaning. "Which means that you, too, are somehow involved in this."

. . .

Russo's car was half a block down, parked in front of a hydrant, where Lucas had left him. He was staring at his phone. There was a parking ticket on the window.

When Lucas kicked the door, Russo jolted. He looked over, saw Lucas, and pushed the door open.

Lucas got in and held up his alloy hand.

Russo took the polyethylene evidence bag and an elastic from the dashboard, and momentarily glanced at the ticket now stuck to the window with rain. "Fuck," he said, before looking at Lucas's outstretched arm. "How'd it go?"

"I got thrown out."

Russo smiled as he slid the bag over Lucas's green hand. "Your life is absolute clown shoes, ain't it?"

Lucas held the bag while Russo secured it with a zip tie.

Russo opened the window and scraped the parking ticket out from beneath the wiper. It came apart and he threw the pieces onto the street and closed the window. "Fuck."

Lucas tried not to sound too irritated when he said, "Can we get going?"

He would change arms at home, and this one would go to the lab to have Vaughan's DNA sequenced, then compared against Delmonico's fetus. The FBI lab would usually handle this particular detail, but the investigation into Delmonico's death had been started by Russo, so it was still in the NYPD's wheelhouse. Having their lab do the work would knock a few hours off the administrative paperwork.

The thing was, neither a positive nor a negative match would answer any of the real questions that were the foundation of the investigation—it would simply add more.

Russo closed the window and wiped his wet fingers on his coat. "So what will all this prove?"

"That either Vaughan is telling the truth. Or lying."

Russo's face went blank as he worked the chart out. "Which might give him a motive in the killing."

Lucas was glad Russo was trying to spin all the plates; they weren't going to solve this one with baseline thinking. "It might give Vaughan a motive, but it might also give Delmonico's husband a motive. Or if the husband was seeing someone, maybe *that person* found out and thought it might jeopardize things."

And there it was.

More questions. Fewer answers.

"You think this thing is *that* complicated?"

"I *know* it's that complicated; otherwise I would have figured it out by now."

"I'm not even going to ask if you meant to say 'we.'" Russo started the car. "After you switch out arms, how about we go get some breakfast? I know a great place over on—"

"No."

Russo shook his head. "I don't know. You know, if you hadn't been born, somebody would have had to invent you."

"Yeah, well, good luck with that."

67

26 Federal Plaza

For the first time Lucas could recall—which very possibly translated into the first time ever—Kehoe looked rough around the edges. He had showered. Shaved. And of course changed his suit and shirt (not forgetting to rotate accessories). But he resembled a baseball that had been used for a single grounder straight out of the box, then polished and waxed—the stitching was tight and the leather still new, but it was no longer perfect.

Kehoe glanced over as they strode down the hall, not even remotely in step, and said, "Page, you look a little . . . frightening," ending the *Who looks worse?* discussion Lucas was having in his head.

"You get any sleep?"

Lucas added the two hours he had fallen asleep on the sofa, only to be simultaneously woken by Alisha and Hoffner, with the two hours he had put into the bank after talking to the headshrinker in his museum of the macabre. "Loads."

"Can you think straight?"

"As long as I don't have to chew gum at the same time."

"What did you say to Vaughan?"

"Only that I see he's involved in too many parts of this thing for it to be a coincidence. And that if he has anything to say, now would be the time."

"And?"

"And he asked me to leave."

"I see."

Lucas waved it away. "It happens all the time."

"How did he appear?"

"The guy was wearing a robe with Idi Amin epaulettes, his hair looked like it had been styled with a Tesla coil, and he showed me his not-insignificant collection of shrunken human heads"—Lucas smiled involuntarily—"which was in his fucking kitchen."

"Did he look nervous?"

"I don't think it's possible to make a guy who has a collection of human heads nervous."

"Is he responsible for this?"

"I don't know. If he's guilty, he's certainly acting innocent."

Kehoe nodded as if that was the expected answer. "Our people filled in a lot of blanks last night." He slapped Lucas in the chest with the file he was carrying. "Dr. Matthias Vaughan spent a lot of time doing not-nice things for our government."

"I read some of his articles. They were couched in academic nomenclature, but he's big on experiments that manipulate social psychology." They took another hallway that would eventually get them to the operations room Hoffner was running.

Kehoe kept talking. "Well, there were some things that weren't in the file that we got from the DOJ. He helped develop enhanced interrogation techniques at Parwan Detention Facility two decades back when it was still called the Bagram Theater Internment Facility. Then, through a transfer from an unknown governmental body—most probably the NSA under directions from the CIA—he did a stint at Guantánamo Bay, working on 'special projects,' which is a term that *always* makes me nervous when used in conjunction with the word 'government.'"

Lucas was surprised by that. "How did he get the gig at the Manhattan Psychiatric Center?" It was impossible to miss the hippy frequency beeping off the guy like a radio signal.

"We don't know. He was well connected at both the DOJ and the State Department, which I again interpret as meaning the NSA and CIA. He most likely screwed up, and was sent there for penance."

"None of that assuages any of my unease."

"It wasn't supposed to; it was simply information."

Lucas now *knew* that Kehoe was tired; he was not a man given to over-explaining himself.

They got to the operations room and a junior agent opened the door for Kehoe without being asked. The SAIC nodded a thank-you, and waved Lucas in.

Kehoe headed over to the row of analysts who were sequestered against one of the walls. "I have something you need to see."

He went to Agent Mace's station. "Agent Mace, would you run through the findings that you and Special Agent Hoffner brought to my office earlier."

Mace swallowed and nodded. "Yessir. It's right here, Special Agent in Charge, sir." Mace thumped away on the keyboard. "Here it is."

Lucas leaned in, his eyes automatically going to the top of the digitized form. It was an old-school scan, and it was slightly lopsided, but it was legible and clear. It was a form specifying the cessation of artificial intervention for Denise Moth's son, Matthew.

Mace scrolled through until they arrived at the signature at the bottom and said, "It was authorized by Dr. Nellie Kozik."

Lucas felt another piece pop into its respective position: Nellie Kozik committed suicide. Four months before Denise Moth tried to kill Leonard Ibicki.

Lucas looked up and Whitaker was beside them. She held two coffees, one of which she was holding out for him. "Did I miss anything?" she asked.

Lucas said, "Nellie Kozik signed the orders to cease life support on Denise Moth's son—it was an insurance case, and the company felt there was no point in continuing care for someone who was little more than a collection of internal organs. Because of Kozik's signature, Moth's son was parted out like a Mazda."

"So we have Moth?"

"Yes."

Mace closed the form and brought up surveillance footage. "And two of our field agents found this." It was a CITGO gas station at nighttime. A thin black man was filling a jerry can at one of the pumps, beside a Toyota. "That," said Mace, "is Darrel Moncrieff. This is Highway Twenty-Seven, near Montauk, taken at eleven thirty-three P.M. the night Dove Knox was killed."

Lucas leaned in. "I know that station. It's about five miles west of the Lobster Roll."

Which meshed with Darrel Moncrieff being on the other end of the call the night Dove killed himself—threatening to burn his wife alive would have been all the incentive he needed.

Whitaker froze in the midst of taking a sip. "Holy shit, you were right."

Lucas shrugged. "I wish you'd stop being surprised by that."

68

Broadway and Howard Street

Arlo Reed and Ludwig Kling wore middle-class clothing, had middle-class haircuts, and sported middle-class watches on their wrists. There was nothing unusual, or even memorable, about the two men and, if plugged into a bell curve, they would fall right at the apex of suburban expectations straight across America. Which was not as much of an accomplishment for two clinically certified psychopaths as it would first appear.

And anyone passing them on Broadway would have been shit-stone freaked out to learn that they had murdered Dr. Jennifer Delmonico. And a lot of other people as well.

They felt safe in their anonymity because the photo stills that had been lifted from the surveillance cameras on the Brooklyn Bridge that night had all the detail of the Zapruder film—minus the color— which meant that every nondescript middle-class man in America was a potential suspect. And they considered their position at the top of the FBI's hunting list to be a hilarious distinction.

They were heading slowly up Broadway, just north of Canal Street, taking in the store windows, which were always interesting in this neighborhood. They had lunch at the Hop Kee on Mott Street— soft-shell crab with some friends (who knew them as Marv and

Dale). The crab had been excellent and they had allowed themselves two Tsingtaos each, which was unusual. They now had two hours of window-shopping on their long walk up before hitting the gym in a couple of hours. It was, in every sense of the term, a lazy day.

They were in front of a record store—which they were both surprised had not gone the way of Blockbuster—when their business cell buzzed.

Ludwig carried the phone today and he didn't bother checking caller ID—only two people had this number. "Yes?"

"You're on the clock."

"Okay."

"Today."

Ludwig checked the digital watch he had purchased in some forgotten airport gift shop an unremembered amount of time ago. "That isn't a lot of time."

"It doesn't matter. Pretend it's the old days."

It would have been better to know about this before the beer. "Who is it?"

"It's a *they*—plural, not pronoun."

"How many?"

"Two. FBI agents. A woman named Whitaker and a man named Page—Special Agent Alice and Dr. Lucas, respectively. She's black; he's a double amputee."

Ludwig never asked why because one reason was as good as another. "Accident?"

"It doesn't matter as long as they don't get back up."

"Where do we find them?"

"One of you stake out Page's place; the other should follow your favorite detective from the Nineteenth. Hit them when they're alone."

Ludwig didn't bother nodding. "It's done. But we don't have any time to plan for any finesse—it's going to be loud." He looked over at his partner. "Messy."

"I don't care." And the call disconnected.

Arlo turned away from the rack of 180-gram jazz classics in the window. "How many?"

"Two."

"When?"

"Today."

"We shouldn't have had those beers."

Ludwig waved his concerns away. "It's okay. These don't have to look like accidents."

69

Metropolitan Detention Center
Brooklyn

Denise Moth was the same unmoving paragon of stoicism as the other day, but Lucas was doing his best to pry a corner of her head open to get at the emotions hiding in the VIP room.

"You are two years into a seven-year sentence for attempting to murder Dr. Leonard Ibicki. We offered to scrub your sentence the last time we were here. And even if we don't, you come up for parole in another year. But that was before we learned that in exchange for you murdering Dr. Ibicki, someone else had to kill Dr. Nellie Kozik."

Moth was doing a pretty good job of controlling the fear and rage that had to be strobing through her system. She stared straight at him without shifting from eye to eye. She didn't even blink.

"Nellie Kozik signed the papers for the insurance company so they could legally cease providing care for your son. But it was an administrative decision, not a medical one, so it wasn't in your son's file, and we missed it. We don't even know how you found out—it's supposed to be a double-blind system. But because of her, your son was taken off of life support. I can understand how that made you feel. And a judge will understand how that made you feel. But someone killed her for you, and in exchange you were to kill Leonard Ibicki, the pathologist who misdiagnosed Albert Hess's great-niece's biopsy. You fucked that up, and Ibicki was eventually murdered by someone else. Which means that you are now part of a conspiracy. You are going to spend the rest of your life in prison along with every other asshole who signed up for your little troop."

Her eyes filled with tears, but she didn't say anything. Or move. Or even blink. The rage wafted off her like cold dropping out of a freezer.

Her lawyer, who looked less irritated to be here than last time, leaned over and whispered something in her ear from behind a cupped hand. Then he looked up at Lucas and asked, "Unless?"

"Unless she tells me everything she knows." He shifted focus back to Moth. "I want to know how she met these people. How they organize. How they pick their targets. I want names. Or addresses. Or whatever else she has." Lucas pulled off his glasses and leaned in, so that there would be no misinterpreting his offer. "These people tried to kill my wife, and I am not going to stop. You understand revenge better than most people, don't you, Denise?"

The tears were shaking loose now and her bottom lip trembled, but Lucas wasn't about to stop.

"You know that hate you have, that anger that you feel in your stomach all night like a frozen fist whenever you remember your son? I *know* that anger. I *have* that anger. But I have the federal government on the side of mine. And I am going to figure out what's going on, and I am going to close it down."

Moth's tears were streaming down her cheeks, but she didn't wipe them away. She just stared at Lucas while the monsters in her head began to disassemble the place.

She shook her head.

Her lawyer leaned in and whispered in her ear. She didn't let him finish his sales pitch; she simply shook her head once again.

Lucas stood up. "I don't know why you're doing any of this, but I hope it turns out to be worth it."

And he left her alone.

With her lawyer.

And her misery.

70

The Upper East Side

Ludwig stood at the corner of Fifth Avenue, under the superstructure of Erector set scaffolding. He had traded the suburban lifestyle fashion from his lunch in Chinatown for Upper East Side show-offery, which was a Prada jogging suit—manufactured out of something that they marketed as *Recycled Double Technical Polyester Yarn*. The outfit was made out of recycled plastic water bottles, which technically made the three-thousand-dollar price tag both an insult and a dare, which was a difficult combination to pull off in retail, and he wondered what kind of an idiot bought shit like this. But it was the perfect camouflage for this neighborhood and no one would think that he was here to take two lives.

Due to the truncated schedule, he and Arlo hadn't been able to do either research or surveillance on their targets. But that was not as unusual as it should have been—in the two decades Ludwig had spent hunting human beings, most of the jobs had been put together on the fly, with little more than a name and a photograph. Sometimes they operated with less. Like now.

Ludwig leaned against the metal structure, pretending to look at his phone. But his eyes were aimed down the street, toward the brownstone beside the French consulate. He had no idea if Page was home, or if Whitaker was on the way. In point of fact, it was possible that neither of them would present themselves and his partner, Arlo, would get to bag both of them.

The front door to the Page home opened, and a guy with two mechanical drumsticks came out.

Ludwig shifted into meat-eating mode, pocketing the phone and instinctively checking the pair of Spyderco knives. But his eyes stayed locked on target.

Something was wrong; Page was supposed to be missing one leg and one arm—this guy was missing two legs. They weren't shaped like regular feet—they looked like molded hockey sticks in bright orange. But a double amputee was a double amputee—what were the chances of two guys missing major parts living in the same place?

It had to be him.

The guy on the hockey sticks came down the steps, looked east, then west, and went into a jog, which made up Ludwig's mind for him.

Hockey Sticks kicked off in a light run. Nothing hard, just good cardio that would keep his heart rate up for however long his routine was. The weird flanges he used as legs gave him a decent spring, but how good could he be at lateral movement? Or in a fight? And even a physically typical guy was at a marked disadvantage against a knife. Never mind two. Especially in the hands of someone who knew how to use them.

Hockey Sticks passed on the opposite side of the street, stopped at the corner of Fifth Avenue, checked traffic with a sweep of his head that brought Ludwig straight into his line of vision, then headed across the intersection to the park.

Ludwig put on his hood and started after him.

71

The 19th Precinct
East 67th Street

Arlo watched the wildlife. There were police of every discernible genus on display. In all shapes. Sizes. Races and sexes. Occupying themselves with all manner of activity that had nothing to do with serving or protecting or even paying attention to the world at large. There were uniformed officers drinking coffee; plainclothesmen looking at pictures on their phones; a couple of the tactical guys in black nylon and knee pads arguing over something; three horsemen in helmets and black pants with yellow stripes from the mounted unit feeding something that looked suspiciously like Soylent Green to their horses.

But Arlo was not interested in the genus as a whole; he was waiting for a specific species—that of Detective—who belonged to the rarefied subspecies of Homicide, who was named John Russo.

Russo could lead him to Whitaker and Page.

The motorcycle Arlo was using belonged to a Chinese businessman who was currently overseas. Even if everything snafued and Arlo had to abandon the bike, it could not be traced back to him.

When—or was that *if*?—Russo came out, Arlo would shadow him until he hooked up with the targets. And if Russo didn't lead him to them, Ludwig would pick them off in front of Page's house. Because if nothing else, their two decades of working together had taught them that success was built on redundancy.

An hour into Arlo's wait, Russo came out, stopping to light a cigarette on the precinct steps. He took in a few drags before trotting down the stairs and crossing the street to a nondescript Oldsmobuick.

Russo started the car and Arlo fired up the bike.

The detective pulled out and caught the light.

Arlo was on his bumper by the end of the following block.

72

Weill Cornell Medical Center

Mindy Appelbaum had taken the Lexington Avenue Line to the 68th Street station at Hunter College. She could have opted for a line that would have delivered her closer to the hospital, but her intent had not been ease.

She left her cell phone at home. And had opted for a moderate disguise—"wear clothes that you typically wouldn't," he had suggested. But she didn't think that anyone would recognize her. Or know to look for her. Or even to suspect that she was coming.

Because, after all, she had no motive to do this. Which guaranteed her some sort of retroactive invisibility once she crossed the horizon from the before to the after. When this was over, they would have no reason to look for her, which meant they would have no way to find her. But that did not mean that her stomach wasn't clenched into a cold fist that felt like it was pinching off her blood flow.

As she walked through the entrance, she reminded herself to act as if she belonged—and she forced the action to fill her small sphere of concentration. If she looked like she belonged, no one would ask her why she was here. Or think to remember her. And with more than four thousand employees on-site at any given time, it was doubtful that anyone would.

As soon as she was inside, she unbuttoned her long coat, exposing the blue scrubs that were as ubiquitous to the hospital as the identification badge she wore—she had purchased the outfit from a uniform supplier online and made the ID herself, using a printer and laminating machine at work. The finishing touch on her ID badge was a Yankees lanyard she had received as a door crasher at the home opener last April.

She tried to relax her shoulders and walk with purpose, as if she was an important person with important things to do in this important place. But in truth most of her concentration was taken up with following the colored lines on the floor that connected the various medical neighborhoods.

The institution occupied more than a full city block, but she didn't want to rush this; people who rushed made mistakes—the proof was that she was here. If the doctors hadn't rushed with Patrick, he would still be alive. In her life. And she wouldn't have been forced to become like them.

Mindy took the steps to the food court on the mezzanine to purchase a coffee. It seemed like another smart prop—everyone carried coffees. And she needed the extra few minutes to build up her courage.

After getting a *venti misto* with steamed whole milk and one sugar (which she hoped would dent the cold lump in her chest), she took off her coat and found a seat in the high-ceilinged area by the windows.

She drank her coffee, went over her plan, and told herself that she was ready for this. But even if she wasn't, she had committed, and there were no takebacks once you put your foot on the gas pedal. Besides, the whole thing had been in motion for too long at this point to make any changes. Not after the promise she had made. Or the price she had paid.

Because there had never been any real choice for her. Not in any meaningful way. She had played all the mental games involving the usual semantics and intellectual dodge ball that human beings resorted to when faced with the unthinkable. But none of it had changed her mind. Or weakened her determination. Or brought Patrick back. So she had ended up right where Destiny had decided.

To kill Dr. Erin Page.

73

Central Park

Ludwig was impressed—his target was doing pretty good for a guy using a pair of salad spoons as feet.

After crossing Fifth, he ran south to the park entrance at 72nd Street, where he cut in on Terrace Drive. From there he swung north, past the model boat pond. But it was November, and a weekday, and no one was out except a guy wearing plastic bags with a bunch of colored paper woven into his beard playing "(I Can't Get No) Satisfaction" on a beat-up harp with four strings, like an alternate version of Keith Richards's Ghost of Christmas Future.

Ludwig's curiosity had kicked in; he had never killed anyone with a disability before. Not unless he included that blind teacher in Afghanistan. But he hadn't known she was blind when he had turned off her darkness for good, which kind of made that one moot. Or at least non-applicable.

He was going to stick this guy with both blades at the same time— one at the base of his skull, the other straight through the ticker— which would blow out his pilot light instantly and permanently.

The bronze Alice in Wonderland statue ahead was one of the most popular tourist draws in the entire city. Back in the day it had always been swarmed by Asians carrying Ralph Lauren bags and firing off pictures with monstrous SLRs. These days it was a perennial favorite of the TikTok generation, who had pouted into the abyss of social media in a way not seen since Narcissus first saw his own reflection.

Spoon man cut right, zipping past the Mad Hatter, and picked up his pace as he hit the open path past the stone base of the statue, heading toward Glade Arch.

And that's when it came together—the path under Glade Arch was one of the darkest sections of the park after the Bethesda Terrace Arcade. Which was another thing that often happened with short-notice jobs—the Fates all lined up and the entire thing unfolded as if it had been scripted by an ancient prophet.

Even if someone was under the bridge when he struck, the entire interaction from knives-out to knives-in to knives-back-out wouldn't last more than the time it would take to snap your fingers. And most people didn't recognize a murder taking place right in front of them because they had no way to identify it—like that apocryphal story about the indigenous population not being able to recognize Columbus's ships when they showed up; they could not see what they had no experience with. True or not, everyone knew how that turned out.

After the bridge, Ludwig would turn west, jump Fifth, Superman his jogging suit three blocks away, and disappear into the city.

And that was all the thinking there was left to do.

The stone bridge was a hundred and fifty yards out when he pulled out the ceramic Airframe knives.

He increased his speed, slowly, so that his footsteps wouldn't echo out of time with his target; the ancient ancestral bud in the back of the human brain that had survived from the time we drank from puddles could sense some remarkable things. Ludwig had seen it kick into action too many times to discount its predictive powers—his own had saved his life twice, once in Crimea and another in Mali.

With each step, Glade Arch grew a little larger.

At fifty yards out, he adjusted his pace one final time.

Fifty yards became forty.

Forty became thirty.

Then twenty.

And ten.

He adjusted the knives in his palms, automatically positioned his thumbs on the studs.

Five yards.

He was beside the man with the prosthetic legs.

The shadow of Glade Arch swallowed them both.

Ludwig flicked the blades open.

And lunged.

74

West 72nd Street and Amsterdam

Lucas watched Russo as he did a food run at Gray's Papaya across the intersection. The place was on the wrong side of town, but since Erin had specified *good* hot dogs and since everyone concerned needed a few calories to keep the machinery running, this was serving as one of those several-birds-with-one-stone exercises. Besides, Lucas, Whitaker, and Russo needed to have a discussion aimed at synchronizing their various realities, and one place was as good as another.

Russo was at the cash register, loading up a pressed-cardboard tray with the five major food groups: grease, cholesterol, fat, salt, sugar—all with a good dose of chemical preservatives thrown in. The only things missing were defibrillators. And an insulin syringe.

Whitaker was providing Marlin Perkins commentary. "... and here we see the wild Russo in its natural habitat. Although it is far from home, it is able to locate its favorite meal, which apparently includes tube steaks and fruit drinks. ..."

Lucas and Whitaker were in Verdi Square, a tiny park diagonally across from the hot doggery. The little green space hosted the entrance to the 72nd Street subway station, which served the IRT

Broadway–Seventh Avenue Line. Several pairs of uniformed NYPD officers stood around, most near the doors of the head house.

As many feared that this was one of the last outdoor days of the year, the park was occupied by lunchtimers, many of whom sat on benches, eating from Tupperware and staring into their phones as pigeons milled about in their continual hunt for anything of nutritive value. Lucas worked on a cup of liquefied caffeine as Whitaker continued to polish her *Mutual of Omaha's Wild Kingdom* narration.

". . . this particular Russo is the rare, one-eyed version, the result of an unknown accident—or, more likely, foolish behavior—at some point in the past. Which helps to explain why it occasionally walks into lampposts and other large objects on its left side. . . ."

Lucas leaned over and added, "Judging by the egregious clothing, it also deeply affects its color coordination and pattern recognition."

Whitaker elbowed him away, and continued channeling *Wild Kingdom* from the 1970s. "Now that the Russo has secured food, it does not wait to get back to its clan to begin feeding, as evidenced by the hot dog it has begun to consume—hands-free—as it prepares to cross the busy intersection to rejoin its friends."

"We're not friends," Lucas said coldly.

Russo crossed 72nd and a wind caught one of the napkins. It lifted out of the box and sailed out over Amsterdam, where it disappeared behind a bus.

Russo, the sausage still clamped in his mouth, stepped up onto the sidewalk in front of the Capital One Bank, and did a one-point pivot to cross Amsterdam to the plot of grass and trees and benches. He looked over and tried to smile, which was a hard move to pull off with a wiener in his mouth.

Lucas didn't bother returning the smile, but he did nod back; he appreciated Russo picking up lunch.

Whitaker continued the voice-over but turned her back on Russo so that she faced Lucas. ". . . the wild Russo is known for its love of alcohol and has a penchant for unbridled optimism, the latter of which can annoy others in its group, particularly the grouchy ones."

Russo winked at Lucas, over-craned his neck to compensate for his bad eye as he checked traffic coming up Amsterdam, then began to turn back.

But the molecules of his face rearranged mid-turn.

Along with his body language.

He swiveled his head south again, began to put the box down on the hood of a car.

Lucas followed Russo's line of sight.

A motorcycle. Blowing the light. The rider lifting a pistol. Bearing down on him and Whitaker.

Lucas started to yell, to warn Whitaker, but time wouldn't let him, and he watched it all unfold in slow motion that he was unable to manipulate.

Across the street, Russo was fighting the gel that was suspending time, and he set the box down on the hood in agonizing slowness. Reached into his coat.

Whitaker was in front of Lucas, oblivious to the ballet playing out behind her.

Russo's gun arm came up.

The motorcycle pulled out, around a car, and crossed to the westernmost lane—the one closest to them—and the scream of its engine rose above the noise of the city.

Lucas tried to reach out. To grab Whitaker. To shield her. To scream.

To.

Do.

Something.

Over Whitaker's shoulder, Russo sighted in.

Acquired.

The motorcycle veered. Lurched toward them.

Whitaker began to turn.

The rider's muzzle came up. Zeroed in. And even from this distance looked large enough to take the world away.

But Russo stepped out of the gel and let loose with his SIG Sauer.

His five shots punched through the lunchtime air.

They walloped through the motorcyclist's leather and meat— *one, two, three, four, five* times.

He shuddered.

Lost control of the bike.

The uniformed cops at the 72nd Street subway station began to spin. To claw at weapons.

And the dynamics of the moment completely reset as the front brake of the bike locked.

There was a split instant when the motorcycle came to a stop. Or at least an optical trick implied that it did. Then the back end launched, and it flipped into the air. The rider was trebucheted forward.

He hit the end of his trajectory, his boot snagged on the brake pedal, and he was yanked back against the path physics had initially chosen for him. The bike completed its flip, and the back end slammed into the asphalt, tearing the seat away and kicking up a stream of living sparks.

TICK!

The rider whipped around, still tethered to the bike, and slapped into the asphalt like a dolphin hitting the ocean. But the molecules of the road were too dense to absorb him, and he made a million sickening simultaneous crunches before the bike began another airborne rotation, once again taking him with it.

Whitaker was into her turn now, her hand instinctively at her holster.

The uniformed cops started to disperse, to move toward the shots. And the tumbling bike.

The motorcycle managed one more powerful rotation, hit, and the front fork splayed, sending the wheel off into the air. Rider once again met street. Once again made a loud smack. And a loud crunch.

TACK!

The bike flipped, zinged by Whitaker, and punched through the back window of her new SUV, straight into the bed, the boneless-chicken rider still tethered to it.

There was a small fraction of silence as everyone recalibrated their playback functions before the Lincoln erupted in a high-pressure fireball that blew out the windows and lifted it into the air. Lucas pulled Whitaker to the ground, and they were pelted with glass and all manner of flaming shit.

TOE!

Across the street, Russo holstered his pistol, picked the tray of food off the hood of the car, and came walking over with the sausage still in his mouth.

75

Central Park

Dingo spotted the man in the expensive black tracksuit milling about on the corner of Fifth Avenue as soon as he stepped out the front door. When he checked traffic, he knew the guy was watching him. When he followed, he understood that something was up. Eighteen years spent as a combat photographer in some of the world's most challenging environments had trained his eye to do two things — find the interesting and assess the dangerous, which were often the same thing. And when he added the man in the tracksuit to the attack on Erin, and the chaos floating around Lucas, he went into threat assessment mode.

The man was doing his best to look casual, but no one in Prada ever looked casual. And no one stood under scaffolding to check their phone for more than a few moments. Not with Central Park right across the street.

Dingo knew something was wrong as soon as the guy started following him down Fifth.

Dingo thought about going back home. But the kids were there. He thought about phoning Lucas, but the poor guy had enough shit to worry about right now without adding bogeymen to the list. He thought about calling the police, but what would he tell them, that he thought some guy was following him? The cops loved getting calls like that.

No, he'd have to figure out just what this guy wanted. And then deal with it accordingly.

Dingo put all the women he had been seeing lately through his head, trying to remember if any of them were married, or dating guys with anger issues, and the exercise made him realize that he had to make better romantic decisions in the future.

But none of that helped him figure out who the guy was. Or what he wanted.

Dingo cut into the park at 72nd, then swung north, toward the Lewis Carroll statue. When he hit the nice, even pavement of Terrace Drive, he put a little more torque into his step, and the carbon fiber blades responded accordingly. He liked the blades, and wore them more than his street feet, but they tended to freak the normals out just a little. He wished he were a little less concerned with what other people thought, but that wasn't the kind of thing that you could take from the theoretical to the practical that easily. Lucas, on the other hand, had passed *I don't give a fuck* so long ago that Dingo often wondered if he even noticed that there were other people in the world except as an impediment.

Dingo passed the Mad Hatter and dropped his pace. The next three hundred yards were wide open, but they'd put him under Glade Arch. And if the man following him had any ill intent, that's where it would happen.

The best course of action would be to slow down enough for the guy to come up right behind him and get in close. That way—gun, knife, fists, club, crossbow, or harsh words—Dingo could rush him.

He put less force into his step, which maintained his rhythm but reduced his speed.

Dingo followed the gentle curve of the path, keeping his rhythm and focusing on the sounds of the steps behind him.

Glade Arch began filling his built-in viewfinder, and the footfalls behind him closed in.

Forty yards.

Thirty.

Then twenty.

Dingo flexed his fingers, pushed the adrenaline into his system, and cleared his head.

Ten.

The footsteps picked up.

Five.

And they were under the bridge.

The footsteps changed. Dingo spun.

An arm came at him. He saw the blade.

The second arm came in, swinging wide with another knife.

Dingo pivoted, transferring all his momentum into his right leg. The prosthetic compressed, absorbed the energy, stored it for an instant, then released, shooting Dingo up.

He grabbed the right wrist as it swung in, pulling it through its arc and bringing his knee up in one fast jolt.

His knee connected with bone and sinew, and he pushed down as hard as he could, breaking the arm at the elbow with a vibrant crunch that came out on a scream.

The first knife clinked off in the dark.

But the other arm was coming in.

Dingo spun away from the second blade. Brought his forearm up. Blocked it.

The arm pulled back.

Built up energy.

Dingo smashed down on the broken arm again, and it ruptured like a broken cigarette, sporking bones through the skin and wringing out another horrid shriek.

Dingo roared, brought his knee up into the downturned fist, grabbed his attacker's hair, and pulled forward as hard as he could.

Face met compound fracture.

There was a sickening crunch as Dingo drove his knee up, spearing his attacker in his brain with his own bone.

He let out a single fearsome *Yawp!*, shat himself, and flopped over dead.

76

Weil Cornell Medical Center

Mindy Appelbaum finished her coffee at the small table overlooking the aluminum and glass atrium. She considered getting another but was present enough to realize that was just a delay tactic. So she walked the empty cup over to one of the stainless-steel tubes that served as a recycling station and dropped the cup in the container marked for paper, the lid in the one identified for plastics. Then she went back to the table and removed a folded Big Brown Bag from the pocket of her coat, which was on the seat of the other chair. She unfolded the bag as if this were one of her regular routines, placed her coat inside, and headed for the bathrooms.

Once in the bathroom, she stuffed the Big Brown Bag into the trash and locked herself in one of the booths where she checked the pair of syringes in her pocket. Both had survived the trip on the subway and she tucked them into separate pockets on the front of her blue nurse's outfit. She then took a quick pee, washed her hands, and checked herself in the mirror.

Unless she tried to pass through a security point where her badge was required, the hospital was hers. There was a chance that she wouldn't get through upstairs, but she had a lot of experience with hospitals—more than she wanted to remember—and the little actions that would make her invisible to both staff and patients. All she had to do was act like she belonged.

Mindy smiled into the mirror, but the happiness had been erased from her muscle memory. Not that most people would notice. But she did. And thought about why.

And about how she had arrived at this place in the universe.

At this time.

She briefly thought about Patrick. About what he'd think about what she was doing. And remembered that she had promised not to do this to herself anymore.

Especially now.

Especially here.

But her heart wasn't listening to all the commands her brain was yelling at her, and her eyes filled with tears that she dabbed away before they picked up steam.

And took a few breaths.

Then she blew her nose, filled her lungs a few times, and tried out the smile once more.

This time it almost looked real.

Act like you belong, she told herself.

And left the bathroom.

She pretended to be absorbed by her phone as she moved through the corridors (which experience had taught her was how most hospital staff spent their time, whether they were working or not). The phone wasn't activated—but it lit up, which was all she needed from it. Every now and then she would glance up and nod a friendly, but distant, hello to someone.

Act like you belong.

She made it to the elevators for the trauma surgery wing, stepped inside, and punched the button for the floor where they kept the neurology patients, where Erin Page was staying as Jane Doe.

Even while she was alone in the elevator, she stared down at her phone. When they went over the security footage afterward, all they would see was a brunette nurse in her thirties checking texts.

Act like you belong.

No one else got on, and when she stepped out into the hall on the floor, she felt the adrenaline start to fill her pistons.

Act. Like. You. Belong.

Turning and running is *not* acting like you belong.

So she took a step. Followed by a second. Then a third. And just like that she was walking down the hall.

As if she belonged.

She kept her eyes on her phone as she moved and even smiled at the screen as if someone had sent her a meme or a joke. She had seen that a lot during her time in the hospital—nurses walking by the sick, looking at their texts and giggling, like they had other places waiting for them. Which she had always found sadistic.

She passed the station where three nurses—two female, one male—were on their phones. No one looked up. Or even noticed her walk by.

Act like you belong.

She was almost there and she thumbed the *sleep* button on her phone, slid it into her pocket, and looked up.

A woman in a suit was sitting on a chair beside the room and Mindy smiled at her, but she barely glanced up—she was too busy staring at her own phone.

Act like you belong.

Mindy walked toward the door, paused a few feet away, and checked her watch. Then she looked up, smiled absently, and pretended to do some arithmetic in her head as she counted off *one-two-three-four* on the fingers of her left hand. When she was done she smiled again, nodded as if she had just verified some important detail to herself, and took a step toward the room.

Like she belonged.

She reached out and grabbed the door handle.

The woman on the chair went back to her phone.

Mindy entered the room, closed the door behind her, and turned to the bed, where Dr. Erin Page was asleep.

77

West 72nd Street and Amsterdam

Whitaker watched the smoke and steam sizzle into the sky as the firefighters did their version of catastrophe mitigation. The SUV had been burned beyond any reasonable facsimile of functionality, and the insurance company would be selling this sucker by the fire-blackened pound. Or at least they would once the motorcyclist Russo had sent to the afterlife was swept out of the debris.

The intersection was blocked off and the various public departments were going through the motions of interviewing, recording, questioning, and analyzing. But a security camera in the bank had caught the shooting, and everyone concerned was satisfied that Russo had acted appropriately. All the cops on-site knew the detective, and he was getting backslaps and offers of drinks later on that he was accepting without the slightest hint of humility.

Crowds had gathered on all the permitted corners and were once again doing their best to somehow make a bad situation even worse.

After finishing up with one of the police officers, Lucas walked over to Whitaker, who was leaning against the iron fence around Verdi Square. "You know," she said, without taking her eyes from the blackened bones of the SUV, "I'm beginning to think that your luck might be just a teeny tiny bit contagious."

"You won't get an argument out of me."

Russo disengaged from the gaggle of cops and walked over. Behind him, the plume of smoke spiraling into the sky was finally beginning to fade. "Sup?" he said, and for a man who had just fired five rounds on a crowded street, killing a man, a motorcycle, and an SUV, he looked remarkably relaxed.

Whitaker cranked her smile up. "Nice shooting."

"Thank you."

"No. I mean *David Soul* kind of shooting." She was eyeing him with new respect. "You didn't learn that on a range. Or as a street cop. Not even in New York."

He put his hands into his pant pockets, rocked up on the balls of his feet, and smiled. "Army Rangers. Thirteen years."

Lucas looked up the street, at all the moving components you had to get just right to make five shots like that line up. All perfect. With a moving target. In a shifting landscape. In a lunch-hour crowd.

Whitaker said, "Complicated shooting environment."

Russo was still smiling—it was obvious he was taking great pleasure in his momentary celebrity. "I spent ten years in an actual war. Sometimes the chaos helps me focus."

A detective walked up, looking like his life wasn't providing the purpose he was searching for. He held up his phone. "The bike belongs to a Hong Kong businessman who has a place on Park Avenue. He's away and no one reported it stolen."

Lucas was playing things through in his head and something had fallen out of place since last night, since he had read Vaughan's file, and he couldn't figure out what it was.

Whitaker looked at him, and her smile flattened out. "What's wrong?"

Russo turned, and examined Lucas. "Something bugging you?"

"I'm just tired." He looked across the intersection to Gray's Papaya. "I need to get Erin some hot dogs."

The blockade of cop cars at the mouth of 72nd and Amsterdam split and their new Lincoln arrived, followed by a black sedan.

The two vehicles nudged through the intersection, drove around the burnt-out former vehicle, and came to a synchronized stop in front of the subway station. A junior agent got out and Whitaker held up her ID and waved him over.

"Special Agent Whitaker?" he asked while looking over at the charred wreckage across the street.

She nodded.

He held up a key fob. "Your new ride, ma'am. And I have instructions from Special Agent Hoffner." He took a step back and, without a hint of humor, flatly said, "He asked if you would prefer that I light this one on fire right now to save you the trouble?"

78

Weill Cornell Medical Center

The ambient hum of her immediate space changed and Erin was aware that someone was in her room. The intruder was trying to be quiet, but some unknown part of Erin picked up on the presence before the scent of perfume told her that it was a woman.

Erin must have been asleep for a while because she wasn't scheduled for a welfare check by the nurses until three. Had she missed Lucas? Had he come by? No. He would have woken her. Especially if he brought hot dogs. He was good with the little things.

And then the presence shifted. And she heard the faint tread of soft-soled shoes and the practiced footsteps of a nurse trying not to wake a patient.

She opened her eyes. And saw her. She was new. At least to Erin. She was locking the door.

And holding a syringe.

79

Erin closed her eyes.

Listened.

Counted footsteps.

Tried to figure out what to do.

She didn't know what was in the syringe, but the nurse had locked the door, which was all the convincing she needed that this was a problem.

Erin was in pain. Virtually immobile.

The nurse was coming around to the side of the bed where the rail was down. The side that Erin used to get up.

The side facing the window.

Erin slowly reached for the bed rail with her right hand and peeked between her lashes.

The woman was coming around the footboard.

Erin's hand found the rail. She locked her fingers around it. Began to pull and her body shifted.

The nurse was beside her now. Erin pulled as hard as she could with her right hand.

Her body swung down. To the right.

As her legs swung out, to the left.

She pulled her knees up.

The nurse pounced, the syringe held high.

Erin screamed. Hulk Zumbaed as hard as she could. Using every ounce of muscle. Every fiber of fear. Every molecule of energy.

Her feet thudded into ribs. The nurse stumbled clumsily back.

Erin tried to get up and rolled off the bed, but her feet just weren't there and she spilled onto the floor.

The nurse hit the window. And there was an instant when it flexed in indecision.

Then it made up its mind, and threw her forward.

Yells from out in the hall.

The nurse sprang back.

Erin tried to crawl under the bed.

Gunshots.

The door shattered.

The nurse lunged.

The syringe came down.

She was on top of Erin. Their eyes met.

And her chest exploded as three gunshots punched home.

She was hammered back. Into the window. It shattered. She was punched out into the sky. Where she hung for a bloody red instant.

Until she didn't.

80

Lucas pointed over his shoulder at the empty parking spot on the corner. "Right there."

Whitaker gave him a smile. "Maybe you're not as unlucky as I thought."

She hit the asshole lights so no one would steal the place, pulled a U-turn, and parallel parked in a seamless maneuver.

She killed the engine and nodded at the Gray's Papaya bag that Lucas cradled in his lap. "You do realize that you're screwing up that new-car smell with those things, right?"

"They smell better than plastic to me."

"That's leather."

"If you say so."

They got out and Whitaker came around the SUV, to the sidewalk. Lucas pushed his door closed and sighted the corner of 68th and York. "Let's do the front entrance. It's closer."

Whitaker stopped to buff an imaginary piece of dirt off the shiny new vehicle just as Lucas heard a crack in the sky overhead.

He looked up. And saw—

Was that a body?

Leaving the building in a perpendicular trajectory.

His mind registered what he was observing, but he could not align it with Newtonian theory—human bodies did not belong in the air. And they most certainly did not move parallel to the ground.

But the body stopped its sideways trajectory, and succumbed to the earth's superior mass. Began to fall.

Lucas had time to take a single step back before the flesh and bone meat-e-orite slammed into the front end of the Lincoln.

The impact shook the ground. The alarm went off.

Whitaker was knocked off her feet and she fell back on her ass with, "What the actual fuck!"

Lucas ran for the hospital entrance.

81

Lucas held Erin's hand as they wheeled her to a new room, one with a window. The Gray's Papaya bag was at the foot of the bed, leaching grease and making the hallway smell a little bit better. Or less sterile. Or some midway permutation thereof.

Kehoe's agent, a small tight-faced woman named Robinson, followed, apologizing profusely. After thirty feet, Lucas stopped the procession to tell her that she needed to piss off. When Robinson opened her mouth to protest, Whitaker steered her away by the elbow with a silent shake of her head.

Police were positioned around the floor and the staff were all walking around in silent mode with looks of disbelief stuck to their faces. Jacobi was up here, flexing his skill set and streamlining the interaction between his people and the police.

Russo came up with two uniformed officers and they were taking care of the paperwork. Another pair of detectives came in to question Erin, then the hospital staff, and finally Robinson, who Lucas insisted should be shot for dereliction of duty.

And after an hour the big question was still the identity of the woman who had tried to kill Erin before shitcanning another of Whitaker's SUVs.

Russo had gone over the body in search of identification, but all he had come back with was a pair of syringes in a polyethylene bag that would be meaningless until the lab had a look at them.

They rolled Erin into her new room and Lucas asked everyone to leave so they could talk. Whitaker, who was markedly silent, stood sentry at the door, coat open, hand on the grip of her service piece. Lucas suspected that a good part of her bad mood had been generated by the loss of the fourth vehicle in as many days.

When they were finally alone, Lucas leaned over and kissed Erin on the forehead. "Are you okay?"

She looked up at him. "Two people have tried to kill me in three days. No, Luke, I'm pretty fucking far from okay."

"Did you recognize her?"

Erin shook her head. "Nope."

"Did she say anything?"

"Nope." She took a deep breath. "Someone really wants me dead."

"Your name is in a pool."

She just stared at him.

His phone buzzed and when he saw it was Dingo he held it up. "I gotta get this." He then answered with, "Dingo, it's not a good—"

"Something happened—don't worry, the kids are fine. But I got attacked in the park."

"Attacked? What do you mean?"

Erin tried to sit up in bed and Lucas mouthed the words, *The kids are fine.*

Dingo said, "I'm with the cops right now. Some guy tried to stab me while I was jogging."

"What?"

"Some guy tried to stab me."

"Did the police catch him?"

"No, um, I, uh, kind of killed him."

"You what?"

"I kind of killed him. Dead. He pulled two knives on me as I was running under Glade Arch. Two knives, Luke. This guy wasn't a mugger—he knew what he was doing. He wanted me dead." There were all kinds of subtext in the statement—including things that Dingo didn't even know he was saying.

"Do you need a lawyer?"

"No, there were witnesses. And the detectives are being great."

"Are you hurt?"

"I bruised the side of my hand."

"Do I want to ask what happened?"

"I disarmed him, broke his arm, and drove his wristbone through his braincase."

Lucas didn't know what to say to that. So he didn't reply.

Dingo came back with, "Look, everything is okay, but there's something else you need to know, man—the guy followed me. From home. He was waiting for me at the corner of Fifth."

"What did he look like?"

"Skinny dude. Late forties. Big pornstache. Good runner."

"Did the police tell you who he is?"

"I checked his pockets before they arrived; he didn't have any ID. Just a phone—the police have it."

Lucas put the past hour through his processor. Three would-be killers, without identification. One after him and Whitaker, one after Erin, and one after Dingo, which was—

And that's when he got it. "He wasn't after *you*."

"No, Luke, he was most definitely after me. He followed me and—"

"He was after *me*."

"How the fuck could anyone confuse me for you? For starters, you're a foot taller."

"To a man with a hammer, everything looks like a nail—a double amputee is a double amputee. It's the only thing that makes sense."

Lucas looked down at Erin, and her expression had moved from one kind of shock into another. "I'll be there as soon as I can. What are the detectives' names?"

"Detectives Cristo and Finnegan."

Lucas said, "Hold on," to Dingo, then snapped his fingers at the doorway. Both Whitaker and Russo stuck their heads in.

Lucas pointed at Russo and held up his phone. "Detectives Cristo and Finnegan are at my house right now. Freddie Mercury just tried to kill my friend Dingo while he was jogging in the park. Freddie's dead."

Russo came in. "Does the Corleone family have a baptism I don't know about?"

Lucas knew he was just blowing off steam—they were all keyed up and surfing on multiple adrenaline spikes. But he wasn't in the mood for jokes right now. "Are they decent cops?"

Russo nodded. "You met Cristo—he's solid. Finnegan is a good cop, but he's like you—no sense of humor."

Lucas went back to the call. "Okay. I'm at the hospital with Erin— someone tried to kill her, too. Let me straighten shit up over here and then I'll head home. Make sure the cops stay there until I arrive."

"Kill Erin? Is she—?"

"She's fine."

Russo held up his phone on the other side of Erin's bed. "Don't worry. I'll send some people to watch the place."

Dingo said, "I'm sorry, man. I—"

"You have nothing to be sorry about. Just hold tight." Lucas swiped left and pocketed the phone to see Erin staring straight into him, so he dropped it on her. "Dingo was attacked in the park; somebody tried to stab him. He killed the guy. He's home and the kids are fine."

Her eyes narrowed. "It's not the kids I'm worried about; it's you and me. Just what, specifically, is going on?"

Lucas summoned Whitaker in from the hallway.

"Yeah?" she said, her eyes on the door beyond the room, still in combat mode.

"Freddie Mercury tried to kill Dingo. Followed him from our house and pulled a pair of knives. Dingo killed him in the fight. No ID, but he was carrying a phone."

Whitaker said, "That's three."

Erin squeezed his arm. "Three *what*, Luke?"

She needed to know what was going on, so Lucas said, "Russo stopped a guy who came after me and Whitaker an hour ago."

"Let me guess—'stopped' is a euphemism for 'shot full of holes'?"

Russo shrugged. "I wouldn't say 'full.'"

Erin's mouth popped open. "And you were going to tell me about this when, exactly?"

Lucas looked at his shoes and said, "I'm telling you now."

There was a knock on the door and everyone looked up to see Lorne Jacobi standing in the frame. He looked like he needed a drink. Or just had a few.

Erin waved him in.

Jacobi looked down at the threshold, closed his eyes, then stepped in. "I'm so sorry about this; I don't know what happened." The apology was directed at Erin, but he was looking at Lucas, and there was something going on behind the words.

Erin shook her head and tried out her little smile. "It's not your fault."

Lucas held up a hand. "Who knew she was in that room, Lorne?"

"Nobody. Just me." He shook his head and repeated, "Just me."

Lucas introduced Lorne to Whitaker and they nodded at each other across the bed. Then Lorne turned to Russo and said, "Nice to see you again, Detective."

Erin, who was the only one trying to look like everything was normal, said, "I didn't know you and Detective Russo were friends."

Lorne shrugged. "The hospital is in the good detective's precinct."

Russo smiled cordially. "I've brought a few people in over the years. Mostly perps. But Dr. Jacobi here has helped put some of our boys in blue back together."

Jacobi held up his hands, demonstrating two nylon sleeves that compressed his wrists—therapy for his carpal tunnel. "Not lately."

Lucas nailed Jacobi with his best *I need help* stare, and asked, "When can Erin leave the hospital?" Subtext: *When can I put her some place I can protect her?*

"The road ahead is all physiotherapy and maybe a few small corrective surgeries. She should stay tonight just to make certain she didn't undo any of the work with that fall of hers. As long as nothing came apart, she can go home tomorrow. I'll personally come by to check on her, if that helps at all."

Erin returned his smile, and it was impossible to miss the fondness and respect. "That's all the assurance I need." She diverted her attention to Lucas. "Besides, it's not like I don't know what to expect—if I have any problems, I'll know."

Whitaker leaned back against the window. "Well, Mr. Genius, if this is taken care of, it's time you dusted off that big brain of yours and put this thing into context, before one of these yahoos gets lucky."

Erin was still looking at Lucas. "We're all going to need therapy after this."

"We can get a group discount." Russo tapped the side of his head. "Therapy ain't so bad—you sit around listening to other people with problems so horrible you start to hope they're not contagious."

Erin looked at him. "Have you ever been in therapy?"

"A better question would be, Have I ever *not* been in therapy." His smile got away from him with that.

There was another knock at the door and two individuals constructed out of oversized FBI building blocks entered—one male, one female—bringing the room to critical mass.

The FBI man nodded a terse greeting to Whitaker, ignored Russo and Jacobi, then turned to Lucas. "Dr. Page?"

"Yes."

"I'm Special Agent Arifi; this is Special Agent Kostas. We were sent down by Special Agent in Charge Kehoe, sir. To protect your wife. I will stay in the hallway, and Special Agent Kostas here will stay in the room. You have our presence until this investigation is put to bed to your satisfaction, sir. The two other agents on our rotation were also chosen by the SAIC; we will introduce them to your wife when they take over our shift. There will be no personnel changes without everyone being notified and you signing off. Is that clear, sir?"

Russo nodded approvingly. "Cool. What about me?"

Special Agent Arifi gave Russo a disinterested once-over, stopping on his glass eye for a second before switching over to the good one. "And *you* are?"

Russo held up his badge. "Detective John Russo." He flicked the brass-plated nickel with his finger. "Homicide."

Special Agent Arifi leaned forward, eclipsing Russo. "I'm sorry, sir, but you are not part of our purview."

82

The Upper East Side

The rain against the iron railing out back was adding a little music to the silence everyone was marinating in and dark had swallowed the sky. The counter was littered with Chinese take-out boxes in various stages of depletion and the kids had moved off into the house to leave the adults to their silence.

Whitaker was at the table with Russo, both of them working on an after-dinner coffee. Dingo was leaning against the island, elbows back on the granite, finishing up his fifth beer. The detectives had left two hours ago, but Russo had positioned a pair of uniformed officers in a cruiser out front.

Whitaker was staring into her coffee as if it contained healing properties. "You stabbed him in the brain with his own bone?"

"Technically I drove it in with my knee."

Russo said, "Remind me never to piss *you* off."

Whitaker turned to Lucas. "And?"

Lucas had just burned ten minutes on the phone with Kehoe, getting updates. "The woman who tried to kill Erin was Mindy Appelbaum. Thirty-two-year-old accountant at a restaurant supply business in the Bronx. The lab analyzed the syringe Russo found in her pocket; it contained enough hydrogen cyanide to kill a pod of blue whales.

"She was the pinch hitter for Ira Alan White. Her husband, Patrick, died of a rare form of blood cancer five years back. He was misdiagnosed and their insurance plan spent some time playing catch-up with their health-care provider, and by the time they had things worked out Patrick was in a tailspin. He died soon after. Mindy sued the insurance company and the doctor who misdiagnosed the cancer and lost."

Whitaker said, "Drumroll, please . . . and the doctor's name was?"

"Annette Kavanagh."

Whitaker looked up. "Kavanagh . . . Kavanagh . . ." She snapped her fingers. "Annette Kavanagh. Oncologist. Fell asleep in bed with a cigarette and died of smoke inhalation."

"That's her."

Russo said, "So according to your theory—"

Whitaker held up her hand. "A *scientific theory* is different than a policeman's *hunch*. It's not a guess; it's an umbrella under which related and verified facts are kept." She smiled up at Lucas. "See? I pay attention."

Russo eyed her for a moment before turning to Lucas. "So under your absolutely certain theory, which is not a theory as I understand it, someone killed Kavanagh for Appelbaum, then Appelbaum went after Erin, but not for the person who killed Kavanagh, but for someone else?"

"Yes."

"This sounds like an awful lot of effort to get to the same destination. I'm having trouble with this."

Whitaker put a hand on his shoulder. "It's fucking brilliant. Think about it. It removes motive from the murder—it's goddamned perfect."

Russo didn't look convinced. "Yet here we are."

Whitaker nodded up at Lucas. "You'll have to thank Dr. Page there for this one. No one believed him. Not Kehoe. Not Hoffner. I wasn't even sure."

Russo asked, "So what are you missing to put this thing to bed?"

Lucas was still uncertain which questions would get them to the big answers. "We need to find out how they're trading murders. Is it double-blind? Do they meet in person? Is this done through an intermediary? A dispatcher? Is this organized online? Do they know that they are part of a broader conspiracy, or does each participant think that only they are involved? Is money involved? Do they get together for Monopoly and pull names out of a hat?" Lucas paced the kitchen, looping around the island and past the stove with the broken glass door. "We need to figure out how this is done."

"And what about the guy Dingo shish-kebrained with his own bone?" Whitaker leaned back on the bench and put her elbows up, which strained her buttons, exposing a black bra under the white Brooks Brothers shirt. "Or the guy Russo shot?"

Lucas had some good news for her. Along with some bad. Two forward. One back. Ad infinitum. "The two assholes from the Delmonico killing—Freddie Mercury and his pal? Once we ID them, we'll figure it out. The phone Mr. Mercury carried received a call just after lunch today. It came from a phone booth in Lenox Hill, at Sixty-ninth and Lex—they tried to find some security footage, but they've got nothing so far."

Whitaker said, "That's only four blocks from Matthias Vaughan's apartment."

Russo shook his head. "And it's two blocks from my precinct—that isn't proof unless they have him on film. And even then . . ." He let the statement trail off.

Lucas knew that they had enough to put this together, but it was like reverse engineering a complicated organism without knowing the sequence in which to assemble its polynucleotide chains.

Russo looked like his head was filled with nothing but question marks. "Haven't they IDed either of these jokers yet?"

"That's the headshaker in the equation. Mr. Mercury's was still intact—relatively speaking. The guy who got smoked in Whitaker's SUV is useless—they were lucky to be able to extract DNA out of the few shards of bone that were left. Mercury's prints haven't shown up anywhere and they ran facial recognition through every available database, from DMVs, the military, and the passport office right on down to local libraries, Costcos, and gym memberships—countrywide. Nothing. It will come down to identifying them through DNA—and that's only if they are on file somewhere. Which I can't see happening if fingerprints haven't generated any hits."

The glasses started rattling in the cupboard as Damien let go upstairs with his electric guitar, and even though there were two floors between them, it needled into Lucas's fillings, and he stood up to go tell the kid to lay off for a while. But Dingo pushed off the island and said, "I got it. You stay here and figure out how to bring down the Brooklyn Illuminati."

Lucas changed focus to the take-out containers. "Kehoe put a team on Vaughan."

Whitaker came back into the conversation. "How do we get to him?"

"We wait to see what happens when the lab finishes sequencing the DNA from our two killers today. If they're in the system, it might point us in a direction."

Russo looked over at him. "And if they're not?"

Lucas put a half-empty (or half-full, depending on perspective) container of shrimp and lobster sauce into the fridge. "I'm working on it."

83

Morning brought more rain. And a visitor.

Lucas answered the door in a pair of jeans with blown-out knees and an old T-shirt from some band he had seen in a bar back in university—which was as cool as he ever got anymore. Kehoe was on the stoop, his usual unreadable expression dialed into concern. He held a file.

Lucas waved him in, leaving Otto Hoffner standing by the SUV like a cigar store Indian on steroids.

Kehoe asked, "Are the kids home?" as he walked by.

"No." Dingo had taken them all to school with a car service. Alisha was with the babysitter and Dingo had not yet come back.

Kehoe headed straight into the kitchen and placed the file on the counter. "DNA on your two would-be hitters came back."

Lucas flipped the cover open. The docket contained two single sheets of paper. He zeroed in on the pixelated photograph in the top corner of the first page. It was clearly a military identification photograph, lifted from a file somewhere. He was younger but already had the big Groucho moustache—their pal Freddie Mercury.

His name was Ludwig Kling.

Below the name was a birth date.

And below the birth date was the date he died—July 21, ten years ago.

Lucas picked up the second sheet, and it was identical to the first in style and format, differing only in the image. The man in the photograph was the mystery motorcyclist who had ended up in a dust bag—and most probably the man who had helped Freddie Mercury kill Jennifer Delmonico. It was grainy like the other image.

Once again, below the image was a name: Arlo Reed.

Below the name was a birth date.

And below the birth date was the date he had died, the same as the other—July 21, ten years back.

Lucas looked up; Kehoe didn't need to hear the questions to start answering them. "We got a DNA match on both those men from their military records. The special warfare department referred me to the Department of Defense, who in turn redirected me to the DOJ. Those came in twenty minutes ago."

Lucas didn't have to tell Kehoe the files were horseshit. Or that someone was lying. Or hiding something. All those were givens. So he asked, "What can we do?"

"I'm not releasing the bodies: I've had them sent to storage, with no paperwork so no one can find them unless I want them to. That way the DOJ can't confiscate them and tell me that I never had them in the first place. I've got legal going after the DOJ, and I've called the mayor, the governor, and a friend who works at the Southern District to help me deal with this. Those two men tried to kill my people in my city and I'm not going to let that kind of thing go. I don't care *who* they are. Or *who* they work for."

Lucas put his metal hand down on the file. "What does this mean?"

"My initial guess would be that they're CIA, but Central Intelligence doesn't let their people work on American soil. Or at least they're not allowed to by mandate.

"They might be retired. Or moonlighting. But I would think that if that was the case, the Department of Defense would have something to say about ex-personnel killing American citizens."

Lucas looked at the two single pages. "There's nothing else on them?"

Kehoe shook his head. "We took every database in the country apart and they don't show up anywhere. Their files have been scrubbed, and very few governmental bodies have the power to do that. And even fewer have the power to *undo* it. We won't know anything about them for weeks." He stared straight into Lucas's good eye. "If ever." There was something going on in his head, and the way he examined Lucas meant he expected it to be recognized.

Lucas responded by picking up the file and heading out of the kitchen. "You can show yourself out."

"Where are you going?" Kehoe called after him.

"To change my clothes. And get some answers."

84

Wall Street

Paul Knechtel was one of those men who was getting better looking with age, and the contrast between his ascending appeal and Lucas's jalopy approach to aging was hard to miss. If graphed out on a
symmetrical Laffer curve, they would be at exactly the same point
on the y-axis, but on opposing sides of the center.

They met at MIT, where Knechtel had been doing his dissertation on a theoretical branch of jet propulsion and Lucas had been
writing his second doctoral thesis. But school for Knechtel hadn't
been a training ground for his eventual career—it had been a way for
him to limber up his thinking before taking over the family business.
Knechtel Investments was a perennial firm on Wall Street, and so
successful that it had never been—nor was it likely to be—available
to the general public. Its main focus was the financing of infrastructure deals for nation-states via international corporate investment.
Knechtel was the only banker Lucas could stand talking to, mainly
because he was the sole non-sociopath he had ever encountered in
the trade.

Knechtel sat back in the sofa. Most people would focus on the
massive taxidermy display behind him—an aurochs with silver-
tipped horns locked in battle with a monster Kodiak bear. Lucas

thought the display clumsy and heavy-handed, but he was certain that clients were impressed. After all, if you were financing actual countries in the hopes of making a buck, your worldview had to be both cynical and self-important.

"How important is this?" Knechtel asked. He appeared calm and disinterested, but Knechtel was literally one of the smartest men Lucas had ever met, and he knew there were millions of tiny computations going through the man's head.

Lucas took off his glasses and pointed his good eye straight into Knechtel's skull. "They tried to kill my wife, Paul. Twice. I need to stop these people."

Knechtel was silent for a few seconds and Lucas knew his brain was compiling millions of calculations, all of them focused on blowback. In what seemed like a long time but clocked out at twenty-two seconds, Knechtel stood up, picked up the two pages Kehoe had given Lucas that morning, and said, "Give me five minutes."

Knechtel walked out, leaving Lucas alone in the office. But like everything else in Knechtel's life, calling the space an *office* was a massive understatement. The room was close to a gymnasium in size, which was quite the feat in an area known for ridiculous cost-per-square-foot ratios. In most rooms the taxidermy display would overpower the rest of the space, but in here it was relegated to the role of accessory. There wasn't much in the way of furniture—an Art Deco Macassar ebony desk, probably by Jules Leleu; a pair of armoires by Carlo Bugatti; two tufted sofas; and a coffee table. But the space transcended the concept of an office due to the three-story library that wound up into the ceiling, capped off with a nineteenth-century Belle Époque wrought-iron skylight thirty feet in diameter.

Lucas spent some time perusing the library, which he knew had taken decades to put together. He understood why some people—techno-junkies, mostly—considered the concept of a library to be antiquated. Did the world really need a million copies of *On the Origin of Species,* or was one digital copy, available to everyone, the smart route?

He finished counting all the books in the library—twice—when Knechtel came back. He handed the two pages to Lucas and checked his watch—a massive pink gold Panerai. "Be at the West Thirtieth Street Heliport in one hour, fifty minutes. A black Airbus H155 will touch down and a man in a black boiled-wool overcoat and a blue silk scarf will get out. He will be carrying an aluminum Halliburton briefcase. He will walk into the BLADE Lounge, where you will be waiting at the table in the northwest corner, facing the door. He will sit down, open his briefcase, and place some reading material on the table. You will have fifteen minutes to go through it in front of him, after which time he will place it back in his briefcase and leave without saying anything."

"Do I give him money? Do I—?"

Paul shook his head and handed the two pages back to Lucas. "You don't say anything to him. Not 'hello,' not 'thank you.' You just let him give you whatever he gives you. You look at it. You take your fifteen minutes. And you let him leave. After that you forget him."

Lucas looked up at Knechtel, and realized that he had put a lot of muscle into getting this done. "Thank you, Paul. I appreciate this."

Knechtel waved it away. "Don't. Just go save the world."

85

West 30th Street Heliport

One hour and fifty minutes after his meeting with Paul Knechtel, Lucas watched the Airbus H155 touch down from his assigned perch at the table in the northwest corner of the informal lounge/bar/snack counter. A man who looked to be anywhere from a hard fifty-five to a fit seventy got out. He had the square shoulders, bad haircut, and physical bearing of a career military man, and Lucas figured he at least carried the designation of "colonel," maybe even "general."

Lucas had already figured out that Knechtel had pulled some important strings to make this happen. The first hint was that he was able to dig up information on something the DOJ had no interest in releasing—very few individuals could accomplish that particular trick. The second hint was in the helicopter and timing. Lucas had looked up the craft, and it had a cruising speed of just under 175 miles an hour. When he factored in a lead time of fifteen minutes to gather material and make it to a helicopter pad, the only logical point of origin was Langley, Virginia, which was 234 miles away, and home to the Central Intelligence Agency. No other locale fit the requirements. Except maybe the Pentagon. Which was also a possibility. After all, Knechtel's business model helped him prop up foreign nation-states, which no doubt made for interesting and influential bedfellows.

Lucas watched the colonel/general walk stiffly to the doors at the far end of the clubhouse. Other than the expensive overcoat and very nice suit, he looked like a composite drawing of a retired soldier in a prepper catalogue—flattop, aviators, and a face that had had the emotions surgically removed sometime between Vietnam and Operation Iraqi Freedom.

He walked into the lounge, headed straight to Lucas's table, and placed the aluminum Halliburton down on the stool. He popped the catches, removed two thick files, and put them down in front of Lucas. He then closed his briefcase, put it on the floor under the table, and sat down in the other chair.

Lucas was not generally given to warm interactions with people out in the world, but even he found their non-communication a little weird. But Knechtel had been specific, so he looked down, and opened the file on Ludwig Kling.

• • •

Fifteen minutes later, Lucas watched the Airbus H155 fuel-powered mechanical insect lift gracefully off the pad, bank low out over the Hudson, then head north along the river. When it was swallowed by the rain, he left the lounge, walked through the big gate in the chain-link fence, and headed across Twelfth Avenue, to Whitaker's Lincoln.

After reading the files, there were no doubts left that the man in front of him had been from Central Intelligence. The files were straight out of the archives, and every page had a CIA designation in either a watermark, stamp, header, footer, or seal. And Lucas knew that what he had just done was more than likely illegal.

Which he rationalized by contrasting it against hiding the identity of murderers.

He had gone through nearly five hundred pages on Ludwig Kling and Arlo Reed, two men who were, in the parlance of spy novels, government assassins. They had both been career soldier bees for the CIA hive, with histories that read like demons' résumés. Their births and education and early lives could have been anyone's— parents with regular jobs who had children they probably expected to grow up and become contributing members of society. But by the time Reed and Kling finished their training under the tutelage of one of the American government's special warfare divisions, neither would ever again be fit for public consumption.

Their initial career trajectories put them in different parts of the world, but by the time they were in their early thirties a joint operation in Mali had changed their respective paths forever. After, they only worked together, and Lucas counted a total of seventy-nine people they had *maximally demoted* (in the sterile nomenclature of institutionally organized assassination) as a team. The names of these targets had been redacted, but their occupations had not, and Lucas was horrified at the number of unsuspecting schoolteachers and dentists and artists and businessmen who had been murdered just because they presented some minor ideological inconvenience for unclear American interests in some foreign land.

The hit men's work eventually brought them to Afghanistan, where they engaged in a rash of joint CIA–Karzai Transitional Administration sponsored assassinations, mostly civilians, with a particular focus on journalists.

They operated for two years in Kandahar, depleting the population one unsuspecting citizen at a time, before the CIA decided their psychosis would better serve US interests in Bagram. By this point, the American government had grown dissatisfied with Karzai's administration, and Reed and Kling were retasked to a pilot program under the acronym MISO, which stood for military information support operations. MISO was a pseudonym for PSY OP, and they set about a new rash of assassinations designed to undermine local commerce alliances with the very noble goal of selling more American-owned crap.

Lucas was lucky with the light, but he stopped, and checked traffic both ways. After what he had just read, he understood that he was dealing with people who would have no qualms about turning him into a traffic fatality statistic. So he was careful crossing. But his paranoia was just that, and he made both the southbound and north-bound lanes of Twelfth Avenue without hitting yellow, or getting flattened by a "runaway" truck.

Whitaker was parked up on the sidewalk on 30th Street, intently watching him. As he approached, she smiled, and the deep thump of music inside the car dropped off precipitously. She fired up the en-gine as he crossed in front. He opened the door and climbed inside.

Whitaker held the tablet out for him, and he knew what she was going to say, so he cut her off with, "Russo sent Vaughan's DNA results and he's the father of Delmonico's fetus, right?"

Her mouth fell open and she said, "I'm starting to feel like you don't need me anymore."

"Don't be ridiculous. I don't drive, remember?"

He sat there in silence for a few seconds, adding it all up. "It's Vaughan. All of it. He's our guy."

86

The Upper East Side

Two dozen law-enforcement vehicles simultaneously converged on Dr. Matthias Vaughan's address. It was a textbook example of coordination, and Lucas knew that everyone would be vying for credit in the aftermath, taking unearned bows for their part in solving a far-reaching conspiracy of serial murder. He also knew that their collective cognitive dissonance would not allow them to admit that they had all been unable to see the initial problem. There would be buck-passing and blame sharing, but the truth was that no one had seen this except for him. As usual, he took solace in knowing that he had once again been right.

But they weren't done with this thing—there were still twenty-eight murderers to find. Or, to be more succinct (which in this particular instance simply meant less wrong), there were the murderers of twenty-eight people to find. After all, it was possible that some of the people involved had killed more than one doctor. And they also knew that in the Delmonico homicide there had been more than one perpetrator—there could be more instances of the same.

No one expected Vaughan to put up any sort of a fight. The behavioral people said he was most probably a psychopath, but they were also relatively certain that he was a narcissist, and he had gone unpunished for so long that it wasn't much of a stretch to assume that he saw himself as untouchable. It was a common characteristic of serial killers—people assumed that they wanted to get caught because of how brazen they often were with their crimes, but the truth was that they never considered getting caught as a possibility; their track record was personal proof positive that they were just too smart for The Man. The behavioral people predicted that he was so high on *Vitamin I* that he would probably attempt to represent himself in court.

Kehoe had the analysts map out a timeline before sending in the Marlboro men, and it hadn't been much of an effort to put Arlo Reed and Ludwig Kling in Vaughan's general (and, arguably, specific) orbit back when he had been sculpting "special projects" for the US government in the Afghan theater of war.

Vaughan was posted at the Bagram prison at the same time the CIA file showed Arlo Reed and Ludwig Kling were there. Their stay overlapped with the good psychiatrist for twenty-one months, coinciding with his publishing blitz on social psychology, specifically the ability to shape public opinion and social trends through selective pressure on civic leadership roles—during which time Kling's and Reed's files outlined killing after killing after killing.

In September of 2004, a month before an investigation into personnel at the prison was launched, and under orders from an unnamed governmental agency (most likely the CIA), Vaughan was quietly dismissed. A few months later he turned up stateside, as head of the Manhattan Psychiatric Center. A month later, the *New York Times* broke the story about the abuses and psychological torture endured by enemy combatants at Bagram. Vaughan's file showed he had been there, but he never showed up in any of the reports—which was odd.

Around the same time, Arlo Reed and Ludwig Kling were also rotated out. Again, under orders from an unnamed American agency.

Between 2005 and 2012, Vaughan had taken three long-term

absences from his work, all of which coincided with overseas dates cited in Reed's and Kling's files. More papers published. More governmental work. And more killings.

The connections were all circumstantial; the connections were all coincidental; the connections were all logical.

So here they were.

Lucas stood in the hallway, trapped in one of those in-the-moment experiences that the New Agey mindfulness people were always trying to sell in their online ads. He was staring at the floor, collecting the individual frequencies in the music behind the thick oak door, and reassembling them into a whole. Which was a weird thing to be doing while a SWAT team worked its way upstairs to serve a no-knock on Dr. Matthias Vaughan.

Whitaker was across the hall, in the stairwell doorway, waiting for the cue that it was okay to come up. Her coat flap was back, and she was resting her hand on her holster, index down, over the Kydex, in one of those automatic actions that she probably didn't even know she was doing. Russo stood just beyond the door, in the stairwell proper, sipping booze from his ever-present mug. They had called him as a courtesy, and he was waiting in his car on the corner when they showed up, all smiles that he had been right.

Lucas had his eyes closed as he tried to actually hear the song. It was a faint vibration that traveled through the concrete, grounded out in his prosthetic leg, made the jump to his skeleton, then activated the neurons in his somatosensory cortex—which was a type of hearing, but not in a literal way. It was being played at very respectable apartment volume and Lucas doubted that anyone else would be able to zero in on it. Which was the weird thing about the *Event*—it had put a dent in all of his major systems, obliterating some of them entirely, but all of the small subsystems related to his hearing felt like they had been replaced by ones modeled on a fruit bat.

He titled his head, and there was no missing that the tune was built on bass and drums, with some treble thrown in to offset the thunder. Whoever was handling vocals had highs that could blow a hole in a sand dune if they wanted to. But it was so distant that for a few seconds he thought it might just be radio interference—maybe the unusual combination of his metal parts was acting as an FM antenna. Then he realized that the person in 33D was listening to "Baba O'Riley." Then *that* realization was offset by a second—that all of his kids thought this was music from the stone age. Except for Damien, who had an old-timey rock-and-roll thing going that Lucas hoped he would never lose.

Lucas was basking in the small personal victory when the unmistakable crash of the SWAT team taking Vaughan's door off the hinges upstairs cut the interlude short, and all the little vibratory nuance disappeared from his universe.

The tactical team went through the apartment and their intermittent declarations of "Clear!" . . . "Clear!" . . . "Clear!" echoed down the stairs and through the open door.

Lucas looked over at Whitaker, who held up a finger, signaling that they still needed to wait. Which was an unnecessary action on her part—Lucas had no intention of storming the beaches with the soldiers.

It took the SWAT men seconds to check the entire apartment, but there was a long lag between the last yell of "Clear!" and the signal that it was okay to come up.

Lucas followed Whitaker and Russo up the stairs. All eight SWAT men were out in the hall. But there was no Vaughan. Or smiles.

The leader of the squad, a small man named Friedman, waited at the door. He had his helmet under his arm and his single eyebrow was creased, complementing the frown he wasn't bothering to hide.

"He home?" Whitaker asked.

"He's home," Friedman said.

By his tone, Lucas knew that he was correct in his suspicions.

Friedman led them into the place, unceremoniously kicking a big splinter of wood from the door aside. The door itself had swiped half a dozen of the Sheriff photographs off the wall, and they lay strewn about, gilt frames broken, glass shattered, images lost forever. The door itself was up against the wall.

Glass cracked under the soles of Friedman's boots as he took them down the hall, past the kitchen. Lucas looked in to see the audience of human heads in their case, each in its own protective cloche, a diminutive blinded mute audience to unknowable horrors.

Friedman took Whitaker, Lucas, and Russo into the living room, which Lucas hadn't seen the other day, and knew he would remember forever.

Friedman nodded at the back corner of the apartment. "Bathroom. I'll be outside."

Whitaker looked over at Lucas, who decided that he'd let them take the first peek.

Russo headed back, in the direction Friedman had pointed.

Russo passed the piano, ducked around a tall Tiffany slag glass floor lamp, and moved the maroon velvet curtain with the braided gold pull aside, exposing the bathroom door.

He stood in the doorway, outlined by the incandescent halo in much the same way Kehoe had been last night in front of the wall of monitors. He didn't move. And he was uncharacteristically silent.

Whitaker walked up behind him and looked in. "Oh my God." She turned away, looked over at Lucas, and shook her head. "Don't," she said.

Lucas did not want to see what was in there, but he walked over anyway, as if his central program would not let him forego the sight.

Russo stepped aside and put a hand on his shoulder as he moved by.

But death has many personalities, and he didn't know the specific hat it had worn when it visited the psychiatrist.

And even if he had bothered with a guess, he would not have imagined the possibility.

Vaughan lay in the bathtub. Floating in water that looked like it was mostly blood. Or at least his body did.

His head sat on an antique enamel medical cabinet with glass doors. Above the glass apothecary urns with chrome lids containing cotton balls and Q-tips and dental picks.

He faced slightly left, toward the mirror. But he did not stare at his own reflection—he could not—because his eyes had been sewn shut. The lids were tied closed with three knots, needles dangling off the end of the line—standard surgical sutures.

Vaughan's mouth was similarly fastened, the only noticeable difference being the number of knots—five. Two of the needles were lost in his blood-soaked beard.

Lucas backed away, turned, and ran out of the apartment.

87

After their visit to Dr. Vaughan's apartment, Lucas was both grateful and resentful that the police were still positioned outside of his house. Russo stopped for a little small talk with the two uniformed officers before following Lucas and Whitaker inside.

Dingo and the kids were in bed, leaving Lucas, Whitaker, and Russo to their conversation. Russo was the only one who had an appetite, and he had uneceremoniously microwaved a can of Chef Boyardee spaghetti, which Lucas thought was a very poor choice after the Tarantino masterpiece they had seen at Vaughan's.

"Can we all agree that the good psychiatrist did not commit suicide?"

Whitaker looked away from Russo's plate. "Can you dial it back just a tiny bit?"

"Of course. Sorry. I forget shit like that makes a lot of people uncomfortable."

Whitaker picked up her mug, but she just looked at it, then placed it back on the table. "You didn't find that horrifying?"

Russo wiped his mouth and shrugged. "I spent too much time in Klusterfuckistan, chaos on earth; my idea of horror was recalibrated a long time ago." He twirled up a big forkful of spaghetti and dusted it with a lump of plastic cheese shavings before happily inserting it into his mouth.

They lapsed into silence while Russo worked on his food. Lucas was making a concerted effort to put his coffee into the tank—he needed the caffeine—but his esophagus was refusing to let anything down.

Whitaker wasn't even trying to drink, and just stared at the subway tile, no doubt doing the impossible of trying to forget what she had seen by thinking about it too much, which was a conundrum Lucas thoroughly understood.

"You okay?"

Whitaker blinked, and transported back to their conversation from her trip through time to see a headless psychiatrist. Or was that a bodiless psychiatrist? "That was not disguised to look like an accident."

"Or a suicide," Russo offered, once again giving them a poorly timed smile. "Okay. Christ. I'll stop."

Vaughan had been decapitated with a large knife with a thick blade, six to seven inches in length. Whoever killed him had done that type of thing before—they had an understanding of how to remove a human head, which apparently wasn't as simple as the movies made it appear. And they brought their own sutures along—none were found in Vaughan's apartment.

The knots securing Vaughan's eyes and mouth were all identical—simple surgeon's knots. The ME said they were relatively accurate but not all uniform and he didn't think the murderer had a lot of experience tying them even though they knew the technique.

Whitaker picked up her coffee, looked into the mug, didn't find whatever she was looking for, and once again put it down on the table with a thud. "So walk me through this again."

Lucas opened his hands, and noticed that the finish on a few of his fingertips was down to the aluminum. How had that happened? "Let's say a patient came into Vaughan's office who blamed a doctor for some misdeed. Or maybe they came in to deal with the grief of losing a loved one and he steered them toward the blame game. After who knows how many sessions of being primed by a very effective clinical psychiatrist, they're presented with the option of avenging their dead loved one—maybe in group therapy with a bunch of other patients that he's worked his mental magic on. Possibly everyone in the group is in on it. Maybe only a few. I haven't figured it out.

"So Vaughan proposes a solution—a member of the group will kill your doctor, and in return, you will be required to do the same for yet *another* member. Maybe they sit around in a circle and actually trade killings, like baseball cards, or Pokémon cards, or non-fungible tokens, or whatever the fuck kids trade these days. And the selling point is that when they pull the crisscross, there is no motive for their killing, which means no way to get caught. Round and round.

"I assume that not everyone is easy to push over that line, so maybe standard protocol was that Vaughan had Kling and Reed kill the doctor for the patient he was grooming, which put them on the hook for murder—what's a little emotional leverage and blackmail on top of homicide? And I wouldn't be surprised to learn that someone backed out, or tried to back out, of their deal. If that happened, Kling and Reed visited them, and they ended up on the Medical Examiner's slab, their homicide ruled a suicide or an accident. That would be a good explanation for why Moth wouldn't speak to us— she's afraid. Like I said, it was a pretty smart setup. Vertically integrated group homicide. Soup to nuts."

"I see the nuts," Russo said through a big mouthful of spaghetti. "Not the soup."

Lucas nailed him with his *Shut the fuck up* face, and Russo once again said, "Sorry. Jeez."

Whitaker held up her hand. "So why send Kling and Reed after you and me? Why not after Russo here? We all visited him. We were all involved in the case. And even if he *had* killed all of us, it doesn't make sense as a move—the investigation was already going on. You don't stop a case by killing an investigator."

"I don't know." Again—fewer answers, more questions.

"Did Vaughan have Delmonico killed?"

That was another one that had no obvious through line. "She was carrying his child. Maybe she wanted a commitment. Maybe she *didn't* want a commitment. Maybe she wanted to leave her husband. Or wouldn't. She was planning an abortion. Or refusing one. It's possible that he shared his little crisscross murder network with her—pillow talk, a confession after a couple of glasses of wine.

"Or maybe Delmonico was involved—maybe she was on the hook for the murder of a colleague. Maybe she wouldn't fulfill her end of things, and he had those two mooks throw her ass into traffic." He straightened up and managed to push a mouthful of coffee down his pipe. "He already had Reed and Kling in place—hit men on call. When you're used to swinging a hammer, you get blasé about banging in nails."

Russo nodded at that. "You really think he had those two guys kill some of the doctors?"

Lucas shrugged again. "Why not?"

Russo finished the concoction in his ever-present travel mug, shook it, took one more pointless shot at the contents, put it down, then reached over, picked up Whitaker's coffee, and took a loud slurp.

"Hey!"

"Were you drinking that?"

"Not anymore." Whitaker, who still looked lost, turned to Lucas. "What was Vaughan's motivation for organizing these doctor-hunting parties?"

Another good question. "It's not like the God complex isn't a well-known pathology in the field of medicine. Maybe he just got a kick out of it; he was a run-of-the-mill sociopath. Maybe he enjoyed manipulating people. This was his version of game night."

Russo finished a mouthful of spaghetti, took another big slurp of Whitaker's coffee, and smiled. "I personally think that Battleship rocks."

Whitaker, ignoring Russo, said, "So who killed Vaughan?"

Lucas took a sip of coffee, and it had crossed the Rubicon from barely warm enough to too cold, and he pushed it away. "The more important question is *why?*"

"I don't understand."

"Because there's been a change in the pattern over the past week. Before Delmonico, we were looking at roughly twenty-five days between killings. In the past seven days we've had Delmonico, Knox, and Solomon killed. Erin has had two attempts on her life. They got Vaughan. And they went after you and me. It's a classic example of an exponential—what caused it?"

"Any ideas?"

"Whoever killed Vaughan knew him and had been in that apartment before; they brought those sutures along. Which means they knew about Vaughan's shrunken-head collection. They were making a point."

"Of?" Russo asked.

"I don't know. Maybe he had given them the same monologue about the Jivaro using shrunken heads to gain the power of their former enemies. Maybe it was just a symbolic fuck you."

The doorbell rang, and Lucas pushed off the island.

Lemmy came ripping down from upstairs and Lucas told himself to remember to turn the lights on when he went to bed—the runners would be bunched up, and the last thing he needed to add to the current multiple crises was a broken hip.

He peeked through one of the small beveled panes and was surprised to see Lorne Jacobi standing out in the rain.

Lucas opened the door, waved to the policemen who were on the sidewalk, hands on holsters. "It's okay, Officers; he's a friend."

Lorne stepped inside, and Lucas closed the door. "Is everything okay?" he asked as they went through their patented fist bump.

Lucas wondered if he had really just asked that—because the only answer that made any sense at all was a big fat no. "What's going on, Lorne? Why are you here?"

"I heard that Matthias Vaughan was murdered."

Lucas checked his watch and was once again impressed at how quickly bad news traveled. "Yeah." Which was about as much detail as he wanted to clog up his RAM with.

"First Jennifer Delmonico, then Arna Solomon, an attempt on Erin, and now they killed Matthias Vaughan. What's going on, Luke?"

Lucas gestured down the hall. "Come on in. Have a coffee."

When they walked in, Lucas said, "I think you all know one another."

The handshaking began, and when he and Russo connected, Lorne winced and pulled his hand away. "Sorry—hand problems."

Lemmy circled the island, then the table, sniffing the floor for anything that might smell, and therefore taste, good.

Russo pulled his hand away. "Forgot."

Lorne took off his coat and looked around the room as if just figuring out that this was the point in the movie where they rolled out a table full of guns and were about to begin loading them. "Have I come at a bad time?"

Maude, wrapped in Erin's old blanket robe, came in. "Hey, Uncle Lorne. I heard your voice." She looked around. "Is Uncle Neville with you?"

She gave Lorne a quick hug and Lucas found a lot of solace in that little intimate moment.

"No. It's just me. But I was telling your dad that we'd love to come visit you guys."

Maude looked over at Lucas, and said, "Well?"

"Of course." He was thrilled that she was finding time to be a kid in all the crap that was going on, which didn't give him any sort of a choice. "We'll figure something out. Now go back to bed."

She left, but not before scowling at Whitaker and giving Russo Erin's look of dismissive disdain. Lemmy went with her.

Lorne took a seat and Lucas realized that they had figured out as much as they were going to and maybe Lorne's presence could help them recalibrate their moods. "How do you take your coffee?" he asked.

Lorne nodded as if his head were made of ironwood; the past week had chopped holes in his life as well. "Black, please."

While Lucas filled a mug, he asked Lorne, "How difficult would it be to find a therapy group that gets together once a week if you didn't have any sort of a starting point?"

"Do you know what the group's mission statement is?"

"Nope."

Lorne's mouth did a reverse scimitar as he thought it out. "At any given point in time there have to be ten thousand weekly group meetings in the five boroughs to help people deal with any number of issues. Roughly half of those are not sponsored or affiliated with any national or parent organization. Many are anonymous — Alcoholics and Gamblers and Sexaholics and Internet and Technology Addicts Anonymous, for example. You could check with the usual venues — civic centers, community halls, churches and temples, schools, clubs, and rental halls. Maybe community or specialty bulletin boards on neighborhood websites. But even then, many of these groups would not have rosters, or any official membership — just weekly meetings where nameless people show up."

Lucas brought Lorne's coffee to the table. "You make it sound impossible."

Lorne shrugged. "Let's just say that I think it to be an improbable undertaking."

88

It was midmorning, and today it looked like Sauron was in charge of the weather. Wind lashed the street, using the rain as a weapon, and the sky was rendered in a pixelated gray that pulsed like a black sail. But there was no lightning. Or dragons. Both of which would have been understandable and, in a way, really cool.

Lucas had a car service bring them home. He hadn't bothered picking up the loaner from the insurance company and Erin did most of the driving anyway—which she was in no shape to do, and wouldn't be for a while. And this way the kids got a ride in a limousine, which had to earn him some cool points. Or Likes. Or whatever they were calling social currency these days.

Lucas was doing his best not to think about differentiating the guys in the black hats from the guys in the white hats. He needed to be present in his own life. At least for now.

The kids spilled out onto the curb and ran for the stairs like a demonstration on entropy.

Lucas helped Erin out while the kids tripped over themselves to get up the steps and be the first to open the door.

Russo's two uniformed officers were in their car, almost directly in front of the house. Lucas gave them a small metal-fingered salute, and they both nodded back. He knew that they resented being here, but they had their orders. And they were definitely providing a little emotional security.

Lucas, Erin, and the kids got up the stairs, and Dingo and Lemmy and Bean were waiting inside in a perfect Downton Abbey line. Dingo had on a tuxedo T-shirt; Lemmy wore a bow tie; Bean's formal wear consisted of a single happy face sticker on his bum.

There was a kid-made (which Alisha had informed Lucas was most definitely *not* the same as handmade) banner over the study door exclaiming *WELCOME HOME, MOM!* in a million colors, and decorated with hand-drawn images of everything from butterflies to kisses to guitars.

The kids came and all took a piece of an elbow and started to help her up the stairs and Lucas could see that Erin was doing her best to smile even though she was in pain.

Dingo came over and put his hand on Lucas's shoulder. "Why do you have that look on your face?"

Lucas was watching Erin take the steps in that slow way people who haven't been on their feet for a few days adopt. "What look?"

"The kind that a kid sitting down for dinner has while his friends are outside, playing cricket."

"This is America, Dingo—nobody plays cricket."

Erin got to the top of the stairs, and turned. Their focus intersected for a few seconds, and she stared at Lucas intently. Her brow furrowed. Then released. And she nodded at him. Smiled. *It's okay*, she mouthed. *Go.*

The Town Car was still parked at the curb, and Lucas signaled the driver, who nodded and held up his hand to convey that there was no rush.

Lucas looked back up at Erin and blew her a kiss off his metal hand.

She smiled, told him a thousand little things with her eyes, then let the kids prod her into the bedroom.

Lucas paused on the threshold. "Watch the place," he said to Dingo, then walked down the steps in the rain.

89

The Hayden Planetarium
Museum of Natural History

They had not been able to get a list of Dr. Vaughan's patients—the judge hadn't been convinced that the broader good was being served by exposing thousands of patients on the dead psychiatrist's roster to scrutiny when, in point of fact, the bureau was only looking for a couple of dozen at most—and no warrant had been secured.

Lucas stared up at what his mind understood to be a domed ceiling but his eyes interpreted as an infinite horizon. In place of the familiar images of the cosmos was a sky congested with data. Spreadsheets. Invoices and payment records. Electronic copies of every conceivable financial record available—ATM and credit card statements, utility bills, electronic payments, Uber and Lyft accounts, rewards programs, parking tickets, and debit card purchases. MetroCards and grocery bills. Gym memberships and Costco purchases.

Along with the physical addresses associated with all purchases, transactions, and activities.

The Zeiss IX projector's horizon-to-horizon capabilities enabled them to saturate the curved viewing surface of the planetarium with information. Even with just half of his factory-original ocular hardware still running, Lucas could view massive amounts of data, and his core processor was running flat-out.

The data in the sky cycling by was being siphoned in from the FBI's main computer lab at Quantico, Virginia, where monstrous computational firepower cross-referenced every piece of information against every other piece of information.

The room was filled with numbers from horizon to horizon and Lucas had room to pace as he stared up at a cosmos of data, searching for a group of serial killers.

Kehoe had okayed the project, signing off with a three-word motivational slogan plagiarized directly from Nike.

But it had been Lucas who secured the space through a mix of calls to the appropriate people and a calculated use of threats, compliments, and promises of credit. The projector's head operator—a young man named Clive Bower—was excited about using the environment in an unconventional way, and he was getting along with Bobby Nadeel, whom Lucas needed because they thought in a similar manner. At Kehoe's insistence, Agent Mace was along for the ride, and was doing a good job of stepping out of his comfort zone. A handful of analysts sat in a corner on standby, in case Nadeel got tired.

Lucas was focusing on the knowns, and the one constant—even after Lucas became involved—was that none of the murders took place on a Tuesday.

Which was either a complete accident. Or a part of the equation.

And if it was part of the equation, then it had a purpose. A reason.

And the only reason Lucas could imagine was that was the day that Dr. Vaughan's group got together.

Lucas had his small team zero in on their five known murderers and would-be murderers—Trina and Darrel Moncrieff, Albert Hess, Ira Alan White, and Mindy Appelbaum, who had killed, or tried to kill, Dr. Dove Knox, Dr. Arna Solomon, and Erin, respectively.

Nadeel and Mace, with Bower's help, went through the suspects' lives, focusing on Tuesdays, going back to six months before the first doctor on their list had been murdered.

Their respective worlds were disassembled, from front to back, beginning with financial records and filtering through their various digital lives, ending up with social media accounts.

The breakthrough came in bursts, and the first one just floated by, a single data point in a universe of unrelated information. When Lucas saw the second, he began a list in his head. By the third, he began to suspect what he was looking for. And by the fourth, he had it.

They had all worked very hard to stay invisible. But technology has become so interwoven with human life that they probably never realized they had made mistakes, not even after the fact.

—Trina Moncrieff had made three separate purchases at three separate bodegas on three separate Tuesdays, all within a nine-month period. The purchases were on separate cards. All were made between 9:15 and 9:30 P.M.

—Darrel Moncrieff had a single parking ticket issued to him at 8:03 on a Tuesday night. The date was different from the three Trina had made her purchases on. The license and make of the car matched the one at the CITGO out in Montauk on the night Dove Knox was murdered.

—Mindy Appelbaum made four separate purchases on four separate Tuesdays—all small sales at the same liquor store. Two of the transactions occurred between 7:20 and 7:30 P.M.; two were between 9:12 and 9:22 P.M. They were also months apart.

—Ira Alan White had made three purchases, all on separate Tuesdays—a MetroCard at the automatic machine at the 18th Street subway station (at 9:41 P.M.), and two cash withdrawals at different ATMs (7:04 and 7:21 P.M.).

There was nothing unusual about these transactions. They demonstrated nothing out of the ordinary in any meaningful way. Except that they had all occurred in Chelsea, where none of these people lived or worked.

Which gave Lucas his starting point.

Nadeel brought up a map of Chelsea and marked the location of all ten transactions and the single parking ticket; they had occurred within a single block of one another.

The team ran all the businesses, looking for one that would be a suitable meeting place every Tuesday between the hours of 7:30 and 9:00 P.M.

There were three diners on the block.

And one had a separate area at the back that could accommodate a group—the Chelsea Bird.

Lucas now knew where they met. But he didn't know who *they* were.

Bobby Nadeel was at the console, lit up like deadmau5. He hammered away at the keyboard to keep Lucas sated with visual data while Clive Bower handled the migration of information from Nadeel's laptop to the big Zeiss IX projector, wallpapering the ceiling of the planetarium in endless transactions.

Lucas took a sip of coffee, put the paper cup back down, and nodded at the skein of digits suspended in the night sky overhead. "We need to ask Little Brother for help."

Nadeel raised his hand. "You mean *Big Brother*."

"No, I do not." Lucas looked away from the ceiling, and something in his neck popped—which was long overdue. "It's not massive government surveillance that your average citizen has to worry about; it's the army of Little Brothers we've turned ourselves into— we're crowdsourcing our own surveillance state."

"Um . . . okay?"

"What I need is a list of everyone who has been in the Chelsea Bird on any Tuesday night over the past three years—let's say with a purchase between seven and ten thirty P.M. Then we look at their social media accounts and anyone who made a post that provides them with an alibi on any of the twenty-eight outstanding murders gets put on a list."

Nadeel held up his hand again. "That will net you thousands of people."

Lucas turned back to the ceiling. "You let me worry about that."

90

Chelsea

When Lucas walked in, the little bell on the spring over the door gave off a flat ding-a-ling that no one bothered to pay attention to.

The diner was classic Art Deco—chrome and stainless steel over Portoro marble and red imitation leather, all wrapped up in a quarter mile of glass.

Over the course of its life, hundreds of thousands of customers had rotated through. Everyday people. Hardworking people. Lazy people. Movie stars, musicians, and mobsters. It had been the target of sixty-three robberies and five of the would-be thieves were shot in the restaurant, four by police, one by a cook. There had been fifteen gang killings over the years, the last one occurring in February of 1978. The restaurant had appeared in seventeen TV shows, nine movies, sixteen commercials, and two music videos. Eight hundred and seven marriage proposals had occurred on the premises. Nine babies had been born under its roof. Twenty-eight people had died while eating there.

Lucas nodded a hello to the waitress at the front, and indicated the group at the back with a green anodized finger that clearly freaked her out a little.

They were decorating, and boxes of Christmas ornaments took

up six feet of counter space. Silver and blue tinsel garlands, plastic Santa Clauses. Fat little snowmen with fake carrot noses. Bluetooth Bing Crosby was singing "Silver Bells."

Tonight, like every Tuesday for the past three years, the group occupied a cluster of tables in the sunken area at the back, separated from the rest of the space by two half walls and beaded curtains. They could have been attending an Alcoholics Anonymous meeting, a get-together for the American Communist League, or a Game of Thrones club.

Lucas walked straight through to the back, and parted the beaded curtain to find nineteen people divided unevenly between six tables.

Conversation stopped cold. All nineteen faces turned to him.

"Sorry, man. This is a private meeting," a heavyset man in a Carhartt jacket said. He didn't try to be friendly. Or even polite.

Lucas walked over and sat down in front of him, and it wasn't difficult to see that this clearly irritated him.

He took off his sunglasses and stared the man down. After eight long seconds, the guy looked away, reorganized his composure, then turned back. "Private," he repeated.

Lucas shifted his attention to the group, taking each face in, one at a time. Some stared back; others looked away. But they all remained quiet.

After his visual tour, he turned back to the man in the Carhartt jacket. "John Cerrone, my name is Dr. Lucas Page, Federal Bureau of Investigation. We would like to question you about your part in the murder of Dr. Edward Lu."

Cerrone's mouth popped open—sound effect included—before he shut it. "I don't know what you're talking about."

A woman one table over said, "What is this about?"

Lucas turned to her. "Shirley Shipley, the FBI would like to question you about the murder of Dr. Arthur Fossner."

Another look of surprise.

Lucas swiveled his head, nodding at each person in turn. "Benjamin Rojas, you are wanted for questioning in the murder of Dr. Carol Villeneuve; Elizabeth Kline, you are wanted for questioning in the murder of Dr. Chester Vance; Moshe Kominsky, you are wanted for questioning in the murder of Dr. Dawn Ryan; Abigail Ratner, you are wanted for questioning in the murder of Dr. Paul Ho—"

On and on, around the room, he went.

One. By. One.

Case. By. Case.

Homicide. By. Homicide.

They began to stand. To put on coats. No one made eye contact. Or spoke. But they operated as a herd, running for safety.

As the first one—Dominic Lester, wanted for questioning in the death of Dr. May Arora—opened the beaded curtain, Whitaker came in. She was followed by the windbreaker brigade.

Whitaker was professional when she said, "Ladies and gentlemen, if you would all please place your hands on the table in front of you, no one will get shot."

And through the entire process, no one said a word.

91

26 Federal Plaza

Lucas sat in the leather and chrome Corbusier chair in Kehoe's office, feeling as if he were a supporting character in someone else's novel rather than the main character in his own. His existential angst was no doubt fueled by exhaustion—he was so tired that he could not delineate where his body ended and the chair began, and he wondered if Kehoe would just let him keep it so he wouldn't have to stand ever again. He could order some wheels from Amazon, maybe one of those little orange flags, and a cooler for snacks—he'd be golden.

Whitaker was off with Hoffner and his people, where they were going through the unenviable process of interviewing fourteen suspected murderers in different rooms, all at the same time. Five people who had been present at the diner didn't fit the equation. At least not yet. And they had all been let go with orders not to leave town. Three others were on the way in. More were being sought out. It was all coming down.

Hoffner, who was an imposing sight at the best of times, had looked positively fearsome as the unmarked vehicles delivered the suspects to the underground garage, one at a time. Hoffner had given each of them the same speech, delivered to the same stunned face—

the first to open up would get a deal while the rest spent eternity locked away in a greasy little concrete room that smelled of things best left unmentioned.

They were coming up on an hour into the process and Lucas wondered why Whitaker hadn't come back with good news—there was no way that all the suspects were keeping quiet. Hardened mob hit men cracked when a deal was floated in front of them—a bunch of nobodies from a self-help group most certainly didn't have the necessary stoicism.

Kehoe's cantilevered ten-foot floor-to-ceiling door swung in and Whitaker came around the front of the chair, saving Lucas from going through the process of turning his head.

He looked up, expecting to see one of her great white shark smiles. She looked glum as fuck. "They won't talk."

Without realizing that he had instigated the command—and completely surprised by it—Lucas was on his feet. "What do you mean?"

"Nothing. Nada. Not one of them is willing to give us what we need. We have half of them cold and we'll have the other half by the time the sun comes up. Double counts of murder one, conspiracy, and a dozen other felonies thrown in just because we can, and not a single one of those people will say *anything*."

"I don't get it."

"They're presenting like battered wives." Whitaker did a round of Kehoe's empty office—Kehoe was with the troops, hopping from anteroom to anteroom, looking through two-way mirrors at unsmiling people sitting at small tables, cups of coffee in their hands.

"Half have asked for lawyers; half of those have shown up. And all of them refuse to talk." Whitaker suddenly stopped as if she were seeing him for the first time. "If you don't lay down soon, you're going to lay down permanently."

"I look that bad?"

"You look like Bernie Lomax."

"How about we go get some food."

"Which means hot dogs, right?"

"Absolutely." Lucas held the door open for her. "Because life is about the little pleasures."

"You do realize that only rich white people say shit like that, right?"

They headed for the elevator.

"Are we still using your MetroCard to get around?"

Whitaker held up a key fob. "I'm back in the saddle."

The elevator was waiting for them, and Whitaker punched in for the second level in the garage, which was not their usual floor.

After descending into the concrete guts of Federal Plaza, the doors opened onto a security entrance identical to their usual floor. Whitaker carded them through the sally port, into the garage.

Lucas was used to two types of bureau vehicles—nondescript sedans and the testosterone-laden black Navigators that exuded the word "official." This level was a mix of vehicles, from Range Rovers to Coopers.

Lucas hoped that Whitaker hadn't been allotted some ancient beater simply because she had killed a bunch of FBI vehicles. None of the dead SUVs had been her fault—except maybe the one she had killed getting Erin to the hospital, and even that one could be argued away on semantics. And the two that had absorbed falling bodies could technically be written off as acts of God—or whatever label the FBI insurance rider substituted for that little chunk of nonsecular nomenclature. And the one that had been reduced to charcoal when Russo took out Arlo Reed could technically be written off as regular company wear and tear.

"No Navigator?"

"I'm afraid that my Navigator days are over."

"I am going to talk to Kehoe," Lucas said as Whitaker headed up a lane.

"About?" she asked without turning around. Or stopping.

"About getting you another Navigator." He slipped from pause into full-stop mode. "I agree that killing so many vehicles in such a short period of time *is* unusual, but like Motzkin demonstrated, and this case has *proved*, unusual and unlikely things happen *all the time*."

"So you're not coming?"

He resisted the temptation to stamp his feet. "Let me straighten Kehoe out first. He can't say no to me. And I don't know if I'll ever have the energy to come back here ever again."

Whitaker, who was now thirty paces ahead, waved over her shoulder and said, "Suit yourself," before ducking into the line of cars.

Lucas stood there, trying to calculate which would take fewer calories—getting into another combat of silences with Kehoe, or simply getting into whatever car Whitaker had been relegated to.

He heard a car door open. Then close. An engine fire up. Then Whitaker reversed out of the spot and backed down the lane, stopping beside him in a very ugly car.

She opened the passenger window and leaned over the armrest. "Are you getting in?"

Lucas stood there, staring at the car, while Whitaker flexed the engine, which sounded like Tom Waits playing a didgeridoo. "Just what, precisely, is this?" Even from three feet away, the new-car smell overrode the stink of exhaust.

"A Ferrari SF90."

Lucas looked it over. "Isn't it a little . . . juvenile?" But he opened the door and slid cautiously into the seat, which felt like it was inches from the ground—because it was.

He managed to find the seat belt, a complicated five-point affair, and began the process of harnessing himself in. He had to leave the right-side harness loose to accommodate for his ribs, which were starting to feel like they might get better after all.

Whitaker hit the gas a few times, sending the RPMs into peak dead-dinosaur burning territory, and spoke loudly over the massive display of horsepower. "They use cars like this in sting operations involving rogue Arab sheiks who dabble in arms sales. Pablo Escobar wannabes. That kind of thing. There are only three hundred of these suckers in the world, and the FBI owns one of them."

Lucas looked around at the small-dick energy, taking in the colored stitching, the bright gauges, and the fire extinguisher bolted to the floor. "How the fuck did you get Kehoe to let you sign this out?"

"I didn't sign it out. You did."

Then she punched down on the pedal, launching the red supercar up the ramp.

92

The Upper West Side

Lucas stayed in the fancy car while Whitaker ran into Gray's Papaya to pick up their meal. Although "meal" was technically a misnomer—"simulated food product" was more apt.

A crowd gathered around the car while Lucas waited for Whitaker. They took pictures and narrated videos, all while twisting their fingers up in pseudo gang signs, and Lucas found the entire experience bewildering and sad.

The ride up here had been an exercise that demonstrated many of the laws of physics, putting a few of them to the test. From the first time they had been put together during the winter sniper case, she had been heavy-footed. But now, with this ridiculous amalgamation of bad taste and horsepower to captain, she was a true danger. Playing hooky with such a pricey ride made it impossible to miss the Ferris Bueller analogy and Lucas thought about dialing the English Beat up on Spotify.

He was trying to calculate how many miles of colored yarn and gallon drums of pushpins they would need to connect all the spiders in Vaughan's criminogenic web when his phone went off.

He was grateful to see that it was Erin and hit *speaker*.

"Hey, baby."

"Hey yourself, Mr. Man. Have you remembered to eat?"

He smiled at that. "We're at Gray's Papaya right now. We're celebrating a little."

"So you got the guy?"

"It wasn't a guy; I'll fill you in when I get home. It's complicated." Lucas knew the message was warbled, but it would take a hundred thousand words to do it justice.

"So you can come home? Be with the kids? And me?" He could hear that she had her little chipmunk smile dialed up.

"Yes."

"Excellent." She sounded at peace. Happy. Which he knew was a momentary indulgence, because life was like that. "Lorne is coming by to check on me; he's dropping off a book that Neville sent. They're sweet."

"I told him to come out to the beach house with Neville at Christmas. With Whitaker and her son, I think everyone will have a little much-needed fun. We can bake some, um . . . what *do* you bake?"

"Cookies, Luke. You bake cookies."

"Excellent! We can bake cookies. Where do we buy the components? Do we have to order them or—"

"They're ingredients, not components, and no, we don't have to *order* them. Flour, sugar, some chocolate chips, eggs, and you're set."

"Great. Cookies it is."

"What about your friend Russo?"

"He's not my friend."

She snorted her little laugh again. "Yes, he is. I saw you with him. He's now the Third Amigo. You have to invite him. Does he have a family?"

Lucas shrugged. "We're not at the what's-your-address-so-I-can-put-you-on-my-Christmas-card-list point in our relationship. His wife died. Or they got divorced. Or she died after they got divorced. I think it's complicated."

"Well, I think it's sweet the way he very obviously admires you.

And even if you don't like him, everyone else does, so invite him for the holidays. Just two days. And Lorne will know what's happening by then. He'll either have a package, or he'll be back at work."

"What package?"

It was hard to miss that she was sleepy, but trying not to be. But that's what people did when they had been shot. "His CTS isn't getting any better. He tried everything—I mean absolutely everything, including acupuncture. He even tried Neurontin, which has no clinical proof of efficacy, so that tells you how desperate he is. After the two operations Delmonico performed on him didn't work, he tried physio, steroids, splinting. He's even been doing yoga and B6 injections. But it's coming up on three years, and if he can't operate anymore, the board is considering replacing him. He's been out of the OR for two years, and that's a long time."

Whitaker came out of the hot dog joint with a tray and a bag, and when the would-be Instagrammers saw the pistol on her waist, they backed off a little but kept taking pictures.

"Whitaker's coming back with our food. I gotta go."

"So you'll invite Russo for Christmas? Even Lorne likes him. And he likes fewer people than you do—so Russo is a statistical unicorn."

"I'll think about it."

Lucas hung up and Whitaker opened the door and handed the bag and tray over the console. "I hope this was worth driving all the way up here when there are, oh, I don't know, like *thirty-five thousand* restaurants closer to the office." She got in, all smiles.

But Lucas was going over the conversation with Erin. And something was wrong.

What was it?

And then it fell into place with all the other broken snippets of code that were meaningless on their own.

"We need to locate a cell phone and track it."

"Sure. I just have to call the office."

He opened the door and placed the food on the ground, between the car and the curb.

"What the fuck? I just waited in line for—"

He slammed the door and said, "Call."

She stared blankly at him for a few seconds, then dialed the office via the car's Bluetooth.

Hoffner's deep baritone came on over too many speakers. "Yeah, Whitaker, what is it?"

"It's Page. I know why they won't talk. I know who killed Vaughan. And we need to find him *right now*."

93

The Upper East Side

Lorne Jacobi was early, which was better than being late. Especially at this hour.

He was in the traditional Upper East Side outfit of a quilted Barbour jacket, corduroy pants, and English boots—with the seasonal necessity of a traditional black umbrella. On Sundays, when he wore this outfit to the park with Neville, he looked like a thousand other men from the neighborhood. And in some odd way, he enjoyed the anonymity.

He had his doctor's bag with him, which was a bit of a painful experience in that it was one of those reminders of a life he had worked so hard to have and might soon be gone. But he was also enough of a realist to understand that things continually changed, and if you didn't change with them, you would be left behind like some relic from your own life.

He waved to the two policemen in front of the Page house, and they nodded back. They looked bored and uninterested, but what could you expect from two men cooped up in a car all day long?

All the lights were on and Maude answered a few moments after he rang the bell. "Mr. Lorne!" she said, and waved him in with a wet paintbrush as if it were a wand.

"Hey, Maude. I know it's late, but I told your mom I was coming by."

"Yeah. I heard. Did you say hello to the cops?" She leaned out the door and waved at the policemen, who waved back. "I think they're bored." The combination of fingerprint-marked jeans and paint-splattered T-shirt looked good on her, and for a moment Lorne envied her youth.

Lorne handed Maude his bag while he took his boots off and hung his coat on the Art Deco hall tree by the stairs.

When he was done, Maude held the bag out. "She's upstairs. In bed. You want a juice box or something?"

"I'm okay. But thank you for asking." He tapped the side of the bag. "Neville sent a book over for your mom."

Maude smiled, and put the paintbrush into her jeans pocket. "She said you and Mr. Neville might be coming out to the beach for Christmas."

Lorne liked how direct she was. He was so used to the bullshit politics at work that speaking to a teenager was both refreshing and reinvigorating. Then again, Erin was like that, too—she avoided all the petty jealousies and chest-thumping that he had long ago accepted as a departmental pathology. "We'll know next week—we have a lot going on. If we do, is there anything you want for Christmas?"

Her face scrunched up at that. "No gifts. There are five of us and you'd go broke. Plus, we don't need anything."

"Gifts don't have to be about *needing*; they can be about *wanting*."

She shrugged. "I think we're all good. Except for Damien. He needs a smaller mouth. Just make a donation to a kids' charity or something; that would be very cool. And bring some pastries or stuff—we all like pastries."

"Noted." Lorne headed upstairs. "If you need me, I'll be with your mom."

94

Russo was pretty drunk as he barreled up Madison. He had the monkey magnets on, but the siren was off. He was doing about seventy, which was fast enough and too slow both at the same time. But driving with an elevated blood alcohol content was routine for him, and even if he got pulled over, this was his neighborhood, his precinct.

When he hit Page's street, he killed the lights and turned left, which was the wrong way.

The two cops in the cruiser popped up behind the windshield, which was the appropriate action when a car went the wrong way down a one-way street.

Russo double-parked directly across from Page's, the nose of his car pointing toward Fifth Avenue, and got out of the car. He nodded at his men across the street, and they visibly relaxed.

It was cold and raining and he put his gloves on. Crossed his arms. Looked up at the house.

The front windows were all lit up. Shadows moved. He could hear the distant sounds of life going on inside. Everything looked good in Page Land.

Russo crossed to the cruiser, and when the window opened, his two men nodded in unison.

"Detective," the officer named Hoi said.

Miller, his partner, just smiled and nodded as if he had been raised on lead paint chips and nitrous oxide.

A box with the word *Pizza!* stenciled onto the lid was wedged onto the dash, along with two coffees that had fingerprinted rings of steam on the glass.

"Anything happening?" Russo asked.

Hoi shook his head in disappointment. "Nada, sir. Their friend from last night dropped by—he's there now."

"Lorne Jacobi?"

Hoi shrugged. "I don't know. The same guy that visited while you were here."

That had to be Lorne Jacobi. He had promised to look in on Erin. But it was kind of late for house calls.

Russo's phone rang, and he recognized Lucas Page's ringtone.

Both uniformed cops looked at him like they expected him to answer it.

He knew he'd look suspicious just standing out here, not answering. So he reached into his pocket, took out his little just-in-case revolver, and shot both men in the face.

95

Central Park

Whitaker was a perfectly timed machine, paddle shifting, steering, counter-steering, and braking the Ferrari through the park on the 66th Street crossing. They were doing almost a hundred and twenty, stirring up leaves and mist with the gaudy red Batmobile. Every time she hit the gas, they tore through another time zone.

Lucas was listening to his phone ring. And ring. And fucking ring some more.

Erin's voice finally came on. "Hey, honey. I'm here with Lorne and—"

"Listen to me! It's Russo! Don't answer the door. Don't let anyone in. It's Russo. He's Vaughan's partner. They fucking knew—"

—the distant sound of gunshots—

"Oh my God, Luke! I just heard two gunshots. Right outside."

"Get the kids in our room. Lock the door."

"What—? *Kids!*" she screamed, and the line went dead.

Dingo was at the dojo, way up in the Bronx. So that was out.

How had he missed this?

Whitaker's phone rang over Bluetooth, and without taking her eyes from the road she punched the call through.

Lucas almost screamed, "What?"

Hoffner's voice came on in calm surround monotone. "I've got a team rolling. They're on their way. I also have a call into the Nineteenth—they're sending people."

"It's Russo! It's fucking Russo! Those are *his* people. Tell them to shoot that motherfucker on sight!"

"Page, calm down."

"Don't fucking tell me to—"

"Page, listen to me—everyone is on the way. It doesn't make sense for Russo to do anything; he—"

"This isn't about *making sense*, you moron! *He's fucking nuts!* This is about his revenge. Erin is the one victim who survived. This is personal for him. *Personal.*"

"Shit."

"That's what you got? *Shit?* Fuck you!" Lucas reached over and disconnected the call.

Whitaker rocketed out of the park on the 65th Street exit, straight into a red light and a wall of cars.

She downshifted and braked and the tires screamed as she skidded through a small opening between two cars, then punched the gas.

Brakes squealed. Cars collided.

She steered around a white SUV, then zipped through the intersection as if protected by divine intervention. The Ferrari bounced on a rut, bottoming out, and she straightened out and hit the gas.

And they were through. On 65th, heading to Madison at three times the speed limit.

The Ferrari swallowed the full block in seconds, and Lucas grabbed the door handle and hoped for more deific protection at Madison, where Whitaker once again downshifted and swung the big powerful ass of the Ferrari through the light, and around the corner, in a wide arc of noise that threw up water and summoned an angry opera of horns.

Madison ahead was empty. And she floored the fucking pedal.

The big V12 lit up like a warhead and they ate Madison Avenue.

Crossing 66th.

Then 67th.

68th.

69th.

70th.

Then they were there, and Whitaker downshifted and threw the Ferrari around the final corner, the wrong way down Lucas's street.

"There." Lucas squinted into the dark. "That's Russo's car." It was double-parked and facing west.

Whitaker punched up the block and Russo materialized from behind the cruiser that was parked at the curb.

He stopped in the middle of the street.

Whitaker yelled, "Get down!" just as Russo went into a classic Weaver stance.

But the racing harnesses held them in place like a lead hand. They couldn't duck.

Whitaker jerked the wheel and hit the brakes just as Russo fired, and the high-pitched *CRACK!* hit the corner of the windshield as they went sideways on the asphalt.

"Sonofabitch!" Whitaker yelled, and slammed the car into *reverse*.

Russo fired on them in rapid succession.

One!

Two!

Three!

She wibbled the wheel as they launched in reverse, and all the shots missed, taking angry bites out of the windshield.

There was an instant of silence and Whitaker had her piece out. She pointed through the spiderwebbed glass, sighted Russo in, and fired off three shots.

Russo tumbled sideways, and ripped the door to his car open. Got inside. And sped away.

"Page, you okay?"

"Go! Go!" he bellowed, picking glass out of his face.

Whitaker shifted into first, and went after the fucker.

But the windshield was shattered, and the light refracting through the mosaic surface was impossible to see through.

Whitaker shifted twice before the end of the block, and they roared onto Fifth Avenue, once again passing through a flock of honking vehicles with impunity.

"I can't see," she said calmly.

Lucas punched at the windshield with his prosthetic, hitting it a dozen times in the corner before taking it out of the frame on his side.

He hit it again. And again. And again. Until it lay across the dash, still connected on her side, where he couldn't reach.

"I can't—" he began.

Whitaker wrenched the wheel violently to the right and the windshield shot off the dash, bounced on the hood, then went over the side of the car. It slapped against the door, buffeting like a torn sail.

Russo's sedan slalomed through traffic up ahead, rocking back and forth on its springs.

The windshield thwacked against Whitaker's door, and she veered to the left, sideswiping a line of cars. The windshield—and her mirror—tore away.

Emergency lights appeared in the mirror on Lucas's side. Cop cars. At least five of them.

At this speed, wind and rain whipped them in the faces, nuggets of glass swirled around.

Lucas was protected by his sunglasses, but Whitaker squinted into the shit pelting them.

She opened both of their windows, which helped redirect the airflow.

They ripped through 66th, then 65th, and cars were strewn about from their last trip through, when they had crossed the right-angle transept.

The avenue ahead was relatively clear, and Whitaker punched it. They gained on the sedan.

Russo had the car flat-out on Fifth, but Whitaker ate up the road more efficiently.

They crossed 63rd and Russo was five car lengths ahead.

By 62nd, it was two.

At 61st, Whitaker was right on his ass, and she slipped into his stream, and the wind in their faces let off.

They sat in the pocket for a few heartbeats, and then she pulled out.

There was a second when they headed away from Russo's car, on a direct path to hit the Grand Army Plaza loop.

"Hold on!" she yelled over the wind and rain and the scream of the power plant.

She steered hard to the left, downshifted, and hammered the fuel.

At the 59th Street intersection, the front end of the Ferrari connected with the back right quarter panel of Russo's sedan in a perfect PIT maneuver.

There was a brain-blinding scream as the front end of the sports car crumpled.

Then the racing cage within connected with Russo's back axle, and the lighter vehicle's stored momentum transferred to his back end, pushing it violently sideways.

The airbags in the Ferrari deployed.

Russo swerved. Then skidded. Tried to counter-steer. But he lost control.

The Ferrari spun around.

Russo's front wheels hit the curb, and the vehicle lifted off the wet asphalt, launching forward, toward the Fifth Avenue Apple Store.

The Ferrari spun down the street, pinballing off the parked cars in a drumroll of dents, sparks, flashing lights, and alarms.

Russo's car tumbled on the long axis, and when the back end slammed into the concrete, the trunk opened, scattering Gatorade and vodka bottles and papers into the rain.

The Ferrari completed one last rotation, slammed into a row of parked cars, and came to a stop.

Russo's ride tumbled twice more, and sledgehammered into the side of the engineered glass cube. The massive panel bent—actually flexed—for an instant, and it looked like it might stop the car.

But the glass reached the end of its tolerances, disintegrating in a loud crash, and the car was injected into the building.

It tumbled one more quarter turn, sending shattered everything through the air, before slamming into the glass staircase, where it stopped, suspended like an insect in amber.

Lucas looked over and Whitaker was still. She had a deep gash on her forehead, and blood was streaming onto her face. She was pounding on the racing harness, but she couldn't get free.

"Are you okay?" he asked.

She looked over at him and nodded a single, painful time. "My harness is stuck. Go," she said, holding out her pistol. "Get that fucker."

Lucas looked at the weapon, shook his head, and pulled the door handle. Nothing happened.

He hit the door with his shoulder and it popped open with a very expensive groan. But he didn't leave—he turned and hit Whitaker's buckle with his metal fist. She grunted, and the harness popped open.

He pushed her door open for her and it fell off. She began to climb out.

Lucas headed for the giant crystal cube.

96

The Upper East Side

The police cars surrounded them like nineteenth-century cavalry on a genocidal mission.

Cops emptied out. Drew their weapons. Took cover behind vehicles.

"Freeze!" three different voices yelled at varying degrees of volume, all set to eleven on the threat scale.

Lucas stopped.

Behind him, Whitaker, weapon still in hand, swayed on her feet. "I am a federal agent!"

"Drop it, lady!"

Whitaker slowly turned her head toward the command but didn't drop the pistol. "I repeat, I am a federal agent—Special Agent Alice Whitaker, Federal Bureau of Investigation. You are interfering with—"

"Sure, lady. And I'm Ryan Reynolds. Drop your fucking gun!"

Russo's car hung in the center of the big glass cube like a factory second by Damien Hirst. The entire thing was smoking, and the cube was quickly filling with a dense black cloud.

"You too, asshole!" one of the cops yelled at Lucas. "On your knees!"

Which was a command that Lucas couldn't follow if he tried—his prosthetic would not allow it.

"In three seconds, you are on the way to the morgue. Do you—?"

That was when a troop of FBI SUVs—lights flashing—descended on the scene like velociraptors on a hunt. The doors opened, and a dozen men sporting semi-automatic carbines got out, all in their famous windbreakers. A helicopter appeared in the air overhead, three large yellow letters on the bottom.

Hoffner got out of the SUV nearest the man ordering Whitaker down. "This is an FBI operation. We are—"

The cop sighting in on Whitaker said, "That bitch has to—" But the sentence ended with his head in a windshield.

"We have this!" Hoffner roared, and the cops all lifted their guns.

Lucas's and Hoffner's stares met over the square, and the big man nodded and said, "Go."

The front door was gone, and Lucas stepped into the glass enclosure. It smelled of fried car parts and gasoline.

Russo's car was suspended at a right angle to the ground, facing straight into the earth.

Lucas took a dozen steps down until he was level with Russo, who hung loosely in his seat belt. His face looked like it was on inside out and some of his teeth were embedded in the steering wheel. But he was staring straight at Lucas.

Lucas crouched down to better see the cop. The curved glass banister was between them, and he used it to support himself. One of Russo's shoes lay on the step below, upside down and bloody.

Russo looked over. Gave Lucas that loony smile of his. "Page." His glass eye was gone, or at least it looked like it was—it was hard to tell. "How ya doin'?"

Lucas had no idea what he was supposed to say. "Why?"

"Why, what?" Russo asked, and laughed, which quickly converted to a cough.

Gas was cascading down the side of the car, hitting the stairs on its way to the lowest point somewhere in the retail space below.

"Why all of it?"

Russo looked at him for what felt like a long time, his smile slowly converting to a bloody rictus grin that was more space than teeth. Then he raised that little pistol of his. "Just in case," he said, and pulled back the hammer.

"Russo, no!"

But Russo pulled the trigger and the pistol roared and the round splatted against the curved glass banister.

The leaking fuel ignited, and flames blossomed to life in slow motion.

Russo's lone eye widened and he began pounding on his seat belt, which wouldn't let him go.

The flames went from slo-mo to a conflagration that enveloped the car.

Russo began to scream.

Lucas felt hands grab him, begin to bear him away. He was pulled toward the upper deck just as Russo, absorbed by the roiling cauldron, placed the barrel of the little gun into his mouth.

Lucas was dragged to street level and the men supporting him lunged for the portal. More first responders rushed forward, and arms bore him away.

Behind him, the glass building filled with flames and there was an ear-puncturing flash as the cube disintegrated, throwing Lucas and the first responders to the concrete.

Glass and metal and a billion dollars of Chiat/Day marketing blew into the sky. Rained down on the concrete.

Lucas turned back to the burning hole in the ground and all he could hear—louder than the police sirens and bullhorns and confusion, louder than Russo's final screams, louder than the explosion and chaos—was the echo of the empty chamber when Russo had pulled the trigger that final time.

97

Fifth Avenue was being rerouted below 57th and above 60th, which basically meant they had a four-block perimeter that was causing all kinds of havoc with traffic, even at this hour. The rain was coming down, but it didn't have any conviction, and the big glass no-longer-a-cube was a smoking square hole in the concrete, its open maw belching heat and steam like a portal to the underworld designed by Albert Speer. The street was pulsing with all manner of emergency and task lighting and everyone from the FDNY to the NYPD was on-site, securing the area and keeping the phone-camera clownarchy far enough away that their psychopathy was reduced to a distant hum.

Lucas and Whitaker sat on the back bumper of an ambulance, and the rain was causing all kinds of visual noise for Lucas. But the big white bandage over Whitaker's left eyebrow—covering seven field stitches—gave him something to focus on.

"You know," Whitaker said as she watched a dozen firemen pump water into the Apple void. "You're like natural selection in real time."

Lucas smiled and let himself enjoy the fatigue that was setting in. "I clearly remember *you* doing the driving."

"I am *so* fired."

Lucas waved it away. "Don't worry, I'll talk to Kehoe."

She snorted loudly and slapped his knee, which almost upended his precarious balance on the bumper. "Please don't."

The fire had migrated into the retail Apple space below and taken on a life of its own, eating through the electronic inventory. The intermittent burst of cell phone batteries and other lithium-powered devices as they exploded offset the commotion up here, adding texture to the scene.

Hoffner was near the line of black SUVs, standing over one of the NYPD power players and refusing to apologize for putting Ryan Reynolds's melon into a windshield. Even from this distance, Lucas could tell that the policeman was losing and, more importantly, he could tell that the policeman knew he was losing, which brought its own reward. After Russo, Lucas doubted he'd make friends with any more cops for a while. Hoffner probably felt the same way.

Whitaker interrupted his little interlude when she said, "Thank God it's over."

"Special Agent Whitaker," he said, sounding very official, "God has been officially dead since Zarathustra walked down the mountain and kicked Nietzsche in the shin."

She side-eyed him and shook her head. "How did you figure out it was Russo?"

"The final bolt in the thing was something Erin said on the phone. And it fit in with everything else. It was there the whole time, from our first encounter. I just didn't see it. Fuck. Me."

"Um, that's not an answer."

Lucas straightened out his back and nothing popped, which was a minor miracle. "Okay, so when Russo showed up at Hess's hospice in Westchester, he was waiting for us—*in case* we went to visit Hess, which he knew meant that I had started to figure things out. When we showed up, it confirmed his suspicions and he insinuated himself into our investigation to keep abreast of our information flow."

She looked over and her mouth was hanging open. But just for an instant. "Classic perp behavior."

"And he told us right there that seven of the homicides had happened in his precinct and that his people were the first on-site in all seven deaths. Seven out of thirty-one murders. That's almost twenty-three percent, which is approaching a quarter of the homicides. That is significant. And I missed it." He paused for a moment as another piece fell into the pocket. "He was also first on the scene when Ira Alan White tried to kill Erin; he was probably waiting a few blocks away while it went down.

"He also brought up therapy a bunch of times—in Erin's hospital room, that night at my house. He said it was sitting around with a bunch of people who have problems so bad you hope they're not contagious. I bet you that Ferrari over there that when we get a warrant to see if Russo's name is in Vaughan's files it'll be there, somewhere. They did this together."

Whitaker looked over at the Ferrari, which was now a car in name only. "That thing ain't worth a peso, my man."

Lucas continued gaming it out, knowing that enough of it was true that they could move each detail a few columns this way or that and it would still come out the same. "And the way he took out Arlo Reed? Russo saw him coming because he was *looking for him*. I bet they were all in Afghanistan together in some way. Maybe they all worked with Vaughan on his 'special projects.'"

The reel-to-reel in Whitaker's head was taking this all in and sending it to the analytical software and she was slowly nodding. "That's cold; I mean mother-in-law kind of cold."

Lucas looked toward the smoking square in the concrete as another burst of exploding batteries echoed up from below. The temperature differential between the water from the fire hoses and the air was generating a localized fogbank, and figures faded in and out of focus like phantasms. "And he handled the Delmonico killing all wrong. Or at least it was handled incorrectly in hindsight. He didn't show us that dash-cam footage until *after* our people requested the CCTV footage from the Bridge Authority. I was sitting in the diner in Washington Heights after Trina Moncrieff jumped off her balcony and he called. He said, 'I just saw the rec your people put in for the surveillance footage from the Brooklyn Bridge on the night that Jennifer Delmonico was killed, and there's some sister footage that I got from a dash cam that you'll want to see'—that's verbatim. He had *already seen* the bridge footage—he had it immediately after her death—but he didn't mention it until he knew *we* were going to see it. And I should have realized that for such a smart guy, he missed that timing game with Arlo Reed and Ludwig Kling when they tag-teamed Delmonico on the bridge." The phantasms over by the burning square gate to the underworld were haloed in light, lesser demons cooling down the portal to Hades. "And I don't know how I didn't see it, but Russo was the father of Delmonico's baby."

Whitaker jumped to her feet. "NO! NO! NO!"

"Please, turn off the cap locks."

"Sorry. But no way! *You* got Vaughan's DNA sample."

"You're missing the subterfuge here."

"*Subterfuge?* Who are you, Harvey Keitel?"

Lucas watched the haloed demons run their hoses. "I collected the sample, but who handed it in?"

She opened her mouth to answer, then closed it and shook her head. "Fuck me."

"I got Vaughan's DNA sample and Russo bagged it. From there the chain of custody goes to Russo. *He* delivered it to the NYPD lab because they had already sequenced the DNA from Delmonico's fetus. He must have removed Vaughan's DNA and put his own DNA on it because he knew that it was his child. Russo was the older guy who lived on the Upper East Side and was funny—he said it himself. Verbatim."

"How did you figure that out?"

"The anodizing on my fingers was worn through after I got it back from the lab. They wouldn't have used something to clean it that would strip the anodizing—that's a chemical process. So Russo must have scrubbed it with an SOS pad or something."

Whitaker was walking in small circles. "Go on."

"And Jacobi knew Russo from the hospital. I bet we look into the schedules and time sheets and we can put Russo and Delmonico in Emerge at the same time, probably more than once. Delmonico worked on one of Russo's co-workers, or she was there one of the nights he brought in a perp. They started seeing each other. Maybe he needed her to get access to patient files or something. I don't know all the nuances, but she got pregnant, and maybe she wanted to leave him, maybe she wanted a commitment and he didn't, and he had Arlo Reed and Ludwig Kling kill her. Maybe she found out he *was* accessing files through her computer and threatened to report him— who knows? And I always found it weird that he was proud of that 'Number One Ex-Husband!' mug, yet said he was a widower. And Delmonico's mother said Jennifer was seeing a widower."

"But why kill Kling? Kill Reed? They were all in this together."

"Were they?"

"What do you mean?"

Lucas was surprised she hadn't seen the correlation. "Think about it—with Vaughan, Reed, and Kling dead, nothing leads to Russo. Even if we got confessions out of all the people we dug up—"

Whitaker held up her hand. "And by 'we' you mean *you*."

Lucas ignored the remark. "Even if we got confessions out of all the people *we* dug up, there isn't any proof—it would be the word of a bunch of murderers against an NYPD detective. Nothing leads back to him. And if we combine Moncrieff jumping off her balcony with all the sealed lips down at Federal Plaza tonight, I think it's safe to assume that most of them, if not all, are closed doors. And all the hard evidence actually points to Vaughan, not Russo."

"So Russo killed Vaughan?"

That was another thing that had been bothering Lucas. "It had to be. He was waiting for us at the corner the night the men in black stormed Vaughan's apartment—he was there *before* us. And a homicide detective would know how to cover his tracks—a rain suit, rubber gloves, and some electrical tape go a long way. And the ME said that whoever took Vaughan's head off had used a knife with a six-to seven-inch blade and it wasn't the first time they had decapitated someone. That blade length fits in with a combat knife—a Ka-Bar or something similar—and I think we can safely assume that there's a good chance he had done that before."

"But why decapitate Vaughan? Why sew his eyes and mouth shut?"

Lucas shrugged; some mysteries were precisely that—mysteries. "I think he was making a point. Maybe for the members of the group, so they'd realize that there was a bigger badder voodoo daddy out there. We know that he had the potential to frighten people. I thought that Trina Moncrieff chose to jump off her balcony rather than face us. Maybe she was afraid of facing Russo. Moth wouldn't talk to us even though we had her cold. Why? She knew that Vaughan had control of her life in a way—he could always speak to a parole board, or maybe even have her forcibly medicated and silenced. But with a maniac like Russo as an attack dog? The fear factor had to be unbearable. And don't forget, it was Russo who found Moth, just like Ira Alan White—*before the bureau did*. He knew Moth wouldn't say anything. I wonder what he threatened her with?"

"That poor woman."

Lucas had been thinking about that, too, and he nodded. "Yeah, that poor woman."

Whitaker still looked dazed, which the blood and bandages somehow accentuated. "But that doesn't explain the sutures on Vaughan's eyes and mouth. Wouldn't a simple decapitation—Jesus, fuck, listen to me—'simple decapitation.'" She picked up pacing in small circles again. "Wouldn't a decapitation be enough of a message? I don't understand the sutures."

Lucas shrugged. "You're forgetting something."

"Yeah? What?"

"That Russo was fucking nuts. Maybe that's all the reason there is. Maybe we'll learn something later. Who knows?" And he was willing to let that be an answer to this entire case. Some things were just never meant to be figured out. And some things simply didn't matter.

Whitaker dropped back down onto the bumper of the ambulance. "Have you figured out the big *why* in this one? You said this one was driven by motive."

"It was sold as a revenge narrative to a lot of the people committing the homicides, and maybe that's what holds it together—maybe Russo lost his eye because of a doctor. But maybe it's even simpler than that—maybe Russo just got a kick out of killing people and he thought of himself as the smartest person in the room."

"Then why stop?"

"I think when you beat him out of his hundred bucks with my numerical recall, he realized that his self-evaluation had been a gross misconception. I think he figured out that with Vaughan, Reed, and Kling unplugged, there was nothing to tie him to all of this. I think he was cleaning house, tying up loose ends before closing shop and shutting everything down. At least for a while. I bet if we go back and look at all of the murder investigations he was ever involved in, we'll find some strange coincidences and weird little through lines—I think he's been active for years. He's just been careful. And he probably investigated a few of his own murders, which is an easy way not to get caught."

Whitaker nodded as if it all sounded plausible—which was all anyone could expect at this point. Maybe months down the road, after the bureau had folded it all up and packed it away in a file somewhere out there in the cloud, a few details might be off. But so what? "What was the thing that Erin said on the phone that put it all together for you?"

Lucas looked back up at the fog and smoke and the indistinct forms moving through the night. "She said something that was similar to something you said earlier—that Russo liked me, which made him a statistical unicorn. And Erin always says there are two kinds of people in the world—those who like me, and those who have met me. And, well . . ." He let it trail off. "I knew that he had been lying."

She was looking at him and he saw something odd in her eyes and he held up his hand. "I'd much rather be correct than be liked."

"Then you're succeeding." But she did give him her big smile. "And you always got me."

"That's real swell, but we can't sit around on the weekends watching TV like George and Weezie." He knew he needed to stand up, but he wasn't certain that he could depend on his body to obey the neural commands. Besides, Newton's First Law of Motion stated that a body at rests tended to stay at rest, and who was he to argue with one of the three greatest minds in human history? "You have that guy you met upstate last month. The deputy who brought you flowers in the hospital. What was his name?"

"Owen McCoy." Whitaker held up her phone for illustrative purposes. "I have received thirty-one messages from Deputy McCoy since the night I met you at the pizza joint."

"Maybe if you explained that you were busy, he would understand."

Whitaker looked over at him as if his prosthetic eyeball had hatched an octopus. "You think I can put up with some needy dude who sends me thirty-one messages in a week?" She hit the *delete* command and the messages blipped out.

Lucas allowed himself a little laugh. "I guess not."

A figure that moved like a Coke machine with legs materialized out of the mist, followed by a smaller one with a finely tailored outline.

"Dr. Page, Special Agent Whitaker." Kehoe's voice was even, but there was an undercurrent of irritation. But what could they expect? They had just obliterated one of the city's landmarks.

Whitaker said, "Sir," nodding like a peasant greeting a lord.

Lucas waved with his aluminum hand but didn't bother standing.

Kehoe looked up and down the street, his gaze momentarily stopping on errant bits of visual information. He nodded a few times, none of them in a good way, then turned his attention to them. "Are you two finished for the night?"

Lucas nodded heavily. "Yeah."

Kehoe took a long look around. When he was done, he bounced his focus between Lucas and Whitaker. "I believe I saw a car down on Forty-Sixth that isn't destroyed—you two might want to swing by with a couple of hammers on the way home. You know, just to be thorough."

Hoffner stood silently by, doing something Lucas had never thought possible—smiling—and for the first time, Lucas noticed a wide diastema in his front teeth.

Kehoe threw a large plastic evidence bag onto the deep bumper. It was wet, and torn, but there was no missing the contents—the clothing that Dove Knox had worn to the gala that night. "That was in Russo's trunk."

Lucas picked the bag up and wiped the water off with his original hand. Dove's suit was neatly folded, no doubt one of his final actions, and Lucas felt a bolt of sadness hit him—in the adrenaline-fueled hours since Knox's death, he had not had the time to mourn. "Thank you."

Whitaker took a stiff step toward Kehoe and, like a young George Washington holding an axe, went into confession mode. "I'm sorry about the Ferrari, sir."

Kehoe examined her for a moment, then looked back up the street, where the dead sports car was being loaded onto the dead sports car carrier by the dead sports car people. When he looked back he said, "What Ferrari?" and walked away.

98

The Upper East Side

Erin was propped up by all those pillows that Lucas never understood from any practical perspective. She was working on the Patti
Smith biography that Lorne Jacobi had given her. Her glasses were
low on her nose, and her hair framed her face in a blunt cut, which
was new for her. Maude had done the job, removing the burnt and
singed patches, and taking it down to what was considered short
for Erin (but which most women would still consider long), and the
Rossetti model was still an easy comparison to make, even with the
bandages.

She looked up and smiled. "Is that breakfast?"

"That depends."

"On?"

"On whether you consider pizza bagels and coffee to be breakfast."

She closed the book and tossed it into the mountain of pillows,
which then stirred, Bean emerging. "Who doesn't?"

Lucas put the tray down across her lap, and took up position at
the end of the bed—one of the benefits of her five-foot-one-and-
one-half-inch height was that he never had to worry about sitting
down on her legs.

She surveyed the tray and rubbed her hands together. "This looks tasty!"

There were two pizza bagels—microwaved—and a big mug of coffee. He had put a little plastic flower into a Play-Doh bud vase that he found in the library (it looked like Alisha's work but might have been Hector's—he wasn't big on effort in any exercise that wasn't self-initiated). But the breakfast component he was most proud of was the real estate listing.

He found a place he thought Erin and the kids would like, an eighteenth-century stone cottage on a tiny Irish island called Arranmore. The island was crime-free, boasted a population of less than six hundred people, and was three and a half miles from the Irish coast. It even had a few trees. It looked like the place they made Christmas movies about.

She reached for a pizza bagel and her hand paused over the plate before picking up the listing. "What is this?" she asked, unfolding it.

"It's a real estate listing," Lucas said proudly.

She stopped, and looked up at him. "What *kind* of real estate listing?"

"You said you wanted us to leave New York. To move away." He smiled. "Somewhere with trees."

"When did I say that?" She looked shocked.

"In the alley that day."

"*What* day?"

"The day you were shot. After I pulled you out of the car."

Without taking her eyes from him, she refolded the printout and gently placed it back on the tray. "I was in shock, Luke. Who knows *what* I said?"

"I do. You said that you wanted to move."

She shook her head, still looking confused. And more than a little concerned. "Well, I don't. I like it here."

"But you said—"

"I. Was. In. Shock. We're not moving."

"Are you su—?"

"Positive."

"That is the best news I've had all day!"

Erin picked up a bagel and tore it in half, using both hands, which meant that the strength was coming back to her fingers. "Can you imagine us on a tiny island off of Ireland?"

He smiled. "Why not?"

"First, there's not enough stuff there for you to blow up. Second, with a population of six hundred people, you're statistically unlikely to find a single friend. Besides, we're New Yorkers. All of us. We'd have to homeschool the kids. I'd have nowhere to work. And we'd always be outsiders."

Bean made a run at the bagel in Erin's fingers and Lucas scooped him up with his aluminum hand. "A lot of people would consider those to be selling points."

"Yeah, well, you and I are not a lot of people." She shook her head. "Can you imagine uprooting the kids and moving across the Atlantic?"

"I can't imagine us moving across the street."

"So that settles it?"

Lucas reached over and plucked the real estate listing off the tray and tucked it into his pocket. "Apparently so, yes."

The kids came ripping upstairs. Lemmy was the front-runner, and he came bounding into the room like a gazelle. He dropped his snout onto the tray, upending the Play-Doh vase and plastic flower just before the kids stormed the room like Vikings rushing a village—Vikings in footsie pajamas.

Dingo was with them, but he stayed in the doorway. "Um, Luke? There's a delivery from your friend Kehoe downstairs."

"Can you sign for it?"

Dingo held up the slip, smiling. "Done."

Erin gave him one of the looks she usually reserved for Lucas when he wasn't paying attention. "So what's the problem?"

"Look out the window."

Lucas and the kids walked over and pulled the curtains. All eleven eyes rotated down, to the street.

A flatbed was double-parked in front of the house with the man-gled Ferrari on the back. The driver was trying to unload it into an empty parking space, but the car had no wheels that turned, and it was squealing with the friction. But it was clear the guy unloading it wasn't going to give up just because of a little noise and a few sparks.

Holy shit, Brett Kehoe had a sense of humor. Demonstrating once again, that unusual things happen all the time.

Dingo came over and slapped Lucas in the chest with the delivery slip. "There's a note," he said.

As expected, Kehoe's handwriting was perfect.

Luke,

I heard your Volvo was in the shop—please feel free to use this in the interim.

BK

99

Metropolitan Detention Center
Brooklyn

It was early, and Denise Moth looked tired. More tired than last time. But she sat down, folded her arms across her chest, and leveled her stare at Lucas, going straight to his working eye, which impressed him—she had a good memory.

Her lawyer had once again agreed to be present, which said something about his dedication—the legal types tended to be of the *Fool me once, shame on you; fool me twice, shame on me* mind-set. And this was their third time at the table.

A man in a very expensive suit stood in the corner by the door, here as one of the few favors Lucas had ever asked of Brett Kehoe.

Lucas took off his glasses so there would be no misunderstanding, then put his metal hand down on the manila envelope on the table. Her focus shifted for a second, then she looked back up, and Lucas wondered if she had any hope, or happiness, or dreams left.

Not that he needed her for this; most, if not all, of Vaughan's former patients back at Federal Plaza would soon be trying to eat one another for a place in the lifeboat.

And there was only one seat.

Lucas and Moth stayed locked in a staring contest for a few

moments, which was quite the accomplishment against a man whose ocular setup was 50 percent special effects.

After they dragged the uncomfortable silence out for as long as it took for her lawyer to start sighing, Lucas pushed the envelope across the table.

Moth glanced down at it, then back up, which said a lot about her. Mrs. Page used to have a word for that—"chutzpah."

"Open it," he said.

Moth stared at him a little longer, then picked up the envelope, turned it over in her hands, and pulled the flap back. She took out the photographs and placed them on the dented stainless tabletop.

Lucas reached over and fanned them out, displaying official-looking images of Dr. Matthias Vaughan, Detective Jonathan Russo, Arlo Reed, and Ludwig Kling.

Tears filled her eyes, migrated to her lashes, but she didn't look up. Or move.

Lucas kept his voice even as he laid it out. "You went to Vaughan for help, to find some way to deal with losing your son. He had Reed and Kling kill the doctor who signed off on ending your son's care— Nellie Kozik. Then he used that information to blackmail you, forcing you to go after Dr. Ibicki—and if you refused, he had you on the hook for Kozik's murder, a homicide that Reed and Kling had committed. Russo was insurance for you not to talk—a murderous police officer has all the hallmarks of immunity. You were told no one would believe you.

"So you tried to kill Ibicki, but didn't succeed. I read the file and I think you failed on purpose. So Russo spoke to his friends, who were handling the case, and they brought in Matthias Vaughan as a character witness. They held you hostage, Denise."

Moth's bottom lip was trembling. But she stayed immobile, not looking up, not turning away, not saying anything.

Lucas reached across and pulled the photographs away—she did not need to see her tormentors anymore. Not in her head. And certainly not shoved in her face.

"But all you are really guilty of—other than a lot of understandable anger—is *trying* to kill Dr. Ibicki. You failed, and someone else completed the task."

Lucas didn't bother putting the photographs back into the envelope—with his mechanical hand, it would take him ten minutes. So he just tore them in half. "All of these men are dead." He paused, so she could absorb that one detail. "I'll share the specifics if you're interested, but I think you've had enough death to last you the rest of your life. But here's what's going to happen." He ducked his head and leaned low over the table to see her. She lifted her eyes just a little, but it was enough for them to connect. "Or at least what I *hope* happens."

Lucas jabbed a metal thumb over his shoulder at the man in the expensive suit, who remained silent and unmoving. "That is Joseph Martucci, and he is a special prosecutor appointed by the Southern District of New York. He is here to take your statement. That's all he needs—an hour of your time. You have to tell the truth, no matter what that turns out to be, and after that, you walk out of here and into the rest of your life. Today. Your sentence is commuted and you are granted immunity from any further prosecution for any involvement with Vaughan and his coterie of killers."

Moth lifted her gaze, and the tears in her eyes broke free, following the lines in her face and dripping down into her orange prison shirt. The detail reminded Lucas of the gasoline from Russo's car, and he pushed it away—Denise Moth wasn't the only one with memories.

"Counselor Martucci is here as a favor to me—I asked that you be the first to receive this offer. Most of the people involved in Vaughan's little doctor-killing group have been arrested. The rest are identified and will be brought in soon. No one but me cares who the first one to take the deal is—it should be you." He paused again so she could absorb this second important detail. "Dr. Vaughan and Detective Russo are both dead and they can't come back at you and your silence isn't helping you or anyone else anymore."

Lucas nodded over at her lawyer, who leaned in and whispered in her ear.

Moth looked up, wiped a forearm across her eyes, and nodded a single time. "Why me?" she asked, barely above a whisper.

Lucas pulled his final contribution from his inside coat pocket. He unfolded the paper and handed it to Moth, knowing she wouldn't care about the pizza bagel residue in the corner.

She looked at it, and curiosity creased her brow. "What is this?"

"It's a little cottage on a tiny island off the coast of Ireland. It was purchased just in case someone needed it." He smiled—or at least his face made the closest approximation it could. "And you look like that someone."

The prosecutor from the Southern District of New York came forward, handed Denise Moth a handkerchief, and sat down.

Acknowledgments

I once again need to thank my editor, Keith Kahla, for expecting as much from Lucas as I do. And who took the necessary time to get me from there to here—his input (and time) on the two initial drafts was indispensable. Thank you for saying the exact three things I needed to hear, at the precise time I needed to hear them.

Kelley Ragland, Alice Pfeifer, and the people at Minotaur Books, the invisible (and indispensable) force who take the pile of words I hand in and transforms them into something that ends up being so much greater than the sum of its parts—all while giving me the credit.

My literary agent and friend, Jill Marr, who keeps my career on track even though I refuse to get a cell phone and often disappear to my cabin for weeks at a time—I can never thank you enough for all the ways you changed my life.

My agent, Andrea Cavallero, who keeps the movie people away from me even though her job is technically the exact opposite. Please keep telling them that I'm gone and can't be reached.

Sandra Dijkstra (and all the people she puts at my disposal)—your presence (and theirs) enables me to concentrate on the writing.

I also need to thank my dear friend Kenneth Meany for all the time he spent talking this one through. And for letting me steal everything he says. I could never repay the debt.

Lieutenant-General Yvan Blondin—RCAF (Ret.), whose input and notes on the first draft helped me find the blind spots.

Dr. Amanda Hakala for answering a lot of questions early on in the process—I hope I didn't veer too far off the path.

My friend Johnny Russo for always calling at three A.M. Or sometimes even four. And for never being sober when he calls. And for never remembering that he called. And then for not remembering that he's not supposed to call the next time. And then for calling back. Ad infinitum. I appreciate the levity. My Little Lady? Not so much.

My friend Stan Tranter for the 3,317 times he asked me how the book was going.

My ninth grade typing teacher—Mr. White. Who taught me one of the most important skills I have—I think you every day I sit down and face the page.

My foreign publishers, who have changed my life in ways I never saw coming—thank you so much for taking a chance.

And I need to thank my readers for trusting me with their time. Having you out there has made all the nights in front of the blank page (which can be terrifying to a writer) worth every syllable. Thank you for taking these little trips with me and Lucas Page—I cannot imagine a better life. Or a greater privilege.

And as always—Rod Whitaker. For the endless inspiration.

THRILLINGLY GOOD BOOKS FROM CRIMINALLY GOOD WRITERS

CRIME FILES BRINGS YOU THE LATEST RELEASES FROM TOP CRIME AND THRILLER AUTHORS.

SIGN UP ONLINE FOR OUR MONTHLY NEWSLETTER AND BE THE FIRST TO KNOW ABOUT OUR COMPETITIONS, NEW BOOKS AND MORE.

VISIT OUR WEBSITE: WWW.CRIMEFILES.CO.UK
LIKE US ON FACEBOOK: FACEBOOK.COM/CRIMEFILES
FOLLOW US ON TWITTER: @CRIMEFILESBOOKS